MISS GRIEF

and

OTHER STORIES

MISS GRIEF
AND OTHER STORIES

*Constance
Fenimore Woolson*

. . . .

EDITED BY *Anne Boyd Rioux*

FOREWORD BY *Colm Tóibín*

W. W. NORTON & COMPANY
Independent Publishers Since 1923
NEW YORK   LONDON

For information about permission to reproduce
selections from this book, write to
Permissions, W. W. Norton & Company, Inc.,
500 Fifth Avenue, New York, NY 10110

For information about special discounts for bulk
purchases, please contact W. W. Norton Special Sales
at specialsales@wwnorton.com or 800-233-4830

Manufacturing by Quad Graphics Fairfield
Book design by Barbara Bachman
Production manager: Lauren Abbate

ISBN 978-0-393-35200-9 (pbk.)

W. W. Norton & Company, Inc.
500 Fifth Avenue, New York, N.Y. 10110

www.wwnorton.com

W. W. Norton & Company Ltd. Castle House,
75/76 Wells Street, London W1T 3QT

1 2 3 4 5 6 7 8 9 0

CONTENTS

. . . .

FOREWORD

by Colm Tóibín

THE HOUSE KNOWN AS VILLA BRICHIERI-COLOMBI, WHICH the American writer Constance Fenimore Woolson began to rent in 1887, still stands on the hill of Bellosguardo, overlooking Florence with a commanding view of the city and the Arno valley. The gardens are still surrounded by high walls, offering the house the sort of privacy that Woolson considered necessary for her happiness. Woolson wrote to a friend to say that her new accommodation was "an immense success in every way. . . . The situation is unrivalled. . . . Everywhere, when I raise my eyes from either drawing room (there are two), dining-room, bedroom, dressing-room or writing-room, I see the most enchanting landscape spread out before me; mountains, hills, river, city, villages, old castles, towns, campaniles, olive groves, almond trees and all the thousand divine 'bits' that make up Italian scenery."[1]

While Woolson was an inveterate traveler, having wandered a great deal in the American South, in the Orient, in England, Germany, and Switzerland, Italy seems to have been the place that fascinated her most. To another correspondent she noted that, fifty years before her first visit, her granduncle James Fenimore Cooper had also been in Florence with his family. "They remained ten months," she wrote, "living first in an old palace in the city, and then in a Villa outside of the walls. . . . We have been much interested in finding at a library here a book of Uncle Fenimore's which we had never seen—Excursions in Italy. It was published in Paris in 1838, and gives an account of their Italian journeyings."[2]

Farther up the hill of Bellosguardo lie two buildings facing each other that are rich in literary history. On the left-hand side of a small dusty square is Villa Montanto, with its battlemented watchtower. This is where Nathaniel Hawthorne wrote a draft of *The Marble Faun*. ("Hawthorne wrote the Marble Faun there one summer, you know," Woolson wrote to her cousin. "Perhaps one could catch a breath of his spirit."[3]) Opposite is Villa Castellani, in one of whose apartments lived the Bostonian Francis Boott with his daughter, Lizzie. Henry James, who knew the Bootts well, used their apartment and indeed aspects of their personalities and their relationship with each other in the creation of Gilbert Osmond and his daughter, Pansy, in *The Portrait of a Lady* and later in the making of Adam Verver and his daughter, Maggie, in *The Golden Bowl*.

Constance Fenimore Woolson met Henry James first in 1880, when he was in Florence writing the early sections of *The Portrait of a Lady*. She wrote to a friend that despite his busy schedule, "he found time to come in the mornings and take me out; sometimes to the galleries or churches, and sometimes just for a walk in the beautiful green Cascine."[4]

Woolson drew on these encounters for her story "A Florentine Experiment," just as James used them, perhaps more obliquely, in the scenes in *The Portrait of a Lady* depicting Osmond and Isabel after their betrothal. Over the next seven years, Woolson and James met in Switzerland and in England. They had much in common. They were both solitary souls who sometimes needed society—James more than Woolson—but they both also dreaded too much company and all forms of intrusion. They both paid great care and attention to their work. Woolson wrote to a friend: "I don't suppose any of you realize the amount of time and thought I give to each page of my novels; every character, every <u>word</u> of speech, and of description is thought of, literally, for years before it is written out for the final time. . . . It takes such possession of me that when, at last, a book is done, I am pretty nearly done myself."[5]

On August 30, 1893, she wrote from Venice, describing her daily schedule: "I am now called at 4.30 every morning, and then, after a cup of tea, I sit (in a dressing gown) and write until 9.30, when I have breakfast. This is to get the cool hours for work. Then I dress and go on writing until 4 p.m., when I go to the Lido and take a sea-bath."[6]

In 1887, Woolson returned to Florence, wishing to rent an apartment or house on Bellosguardo. She found the Villa Brichieri-Colombi and, before she moved in, invited Henry James to sublease the villa while she was staying in an apartment in the nearby Villa Castellani. The two writers saw each other every day. When James, having moved to Venice, let her know that he was unhappy in the watery city, she invited him to live in rooms on the ground floor of her newly rented villa. On April 24, 1887, James wrote to Edmund Gosse from Villa Brichieri-Colombi: "I sit here making love to Italy. At this divine moment she is perfectly irresistible, & this delicious little Florence is not the least sovereign of her charms. I am fixed, till June 1ˢᵗ, in a villa which in England would be suburban, but here is supercelestial, whence the most beautiful view on earth hangs before me whenever I lift my head."[7]

James was writing *The Aspern Papers*. It was, one imagines, not lost on him, and on Woolson when she came to read the story, that it concerned the legacy of a famous American writer whose first name was Jeffrey (with echoes of James Fenimore Cooper's first two initials), and that it concerned a man in search of shelter, a man who had devoted his life to literary matters who was now in Italy. It also dealt with two spinsters living in a large house, and their gnarled relationship with the visitor.

In 1880, Woolson had published one of her most heartbreaking and dramatic stories, "'Miss Grief,'" about a woman in Italy who is living in great poverty with her aunt. The woman approaches a younger writer with samples of her work. "'Miss Grief,'" dealing as it does with two unmarried literary foreigners in Italy, has interesting echoes in *The Aspern Papers*.

In a preface written for the New York edition of his work, however, James claimed that the roots of *The Aspern Papers* were in a story he heard about the life of Clare Claremont, Shelley's sister-in-law and mistress of Byron, in Florence when she was old and forgotten and in possession of invaluable literary papers. But the inspiration for the story, to some extent, was also in James's own circumstances as the guest of Constance Fenimore Woolson while the story was being composed and, indeed, as a reader of her story "'Miss Grief.'"

While James's knowledge of the United States was severely limited, Constance Fenimore Woolson could write about states of mind and states of the Union that were beyond James's reach. Just as years later Edith Wharton would make

James envious of her intimate knowledge of old New York society, Woolson made clear to him that many parts of his own country, which she knew well and described in stories such as "St. Clair Flats," "Solomon," "Rodman the Keeper," and "Sister St. Luke," were closed to him.

Woolson's letters from Europe are filled with wonder and with vivid description; her earlier letters from the American wilderness are equally vivid as they take pleasure in describing danger, or memories of danger. In one letter she writes in reply to a description of fierce cold: "The cold mentioned made me shudder. It made me 'creep' a great deal more than ever the moccasins did in Florida. I wo'nt [*sic*] say that I am fond of snakes; but I like to look at them from a safe distance. I used to row up the creeks, especially to find them."[8] In another letter, written from Florida, she described her exotic life in the wilderness: "[O]n other days I take a row boat and go prowling down the inlet into all sorts of creeks that go no one knows where; I wind through dense forest where the trees meet overhead, and the long grey moss brushes my solitary boat as I pass. I go far up the Sebastian River as utterly alone as Robinson Crusoe. I meet alligators, porpoises, pelicans, cranes, and even deer, but not a human soul."[9]

Woolson could become familiar, then, with creatures from the wild and prowl among them and also associate on equal terms with Henry James in London, Geneva, Florence, and Rome. She could re-create the atmosphere of the solitary places in a story as full of atmosphere as "St. Clair Flats," in which she writes about light and water with the same sonorousness and clarity as Joseph Conrad. She could write about the legacy of history in "Rodman the Keeper," in which the bitterness and destruction arising from the Civil War are dramatized. In her stories about artists, she could include the figure of Solomon in the story of that name, a failed artist living in poverty in the coal country of Ohio.

What these stories have in common with the work of Henry James is their refusal to offer the reader a happy ending, or an easy sense of redemption. Also, Woolson tended to narrate her story through the eyes or the voice of one single protagonist, thus achieving a sort of intensity as the story proceeds.

As well as being an intrepid traveler, Woolson became an adventurous and brave explorer in the territory of human disappointment. None of her characters is allowed to prevail. If there is an artist, as in "Solomon" and "'Miss Grief,'" then the art will go unrecognized; if there is an evocative landscape, then it will spell death and decay. And if there is travel and adventure, it will lead to misfortune or an ambiguous solution.

Woolson is at her most brilliant and her most complex when she writes about disappointment in love, as she does in "A Florentine Experiment" and "In Sloane Street," two stories about Americans in Europe. Both stories deal with a triangle that in less subtle hands could be called a love triangle, but in Woolson's stories is presented as stranger and more interesting and dynamic.

In the first of these two stories, set in Florence, Mrs. Lovell, who has lost her husband, is being pursued by Trafford Morgan, a desultory American. When it becomes clear that Morgan cannot or will not win her, the intelligent and self-effacing Margaret Stowe, who lives with her aunt, begins to move in his orbit. They may or may not love each other, and what is questioned in this most nuanced drama is the contingent nature of love itself. Woolson is clever enough to allow the story to become mysterious and open-ended and the theme to be filled with shade.

In her book *A Private Life of Henry James*, Lyndall Gordon ponders the relationship between the character of Margaret Stowe in this story and her creator. "Woolson draws an obvious self-portrait in her heroine," she writes.[10] Trafford Morgan, who is the same age as Henry James when Woolson got to know him, is an expatriate wanderer, diffident, hard to pin down. Margaret and he walk in the Cascine, where Woolson and James also walked (and where Isabel Archer and Gilbert Osmond walked). What is remarkable about the story is how elusive and filled with misdirection their relationship is, how oddly they circle each other, as though the author realized that the age of romance for serious novelists had come to an end. The story is bathed in the sort of irony and brittle wisdom that was, a generation later, to be found in the work of Virginia Woolf, Katherine Mansfield, and Elizabeth Bowen.

"In Sloane Street," written in 1892, eighteen months before Woolson's death, takes this idea of a triangle of two women and a man a step further. Philip Moore, a novelist, and his wife, who whines, are traveling with their two children and an old friend, Gertrude Remington, who, in Lyndall Gordon's words, "reads deep books, wears tailor-made gowns, and pins back her hair plainly."[11]

What is most notable about the story is its dry command. The dialogue hovers between making the speakers seem ghastly and suggesting that they are in deep pain. Every moment of the story increases the tension. The narrative line moves underneath the action until slowly it surfaces as the story of Miss Remington's isolation. We watch her feeling slighted by Moore's remarks about women writers. But, more important, as the Moores unite, emerging as a married couple, Miss Remington's status as a single woman makes her seem vulnerable, utterly alone. It is Constance Fenimore Woolson's great gift that this is done without any obvious effort or display, but with much subtlety, controlled sympathy, and writerly skill.

INTRODUCTION

by Anne Boyd Rioux

DURING HER LIFETIME, THE WORDS MOST COMMONLY used to describe the writings of Constance Fenimore Woolson (1840–1894) were: "original," "powerful," "vigorous," "artistic," "sympathetic," "true," and "real." She wrote five novels for adults and dozens of stories and was often compared with Henry James and George Eliot. The leading magazine and book publisher Harper & Brothers sought and received an exclusive contract with her. Her work was considered by many to be superior to that of any living American woman writer, and some believed she deserved the title of America's "novelist laureate." Henry James paid tribute to her in his collection *Partial Portraits* (1888), discovering in her stories about the Reconstruction-era South "a remarkable minuteness of observation and tenderness of feeling on the part of one who evidently did not glance and pass, but lingered and analyzed." In her landmark essay, "Woman in American Literature" (1890), Helen Gray Cone summed up Woolson's reputation: "Few American writers of fiction have given evidence of such breadth, so full a sense of the possibilities of the varied and complex life of our wide land. Robust, capable, mature—these seem fitting words [to describe her]. Women have reason for pride in a representative novelist whose genius is trained and controlled, without being tamed or dispirited."[1]

When Woolson died in 1894, at the age of fifty-three, after falling from her third-story window in Venice, her friend and editor Henry Mills Alden called her "a true artist" whose writings possessed a "rare excellence, originality, and strength [that] were appreciated by the most fastidious critics." In the *New York Tribune*, the influential poet and critic Edmund Clarence Stedman, comparing her with Jane Austen and the Brontës, called her "one of the leading women in the American literature of the century." Charles Dudley Warner, novelist and collaborator with Mark Twain, declared her "one of the first in America to bring the short story to its present excellence," and wrote that her death was "deplored by the entire literary fraternity of this country."[2]

Nonetheless, Woolson's stellar reputation faded quickly. Already in 1906, a reader wrote to *The New York Times*, "Miss Woolson has done too much for America and Americans to be forgotten and ignored." A tribute to her written by the Irish novelist Shan F. Bullock in 1920 suggests the particular value she had to those few who remembered her: "I venture to say that no writer living compares in power and art with Constance Woolson. . . . Had she lived, it is possible that in time she would have forced acknowledgment from a public that refuses even common notoriety to anything save commercial success. . . . But Miss Woolson, it seems, is forgotten. No one remembers her name, even."[3]

At the height of her career, Woolson had managed that difficult combination of critical and commercial success. Yet none of her novels was as successful as her first, *Anne* (1882), which sold 57,000 copies, nearly ten times as many as Henry James's *The Portrait of a Lady*, published a few months earlier. Some critics, most influentially William Dean Howells, had criticized her portraits of women, charging her with a lack of realism and/or morality, and had objected to the difficult themes of her later work, which tackled such subjects as domestic abuse and love outside of marriage. Still, these cannot explain the precipitous decline of her reputation. The growing suspicion in the modern era of expressions of genuine emotion quickly dated her work, which did not shy away from the portrayal of restrained passion and eruptions of powerful emotions, even though these were never the dominant themes of her work. Of even greater influence was the tendency by male critics to classify all women writers as minor as the American literary canon took shape at the turn of the century.[4] Throughout the twentieth century, the narrative of separate literary spheres for men and women persisted, creating a neat split between the major male realists (such as James and Howells) and the minor female regionalists (such as Sarah Orne Jewett and Mary Wilkins Freeman). Woolson's work, which participated in both movements and crossed the gendered divides of her own day, fell through the cracks of the dominant narrative of American literary history.

Nonetheless, Woolson's name was kept alive by a small cadre of appreciative critics from the 1920s through the 1960s, when Henry James's biographer Leon Edel discovered that she was a significant figure in the famous author's life and made her name once again more widely known.[5] Yet Edel had dragged Woolson out of the shadows only to belittle her as a second-rate writer who had tried to ride the Master's coattails. Feminist scholars, many of whom discovered Woolson through their research on James, helped to repair the damage by confirming the artistic and cultural value of her work and examining her pathbreaking life.[6] Yet her friendship with James continues to overshadow her own significance as a writer, and the fact that her life ended in probable suicide has eclipsed her earlier accomplishments, pigeonholing her as a tragic victim of the male literary world's (and her friend James's) neglect.

Another disadvantage for Woolson's reputation has been the fact that she cannot be aligned with one particular region, such as Jewett's Maine or Kate Chopin's Louisiana. Woolson traveled widely, and her writings reflect the breadth of her experience and vision. Her earliest stories were set in the Great Lakes region, near where she grew up, in Cleveland. After 1873, she set many of her stories in the Reconstruction-era South, particularly Florida, where she spent the winters with her invalid mother. After moving to Europe in late 1879, Woolson continued to set her novels in America but also wrote stories about American expatriates in Italy, Switzerland, and England. As a result, she was a pioneering regionalist without a region to call her own.

Coming of age as a writer at the same time as American literary realism, Woolson also made important contributions to that movement that have been greatly overlooked. She always insisted that her writings were taken directly from life as she observed it, which for her included characters' hidden emotional lives, in addition to their inner consciousness or their social interactions, the usual terrain of most male realists. In his remembrance of her, Warner perfectly captured the essence of her achievement when he wrote, "She was a sympathetic [and] refined observer, entering sufficiently into the analytic mode of the time, but she had the courage to deal with the passions, and life as it is."[7]

CONSTANCE FENIMORE WOOLSON grew up in Cleveland, Ohio, then a village of New England emigrants. Her parents moved there from New Hampshire shortly after her birth in 1840. She was the sixth child but would, by the age of thirteen, be the oldest survivor of the Woolson children, which also included a younger daughter and son. Despite so much sorrow, her parents were loving and nurtured her interests in literature and history. She was especially close to her father, Charles Jarvis Woolson, a stove manufacturer by trade and an avid reader, who had been a journalist in Boston and Charlottesville, Virginia, in the 1830s. He gave twelve-year-old Constance a complete set of Charles Dickens's works and encouraged her early writing, none of which has survived. Her mother, Hannah Pomeroy Woolson, was a niece of the novelist James Fenimore Cooper, whose example would exert a great influence on Constance's career. However, it was her mother's poor health, exacerbated by her grief for her lost children, that left a greater impression on Constance, who would grow up to be her mother's caretaker.

After some early setbacks in the Woolson stove business, the family led an upwardly mobile and socially well-connected life in Cleveland. The Woolsons also had a summer home on Mackinac Island in Lake Huron, and Constance and her father often visited Zoar, the Ohio German separatist community, both of which would become important settings for her early writing. Constance was a precocious reader and writer, but her family saw those activities as decidedly domestic. She was raised to be a cultured, well-educated young woman who would make a fine wife and mother someday. Even though she received a nearly college-level education at the Cleveland Female Seminary, her parents sent her, at seventeen, for a year of finishing school in New York and upon her graduation showed her off at Eastern resorts in hopes of finding her a husband. Woolson accepted her family's view of her future, but she was also ambivalent about the overpowering nature of romantic love for women. During the Civil War, when Woolson was in her early to mid-twenties, she came under the spell of what she would later call "the glamor of the war" and fell in love with Zephaniah Spalding, an officer whom she had known from her summers on Mackinac Island.[8] She expected to marry him; however, after the war, he moved to Hawaii, where he married a sugar heiress. It would be many years before Constance came to terms with the loss of her hopes for marriage and a family.

In the meantime, Constance had become the sole caretaker of her ailing parents. Then, when her father died in 1869, she lost her main emotional support. Unfortunately, he also left her and her mother without enough money to support themselves, and it soon became clear that she would have to find a way to earn a living. With the encouragement of her brother-in-law, George Benedict, part-owner of the *Cleveland Herald*, Woolson began publishing the writing she had been doing largely in secret. In July 1870, her first two publications, both travel sketches, appeared, in *Harper's New Monthly Magazine* and *Putnam's Magazine*, two of the leading monthlies of the day. Soon she was sending witty and observant letters home from New York for publication in the *Herald*. After returning to Cleveland, she also published a children's novel, *The Old Stone House* (1873), but soon decided to pursue her greater ambition for serious recognition as a literary artist, publishing a series of Great Lakes stories in the *Atlantic Monthly*, *Appletons' Journal*, *Scribner's Monthly*, and *Harper's*.

Due to their limited funds and her mother's ill health, Constance moved South in late 1873, staying over the next five years in Florida, both Carolinas, and Virginia. She explored the wild environs of St. Augustine, Florida, where she and her mother spent their winters, often delving into the swamps and pine barrens on her own. They also encountered white Southerners' resentment of Northerners who flocked to the South in search of economic opportunity or a warmer climate. Everywhere, the scars of the Civil War were visible, in the dispirited faces of the people and in the cemeteries full of unmarked graves.

In February 1879, after her mother died from a short illness, Constance descended into a deep depression. She felt as if she had lost the one person in the world who gave her life purpose. Having suffered during the 1870s a few periods of acute depression, a tendency that she inherited from her father, Constance now faced a severe battle with what she once called "this deadly enemy of mine."[9] She had also inherited her father's congenital deafness, which was now becoming severe and would increase her sense of isolation and exacerbate her tendency toward depression.

Hoping to break up Constance's grief, her sister Clara

decided to take her to Europe. They sailed in December 1879, and in Europe Woolson finally began to enjoy her new identity as an independent author. Meeting Henry James in Florence, in April 1880, she found a new friend to help deflect her grief. He found her amiable, despite being hard of hearing, and showed her around the galleries and gardens of Florence. She had hoped to meet him as something of a peer, but he had never heard of her and treated her chivalrously as a woman rather than respectfully as a fellow writer. It would take many more years of friendship, but eventually he would call her his "confrère."[10]

Choosing not to return to the United States with her sister, Woolson stayed on in Europe, spending the winters in Florence or Rome and the summers in Switzerland, England, and Germany, getting to know many of the prominent British and American visitors and expatriates. Although her deafness was beginning to become a distinct social liability, Woolson still made many new friends in the early 1880s, among them William Dean Howells and his family. When the whirl of expatriate society threatened to encroach on her writing, she would often retreat from it to concentrate on her work.

In 1887, Woolson finally settled down in Europe, renting her own villa outside of Florence. There she became close to Henry James's friends the American composer Francis Boott and his daughter, Lizzie, who was an artist and had recently married Frank Duveneck, her former art teacher. When the newlyweds had a child nine months later, Woolson was chosen to be his godmother. Enjoying the companionship of these de facto family members and the comforts of her own home, Woolson experienced the greatest contentment of her adult life, balancing writing in solitude with a supportive community. In the spring of 1887, James also came to visit and lived for a month under her roof in the downstairs apartment, during which time they began to develop a quasi-sibling relationship that would grow in the coming years.

However, when Lizzie Duveneck died in March 1888 and her father subsequently took the baby home to America to be raised by relatives, Woolson became despondent. Compounding her sense of loss were her fears about her precarious finances. In her attempt to maintain her villa, she had racked up large debts, which her nephew kindly paid. Although she earned decent money for her novels as well as modest interest from some American bonds, she worried for the rest of her life about money and her ability to support herself.

Her sister again tried to cure her grief and depression with travel, this time to Greece, Egypt, and the Holy Land. Woolson was enchanted with Cairo, where she stayed on alone for three months in early 1890, during which time she felt herself reborn. She reveled in the exotic atmosphere of these foreign countries and developed a wider view of the world, learning to no longer "look down" on the Middle East from a "superior Anglo-Saxon standpoint."[11]

Although she longed to continue her travels, Woolson returned to England, knowing it would best allow her to work without interruption. She lived for over a year in Cheltenham, but she found it too dull and moved to Oxford in 1891. Now closer to London, she began to see James more frequently and traveled often to the city, where she took in plays and visited galleries. She also tried a new remedy for her growing deafness, artificial eardrums, which worked briefly but then caused severe pains that she found difficult to endure. Meanwhile the Russian flu epidemic had reached England, causing Oxford to shut down for the first time in living memory.

Leaving England for Venice in June 1893, Woolson regretted leaving her friend James behind but hoped he would visit her in Italy as soon as he could. In Venice, she tried to recuperate from the flu she had contracted just before her departure, as well as the depression and physical collapse she often experienced after completing a novel. She spent the summer and fall floating in gondolas through the canals and out among the islands in the lagoon, solidifying friendships within the small expatriate community there and searching for an apartment where she could settle down again. She found temporary lodgings on the Grand Canal and brought her belongings out of storage from Florence, gathering around her the many reminders of her friends Boott and the Duvenecks.

During the six months Woolson lived in Venice, she tried hard to relieve the depression and ill health troubling her and planned to start writing again on January 1, 1894. However, as the new year dawned, she felt writing had become too great a strain for her to continue. She fell ill and began preparing for her death, although the doctor thought she was in no danger. During a sleepless night, around midnight of January 24, she instructed the nurse to fetch a special cup for her milk. When the nurse returned, she found the window open and Woolson on the pavement three stories below. The servants brought her upstairs, but she never regained consciousness, living only a few hours.

Although many believed that Woolson took her own life, her preparations for her death—most important, a will—were incomplete at her death. Weakened by her recent illness, she may have fallen as she opened the window for fresh air. This was her family's firm belief. There are strong indications, however, that Woolson, who despaired of finding a home she could afford and of continuing to make her living as a writer, was ready to die. A firm believer in an afterlife that would solve the "cruel riddles" of this existence, she may have hastened her way there.[12]

Woolson was buried in the Protestant Cemetery in Rome, as she had earlier requested of her caretakers. The funeral was attended by a small group of mourners, expatriates who, like her, had not seen their homelands in many years. One of her closest friends, James, remained in London, prostrated by grief. Her memory would haunt him for many years, making its way into some of his later works, such as *The Beast in the Jungle* and *The Wings of the Dove*, in which he portrayed women who loved selflessly and unrequitedly. Yet Woolson's insistence on being buried in Rome's Protestant Cemetery, amid so many famous foreign writers and artists who had died in Italy, including Percy Bysshe Shelley and John Keats, indicates how much she hoped to be remembered in her own right—as an important writer rather than simply as a tragic inspiration to others.

WOOLSON'S WRITINGS WERE so intimately tied to the places she traveled to and lived that they can be divided into three periods: the Great Lakes fiction of the early- to mid-1870s, the Southern fiction of the mid- to late-1870s, and the European fiction of the 1880s and early 1890s. This classification applies only to the short stories and travel narratives, however. The settings of her novels stayed firmly in the United States, even when she was thousands of miles away. As she once explained, she would never be able to set a novel in Europe because all of her deepest feelings were "inseparably associated with home-scenes . . . [t]he Lake-country & Mackinac, the beautiful South, the farming-country of Ohio."[13]

Her list of "home-scenes" did not include her original home, Cleveland, which she felt had been spoiled by the rise of industry and the spread of blast furnaces and petroleum refineries. Instead, she listed the places she had loved best to visit. Although traditionally women had written primarily from the vantage point of their homes, Woolson was inspired to write by the new scenes she encountered on her travels. The landscapes that most attracted her were those that remained largely untouched. She spent much of her youth exploring nature: rowing, hiking, and studying flora and fauna. In adulthood, she was a devoted botanist, with a particular love of ferns, and many of her American stories are filled with the observations of a naturalist, particularly "St. Clair Flats," "Sister St. Luke," and "The South Devil." She was also drawn to places that bore the marks of Old World influence, through immigration or colonization, such as Zoar and St. Augustine. She regretted the way Americans, particularly in the Midwest, valued the new over the old and thus erased all evidence of the past, be it the American wilderness or earlier human habitation. James would later write of her early stories, "she has a remarkable faculty of making the New World seem ancient."[14]

Critics applauded Woolson for discovering so many new scenes and expanding Americans' view of their nation in the wake of the Civil War. Although some questioned the veracity of her works, Woolson was adamant that she drew strictly from life in the creation of her settings, plots, and characters. She also insisted on the importance of making her readers feel for her characters, who are often misunderstood and overlooked. While many of her contemporaries portrayed their provincial characters comically, Woolson portrayed without sentimentality social outsiders struggling for dignity, love, and respect. Her literary aesthetic can best be described as empathetic realism, a mode that she adapted from George Eliot, the favorite author of her early adulthood, and that she maintained even as she came to know and admire the analytic realism found in James's works.

In spite of practicing what might seem a more feminine version of realism, Woolson (like Eliot) was considered a quasi-masculine writer for writing realistically at all, and she understood herself as entering into a male sphere of literature. She regretted that, in her view, "women are prone to run off into the beautiful at the expense of strength." She had "such a horror of 'pretty,' 'sweet' writing" that she was willing to risk "a style that was ugly and bitter, provided it was also <u>strong</u>." Throughout her career, in fact, she sought out the companionship and support of influential male writers. The first such was the New York poet and critic Edmund Clarence Stedman. With his encouragement—he told her he found her stories as powerful as some of Hawthorne's—she was able to ignore the critics who expected her to write more sentimentally and preferred moral endings (like punishment for evil deeds) rather than what she felt was more "artistic and truthful-to-life."[15]

She became known, in fact, for her refusal to end her stories happily.

Woolson's earliest stories, set in the Great Lakes, many of which were published in *Castle Nowhere: Lake-Country Sketches* (1875), were atypical for women writers of her day, peopled as they were with miners, missionaries, and male adventurers. Often writing from a male point of view, she also exposed the limitations of her male characters, who generally assumed the superiority of their sophisticated, masculine view of the world. In many of these stories, she carefully examined the way some men observed women and held them to a narrow set of expectations, refusing to acknowledge their full humanity. For instance, in "St. Clair Flats," the narrator's male friend can see no pathos in the isolated life of a religious zealot's wife; in "Jeanette," an officer on Mackinac Island who, against his better judgment, falls in love with a half-Indian girl is surprised when she refuses him; and in "The Lady of Little Fishing," a female missionary loses the respect of her all-male flock when she falls in love with a degenerate fur trapper.

As Woolson moved south, she extended her empathetic gaze to new regions, types, and conflicts. Her Southern stories, collected in *Rodman the Keeper: Southern Sketches* (1880), dealt extensively with the effects of the war on the South and the intrusions of Northerners into a beautiful and sometimes hostile region. Although the North was eager to forget the Civil War and Woolson was cautioned by one publisher against writing any more about it, she continued to portray white and black Southerners struggling to rebuild their lives. In stories such as "Rodman the Keeper," "In the Cotton Country," and "Old Gardiston," she acknowledged the bitterness of the former planter class and allowed those who had lost everything to speak for themselves, at a time when their real-life counterparts had virtually no means of telling their own stories. In "King David," she depicted the racism of a white Northerner who has come south to educate freed slaves, ultimately giving voice to one of the students, who rejects David's feeble attempts at understanding. Woolson's Florida stories, such as "Sister St. Luke," "Felipa," and "The South Devil," reveled in the exotic, wild landscape and portrayed Northern visitors who have a hard time accepting the carefree lifestyle of the locals, particularly Minorcans, an ethnic group from the Spanish island of Minorca. Once again, Woolson allowed these marginalized characters, particularly in "Felipa," to speak back to the unwitting tourists trying to understand them.

Having made important contributions to the rise of the short story in the post–Civil War period, Woolson then set her sights on a bid for the Great American Novel, turning to what she knew best, the lives of women. Drawing inspiration from Eliot's *The Mill on the Floss* and Charlotte Brontë's *Jane Eyre*, she wrote *Anne* (1882), the coming-of-age story of an unconventional young woman, much like herself, growing up on Mackinac Island and forced to make her way in the world after the death of her father. The opening chapters are themselves a regional masterpiece, a loving portrait of the island and its remarkable inhabitants, including a New England spinster, a French priest, Anne's mixed-race (Native American and white) half siblings, and her Thoreau-like naturalist-philosopher father. Determined to write a national novel, however, Woolson left Mackinac behind and followed Anne to a finishing school in New York, a fashionable Eastern resort, the battlefields of West Virginia during the Civil War (where Anne is a nurse), and ultimately to the rural hinterland of the Maryland–Pennsylvania border, where Anne must solve a murder in order to free the man she loves. At its core, however, *Anne* remains a story about a young woman discovering her considerable strengths and talents at a time when women were expected to hide them and remain at home. Anne does neither and thus joins the pantheon of literature's iconoclastic heroines.

Woolson's next novel was much less ambitious but more finely crafted. *For the Major* (1883) is the portrait of an isolated mountain village near Asheville, North Carolina, in the aftermath of the Civil War. At its center is a wife's attempts to hide from her husband her former marriage and motherhood. It subtly critiques the infantilization of women as it insists on the wife's noble self-sacrifices for her husband. Ultimately, *For the Major* provides a rather startling exposé of the duplicities that marriage requires. In Woolson's fiction, women know that they must play the roles men want to see them in, if they are to win men's affection.

This theme emerged in many of Woolson's short stories of the period as well. In "A Florentine Experiment" and "The Château of Corinne," for instance, Woolson's female characters openly denounce men's expectations that women behave simply and adoringly. During the early years of her friendship with James, Woolson also returned to the theme of failed artists that she had first explored in "Solomon," one of her Great Lakes stories. "'Miss Grief,'" "The Street of the Hyacinth," and "Château" most vividly portray the defeat of female writers and artists who possess the same serious ambitions that

Woolson harbored, reflecting the crisis of confidence occasioned by her engagement with European art and culture, as well as her friendship with James. A later story, "In Sloane Street," never published in book form until now, again picks up these themes, showing how astutely Woolson observed James and inferred his disapproval of women writers.

In these and other stories, Woolson also began experimenting with the analytical style James was known for, emphasizing description and character analysis over plot. While she felt this style had much to offer, she lamented its lack of feeling. Nowhere does she more overtly seek to redress this deficiency, infusing analysis with intense emotions, than in her third novel, *East Angels* (1886), set in the region near St. Augustine. In this work she answered James directly by rewriting, to a degree, *The Portrait of a Lady*. Woolson had earlier written to James that she couldn't tell whether Isabel Archer really loved Osmond, for if Isabel had, surely "heart-breaking, insupportable, killing grief" would have followed his betrayal.[16] In *East Angels*, Woolson exposes her heroine Margaret's great, suppressed passion, showing the severe emotional costs of the self-renunciation she and similarly Isabel practiced. Woolson wanted to reveal what women, in their ordinary lives, could not. As Margaret explains, "We go through life, ... more than half of us—women, I mean—obliged always to conceal our real feelings."[17] As in so many of Woolson's works, this concealment has both emotional and physical consequences. The mind affects the body in mysterious ways that male physicians are helpless to understand or remedy, a theme Woolson explored most fully in her Italian story "Dorothy."

Her darkest work, her fourth novel, even more fully exposes

the dangers of passionate love for women. *Jupiter Lights* (1889), set in the Carolinas and the Great Lakes, shows how love leads in one character's case to submission to an abusive husband and in another's to thoughts of suicide. While Margaret in *East Angels* resists the forceful persuasion of her would-be lover and thus preserves the inviolability of her deepest self, the heroine of *Jupiter Lights*, Eve, finds herself unable to turn her lover away, however degrading she feels her love for him is. His autocratic form of love renders Eve powerless. Should he even grow to hate her, she realizes, she would be happy simply to be near him and fold his shirts. In *Jupiter Lights*, more than in any other work, Woolson contributed to the development of literary naturalism in her exploration of the inherent weaknesses of her characters, from inherited alcoholism to the self-destructive nature of romantic love.

In her final novel, *Horace Chase* (1894), she strove to be thoroughly modern. Set in Asheville and St. Augustine, it portrayed a self-made businessman of the Gilded Age and his young wife, who has married him for money but later discovers real love for another man. As in so many of her works, Woolson portrayed a pair of women, one ultra-feminine and beloved, the other intellectual and unnoticed. Usually she subtly exposed the silent suffering of the less conventional woman, but here she made her vapid beauty discover the pain of unrequited love. In the end, when the wife confesses her adulterous feelings to her husband, he forgives her, proving himself to be a more noble and complex character than he at first appeared. Outside of the main couple, the novel also contains an array of contemporary types, such as the mannish female sculptor who smokes and determines that men's kisses leave much to be desired and the invalid sister who cynically comments from her couch on the conventional lives of those around her.

After Woolson's death, Harper & Brothers published two volumes of her European stories, *The Front Yard and Other Italian Stories* (1895) and *Dorothy and Other Italian Stories* (1896). The most remarkable of the stories not already mentioned is "A Front Yard," which portrays a sturdy New England spinster (a recurring type in Woolson's fiction) who takes on the care of her ungrateful stepchildren after the death of her Italian husband, all the while trying to create the New England garden of her dreams. "A Transplanted Boy," one of the last stories Woolson wrote, heartbreakingly depicts a young expatriated American boy who has lost all connection with his homeland and nearly starves himself in an attempt to provide for his ailing mother. It expresses the loneliness and financial fears that haunted Woolson in her final months.

Woolson's works deserve wider attention today, not only for the way they broaden our understanding of late-nineteenth-century American literature, but also for the way they capture both the social texture of her time and the inner emotional lives of her characters. Her works contradict our assumptions about women's writing from that era, for Woolson did not seek recognition as a woman writer but as a writer. Thus she often tread on masculine territory in her work, while never trying to simply mimic the successes of her male peers. She sought instead to show them what was missing from their views of humanity, broadening the scope of literature to include the heartaches and triumphs of those most often overlooked, such as impoverished spinsters, neglected nuns, self-sacrificing wives and widows, uneducated coal miners, and destitute Southerners. Most of all her writings reflect what is deeply human in all of us, particularly our need to be loved, to be understood, and to belong, none of which are easily accomplished in her stories, or in life.

A NOTE ON THE TEXTS

The text of each story that follows is taken from its book publication, except for "In Sloane Street," which was never published in a book. As the collections from which the stories come were published by four different publishers, their styles in terms of spacing and punctuation vary. These variations have been silently corrected, conforming to modern usage. For instance, what appeared as "is n't" in the original now appears as "isn't," and spaces around em dashes, which varied widely in the original stories, have been closed. Spelling inconsistencies from one text to the next have been allowed to stand. In a few cases, where spelling inconsistencies existed within the same story, these have been silently corrected or noted. "In Sloane Street" presented special challenges because the original magazine publication is difficult to read and contained more errors than the stories published in books. Obvious errors, as with the few scattered in the other stories, have been silently corrected. Otherwise, the integrity of the original documents has been observed as closely as possible.

MISS GRIEF

and

OTHER STORIES

ST. CLAIR FLATS

"ST. CLAIR FLATS," ONE OF WOOLSON'S FINEST Great Lakes stories from the 1870s, is set in the vast freshwater delta at the mouth of the St. Clair River as it flows into Lake St. Clair, not far from Detroit. Its maze-like marshes evoke the classical myth of Ariadne, who gave a ball of thread, or clew, to Theseus to find his way back from the Labyrinth after killing the Minotaur. The story also refers to American millennialism and the ideological contest between forces that viewed the frontier as ripe for development and those who saw it as a source of inspiration and spiritual sustenance. Much to Woolson's regret, those who wanted development were winning. The story is perhaps her most elegiac portrait of what was lost with the disappearance of the American wilderness. "St. Clair Flats" was published in *Appletons' Journal* (October 4, 1873) and reprinted in *Castle Nowhere: Lake-Country Sketches* (1875).

ST. CLAIR FLATS

. . . .

IN SEPTEMBER, 1855, I FIRST SAW THE ST. CLAIR FLATS. Owing to Raymond's determination, we stopped there.

"Why go on?" he asked. "Why cross another long, rough lake, when here is all we want?"

"But no one ever stops here," I said.

"So much the better; we shall have it all to ourselves."

"But we must at least have a roof over our heads."

"I presume we can find one."

The captain of the steamer, however, knew of no roof save that covering a little lighthouse set on spiles, which the boat would pass within the half-hour; we decided to get off there, and throw ourselves upon the charity of the lighthouse-man. In the mean time, we sat on the bow with Captain Kidd, our four-legged companion, who had often accompanied us on hunting expeditions, but never before so far westward. It had been rough on Lake Erie,—very rough. We, who had sailed the ocean with composure, found ourselves most inhumanly tossed on the short, chopping waves of this fresh-water sea; we, who alone of all the cabin-list had eaten our four courses and dessert every day on the ocean-steamer, found ourselves here reduced to the depressing diet of a herring and pilot-bread. Captain Kidd, too, had suffered dumbly; even now he could not find comfort, but tried every plank in the deck, one after the other, circling round and round after his tail, dog-fashion, before lying down, and no sooner down than up again for another melancholy wandering about the deck, another choice of planks, another circling, and another failure. We were sailing across a small lake whose smooth waters were like clear green oil; as we drew near the outlet, the low, green shores curved inward and came together, and the steamer entered a narrow, green river.

"Here we are," said Raymond. "Now we can soon land."

"But there isn't any land," I answered.

"What is that, then?" asked my near-sighted companion, pointing toward what seemed a shore.

"Reeds."

"And what do they run back to?"

"Nothing."

"But there must be solid ground beyond?"

"Nothing but reeds, flags, lily-pads, grass, and water, as far as I can see."

"A marsh?"

"Yes, a marsh."

The word "marsh" does not bring up a beautiful picture to the mind, and yet the reality was as beautiful as any-thing I have ever seen,—an enchanted land, whose memory haunts me as an idea unwritten, a melody unsung, a picture unpainted, haunts the artist, and will not away. On each side and in front, as far as the eye could reach, stretched the low green land which was yet no land, intersected by hundreds of channels, narrow and broad, whose waters were green as their shores. In and out, now running into each other for a moment, now setting off each for himself again, these many channels flowed along with a rippling current; zigzag as they were, they never seemed to loiter, but, as if knowing just where they were going and what they had to do, they found time to take their own pleasant roundabout way, visiting the secluded households of their friends the flags, who, poor souls, must always stay at home. These currents were as clear as crystal, and green as the water-grasses that fringed their miniature shores. The bristling reeds, like companies of free-lances, rode boldly out here and there into the deeps, trying to conquer more territory for the grasses, but the currents were hard to conquer; they dismounted the free-lances, and flowed over their submerged heads; they beat them down with assaulting ripples; they broke their backs so effectually that the bravest had no spirit left, but trailed along, limp and bedraggled. And, if by chance the lances succeeded in stretching their forces across from one little shore to another, then the unconquered currents forced their way between the closely serried ranks of the enemy, and flowed on as gayly as ever, leaving the grasses sitting hopeless on the bank; for they needed solid ground for their delicate feet, these graceful ladies in green.

You might call it a marsh; but there was no mud, no dark slimy water, no stagnant scum; there were no rank yellow lilies, no gormandizing frogs, no swinish mud-turtles. The clear waters of the channels ran over golden sands, and hurtled among the stiff reeds so swiftly that only in a bay, or where protected by a crescent point, could the fair white lilies float in the quiet their serene beauty requires. The flags, who brandished their swords proudly, were martinets down to their very heels, keeping themselves as clean under the water as above, and harboring not a speck of mud on their bright green uniforms. For inhabitants, there were small fish roving about here and there in the clear tide, keeping an eye out for the herons, who, watery as to legs, but venerable and wise of aspect, stood on promontories musing, apparently, on the secrets of the ages.

The steamer's route was a constant curve; through the larger channels of the archipelago she wound, as if following the clew of a labyrinth. By turns she headed toward all the points of the compass, finding a channel where, to our uninitiated eyes, there was no channel, doubling upon her own track, going broadside foremost, floundering and backing, like a whale caught in a shallow. Here, landlocked, she would choose what seemed the narrowest channel of all, and dash recklessly through, with the reeds almost brushing her sides; there she crept gingerly along a broad expanse of water, her paddle-wheels scarcely revolving, in the excess of her caution. Saplings, with their heads of foliage on, and branches adorned with fluttering rags, served as finger-posts to show the way through the watery defiles, and there were many other hieroglyphics legible only to the pilot. "This time, surely, we shall run ashore," we thought again and again, as the steamer glided, head-on, toward an islet; but at the last there was always a quick turn into some unseen strait opening like a secret passage in a castle-wall, and we found ourselves in a new lakelet, heading in the opposite direction. Once we met another steamer, and the two great hulls floated slowly past each other, with engines motionless, so near that the passengers could have shaken hands with each other had they been so disposed. Not that they were so disposed, however; far from it. They gathered on their respective decks and gazed at each other gravely; not a smile was seen, not a word spoken, not the shadow of a salutation given. It was not pride, it was not suspicion; it was the universal listlessness of the travelling American bereft of his business, Othello with his occupation gone. What can such a man do on a steamer? Generally, nothing. Certainly he would never think of any such light-hearted nonsense as a smile or passing bow.

But the ships were, *par excellence*, the bewitched craft, the Flying Dutchmen of the Flats. A brig, with lofty, sky-scraping sails, bound south, came into view of our steamer, bound north, and passed, we hugging the shore to give her room; five minutes afterward the sky-scraping sails we had left behind veered around in front of us again; another five minutes, and there they were far distant on the right; another, and there they were again close by us on the left. For half an hour those sails circled around us, and yet all the time we were pushing steadily forward; this seemed witching work indeed. Again, the numerous schooners thought nothing of sailing overland; we saw them on all sides gliding before the wind, or beating up against it over the meadows as easily as over the water; sailing on grass was a mere trifle to these spirit-barks. All this we saw, as I said before, apparently. But in that adverb is hidden the magic of the St. Clair Flats.

"It is beautiful,—beautiful," I said, looking off over the vivid green expanse.

"Beautiful?" echoed the captain, who had himself taken charge of the steering when the steamer entered the labyrinth,—

"I don't see anything beautiful in it!—Port your helm up there; port!"

"Port it is, sir," came back from the pilot-house above.

"These Flats give us more trouble than any other spot on the lakes; vessels are all the time getting aground and blocking up the way, which is narrow enough at best. There's some talk of Uncle Sam's cutting a canal right through,—a straight canal; but he's so slow, Uncle Sam is, and I'm afraid I'll be off the waters before the job is done."

"A straight canal!" I repeated, thinking with dismay of an ugly utilitarian ditch invading this beautiful winding waste of green.

"Yes, you can see for yourself what a saving it would be," replied the captain. "We could run right through in no time, day or night; whereas, now, we have to turn and twist and watch every inch of the whole everlasting marsh." Such was the captain's opinion. But we, albeit neither romantic nor artistic, were captivated with his "everlasting marsh," and eager to penetrate far within its green fastnesses.

"I suppose there are other families living about here, besides the family at the lighthouse?" I said.

"Never heard of any. They'd have to live on a raft if they did."

"But there must be some solid ground."

"Don't believe it; it's nothing but one great sponge for miles.—Steady up there; steady!"

"Very well," said Raymond, "so be it. If there is only the lighthouse, at the lighthouse we'll get off, and take our chances."

"You're surveyors, I suppose?" said the captain.

Surveyors are the pioneers of the lake-country, understood

by the people to be a set of harmless monomaniacs, given to building little observatories along-shore, where there is nothing to observe; mild madmen, whose vagaries and instruments are equally singular. As surveyors, therefore, the captain saw nothing surprising in our determination to get off at the lighthouse; if we had proposed going ashore on a plank in the middle of Lake Huron, he would have made no objection.

At length the lighthouse came into view, a little fortress perched on spiles, with a ladder for entrance; as usual in small houses, much time seemed devoted to washing, for a large crane, swung to and fro by a rope, extended out over the water, covered with fluttering garments hung out to dry. The steamer lay to, our row-boat was launched, our traps handed out, Captain Kidd took his place in the bow, and we pushed off into the shallows; then the great paddle-wheels revolved again, and the steamer sailed away, leaving us astern, rocking on her waves, and watched listlessly by the passengers until a turn hid us from their view. In the mean time numerous flaxen-haired children had appeared at the little windows of the lighthouse,—too many of them, indeed, for our hopes of comfort.

"Ten," said Raymond, counting heads.

The ten, moved by curiosity as we approached, hung out of the windows so far that they held on merely by their ankles.

"We cannot possibly save them all," I remarked, looking up at the dangling gazers.

"O, they're amphibious," said Raymond; "web-footed, I presume."

We rowed up under the fortress, and demanded parley with the keeper in the following language:—

"Is your father here?"

"No; but ma is," answered the chorus.—"Ma! ma!"

Ma appeared, a portly female, who held converse with us from the top of the ladder. The sum and substance of the dialogue was that she had not a corner to give us, and recommended us to find Liakim, and have him show us the way to Waiting Samuel's.

"Waiting Samuel's?" we repeated.

"Yes; he's a kind of crazy man living away over there in the Flats. But there's no harm in him, and his wife is a tidy housekeeper. You be surveyors, I suppose?"

We accepted the imputation in order to avoid a broadside of questions, and asked the whereabouts of Liakim.

"O, he's round the point, somewhere there, fishing!"

We rowed on and found him, a little, round-shouldered man, in an old flat-bottomed boat, who had not taken a fish, and looked as though he never would. We explained our errand.

"Did Rosabel Lee tell ye to come to me?" he asked.

"The woman in the lighthouse told us," I said.

"That's Rosabel Lee, that's my wife; I'm Liakim Lee," said the little man, gathering together his forlorn old rods and tackle, and pulling up his anchor.

> "In the kingdom down by the sea
> Lived the beautiful Annabel Lee,"

I quoted, *sotto voce*.

"And what very remarkable feet had she!" added Raymond, improvising under the inspiration of certain shoes, scow-like in shape, gigantic in length and breadth, which had made themselves visible at the top round of the ladder.

At length the shabby old boat got under way, and we followed in its path, turning off to the right through a network of channels, now pulling ourselves along by the reeds, now paddling over a raft of lily-pads, now poling through a winding labyrinth, and now rowing with broad sweeps across the little lake. The sun was sinking, and the western sky grew bright at his coming; there was not a cloud to make mountain-peaks on the horizon, nothing but the level earth below meeting the curved sky above, so evenly and clearly that it seemed as though we could go out there and touch it with our hands. Soon we lost sight of the little lighthouse; then one by one the distant sails sank down and disappeared, and we were left alone on the grassy sea, rowing toward the sunset.

"We must have come a mile or two, and there is no sign of a house," I called out to our guide.

"Well, I don't pretend to know how far it is, exactly," replied Liakim; "we don't know how far anything is here in the Flats, we don't."

"But are you sure you know the way?"

"O my, yes! We've got most to the boy. There it is!"

The "boy" was a buoy, a fragment of plank painted white, part of the cabin-work of some wrecked steamer.

"Now, then," said Liakim, pausing, "you jest go straight on in this here channel till you come to the ninth run from this boy, on the right; take that, and it will lead you right up to Waiting Samuel's door."

"Aren't you coming with us?"

"Well, no. In the first place, Rosabel Lee will be waiting supper for me, and she don't like to wait; and, besides, Samuel can't abide to see none of us round his part of the Flats."

"But—" I began.

"Let him go," interposed Raymond; "we can find the house without trouble." And he tossed a silver dollar to the little man, who was already turning his boat.

"Thank you," said Liakim. "Be sure you take the ninth run and no other,—the ninth run from this boy. If you make any mistake, you'll find yourselves miles away."

With this cheerful statement, he began to row back. I did not altogether fancy being left on the watery waste without a guide; the name, too, of our mythic host did not bring up a certainty of supper and beds. "Waiting Samuel," I repeated, doubtfully. "What is he waiting for?" I called back over my shoulder; for Raymond was rowing.

"The judgment-day!" answered Liakim, in a shrill key. The boats were now far apart; another turn, and we were alone.

We glided on, counting the runs on the right: some were wide, promising rivers; others wee little rivulets; the eighth was far away; and, when we had passed it, we could hardly decide whether we had reached the ninth or not, so small was the opening, so choked with weeds, showing scarcely a gleam of water beyond when we stood up to inspect it.

"It is certainly the ninth, and I vote that we try it. It will do as well as another, and I, for one, am in no hurry to arrive any-where," said Raymond, pushing the boat in among the reeds.

"Do you want to lose yourself in this wilderness?" I asked, making a flag of my handkerchief to mark the spot where we had left the main stream.

"I think we are lost already," was the calm reply. I began to fear we were.

For some distance the "run," as Liakim called it, continued choked with aquatic vegetation, which acted like so many devil-fish catching our oars; at length it widened and gradually gave us a clear channel, albeit so winding and erratic that the glow of the sunset, our only beacon, seemed to be executing a waltz all round the horizon. At length we saw a dark spot on the left, and distinguished the outline of a low house. "There it is," I said, plying my oars with renewed strength. But the run turned short off in the opposite direction, and the house disappeared. After some time it rose again, this time on our right, but once more the run turned its back and shot off on a tangent. The sun had gone, and the rapid twilight of September was falling around us; the air, however, was singularly clear, and, as there was absolutely nothing to make a shadow, the darkness came on evenly over the level green. I was growing anxious, when a third time the house appeared, but the wilful run passed by it, although so near that we could distinguish its open windows and door. "Why not get out and wade across?" I suggested.

"According to Liakim, it is the duty of this run to take us to the very door of Waiting Samuel's mansion, and it shall take us," said Raymond, rowing on. It did.

Doubling upon itself in the most unexpected manner, it brought us back to a little island, where the tall grass had given way to a vegetable-garden. We landed, secured our boat, and walked up the pathway toward the house. In the dusk it seemed to be a low, square structure, built of planks covered with plaster; the roof was flat, the windows unusually broad, the door stood open,—but no one appeared. We knocked. A voice from within called out, "Who are you, and what do you want with Waiting Samuel?"

"Pilgrims, asking for food and shelter," replied Raymond.

"Do you know the ways of righteousness?"

"We can learn them."

"Will you conform to the rules of this household without murmuring?"

"We will."

"Enter then, and peace be with you!" said the voice, drawing nearer. We stepped cautiously through the dark passage into a room, whose open windows let in sufficient twilight to show us a shadowy figure. "Seat yourselves," it said. We found a bench, and sat down.

"What seek ye here?" continued the shadow.

"Rest!" replied Raymond.

"Hunting and fishing!" I added.

"Ye will find more than rest," said the voice, ignoring me altogether (I am often ignored in this way),—"more than rest, if ye stay long enough, and learn of the hidden treasures. Are you willing to seek for them?"

"Certainly!" said Raymond. "Where shall we dig?"

"I speak not of earthly digging, young man. Will you give me the charge of your souls?"

"Certainly, if you will also take charge of our bodies."

"Supper, for instance," I said, again coming to the front; "and beds."

The shadow groaned; then it called out wearily, "Roxana!"

"Yes, Samuel," replied an answering voice, and a second shadow became dimly visible on the threshold. "The woman

will attend to your earthly concerns," said Waiting Samuel.—
"Roxana, take them hence." The second shadow came forward,
and, without a word, took our hands and led us along the dark
passage like two children, warning us now of a step, now of a
turn, then of two steps, and finally opening a door and usher-
ing us into a fire-lighted room. Peat was burning upon the wide
hearth, and a singing kettle hung above it on a crane; the red
glow shone on a rough table, chairs cushioned in bright calico,
a loud-ticking clock, a few gayly flowered plates and cups on a
shelf, shining tins against the plastered wall, and a cat dozing
on a bit of carpet in one corner. The cheery domestic scene,
coming after the wide, dusky Flats, the silence, the darkness,
and the mystical words of the shadowy Samuel, seemed so real
and pleasant that my heart grew light within me.

"What a bright fire!" I said. "This is your domain, I suppose, Mrs.—Mrs.—"

"I am not Mrs.; I am called Roxana," replied the woman,
busying herself at the hearth.

"Ah, you are then the sister of Waiting Samuel, I presume?"

"No, I am his wife, fast enough; we were married by the
minister twenty years ago. But that was before Samuel had
seen any visions."

"Does he see visions?"

"Yes, almost every day."

"Do you see them, also?"

"O no; I'm not like Samuel. He has great gifts, Samuel has!
The visions told us to come here; we used to live away down
in Maine."

"Indeed! That was a long journey!"

"Yes! And we didn't come straight either. We'd get to

one place and stop, and I'd think we were going to stay, and just get things comfortable, when Samuel would see another vision, and we'd have to start on. We wandered in that way two or three years, but at last we got here, and something in the Flats seemed to suit the spirits, and they let us stay."

At this moment, through the half-open door, came a voice.

"An evil beast is in this house. Let him depart."

"Do you mean me?" said Raymond, who had made himself comfortable in a rocking-chair.

"Nay; I refer to the four-legged beast," continued the voice. "Come forth, Apollyon!"

Poor Captain Kidd seemed to feel that he was the person in question, for he hastened under the table with drooping tail and mortified aspect.

"Roxana, send forth the beast," said the voice.

The woman put down her dishes and went toward the table; but I interposed.

"If he must go, I will take him," I said, rising.

"Yes; he must go," replied Roxana, holding open the door. So I ordered out the unwilling Captain, and led him into the passageway.

"Out of the house, out of the house," said Waiting Samuel. "His feet may not rest upon this sacred ground. I must take him hence in the boat."

"But where?"

"Across the channel there is an islet large enough for him; he shall have food and shelter, but here he cannot abide," said the man, leading the way down to the boat.

The Captain was therefore ferried across, a tent was made for him out of some old mats, food was provided, and, lest he should swim back, he was tethered by a long rope, which allowed him to prowl around his domain and take his choice of three runs for drinking-water. With all these advantages, the ungrateful animal persisted in howling dismally as we rowed away. It was company he wanted, and not a "dear little isle of his own"; but then, he was not by nature poetical.

"You do not like dogs?" I said, as we reached our strand again.

"St. Paul wrote, 'Beware of dogs,'" replied Samuel.

"But did he mean—"

"I argue not with unbelievers; his meaning is clear to me, let that suffice," said my strange host, turning away and leaving me to find my way back alone. A delicious repast was awaiting me. Years have gone by, the world and all its delicacies have been unrolled before me, but the memory of the meals I ate in that little kitchen in the Flats haunts me still. That night it was only fish, potatoes, biscuits, butter, stewed fruit, and coffee; but the fish was fresh, and done to the turn of a perfect broil, not burn; the potatoes were fried to a rare crisp, yet tender perfection, not chippy brittleness; the biscuits were light, flaked creamily, and brown on the bottom; the butter freshly churned, without salt; the fruit, great pears, with their cores extracted, standing whole on their dish, ready to melt, but not melted; and the coffee clear and strong, with yellow cream and the old-fashioned, unadulterated loaf-sugar. We ate. That does not express it; we devoured. Roxana waited on us, and warmed up into something like excitement under our praises.

"I *do* like good cooking," she confessed. "It's about all I have left of my old life. I go over to the mainland for supplies, and in the winter I try all kinds of new things to pass away the time. But Samuel is a poor eater, he is; and so there isn't much comfort in it. I'm mighty glad you've come, and I hope you'll stay as long as you find it pleasant." This we promised to do, as we finished the potatoes and attacked the great jellied pears. "There's one thing, though," continued Roxana; "you'll have to come to our service on the roof at sunrise."

"What service?" I asked.

"The invocation. Dawn is a holy time, Samuel says, and we always wait for it; 'before the morning watch,' you know,—it says so in the Bible. Why, my name means 'the dawn,' Samuel says; that's the reason he gave it to me. My real name, down in Maine, was Maria,—Maria Ann."

"But I may not wake in time," I said.

"Samuel will call you."

"And if, in spite of that, I should sleep over?"

"You would not do that; it would vex him," replied Roxana, calmly.

"Do you believe in these visions, madam?" asked Raymond, as we left the table, and seated ourselves in front of the dying fire.

"Yes," said Roxana; emphasis was unnecessary,—of course she believed.

"How often do they come?"

"Almost every day there is a spiritual presence, but it does not always speak. They come and hold long conversations in the winter, when there is nothing else to do; that, I think, is very kind of them, for in the summer Samuel can fish, and his time is more occupied. There were fishermen in the Bible, you know; it is a holy calling."

"Does Samuel ever go over to the mainland?"

"No, he never leaves the Flats. I do all the business; take over the fish, and buy the supplies. I bought all our cattle," said Roxana, with pride. "I poled them away over here on a raft, one by one, when they were little things."

"Where do you pasture them?"

"Here, on the island; there are only a few acres, to be sure; but I can cut boat-loads of the best feed within a stone's throw. If we only had a little more solid ground! But this island is almost the only solid piece in the Flats."

"Your butter is certainly delicious."

"Yes, I do my best. It is sold to the steamers and vessels as fast as I make it."

"You keep yourself busy, I see."

"O, I like to work; I couldn't get on without it."

"And Samuel?"

"He is not like me," replied Roxana. "He has great gifts, Samuel has. I often think how strange it is that I should be the wife of such a holy man! He is very kind to me, too; he tells me about the visions, and all the other things."

"What things?" said Raymond.

"The spirits, and the sacred influence of the sun; the fiery triangle, and the thousand years of joy. The great day is coming, you know; Samuel is waiting for it."

"Nine of the night. Take thou thy rest. I will lay me down in peace, and sleep, for it is thou, Lord, only, that makest me dwell in safety," chanted a voice in the hall; the tone was deep and not without melody, and the words singularly impressive in that still, remote place.

"Go," said Roxana, instantly pushing aside her half-washed dishes. "Samuel will take you to your room."

"Do you leave your work unfinished?" I said, with some curiosity, noticing that she had folded her hands without even hanging up her towels.

"We do nothing after the evening chant," she said. "Pray go; he is waiting."

"Can we have candles?"

"Waiting Samuel allows no false lights in his house; as imitations of the glorious sun, they are abominable to him. Go, I beg."

She opened the door, and we went into the passage; it was entirely dark, but the man led us across to our room, showed us the position of our beds by sense of feeling, and left us without a word. After he had gone, we struck matches, one by one, and, with the aid of their uncertain light, managed to get into our respective mounds in safety; they were shake-downs on the floor, made of fragrant hay instead of straw, covered with clean sheets and patchwork coverlids, and provided with large, luxurious pillows. O pillow! Has any one sung thy praises? When tired or sick, when discouraged or sad, what gives so much comfort as a pillow? Not your curled-hair brickbats; not your stiff, fluted, rasping covers, or limp cotton cases; but a good, generous, soft pillow, deftly cased in smooth, cool, untrimmed linen! There's a friend for you, a friend who changes not, a friend who soothes all your troubles with a soft caress, a mesmeric touch of balmy forgetfulness.

I slept a dreamless sleep. Then I heard a voice borne toward me as if coming from far over a sea, the waves bringing it nearer and nearer.

"Awake!" it cried; "awake! The night is far spent; the day is at hand. Awake!"

I wondered vaguely over this voice as to what manner of voice it might be, but it came again, and again, and finally I awoke to find it at my side. The gray light of dawn came through the open windows, and Raymond was already up, engaged with a tub of water and crash towels. Again the chant sounded in my ears.

"Very well, very well," I said, testily. "But if you sing before breakfast you'll cry before night, Waiting Samuel."

Our host had disappeared, however, without hearing my flippant speech, and slowly I rose from my fragrant couch; the room was empty save for our two mounds, two tubs of water, and a number of towels hanging on nails. "Not overcrowded with furniture," I remarked.

"From Maine to Florida, from Massachusetts to Missouri, have I travelled, and never before found water enough," said Raymond. "If waiting for the judgment-day raises such liberal ideas of tubs and towels, I would that all the hotel-keepers in the land could be convened here to take a lesson."

Our green hunting-clothes were soon donned, and we went out into the hall; a flight of broad steps led up to the roof; Roxana appeared at the top and beckoned us thither. We ascended, and found ourselves on the flat roof. Samuel stood with his face toward the east and his arms outstretched, watching the horizon; behind was Roxana, with her hands clasped on her breast and her head bowed: thus they waited. The eastern sky was bright with golden light; rays shot upward toward the zenith, where the rose-lights of dawn were retreating down to the west, which still lay in the shadow of night; there was not a sound; the Flats stretched out dusky and still. Two or three minutes passed, and then a dazzling rim appeared above the horizon, and the first gleam of sunshine was shed over the level earth; simultaneously the two began a chant, simple as a Gregorian, but rendered in correct full tones. The words, apparently, had been collected from the Bible:—

> "The heavens declare the glory of God—
> > Joy cometh in the morning!
> In them is laid out the path of the sun—
> > Joy cometh in the morning!
> As a bridegroom goeth he forth;
> As a strong man runneth his race.
> The outgoings of the morning
> > Praise thee, O Lord!
> Like a pelican in the wilderness,
> Like a sparrow upon the house-top,
> > I wait for the Lord.
> It is good that we hope and wait,
> > Wait—wait."

The chant over, the two stood a moment silently, as if in contemplation, and then descended, passing us without a word or sign, with their hands clasped before them as though forming part of an unseen procession. Raymond and I were left alone upon the house-top.

"After all, it is not such a bad opening for a day; and there is the pelican of the wilderness to emphasize it," I said, as a heron flew up from the water, and, slowly flapping his great wings, sailed across to another channel. As the sun rose higher, the birds began to sing; first a single note here and there, then a little trilling solo, and finally an outpouring of melody on all sides,—land-birds and water-birds, birds that lived in the Flats, and birds that had flown thither for breakfast,—the whole waste was awake and rejoicing in the sunshine.

"What a wild place it is!" said Raymond. "How boundless it looks! One hill in the distance, one dark line of forest, even one tree, would break its charm. I have seen the ocean, I have seen the prairies, I have seen the great desert, but this is like a mixture of the three. It is an ocean full of land,—a prairie full of water,—a desert full of verdure."

"Whatever it is, we shall find in it fishing and aquatic hunting to our hearts' content," I answered.

And we did. After a breakfast delicious as the supper, we took our boat and a lunch-basket, and set out. "But how shall we ever find our way back?" I said, pausing as I recalled the network of runs, and the will-o'-the-wisp aspect of the house, the previous evening.

"There is no other way but to take a large ball of cord with you, fasten one end on shore, and let it run out over the stern of the boat," said Roxana. "Let it run out loosely, and it will float on the water. When you want to come back you can turn around and wind it in as you come. *I* can read the Flats like a book, but they're very blinding to most people; and you might keep going round in a circle. You will do better not to go far, anyway. I'll wind the bugle on the roof an hour before sunset; you can start back when you hear it; for it's awkward getting supper after dark." With this musical promise we took the clew of twine which Roxana rigged for us in the stern of our boat, and started away, first releasing Captain Kidd, who was pacing his islet in sullen majesty, like another Napoleon on St. Helena. We took a new channel and passed behind the house, where the imported cattle were feeding in their little pasture; but the winding stream soon bore us away, the house sank out of sight, and we were left alone.

We had fine sport that morning among the ducks,—wood, teal, and canvas-back,—shooting from behind our screens woven of rushes; later in the day we took to fishing. The sun shone down, but there was a cool September breeze, and the freshness of the verdure was like early spring. At noon we took our lunch and a *siesta* among the water-lilies. When we awoke we found that a bittern had taken up his position near by, and was surveying us gravely:—

> "'The moping bittern, motionless and stiff,
> That on a stone so silently and stilly
> Stands, an apparent sentinel, as if
> To guard the water-lily,'"

quoted Raymond. The solemn bird, in his dark uniform, seemed quite undisturbed by our presence; yellow-throats and swamp-sparrows also came in numbers to have a look at us; and the fish swam up to the surface and eyed us curiously. Lying at ease in the boat, we in our turn looked down into the water. There is a singular fascination in looking down into a clear stream as the boat floats above; the mosses and twining water-plants seem to have arbors and grottos in their recesses, where delicate marine creatures might live, naiads and mermaids of miniature size; at least we are always looking for them. There is a fancy, too, that one may find something,—a ring dropped from fair fingers idly trailing in the water; a book which the fishes have read thoroughly; a scarf caught among the lilies; a

spoon with unknown initials; a drenched ribbon, or an embroidered handkerchief. None of these things did we find, but we
did discover an old brass breastpin, whose probable glass stone
was gone. It was a paltry trinket at best, but I fished it out with
superstitious care,—a treasure-trove of the Flats. "'Drowned,'"
I said, pathetically, "'drowned in her white robes—'"

"And brass breastpin," added Raymond, who objected to
sentiment, true or false.

"You Philistine! Is nothing sacred to you?"

"Not brass jewelry, certainly."

"Take some lilies and consider them," I said, plucking several of the queenly blossoms floating alongside.

> "Cleopatra art thou, regal blossom,
>   Floating in thy galley down the Nile,—
> All my soul does homage to thy splendor,
>   All my heart grows warmer in thy smile;
> Yet thou smilest for thine own grand pleasure,
>   Caring not for all the world beside,
> As in insolence of perfect beauty,
>   Sailest thou in silence down the tide.
>
> "Loving, humble rivers all pursue thee,
>   Wasted are their kisses at thy feet;
> Fiery sun himself cannot subdue thee,
>   Calm thou smilest through his raging heat;
> Naught to thee the earth's great crowd of blossoms,
>   Naught to thee the rose-queen on her throne;
> Haughty empress of the summer waters,
>   Livest thou, and diest, all alone."

This from Raymond.

"Where did you find that?" I asked.

"It is my own."

"Of course! I might have known it. There is a certain raw-ness of style and versification which—"

"That's right," interrupted Raymond; "I know just what you are going to say. The whole matter of opinion is a game of 'follow-my-leader'; not one of you dares admire anything unless the critics say so. If I had told you the verses were by somebody instead of a nobody, you would have found wonder-ful beauties in them."

"Exactly. My motto is, 'Never read anything unless it is by a somebody.' For, don't you see, that a nobody, if he is worth anything, will soon grow into a somebody, and, if he isn't worth anything, you will have saved your time!"

"But it is not merely a question of growing," said Raymond; "it is a question of critics."

"No; there you are mistaken. All the critics in the world can neither make nor crush a true poet."

"What is poetry?" said Raymond, gloomily.

At this comprehensive question, the bittern gave a hollow croak, and flew away with his long legs trailing behind him. Probably he was not of an æsthetic turn of mind, and dreaded lest I should give a ramified answer.

Through the afternoon we fished when the fancy struck us, but most of the time we floated idly, enjoying the wild freedom of the watery waste. We watched the infinite vari-eties of the grasses, feathery, lance-leaved, tufted, droop-ing, banner-like, the deer's tongue, the wild-celery, and the so-called wild-rice, besides many unknown beauties delicately fringed, as difficult to catch and hold as thistle-down. There were plants journeying to and fro on the water like nomadic tribes of the desert; there were fleets of green leaves floating down the current; and now and then we saw a wonderful flower with scarlet bells, but could never approach near enough to touch it.

At length, the distant sound of the bugle came to us on the breeze, and I slowly wound in the clew, directing Raymond as he pushed the boat along, backing water with the oars. The sound seemed to come from every direction. There was nothing for it to echo against, but, in place of the echo, we heard a long, dying cadence, which sounded on over the Flats fainter and fainter in a sweet, slender note, until a new tone broke forth. The music floated around us, now on one side, now on the other; if it had been our only guide, we should have been completely bewildered. But I wound the cord steadily; and at last suddenly, there before us, appeared the house with Roxana on the roof, her figure outlined against the sky. Seeing us, she played a final salute, and then descended, carrying the imprisoned music with her.

That night we had our supper at sunset. Waiting Samuel had his meals by himself in the front room. "So that in case the spirits come, I shall not be there to hinder them," explained Roxana. "I am not holy, like Samuel; they will not speak before me."

"Do you have your meals apart in the winter, also?" asked Raymond.

"Yes."

"That is not very sociable," I said.

"Samuel never was sociable," replied Roxana. "Only common folks are sociable; but he is different. He has great gifts, Samuel has."

The meal over, we went up on the roof to smoke our cigars in the open air; when the sun had disappeared and his glory had darkened into twilight, our host joined us. He was a tall man, wasted and gaunt, with piercing dark eyes and dark hair, tinged with gray, hanging down upon his shoulders. (Why is it that long hair on the outside is almost always the sign of something wrong in the inside of a man's head?) He wore a black robe like a priest's cassock, and on his head a black skull-cap like the *Faust* of the operatic stage.

"Why were the Flats called St. Clair?" I said; for there is something fascinating to me in the unknown history of the West. "There isn't any," do you say? you, I mean, who are strong in the Punic wars! you, too, who are so well up in Grecian mythology. But there is history, only we don't know it. The story of Lake Huron in the times of the Pharaohs, the story of the Mississippi during the reign of Belshazzar, would be worth hearing. But it is lost! All we can do is to gather together the details of our era,—the era when Columbus came to this New World, which was, nevertheless, as old as the world he left behind.

"It was in 1679," began Waiting Samuel, "that La Salle sailed up the Detroit River in his little vessel of sixty tons burden, called the Griffin. He was accompanied by thirty-four men, mostly fur-traders; but there were among them two holy monks, and Father Louis Hennepin, a friar of the Franciscan order. They passed up the river and entered the little lake just south of us, crossing it and these Flats on the 12th of August, which is Saint Clair's day. Struck with the gentle beauty of the scene, they named the waters after their saint, and at sunset sang a *Te Deum* in her honor."

"And who was Saint Clair?"

"Saint Clair, virgin and abbess, born in Italy, in 1193, made superior of a convent by the great Francis, and canonized for her distinguished virtues," said Samuel, as though reading from an encyclopædia.

"Are you a Roman Catholic?" asked Raymond.

"I am everything; all sincere faith is sacred to me," replied the man. "It is but a question of names."

"Tell us of your religion," said Raymond, thoughtfully; for in religions Raymond was something of a polyglot.

"You would hear of my faith? Well, so be it. Your question is the work of spirit influence. Listen, then. The great Creator has sowed immensity with innumerable systems of suns. In one of these systems a spirit forgot that he was a limited, subordinate being, and misused his freedom; how, we know not. He fell, and with him all his kind. A new race was then created for the vacant world, and, according to the fixed purpose of the Creator, each was left free to act for himself; he loves not mere machines. The fallen spirit, envying the new creature called man, tempted him to sin. What was his sin? Simply the giving up of his birthright, the divine soul-sparkle, for a promise of earthly pleasure. The triune divine deep, the mysterious fiery triangle, which, to our finite minds, best represents the Deity, now withdrew his personal presence; the elements, their balance broken, stormed upon man; his body, which was once ethereal, moving by mere volition, now grew heavy; and it was also appointed unto him to die. The race thus darkened, crippled, and degenerate, sank almost to the level of the brutes, the mind-fire alone remaining of all their spiritual gifts. They lived on blindly, and as blindly died. The sun, however, was left to them, a type of what they had lost.

"At length, in the fulness of time, the world-day of four thousand years, which was appointed by the council in heaven for the regiving of the divine and forfeited soul-sparkle, as on the fourth day of creation the great sun was given, there came to earth the earth's compassionate Saviour, who took upon himself our degenerate body, and revivified it with the divine soul-sparkle, who overcame all our temptations, and finally allowed the tinder of our sins to perish in his own painful death upon the cross. Through him our paradise body was restored, it waits for us on the other side of the grave. He showed us what it was like on Mount Tabor, with it he passed through closed doors, walked upon the water, and ruled the elements; so will it be with us. Paradise will come again; this world will, for a thousand years, see its first estate; it will be again the Garden of Eden. America is the great escaping-place; here will the change begin. As it is written, 'Those who escape to my utmost borders.' As the time draws near, the spirits who watch above are permitted to speak to those souls who listen. Of these listening, waiting souls am I; therefore have I withdrawn myself. The sun himself speaks to me, the greatest spirit of all; each morning I watch for his coming; each morning I ask, 'Is it to-day?' Thus do I wait."

"And how long have you been waiting?" I asked.

"I know not; time is nothing to me."

"Is the great day near at hand?" said Raymond.

"Almost at its dawning; the last days are passing."

"How do you know this?"

"The spirits tell me. Abide here, and perhaps they will speak to you also," replied Waiting Samuel.

We made no answer. Twilight had darkened into night, and the Flats had sunk into silence below us. After some moments I turned to speak to our host; but, noiselessly as one of his own spirits, he had departed.

"A strange mixture of Jacob Bœhmen, chiliastic dreams, Christianity, sun-worship, and modern spiritualism," I said. "Much learning hath made the Maine farmer mad."

"Is he mad?" said Raymond. "Sometimes I think we are all mad."

"We should certainly become so if we spent our time in speculations upon subjects clearly beyond our reach. The whole race of philosophers from Plato down are all the time going round in a circle. As long as we are in the world, I for one propose to keep my feet on solid ground; especially as we have no wings. 'Abide here, and perhaps the spirits will speak to you,' did he say? I think very likely they will, and to such good purpose that you won't have any mind left."

"After all, why should not spirits speak to us?" said Raymond, in a musing tone.

As he uttered these words the mocking laugh of a loon came across the dark waste.

"The very loons are laughing at you," I said, rising. "Come down; there is a chill in the air, composed in equal parts of the Flats, the night, and Waiting Samuel. Come down, man; come down to the warm kitchen and common-sense."

We found Roxana alone by the fire, whose glow was refreshingly real and warm; it was like the touch of a flesh-and-blood hand, after vague dreamings of spirit-companions, cold and intangible at best, with the added suspicion that, after all, they are but creations of our own fancy, and even their spirit-nature fictitious. Prime, the graceful *raconteur* who goes a-fishing, says, "firelight is as much of a polisher in-doors as moonlight outside." It is; but with a different result. The moonlight polishes everything into romance, the firelight into comfort. We brought up two remarkably easy old chairs in front of the hearth and sat down, Raymond still adrift with his wandering thoughts, I, as usual, making talk out of the present. Roxana sat opposite, knitting in hand, the cat purring at her feet. She was a slender woman, with faded light hair, insignificant features, small dull blue eyes, and a general aspect which, with every desire to state at its best, I can only call commonplace. Her gown was limp, her hands roughened with work, and there was no collar around her yellow throat. O magic rim of white, great is thy power! With thee, man is civilized; without thee, he becomes at once a savage.

"I am out of pork," remarked Roxana, casually; "I must go over to the mainland to-morrow and get some."

If it had been anything but pork! In truth, the word did not chime with the mystic conversation of Waiting Samuel. Yes; there was no doubt about it. Roxana's mind was sadly commonplace.

"See what I have found," I said, after a while, taking out the old breastpin. "The stone is gone; but who knows? It might have been a diamond dropped by some French duchess, exiled, and fleeing for life across these far Western waters; or perhaps that German Princess of Brunswick-Wolfen-something-or-other, who, about one hundred years ago, was dead and buried in Russia, and travelling in America at the same time, a sort of a female wandering Jew, who has been done up in stories ever since."

(The other day, in Bret Harte's "Melons," I saw the following: "The singular conflicting conditions of John Brown's body and soul were, at that time, beginning to attract the attention of American youth." That is good, isn't it? Well, at the time I visited the Flats, the singular conflicting conditions of the Princess of Brunswick-Wolfen-something-or-other had, for a long time, haunted me.)

Roxana's small eyes were near-sighted; she peered at the empty setting, but said nothing.

"It is water-logged," I continued, holding it up in the fire-light, "and it hath a brassy odor; nevertheless, I feel convinced that it belonged to the princess."

Roxana leaned forward and took the trinket; I lifted up my arms and gave a mighty stretch, one of those enjoyable lengthenings-out which belong only to the healthy fatigue of country life. When I drew myself in again, I was surprised to see Roxana's features working, and her rough hands trembling, as she held the battered setting.

"It was mine," she said; "my dear old cameo breastpin that Abby gave me when I was married. I saved it and saved it, and wouldn't sell it, no matter how low we got, for someway it seemed to tie me to home and baby's grave. I used to wear it when I had baby—I had neck-ribbons then; we had things like other folks, and on Sundays we went to the old meeting-house on the green. Baby is buried there—O baby, baby!" and the voice broke into sobs.

"You lost a child?" I said, pitying the sorrow which was, which must be, so lonely, so unshared.

"Yes. O baby! baby!" cried the woman, in a wailing tone. "It was a little boy, gentlemen, and it had curly hair, and could just talk a word or two; its name was Ethan, after father, but we all called it Robin. Father was mighty proud of Robin, and mother, too. It died, gentlemen, my baby died, and I buried it in the old churchyard near the thorn-tree. But still I thought to stay there always along with mother and the girls; I never supposed anything else, until Samuel began to see visions. Then, everything was different, and everybody against us; for, you see, I would marry Samuel, and when he left off working, and began to talk to the spirits, the folks all said, 'I told yer so, Maria Ann!' Samuel wasn't of Maine stock exactly: his father was a sailor, and 'twas suspected that his mother was some kind of an East-Injia woman, but no one knew. His father died and left the boy on the town, so he lived round from house to house until he got old enough to hire out. Then he came to our farm, and there he stayed. He had wonderful eyes, Samuel had, and he had a way with him—well, the long and short of it was, that I got to thinking about him, and couldn't think of anything else. The folks didn't like it at all, for, you see, there was Adam Rand, who had a farm of his own over the hill; but I never could bear Adam Rand. The worst of it was, though, that Samuel never so much as looked at me, hardly. Well, it got to be the second year, and Susan, my younger sister, married Adam Rand. Adam, he thought he'd break up my nonsense, that's what they called it, and so he got a good place for Samuel away down in Connecticut, and Samuel said he'd go, for he was always restless, Samuel was. When I heard it, I was ready to lie down and die. I ran out into the pasture and threw myself down by the fence like a crazy woman. Samuel happened to come by along the lane, and saw me; he was always kind to all the dumb creatures, and stopped to see what was the matter, just as he would have stopped to help a calf. It all came out then, and he was awful sorry for me. He sat down on the top bar of the fence and looked at me, and I sat on the ground a-crying with my hair down, and my face all red and swollen.

"'I never thought to marry, Maria Ann,' says he.

"'O, please do, Samuel,' says I, 'I'm a real good house-keeper, I am, and we can have a little land of our own, and everything nice—'

"'But I wanted to go away. My father was a sailor,' he began, a-looking away off toward the ocean.

"'O, I can't stand it,—I can't stand it,' says I, beginning to cry again. Well, after that he 'greed to stay at home and marry me, and the folks they had to give in to it when they saw how I felt. We were married on Thanksgiving day, and I wore a pink delaine, purple neck-ribbon, and this very breastpin that sister Abby gave me,—it cost four dollars, and came 'way from Boston. Mother kissed me, and said she hoped I'd be happy.

"'Of course I shall, mother,' says I. 'Samuel has great gifts; he isn't like common folks.'

"'But common folks is a deal comfortabler,' says mother. The folks never understood Samuel.

"Well, we had a chirk little house and bit of land, and baby came, and was so cunning and pretty. The visions had begun to appear then, and Samuel said he must go.

"'Where?' says I.

"'Anywhere the spirits lead me,' says he.

"But baby couldn't travel, and so it hung along; Samuel left off work, and everything ran down to loose ends; I did the best I could, but it wasn't much. Then baby died, and I buried him under the thorn-tree, and the visions came thicker and thicker, and Samuel told me as how this time he must go. The folks wanted me to stay behind without him; but they never understood me nor him. I could no more leave him than I could fly; I was just wrapped up in him. So we went away; I cried dreadfully when it came to leaving the folks and Robin's little grave, but I had so much to do after we got started, that there wasn't time for anything but work. We thought to settle in ever so many places, but after a while there would always come a vision, and I'd have to sell out and start on. The little money we had was soon gone, and then I went out for days' work, and picked up any work I could get. But many's the time we were cold, and many's the time we were hungry, gentlemen. The visions kept coming, and by and by I got to like 'em too. Samuel he told me all they said when I came home nights, and it was nice to hear all about the thousand years of joy, when there'd be no more trouble, and when Robin would come back to us again. Only I told Samuel that I hoped the world wouldn't alter much, because I wanted to go back to Maine for a few days, and see all the old places. Father and mother are dead, I suppose," said Roxana, looking up at us with a pathetic expression in her small dull eyes. Beautiful eyes are doubly beautiful in sorrow; but there is something peculiarly pathetic in small dull eyes looking up at you, struggling to express the grief that lies within, like a prisoner behind the bars of his small dull window.

"And how did you lose your breastpin?" I said, coming back to the original subject.

"Samuel found I had it, and threw it away soon after we came to the Flats; he said it was vanity."

"Have you been here long?"

"O yes, years. I hope we shall stay here always now,—at least, I mean until the thousand years of joy begin,—for it's quiet, and Samuel's more easy here than in any other place. I've got used to the lonely feeling, and don't mind it much now. There's no one near us for miles, except Rosabel Lee and Liakim; they don't come here, for Samuel can't abide 'em, but sometimes I stop there on my way over from the mainland, and have a little chat about the children. Rosabel Lee has got lovely children, she has! They don't stay there in the winter, though; the winters *are* long, I don't deny it."

"What do you do then?"

"Well, I knit and cook, and Samuel reads to me, and has a great many visions."

"He has books, then?"

"Yes, all kinds; he's a great reader, and he has boxes of books about the spirits, and such things."

"Nine of the night. Take thou thy rest. I will lay me down in peace and sleep; for it is thou, Lord, only, that makest me dwell in safety," chanted the voice in the hall; and our evening was over.

At dawn we attended the service on the roof; then, after breakfast, we released Captain Kidd, and started out for another day's sport. We had not rowed far when Roxana passed us, poling her flat-boat rapidly along; she had a load of fish and butter, and was bound for the mainland village. "Bring us back a Detroit paper," I said. She nodded and passed on, stolid and homely in the morning light. Yes, I was obliged to confess to myself that she *was* commonplace.

A glorious day we had on the moors in the rushing September wind. Everything rustled and waved and danced, and the grass undulated in long billows as far as the eye could see. The wind enjoyed himself like a mad creature; he had no forests to oppose him, no heavy water to roll up,—nothing but merry, swaying grasses. It was the west wind,—"of all the winds, the best wind." The east wind was given us for our sins; I have long suspected that the east wind was the angel that drove Adam out of Paradise. We did nothing that day,—nothing but enjoy the rushing breeze. We felt like Bedouins of the desert, with our boat for a steed. "He came flying upon the wings of the wind," is the grandest image of the Hebrew poet.

Late in the afternoon we heard the bugle and returned, following our clew as before. Roxana had brought a late paper, and, opening it, I saw the account of an accident,—a yacht run down on the Sound and five drowned; five, all near and dear to us. Hastily and sadly we gathered our possessions together; the hunting, the fishing, were nothing now; all we thought of was to get away, to go home to the sorrowing ones around the new-made graves. Roxana went with us in her boat to guide us back to the little lighthouse. Waiting Samuel bade us no farewell, but as we rowed away we saw him standing on the house-top gazing after us. We bowed; he waved his hand; and then turned away to look at the sunset. What were our little affairs to a man who held converse with the spirits!

We rowed in silence. How long, how weary seemed the way! The grasses, the lilies, the silver channels,—we no longer even saw them. At length the forward boat stopped. "There's the lighthouse yonder," said Roxana. "I won't go over there to-night. Mayhap you'd rather not talk, and Rosabel Lee will be sure to talk to me. Good by." We shook hands, and I laid in the boat a sum of money to help the little household through the winter; then we rowed on toward the lighthouse. At the turn I looked back; Roxana was sitting motionless in her boat; the dark clouds were rolling up behind her; and the Flats looked wild and desolate. "God help her!" I said.

A steamer passed the lighthouse and took us off within the hour.

Years rolled away, and I often thought of the grassy sea, and intended to go there; but the intention never grew into reality. In 1870, however, I was travelling westward, and, finding myself at Detroit, a sudden impulse took me up to the Flats. The steamer sailed up the beautiful river and crossed the little lake, both unchanged. But, alas! the canal predicted by the captain fifteen years before had been cut, and, in all its unmitigated ugliness, stretched straight through the enchanted land. I got off at the new and prosaic brick lighthouse, half expecting to see Liakim and his Rosabel Lee; but they were not there, and no one knew anything about them. And Waiting Samuel? No one knew anything about him, either. I took a skiff, and, at the risk of losing myself, I rowed away into the wilderness, spending the day among the silvery channels, which were as beautiful as ever. There were fewer birds; I saw no grave herons, no sombre bitterns, and the fish had grown shy. But the water-lilies were beautiful as of old, and the grasses as delicate and luxuriant. I had scarcely a hope of finding the old house on the island, but late in the afternoon, by a mere chance, I rowed up unexpectedly to its little landing-place. The walls stood firm and the roof was unbroken; I landed and walked up the overgrown path. Opening the door, I found the few old chairs and tables in their places, weather-beaten and decayed, the storms had forced a way within, and the floor was insecure; but the gay crockery was on its shelf, the old tins against the wall, and all looked so natural that I almost feared to find the mortal remains of the husband and wife as I went from to room to room. They were not there, however, and the place looked as if it had been uninhabited for years. I lingered in the doorway. What had become of them? Were they dead? Or had a new vision sent them farther toward the setting sun? I never knew, although I made many inquiries. If dead, they were probably lying somewhere under the shining waters; if alive, they must have "folded their tents, like the Arabs, and silently stolen away."

I rowed back in the glow of the evening across the grassy sea. "It is beautiful, beautiful," I thought, "but it is passing away. Already commerce has invaded its borders; a few more years and its loveliness will be but a legend of the past. The bittern has vanished; the loon has fled away. Waiting Samuel was the prophet of the waste; he has gone, and the barriers are broken down. Farewell, beautiful grass-water! No artist has painted, no poet has sung your wild, vanishing charm; but in one heart, at least, you have a place, O lovely land of St. Clair!"

SOLOMON

❧

"SOLOMON" IS AN EXCELLENT EXAMPLE OF WOOL-
son's belief that literature should strive to make the
humanity of those who are overlooked and marginalized known to readers. The story also introduced into
her works the theme of the frustrated or failed artist,
which would reappear throughout her career. "Solomon" takes place in the German separatist community
Zoar, founded in 1817 on the banks of the Tuscarawas
River in eastern Ohio, a region rich in coal. Zoar was
named for the Biblical town that God spared when he
sent fire and brimstone to destroy Sodom and Gomor-
rah. The separatist community's first residents fled
Württemberg, Germany, due to oppression for their
refusal to acknowledge religious authorities. The village that grew up in Zoar resembled a traditional German town and became a popular tourist attraction in
the late nineteenth century. Like the women in the

story, Woolson had often visited the Zoar community during her young adulthood. "Solomon" was Woolson's first story published in the prestigious *Atlantic Monthly* (October 1873), and it was reprinted in *Castle Nowhere: Lake-Country Sketches* (1875).

SOLOMON

. . . .

Midway in the eastern part of Ohio lies the coal country; round-topped hills there begin to show themselves in the level plain, trending back from Lake Erie; afterwards rising higher and higher, they stretch away into Pennsylvania and are dignified by the name of Alleghany Mountains. But no names have they in their Ohio birthplace, and little do the people care for them, save as storehouses for fuel. The roads lie along the slow-moving streams, and the farmers ride slowly over them in their broad-wheeled wagons, now and then passing dark holes in the bank from whence come little carts into the sunshine, and men, like *silhouettes*, walking behind them, with glow-worm lamps fastened in their hat-bands. Neither farmers nor miners glance up towards the hilltops; no doubt they consider them useless mounds, and, were it not for the coal, they would envy their neighbors of the grain-country, whose broad, level fields stretch unbroken through Central Ohio; as, however, the canal-boats go away full, and long lines of coal-cars go away full, and every man's coal-shed is full, and money comes back from the great iron-mills of Pittsburgh, Cincinnati, and Cleveland, the coal country, though unknown in a picturesque point of view, continues to grow rich and prosperous.

Yet picturesque it is, and no part more so than the valley where stands the village of the quaint German Community on the banks of the slow-moving Tuscarawas River. One October day we left the lake behind us and journeyed inland, following the water-courses and looking forward for the first glimpse of rising ground; blue are the waters of Erie on a summer day, red and golden are its autumn sunsets, but so level, so deadly level are its shores that, at times, there comes a longing for the sight of distant hills. Hence our journey. Night found us still in the "Western Reserve." Ohio has some queer names of her own for portions of her territory, the "Fire Lands," the "Donation Grant," the "Salt Section," the "Refugee's Tract," and the "Western Reserve" are names well known, although not found on the maps. Two days more and we came into the coal country; near by were the "Moravian Lands," and at the end of the last day's ride we crossed a yellow bridge over a stream called the "One-Leg Creek."

"I have tried in vain to discover the origin of this name," I said, as we leaned out of the carriage to watch the red leaves float down the slow tide.

"Create one, then. A one-legged soldier, a farmer's pretty daughter, an elopement in a flat-bottomed boat, and a home upon this stream which yields its stores of catfish for their support," suggested Erminia.

"The original legend would be better than that if we could only find it, for real life is always better than fiction," I answered.

"In real life we are all masked; but in fiction the author shows the faces as they are, Dora."

"I do not believe we are all masked, Erminia. I can read my friends like a printed page."

"O, the wonderful faith of youth!" said Erminia, retiring upon her seniority.

Presently the little church on the hill came into view through a vista in the trees. We passed the mill and its flowing race, the blacksmith's shop, the great grass meadow, and drew up in front of the quaint hotel where the trustees allowed the world's people, if uninquisitive and decorous, to remain in the Community for short periods of time, on the payment of three dollars per week for each person. This village was our favorite retreat, our little hiding-place in the hill-country; at that time it was almost as isolated as a solitary island, for the Community owned thousands of outlying acres and held no intercourse with the surrounding townships. Content with their own, unmindful of the rest of the world, these Germans grew steadily richer and richer, solving quietly the problem of co-operative labor, while the French and Americans worked at it in vain with newspapers, orators, and even cannon to aid them. The members of the Community were no ascetic anchorites; each tiled roof covered a home with a thrifty mother and train of grave little children, the girls in short-waisted gowns, kerchiefs, and frilled caps, and the boys in tailed coats, long-flapped vests, and trousers, as soon as they were able to toddle. We liked them all, we liked the life; we liked the mountain-high beds, the coarse snowy linen, and the remarkable counterpanes; we liked the cream-stewed chicken, the Käse-lab, and fresh butter, but, of all, the hot bretzels for breakfast. And let not the hasty city imagination turn to the hard, salty, saw-dust cake in the shape of a broken-down figure eight which is served with lager-beer in saloons and gardens. The Community bretzel was of a delicate flaky white in the inside, shading away into a golden-brown crust of crisp involutions, light as a feather, and flanked by little pats of fresh, unsalted butter, and a deep-blue cup wherein the coffee was hot, the cream yellow, and the sugar broken lumps from the old-fashioned loaf, now alas! obsolete.

We stayed among the simple people and played at shepherdesses and pastorellas; we adopted the hours of the birds, we went to church on Sunday and sang German chorals as old as Luther. We even played at work to the extent of helping gather apples, eating the best, and riding home on top of the loaded four-horse wains. But one day we heard of a new diversion, a sulphur-spring over the hills about two miles from the hotel on land belonging to the Community; and, obeying the fascination which earth's native medicines exercise over all earth's children, we immediately started in search of the nauseous spring. The road wound over the hill, past one of the apple-orchards, where the girls were gathering the red fruit, and then down a little declivity where the track branched off to the Community coal-mine; then a solitary stretch through the thick woods, a long hill with a curve, and at the foot a little dell with a patch of meadow, a brook, and a log-house with overhanging roof, a forlorn house unpainted and desolate. There was not even the blue door which enlivened many of the Community dwellings. "This looks like the huts of the Black Forest," said Erminia. "Who would have supposed that we should find such an antique in Ohio!"

"I am confident it was built by the M.B.'s," I replied. "They tramped, you know, extensively through the State, burying axes and leaving every now and then a mastodon behind them."

"Well, if the Mound-Builders selected this site they showed good taste," said Erminia, refusing, in her afternoon indolence, the argumentum nonsensicum with which we were accustomed to enliven our conversation. It was, indeed, a lovely spot,—the little meadow, smooth and bright as green velvet, the brook chattering over the pebbles, and the hills, gay in red and yellow foliage, rising abruptly on all sides. After some labor we swung open the great gate and entered the yard, crossed the brook on a mossy plank, and followed the path through the grass towards the lonely house. An old shepherd-dog lay at the door of a dilapidated shed, like a block-house, which had once been a stable; he did not bark, but, rising slowly, came along beside us,—a large, gaunt animal that looked at us with such melancholy eyes that Erminia stooped to pat him. Ermine had a weakness for dogs; she herself owned a wild beast of the dog kind that went by the name of the "Emperor Trajan"; and, accompanied by this dignitary, she was accustomed to stroll up the avenues of C——, lost in maiden meditations.

We drew near the house and stepped up on the sunken piazza, but no signs of life appeared. The little loophole windows were pasted over with paper, and the plank door had no latch or handle. I knocked, but no one came. "Apparently it is a haunted house, and that dog is the spectre," I said, stepping back.

"Knock three times," suggested Ermine; "that is what they always do in ghost-stories."

"Try it yourself. My knuckles are not cast-iron."

Ermine picked up a stone and began tapping on the door. "Open sesame," she said, and it opened.

Instantly the dog slunk away to his block-house and a woman confronted us, her dull face lighting up as her eyes ran rapidly over our attire from head to foot. "Is there a sulphur-spring here?" I asked. "We would like to try the water."

"Yes, it's here fast enough in the back hall. Come in, ladies; I'm right proud to see you. From the city, I suppose?"

"From C——," I answered; "we are spending a few days in the Community."

Our hostess led the way through the little hall, and throwing open a back door pulled up a trap in the floor, and there we saw the spring,—a shallow well set in stones, with a jar of butter cooling in its white water. She brought a cup, and we drank. "Delicious," said Ermine. "The true, spoiled-egg flavor! Four cups is the minimum allowance, Dora."

"I reckon it's good for the insides," said the woman, standing with arms akimbo and staring at us. She was a singular creature, with large black eyes, Roman nose, and a mass of black hair tightly knotted on the top of her head, but pinched and gaunt; her yellow forehead was wrinkled with a fixed frown, and her thin lips drawn down in permanent discontent. Her dress was a shapeless linsey-woolsey gown, and home-made list slippers covered her long, lank feet. "Be that the fashion?" she asked, pointing to my short, closely fitting walking-dress.

"Yes," I answered; "do you like it?"

"Well, it does for you, sis, because you're so little and peaked-like, but it wouldn't do for me. The other lady, now, don't wear nothing like that; is she even with the style, too?"

"There is such a thing as being above the style, madam," replied Ermine, bending to dip up glass number two.

"Our figgers is a good deal alike," pursued the woman; "I reckon that fashion ud suit me best."

Willowy Erminia glanced at the stick-like hostess. "You do me honor," she said, suavely. "I shall consider myself fortunate, madam, if you will allow me to send you patterns from C——. What are we if not well dressed?"

"You have a fine dog," I began hastily, fearing lest the great, black eyes should penetrate the sarcasm; "what is his name?"

"A stupid beast! He's none of mine; belongs to my man."

"Your husband?"

"Yes, my man. He works in the coal-mine over the hill."

"You have no children?"

"Not a brat. Glad of it, too."

"You must be lonely," I said, glancing around the desolate house. To my surprise, suddenly the woman burst into a flood of tears, and sinking down on the floor she rocked from side to side, sobbing, and covering her face with her bony hands.

"What can be the matter with her?" I said in alarm; and, in my agitation, I dipped up some sulphur-water and held it to her lips.

"Take away the smelling stuff,—I hate it!" she cried, pushing the cup angrily from her.

Ermine looked on in silence for a moment or two, then she took off her neck-tie, a bright-colored Roman scarf, and threw it across the trap into the woman's lap. "Do me the favor to accept that trifle, madam," she said, in her soft voice.

The woman's sobs ceased as she saw the ribbon; she fingered it with one hand in silent admiration, wiped her wet face with the skirt of her gown, and then suddenly disappeared into an adjoining room, closing the door behind her.

"Do you think she is crazy?" I whispered.

"O no; merely pensive."

"Nonsense, Ermine! But why did you give her that ribbon?"

"To develop her æsthetic taste," replied my cousin, finishing her last glass, and beginning to draw on her delicate gloves.

Immediately I began gulping down my neglected dose; but so vile was the odor that some time was required for the operation, and in the midst of my struggles our hostess reappeared. She had thrown on an old dress of plaid delaine, a faded red ribbon was tied over her head, and around her sinewed throat reposed the Roman scarf pinned with a glass brooch.

"Really, madam, you honor us," said Ermine, gravely.

"Thankee, marm. It's so long since I've had on anything but that old bag, and so long since I've seen anything but them Dutch girls over to the Community, with their wooden shapes and wooden shoes, that it sorter come over me all 't onct what a miserable life I've had. You see, I ain't what I looked like; now I've dressed up a bit I feel more like telling you that I come of good Ohio stock, without a drop of Dutch blood. My father, he kep' a store in Sandy, and I had everything I wanted until I must needs get crazy over Painting Sol at the Community. Father, he wouldn't hear to it, and so I ran away; Sol, he turned out good for nothing to work, and so here I am, yer see, in spite of all his pictures making me out the Queen of Sheby."

"Is your husband an artist?" I asked.

"No, miss. He's a coal-miner, he is. But he used to like to paint me all sorts of ways. Wait, I'll show yer." Going up the rough stairs that led into the attic, the woman came back after a moment with a number of sheets of drawing-paper which she hung up along the walls with pins for our inspection. They were all portraits of the same face, with brick-red cheeks, enormous black eyes, and a profusion of shining black hair hanging down over plump white shoulders; the costumes were various, but the faces were the same. I gazed in silence, seeing no likeness to anything earthly. Erminia took out her glasses and scanned the pictures slowly.

"Yourself, madam, I perceive," she said, much to my surprise.

"Yes, 'm, that's me," replied our hostess, complacently. "I never was like those yellow-haired girls over to the Community. Sol allers said my face was real rental."

"Rental?" I repeated, inquiringly.

"Oriental, of course," said Ermine. "Mr.—Mr. Solomon is quite right. May I ask the names of these characters, madam?"

"Queen of Sheby, Judy, Ruth, Esthy, Po-co-hon-tus, Goddessaliberty, Sunset, and eight Octobers, them with the grapes. Sunset's the one with the red paint behind it like clouds."

"Truly a remarkable collection," said Ermine. "Does Mr. Solomon devote much time to his art?"

"No, not now. He couldn't make a cent out of it, so he's took to digging coal. He painted all them when we was first married, and he went a journey all the way to Cincinnati to sell 'em. First he was going to buy me a silk dress and some ear-rings, and, after that, a farm. But pretty soon home he come on a canal-boat, without a shilling, and a bringing all the pictures back with him! Well, then he tried most everything, but he never could keep to any one trade, for he'd just as lief quit work in the middle of the forenoon and go to painting; no boss'll stand that, you know. We kep' a going down, and I had to sell the few things my father give me when he found I was married whether or no,—my chany, my feather-beds, and my nice clothes, piece by piece. I held on to the big looking-glass for four years, but at last it had to go, and then I just gave up and put on a linsey-woolsey gown. When a girl's spirit's once broke, she don't care for nothing, you know; so, when the Community offered to take Sol back as coal-digger, I just said, 'Go,' and we come." Here she tried to smear the tears away with her bony hands, and gave a low groan.

"Groaning probably relieves you," observed Ermine.

"Yes, 'm. It's kinder company like, when I'm all alone. But you see it's hard on the prettiest girl in Sandy to have to live in this lone lorn place. Why, ladies, you mightn't believe it, but I had open-work stockings, and feathers in my winter bunnets before I was married!" And the tears broke forth afresh.

"Accept my handkerchief," said Ermine; "it will serve your purpose better than fingers."

The woman took the dainty cambric and surveyed it curiously, held at arm's length. "Reg'lar thistle-down, now, ain't it?" she said; "and smells like a locust-tree blossom."

"Mr. Solomon, then, belonged to the Community?" I asked, trying to gather up the threads of the story.

"No, he didn't either; he's no Dutchman, I reckon, he's a Lake County man, born near Painesville, he is."

"I thought you spoke as though he had been in the Community."

"So he had; he didn't belong, but he worked for 'em since he was a boy, did middling well, in spite of the painting, until one day, when he come over to Sandy on a load of wood and seen me standing at the door. That was the end of him," continued the woman, with an air of girlish pride; "he couldn't work no more for thinking of me."

"*Où la vanité va-t-elle se nicher?*" murmured Ermine, rising. "Come, Dora; it is time to return."

As I hastily finished my last cup of sulphur-water, our hostess followed Ermine towards the door. "Will you have your handkercher back, marm?" she said, holding it out reluctantly.

"It was a free gift, madam," replied my cousin; "I wish you a good afternoon."

"Say, will yer be coming again to-morrow?" asked the woman as I took my departure.

"Very likely; good by."

The door closed, and then, but not till then, the melancholy dog joined us and stalked behind until we had crossed the meadow and reached the gate. We passed out and turned up the hill; but looking back we saw the outline of the woman's head at the upper window, and the dog's head at the bars, both watching us out of sight.

In the evening there came a cold wind down from the north, and the parlor, with its primitive ventilators, square openings in the side of the house, grew chilly. So a great fire of soft coal was built in the broad Franklin stove, and before its blaze we made good cheer, nor needed the one candle which flickered on the table behind us. Cider fresh from the mill, carded gingerbread, and new cheese crowned the scene, and during the evening came a band of singers, the young people of the Community, and sang for us the song of the Lorelei, accompanied by home-made violins and flageolets. At length we were left alone, the candle had burned out, the house door was barred, and the peaceful Community was asleep; still we two sat together with our feet upon the hearth, looking down into the glowing coals.

"Ich weisz nicht was soll es bedeuten
    Dasz ich so traurig bin,"

I said, repeating the opening lines of the Lorelei; "I feel absolutely blue to-night."

"The memory of the sulphur-woman," suggested Ermine.

"Sulphur-woman! What a name!"

"Entirely appropriate, in my opinion."

"Poor thing! How she longed with a great longing for the finery of her youth in Sandy."

"I suppose from those barbarous pictures that she was originally in the flesh," mused Ermine; "at present she is but a bony outline."

"Such as she is, however, she has had her romance," I answered. "She is quite sure that there was one to love her; then let come what may, she has had her day."

"Misquoting Tennyson on such a subject!" said Ermine, with disdain.

"A man's a man for all that and a woman's a woman too," I retorted. "You are blind, cousin, blinded with pride. That woman has had her tragedy, as real and bitter as any that can come to us."

"What have you to say for the poor man, then?" exclaimed Ermine, rousing to the contest. "If there is a tragedy at the sulphur-house, it belongs to the sulphur-man, not to the sulphur-woman."

"He is not a sulphur-man, he is a coal-man; keep to your bearings, Ermine."

"I tell you," pursued my cousin, earnestly, "that I pitied that unknown man with inward tears all the while I sat by that trap-door. Depend upon it, he had his dream, his ideal; and this country girl with her great eyes and wealth of hair represented the beautiful to his hungry soul. He gave his whole life and hope into her hands, and woke to find his goddess a common wooden image."

"Waste sympathy upon a coal-miner!" I said, imitating my cousin's former tone.

"If any one is blind, it is you," she answered, with gleaming eyes. "That man's whole history stood revealed in the selfish complainings of that creature. He had been in the Community from boyhood, therefore of course he had no chance to learn life, to see its art-treasures. He has been shipwrecked, poor soul, hopelessly shipwrecked."

"She too, Ermine."

"She!"

"Yes. If he loved pictures, she loved her chany and her feather-beds, not to speak of the big looking-glass. No doubt she had other lovers, and might have lived in a red brick farm-house with ten unopened front windows and a blistered front door. The wives of men of genius are always to be pitied; they do not soar into the crowd of feminine admirers who circle round the husband, and they are therefore called 'grubs,' 'worms of the earth,' 'drudges,' and other sweet titles."

"Nonsense," said Ermine, tumbling the arched coals into chaos with the poker; "it's after midnight, let us go up stairs." I knew very well that my beautiful cousin enjoyed the society of several poets, painters, musicians, and others of that ilk, without concerning herself about their stay-at-home wives.

The next day the winds were out in battle array, howling over the Strasburg hills, raging up and down the river, and whirling the colored leaves wildly along the lovely road to the One-Leg Creek. Evidently there could be no rambling in the painted woods that day, so we went over to old Fritz's shop, played on his home-made piano, inspected the woolly horse who turned his crank patiently in an underground den, and set in motion all the curious little images which the carpenter's deft fingers had wrought. Fritz belonged to the Community, and knew nothing of the outside world; he had a taste for mechanism, which showed itself in many labor-saving devices, and with it all he was the roundest, kindest little man, with bright eyes like a canary-bird.

"Do you know Solomon the coal-miner?" asked Ermine, in her correct, well-learned German.

"Sol Bangs? Yes, I know him," replied Fritz, in his Würtemberg dialect.

"What kind of a man is he?"

"Good for nothing," replied Fritz, placidly.

"Why?"

"Wrong here"; tapping his forehead.

"Do you know his wife?" I asked.

"Yes."

"What kind of a woman is she?"

"Too much tongue. Women must not talk much."

"Old Fritz touched us both there," I said, as we ran back laughing to the hotel through the blustering wind. "In his opinion, I suppose, we have the popular verdict of the township upon our two *protégés*, the sulphur-woman and her husband."

The next day opened calm, hazy, and warm, the perfection of Indian summer; the breezy hill was outlined in purple, and the trees glowed in rich colors. In the afternoon we started for the sulphur-spring without shawls or wraps, for the heat was almost oppressive; we loitered on the way through the still woods, gathering the tinted leaves, and wondering why no poet has yet arisen to celebrate in fit words the glories of the American autumn. At last we reached the turn whence the lonely house came into view, and at the bars we saw the dog awaiting us.

"Evidently the sulphur-woman does not like that melancholy animal," I said, as we applied our united strength to the gate.

"Did you ever know a woman of limited mind who liked a large dog?" replied Ermine. "Occasionally such a woman will fancy a small cur; but to appreciate a large, noble dog requires a large, noble mind."

"Nonsense with your dogs and minds," I said, laughing. "Wonderful! There is a curtain."

It was true. The paper had been removed from one of the windows, and in its place hung some white drapery, probably part of a sheet rigged as a curtain.

Before we reached the piazza the door opened, and our hostess appeared. "Glad to see yer, ladies," she said. "Walk right in this way to the keeping-room."

The dog went away to his block-house, and we followed the woman into a room on the right of the hall; there were three rooms, beside the attic above. An Old-World German stove of brick-work occupied a large portion of the space, and over it hung a few tins, and a clock whose pendulum swung outside; a table, a settle, and some stools completed the furniture; but on the plastered walls were two rude brackets, one holding a cup and saucer of figured china, and the other surmounted by a large bunch of autumn leaves, so beautiful in themselves and so exquisitely arranged that we crossed the room to admire them.

"Sol fixed 'em, he did," said the sulphur-woman; "he seen me setting things to rights, and he would do it. I told him they was trash, but he made me promise to leave 'em alone in case you should call again."

"Madam Bangs, they would adorn a palace," said Ermine, severely.

"The cup is pretty too," I observed, seeing the woman's eyes turn that way.

"It's the last of my chany," she answered, with pathos in her voice,—"the very last piece."

As we took our places on the settle we noticed the brave attire of our hostess. The delaine was there; but how altered! Flounces it had, skimped, but still flounces, and at the top was a collar of crochet cotton reaching nearly to the shoulders; the hair, too, was braided in imitation of Ermine's sunny coronet, and the Roman scarf did duty as a belt around the large flat waist.

"You see she tries to improve," I whispered, as Mrs. Bangs went into the hall to get some sulphur-water for us.

"Vanity," answered Ermine.

We drank our dose slowly, and our hostess talked on and on. Even I, her champion, began to weary of her complainings. "How dark it is!" said Ermine at last, rising and drawing aside the curtain. "See, Dora, a storm is close upon us."

We hurried to the door, but one look at the black cloud was enough to convince us that we could not reach the Community hotel before it would break, and somewhat drearily we returned to the keeping-room, which grew darker and darker, until our hostess was obliged to light a candle. "Reckon you'll have to stay all night; I'd like to have you, ladies," she said. "The Community ain't got nothing covered to send after you, except the old king's coach, and I misdoubt they won't let that out in such a storm, steps and all. When it begins to rain in this valley, it do rain, I can tell you; and from the way it's begun, 't won't stop 'fore morning. You just let me send the Roarer over to the mine, he'll tell Sol; Sol can tell the Community folks, so they'll know where you be."

I looked somewhat aghast at this proposal, but Ermine listened to the rain upon the roof a moment, and then quietly accepted; she remembered the long hills of tenacious red clay, and her kid boots were dear to her.

"The Roarer, I presume, is some faithful kobold who bears your message to and from the mine," she said, making herself as comfortable as the wooden settle would allow.

The sulphur-woman stared. "Roarer's Sol's old dog," she answered, opening the door; "perhaps one of you will write a bit of a note for him to carry in his basket.—Roarer, Roarer!"

The melancholy dog came slowly in, and stood still while she tied a small covered basket around his neck.

Ermine took a leaf from her tablets and wrote a line or two with the gold pencil attached to her watch-chain.

"Well now, you do have everything handy, I do declare," said the woman, admiringly.

I glanced at the paper.

"MR. SOLOMON BANGS: My cousin Theodora Wentworth and myself have accepted the hospitality of your house for the night. Will you be so good as to send tidings of our safety to the Community, and oblige,

"ERMINIA STUART."

The Roarer started obediently out into the rain-storm with his little basket; he did not run, but walked slowly, as if the storm was nothing compared to his settled melancholy.

"What a note to send to a coal-miner!" I said, during a momentary absence of our hostess.

"Never fear; it will be appreciated," replied Ermine.

"What is this king's carriage of which you spoke?" I asked, during the next hour's conversation.

"O, when they first come over from Germany, they had a sort of a king; he knew more than the rest, and he lived in that big brick house with dormel-winders and a cuperler, that stands next the garden. The carriage was hisn, and it had steps to let down, and curtains and all; they don't use it much now he's dead. They're a queer set anyhow! The women look like meal-sacks. After Sol seen me, he couldn't abide to look at 'em."

Soon after six we heard the great gate creak.

"That's Sol," said the woman, "and now of course Roarer'll come in and track all over my floor." The hall door opened and a shadow passed into the opposite room, two shadows,—a man and a dog.

"He's going to wash himself now," continued the wife; "he's always washing himself, just like a horse."

"New fact in natural history, Dora love," observed Ermine.

After some moments the miner appeared,—a tall, stooping figure with high forehead, large blue eyes, and long thin yellow hair; there was a singularly lifeless expression in his face, and a far-off look in his eyes. He gazed about the room in an absent way, as though he scarcely saw us. Behind him stalked the Roarer, wagging his tail slowly from side to side.

"Now, then, don't yer see the ladies, Sol? Where's yer manners?" said his wife, sharply.

"Ah,—yes,—good evening," he said, vaguely. Then his wandering eyes fell upon Ermine's beautiful face, and fixed themselves there with strange intentness.

"You received my note, Mr. Bangs?" said my cousin in her soft voice.

"Yes, surely. You are Erminia," replied the man, still standing in the centre of the room with fixed eyes. The Roarer laid himself down behind his master, and his tail, still wagging, sounded upon the floor with a regular tap.

"Now then, Sol, since you've come home, perhaps you'll entertain the ladies while I get supper," quoth Mrs. Bangs; and forthwith began a clatter of pans.

The man passed his long hand abstractedly over his forehead. "Eh," he said with long-drawn utterance,—"eh-h? Yes, my rose of Sharon, certainly, certainly."

"Then why don't you do it?" said the woman, lighting the fire in the brick stove.

"And what will the ladies please to do?" he answered, his eyes going back to Ermine.

"We will look over your pictures, sir," said my cousin, rising; "they are in the upper room, I believe."

A great flush rose in the painter's thin cheeks. "Will you," he said eagerly,—"will you? Come!"

"It's a broken-down old hole, ladies; Sol will never let me sweep it out. Reckon you'll be more comfortable here," said Mrs. Bangs, with her arms in the flour.

"No, no, my lily of the valley. The ladies will come with me; they will not scorn the poor room."

"A studio is always interesting," said Ermine, sweeping up the rough stairs behind Solomon's candle. The dog followed us, and laid himself down on an old mat, as though well accustomed to the place. "Eh-h, boy, you came bravely through the storm with the lady's note," said his master, beginning to light candle after candle. "See him laugh!"

"Can a dog laugh?" I asked.

"Certainly; look at him now. What is that but a grin of happy contentment? Don't the Bible say, 'grin like a dog'?"

"You seem much attached to the Roarer."

"Tuscarora, lady, Tuscarora. Yes, I love him well. He has been with me through all, and he has watched the making of all my pictures; he always lies there when I paint."

By this time a dozen candles were burning on shelves and brackets, and we could see all parts of the attic studio. It was but a poor place, unfloored in the corners where the roof slanted down, and having no ceiling but the dark beams and thatch; hung upon the walls were the pictures we had seen, and many others, all crude and highly colored, and all rep-

resenting the same face,—the sulphur-woman in her youth,
the poor artist's only ideal. He showed us these one by one,
handling them tenderly, and telling us, in his quaint language,
all they symbolized. "This is Ruth, and denoteth the power of
hope," he said. "Behold Judith, the queen of revenge. And this
dear one is Rachel, for whom Jacob served seven years, and
they seemed unto him but a day, so well he loved her." The
light shone on his pale face, and we noticed the far-off look in
his eyes, and the long, tapering fingers coming out from the
hard-worked, broad palm. To me it was a melancholy scene,
the poor artist with his daubs and the dreary attic.

But Ermine seemed eagerly interested; she looked at the
staring pictures, listened to the explanations, and at last she
said gently, "Let me show you something of perspective,
and the part that shadows play in a pictured face. Have you
any crayons?"

No; the man had only his coarse paints and lumps of
charcoal; taking a piece of the coal in her delicate hand, my
cousin began to work upon a sheet of drawing-paper attached
to the rough easel. Solomon watched her intently, as she
explained and demonstrated some of the rules of drawing, the
lights and shades, and the manner of representing the different features and curves. All his pictures were full faces, flat
and unshaded; Ermine showed him the power of the profile and
the three-quarter view. I grew weary of watching them, and
pressing my face against the little window gazed out into the
night; steadily the rain came down and the hills shut us in
like a well. I thought of our home in C——, and its bright
lights, warmth, company, and life. Why should we come mas-
querading out among the Ohio hills at this late season? And

then I remembered that it was because Ermine would come; she liked such expeditions, and from childhood I had always followed her lead. "*Dux nascitur*, etc., etc." Turning away from the gloomy night, I looked towards the easel again; Solomon's cheeks were deeply flushed, and his eyes shone like stars. The lesson went on, the merely mechanical hand explaining its art to the ignorant fingers of genius. Ermine had taken lessons all her life, but she had never produced an original picture, only copies.

At last the lesson was interrupted by a voice from below, "Sol, Sol, supper's ready!" No one stirred until, feeling some sympathy for the amount of work which my ears told me had been going on below, I woke up the two enthusiasts and took them away from the easel down stairs into the keeping-room, where a loaded table and a scarlet hostess bore witness to the truth of my surmise. Strange things we ate that night, dishes unheard of in towns, but not unpalatable. Ermine had the one china cup for her corn-coffee; her grand air always secured her such favors. Tuscarora was there and ate of the best, now and then laying his shaggy head on the table, and, as his master said, "smiling at us"; evidently the evening was his gala time. It was nearly nine when the feast was ended, and I immediately proposed retiring to bed, for, having but little art enthusiasm, I dreaded a vigil in that dreary attic. Solomon looked disappointed, but I ruthlessly carried off Ermine to the opposite room, which we afterwards suspected was the apartment of our hosts, freshened and set in order in our honor. The sound of the rain on the piazza roof lulled us soon to sleep, in spite of the strange surroundings; but more than once I woke and wondered where I was, suddenly remembering the lonely house in its lonely valley with a shiver of discomfort. The next morning we woke at our usual hour, but some time after the miner's departure; breakfast was awaiting us in the keeping-room, and our hostess said that an ox-team from the Community would come for us before nine. She seemed sorry to part with us, and refused any remuneration for our stay; but none the less did we promise ourselves to send some dresses and even ornaments from C——, to feed that poor, starving love of finery. As we rode away in the ox-cart, the Roarer looked wistfully after us through the bars; but his melancholy mood was upon him again, and he had not the heart even to wag his tail.

As we were sitting in the hotel parlor, in front of our soft-coal fire in the evening of the following day, and discussing whether or no we should return to the city within the week, the old landlord entered without his broad-brimmed hat,—an unusual attention, since he was a trustee and a man of note in the Community, and removed his hat for no one nor nothing; we even suspected that he slept in it.

"You know Zolomon Barngs," he said, slowly.

"Yes," we answered.

"Well, he's dead. Kilt in de mine." And putting on the hat, removed, we now saw, in respect for death, he left the room as suddenly as he had entered it. As it happened, we had been discussing the couple, I, as usual, contending for the wife, and Ermine, as usual, advocating the cause of the husband.

"Let us go out there immediately to see her, poor woman!" I said, rising.

"Yes, poor man, we will go to him!" said Ermine.

"But the man is dead, cousin."

"Then he shall at least have one kind, friendly glance before he is carried to his grave," answered Ermine, quietly.

In a short time we set out in the darkness, and dearly did we have to pay for the night-ride; no one could understand the motive of our going, but money was money, and we could pay for all peculiarities. It was a dark night, and the ride seemed endless as the oxen moved slowly on through the red-clay mire. At last we reached the turn and saw the little lonely house with its upper room brightly lighted.

"He is in the studio," said Ermine; and so it proved. He was not dead, but dying; not maimed, but poisoned by the gas of the mine, and rescued too late for recovery. They had placed him upon the floor on a couch of blankets, and the dull-eyed Community doctor stood at his side. "No good, no good," he said; "he must die." And then, hearing of the returning cart, he left us, and we could hear the tramp of the oxen over the little bridge, on their way back to the village.

The dying man's head lay upon his wife's breast, and her arms supported him; she did not speak, but gazed at us with a dumb agony in her large eyes. Ermine knelt down and took the lifeless hand streaked with coal-dust in both her own. "Solomon," she said, in her soft, clear voice, "do you know me?"

The closed eyes opened slowly, and fixed themselves upon her face a moment: then they turned towards the window, as if seeking something.

"It's the picter he means," said the wife. "He sat up most all last night a doing it."

I lighted all the candles, and Ermine brought forward

the easel; upon it stood a sketch in charcoal wonderful to behold,—the same face, the face of the faded wife, but so noble in its idealized beauty that it might have been a portrait of her glorified face in Paradise. It was a profile, with the eyes upturned,—a mere outline, but grand in conception and expression. I gazed in silent astonishment.

Ermine said, "Yes, I knew you could do it, Solomon. It is perfect of its kind." The shadow of a smile stole over the pallid face, and then the husband's fading gaze turned upward to meet the wild, dark eyes of the wife.

"It's you, Dorcas," he murmured; "that's how you looked to me, but I never could get it right before." She bent over him, and silently we watched the coming of the shadow of death; he spoke only once, "My rose of Sharon—" And then in a moment he was gone, the poor artist was dead.

Wild, wild was the grief of the ungoverned heart left behind; she was like a mad-woman, and our united strength was needed to keep her from injuring herself in her frenzy. I was frightened, but Ermine's strong little hands and lithe arms kept her down until, exhausted, she lay motionless near her dead husband. Then we carried her down stairs and I watched by the bedside, while my cousin went back to the studio. She was absent some time, and then she came back to keep the vigil with me through the long, still night. At dawn the woman woke, and her face looked aged in the gray light. She was quiet, and took without a word the food we had prepared, awkwardly enough, in the keeping-room.

"I must go to him, I must go to him," she murmured, as we led her back.

"Yes," said Ermine, "but first let me make you tidy. He

loved to see you neat." And with deft, gentle touch she dressed the poor creature, arranging the heavy hair so artistically that, for the first time, I saw what she might have been, and understood the husband's dream.

"What is that?" I said, as a peculiar sound startled us.

"It's Roarer. He was tied up last night, but I suppose he's gnawed the rope," said the woman. I opened the hall door, and in stalked the great dog, smelling his way directly up the stairs.

"O, he must not go!" I exclaimed.

"Yes, let him go, he loved his master," said Ermine; "we will go too." So silently we all went up into the chamber of death.

The pictures had been taken down from the walls, but the wonderful sketch remained on the easel, which had been moved to the head of the couch where Solomon lay. His long, light hair was smooth, his face peacefully quiet, and on his breast lay the beautiful bunch of autumn leaves which he had arranged in our honor. It was a striking picture,—the noble face of the sketch above, and the dead face of the artist below. It brought to my mind a design I had once seen, where Fame with her laurels came at last to the door of the poor artist and gently knocked; but he had died the night before!

The dog lay at his master's feet, nor stirred until Solomon was carried out to his grave.

The Community buried the miner in one corner of the lonely little meadow. No service had they and no mound was raised to mark the spot, for such was their custom; but in the early spring we went down again into the valley, and placed a block of granite over the grave. It bore the inscription:—

SOLOMON.

He will finish his work in Heaven.

Strange as it may seem, the wife pined for her artist husband. We found her in the Community trying to work, but
so aged and bent that we hardly knew her. Her large eyes had
lost their peevish discontent, and a great sadness had taken
the place.

"Seems like I couldn't get on without Sol," she said, sitting
with us in the hotel parlor after work-hours. "I kinder miss
his voice, and all them names he used to call me; he got 'em
out of the Bible, so they must have been good, you know. He
always thought everything I did was right, and he thought
no end of my good looks, too; I suppose I've lost 'em all now.
He was mighty fond of me; nobody in all the world cares a
straw for me now. Even Roarer wouldn't stay with me, for all I
petted him; he kep' a going out to that meader and a lying by
Sol, until, one day, we found him there dead. He just died of
sheer loneliness, I reckon. I sha'n't have to stop long I know,
because I keep a dreaming of Sol, and he always looks at me
like he did when I first knew him. He was a beautiful boy
when I first saw him on that load of wood coming into Sandy.
Well, ladies, I must go. Thank you kindly for all you've done
for me. And say, Miss Stuart, when I die you shall have that
coal picter; no one else 'ud vally it so much."

Three months after, while we were at the sea-shore, Ermine
received a long tin case, directed in a peculiar handwriting; it
had been forwarded from C——, and contained the sketch
and a note from the Community.

"E. STUART: The woman Dorcas Bangs died this day. She will be put away by the side of her husband, Solomon Bangs. She left the enclosed picture, which we hereby send, and which please acknowledge by return of mail.

"JACOB BOLL, *Trustee.*"

I unfolded the wrappings and looked at the sketch. "It is indeed striking," I said. "She must have been beautiful once, poor woman!"

"Let us hope that at least she is beautiful now, for her husband's sake, poor man!" replied Ermine.

Even then we could not give up our preferences.

RODMAN THE KEEPER

THE MOST ACCLAIMED STORY TO EMERGE FROM Woolson's Southern sojourns in the 1870s, "Rodman the Keeper" captured the continued sectional strife following the Civil War like no other writer of her generation had. Although reunion romances uniting Northern soldiers and Southern belles abounded, Woolson's story portrayed reconciliation as a more complicated affair. Written from the perspective of a Northerner at a time when the devastated South had virtually no voices to speak for itself, it was a plea for remembering the sacrifices of those who had died as well as those who were still suffering the war's effects. The setting is modeled on the Union cemetery in Salisbury, North Carolina, which Woolson visited in the summer of 1874, writing about it in a letter to the *Cleveland Herald* (October 7, 1874). "Rodman the Keeper" was accepted by William Dean Howells for the *Atlantic Monthly* in June

1875, when federal troops still occupied the South and tensions were beginning to build. Probably as a result of those tensions, he held on to the story for almost two years. Finally it was published in March 1877, after Reconstruction had ended and federal troops had been removed. It became the lead story of *Rodman the Keeper: Southern Sketches* (1880).

RODMAN THE KEEPER

. . . .

The long years come and go,
      And the Past,
The sorrowful, splendid Past,
With its glory and its woe,
      Seems never to have been.
   ——Seems never to have been?
      O somber days and grand,
      How ye crowd back once more,
Seeing our heroes' graves are green
By the Potomac and the Cumberland,
And in the valley of the Shenandoah!

When we remember how they died,—
In dark ravine and on the mountain-side,
In leaguered fort and fire-encircled town,
And where the iron ships went down,—
How their dear lives were spent
In the weary hospital-tent,
In the cockpit's crowded hive,
              ——it seems
Ignoble to be alive!

      —THOMAS BAILEY ALDRICH

"KEEPER OF WHAT? KEEPER OF THE DEAD. WELL, IT is easier to keep the dead than the living; and as for the gloom of the thing, the living among whom I have been lately were not a hilarious set."

John Rodman sat in the doorway and looked out over his domain. The little cottage behind him was empty of life save himself alone. In one room the slender appointments provided by Government for the keeper, who being still alive must sleep and eat, made the bareness doubly bare; in the other the desk and the great ledgers, the ink and pens, the register, the loud-ticking clock on the wall, and the flag folded on a shelf, were all for the kept, whose names, in hastily written, blotted rolls of manuscript, were waiting to be transcribed in the new red-bound ledgers in the keeper's best handwriting day by day, while the clock was to tell him the hour when the flag must rise over the mounds where reposed the bodies of fourteen thousand United States soldiers—who had languished where once stood the prison-pens, on the opposite slopes, now fair and peaceful in the sunset; who had fallen by the way in long marches to and fro under the burning sun; who had fought and died on the many battle-fields that reddened the beautiful State, stretching from the peaks of the marble mountains in the smoky west down to the sea-islands of the ocean border. The last rim of the sun's red ball had sunk below the horizon line, and the western sky glowed with deep rose-color, which faded away above into pink, into the salmon-tint, into shades of that far-away heavenly emerald which the brush of the earthly artist can never reproduce, but which is found sometimes in the iridescent heart of the opal. The small town, a mile distant, stood turning its back on the cemetery; but the keeper could see the pleasant, rambling old mansions, each with its rose-garden and neglected outlying fields, the empty negro quarters falling into ruin, and everything just as it stood when on that April morning the first gun was fired on Sumter; apparently not a nail added, not a brushful of paint applied, not a fallen brick replaced, or latch or lock repaired. The keeper had noted these things as he strolled through the town, but not with surprise; for he had seen the South in its first estate, when, fresh, strong, and fired with enthusiasm, he, too, had marched away from his village home with the colors flying above and the girls waving their handkerchiefs behind, as the regiment, a thousand strong, filed down the dusty road. That regiment, a weak, scarred two hundred, came back a year later with lagging step and colors tattered and scorched, and the girls could not wave their handkerchiefs, wet and sodden with tears. But the keeper, his wound healed, had gone again; and he had seen with his New England eyes the magnificence and the carelessness of the South, her splendor and negligence, her wealth and thriftlessness, as through Virginia and the fair Carolinas, across Georgia and into sunny Florida, he had marched month by month, first a lieutenant, then captain, and finally major and colonel, as death mowed down those above him, and he and his good conduct were left. Everywhere magnificence went hand in hand with neglect, and he had said so as chance now and then threw a conversation in his path.

"We have no such shiftless ways," he would remark, after he had furtively supplied a prisoner with hard-tack and coffee.

"And no such grand ones either," Johnny Reb would reply, if he was a man of spirit; and generally he was.

The Yankee, forced to acknowledge the truth of this statement, qualified it by observing that he would rather have more thrift with a little less grandeur; whereupon the other answered that *he* would not; and there the conversation rested. So now ex-Colonel Rodman, keeper of the national cemetery, viewed the little town in its second estate with philosophic eyes. "It is part of a great problem now working itself out; I am not here to tend the living, but the dead," he said.

Whereupon, as he walked among the long mounds, a voice seemed to rise from the still ranks below: "While ye have time, do good to men," it said. "Behold, we are beyond your care." But the keeper did not heed.

This still evening in early February he looked out over the level waste. The little town stood in the lowlands; there were no hills from whence cometh help—calm heights that lift the soul above earth and its cares; no river to lead the aspirations of the children outward toward the great sea. Everything was monotonous, and the only spirit that rose above the waste was a bitterness for the gained and sorrow for the lost cause. The keeper was the only man whose presence personated the former in their sight, and upon him therefore, as representative, the bitterness fell, not in words, but in averted looks, in sudden silences when he approached, in withdrawals and avoidance, until he lived and moved in a vacuum; wherever he went there was presently no one save himself; the very shop-keeper who sold him sugar seemed turned into a man of wood, and took his money reluctantly, although the shilling gained stood perhaps for that day's dinner. So Rodman withdrew himself, and came and went among them no more; the broad acres of his domain gave him as much exercise as his shattered ankle could bear; he ordered his few supplies by the quantity, and began the life of a solitary, his island marked out by the massive granite wall with which the United States Government has carefully surrounded those sad Southern cemeteries of hers; sad, not so much from the number of the mounds representing youth and strength cut off in their bloom, for that is but the fortune of war, as for the complete isolation which marks them. "Strangers in a strange land" is the thought of all who, coming and going to and from Florida, turn aside here and there to stand for a moment among the closely ranged graves which seem already a part of the past, that near past which in our hurrying American life is even now so far away. The Government work was completed before the keeper came; the lines of the trenches were defined by low granite copings, and the comparatively few single mounds were headed by trim little white boards bearing generally the word "Unknown," but here and there a name and an age, in most cases a boy from some far-away Northern State; "twenty-one," "twenty-two," said the inscriptions; the dates were those dark years among the sixties, measured now more than by anything else in the number of maidens widowed in heart, and women widowed indeed, who sit still and remember, while the world rushes by. At sunrise the keeper ran up the stars and stripes; and so precise were his ideas of the accessories belonging to the place, that from his own small store of money he had taken enough, by stinting himself, to buy a second flag for stormy weather, so that, rain or not, the colors should float over the dead. This was not patriotism so called, or rather miscalled, it was not sentimental fancy, it was not zeal or triumph; it was simply a sense of the fitness of things, a conscientiousness which had in it nothing of religion, unless indeed a man's endeavor to live up to his own ideal of his duty be a religion. The same feeling led the keeper to spend hours in copying the rolls. "John Andrew Warren, Company G, Eighth New Hampshire Infantry," he repeated, as he slowly wrote the name, giving "John Andrew" clear, bold capitals and a lettering impossible to mistake; "died August 15, 1863, aged twenty-two years. He came from the prison-pen yonder, and lies somewhere in those trenches, I suppose. Now then, John Andrew, don't fancy I am sorrowing for you; no doubt you are better off than I am at this very moment. But none the less, John Andrew, shall pen, ink, and hand do their duty to you. For that I am here."

Infinite pains and labor went into these records of the dead; one hair's-breadth error, and the whole page was replaced by a new one. The same spirit kept the grass carefully away from the low coping of the trenches, kept the graveled paths smooth and the mounds green, and the bare little cottage neat as a man-of-war. When the keeper cooked his dinner, the door toward the east, where the dead lay, was scrupulously closed, nor was it opened until everything was in perfect order again. At sunset the flag was lowered, and then it was the keeper's habit to walk slowly up and down the path until the shadows veiled the mounds on each side, and there was nothing save the peaceful green of earth. "So time will efface our little lives and sorrows," he mused, "and we shall be as nothing in

the indistinguishable past." Yet none the less did he fulfill the
duties of every day and hour with exactness. "At least they
shall not say that I was lacking," he murmured to himself as
he thought vaguely of the future beyond these graves. Who
"they" were, it would have troubled him to formulate, since he
was one of the many sons whom New England in this generation sends forth with a belief composed entirely of negatives.
As the season advanced, he worked all day in the sunshine.
"My garden looks well," he said. "I like this cemetery because
it is the original resting-place of the dead who lie beneath.
They were not brought here from distant places, gathered up
by contract, numbered, and described like so much merchan-
dise; their first repose has not been broken, their peace has
been undisturbed. Hasty burials the prison authorities gave
them; the thin bodies were tumbled into the trenches by men
almost as thin, for the whole State went hungry in those dark
days. There were not many prayers, no tears, as the dead-
carts went the rounds. But the prayers had been said, and the
tears had fallen, while the poor fellows were still alive in the
pens yonder; and when at last death came, it was like a release.
They suffered long; and I for one believe that therefore shall
their rest be long—long and sweet."

After a time began the rain, the soft, persistent, gray rain
of the Southern lowlands, and he staid within and copied
another thousand names into the ledger. He would not allow
himself the companionship of a dog lest the creature should
bark at night and disturb the quiet. There was no one to hear
save himself, and it would have been a friendly sound as he lay
awake on his narrow iron bed, but it seemed to him against

the spirit of the place. He would not smoke, although he had the soldier's fondness for a pipe. Many a dreary evening, beneath a hastily built shelter of boughs, when the rain poured down and everything was comfortless, he had found solace in the curling smoke; but now it seemed to him that it would be incongruous, and at times he almost felt as if it would be self-ish too. "*They* can not smoke, you know, down there under the wet grass," he thought, as standing at the window he looked toward the ranks of the mounds stretching across the eastern end from side to side—"my parade-ground," he called it. And then he would smile at his own fancies, draw the curtain, shut out the rain and the night, light his lamp, and go to work on the ledgers again. Some of the names lingered in his memory; he felt as if he had known the men who bore them, as if they had been boys together, and were friends even now although separated for a time. "James Marvin, Company B, Fifth Maine. The Fifth Maine was in the seven days' battle. I say, do you remember that retreat down the Quaker church road, and the way Phil Kearney held the rear-guard firm?" And over the whole seven days he wandered with his mute friend, who remembered everything and everybody in the most satisfac-tory way. One of the little head-boards in the parade-ground attracted him peculiarly because the name inscribed was his own: "—— Rodman, Company A, One Hundred and Sixth New York."

"I remember that regiment; it came from the extreme northern part of the State. Blank Rodman must have melted down here, coming as he did from the half-arctic region along the St. Lawrence. I wonder what he thought of the first hot

Santa Clara County Library
District
408-293-2326

Checked Out Items 9/24/2016 17:28
XXXXXXXXXXXX3334

Item Title	Due Date
1. Greatest hits, volume I II	10/15/2016
33305801982194	
2. Practical ethics	10/15/2016
33305226360091	
3. Miss Grief and other stories	10/15/2016
33305236105833	

No of Items: 3

Amount Outstanding : $12.50

24/7 Telecirc: 800-471-0991
www.sccl.org
Thank you for visiting our library.

Santa Clara County Library
District
408-293-2326

Checked Out Items 9/24/2016 17:28
XXXXXXXXXXXXX3334

Item Title	Due Date
1. Greatest hits, volume I II 33305801982194	10/15/2016
2. Practical ethics 33305226360091	10/15/2016
3. Miss Grief and other stories 33305236105833	10/15/2016

No of Items: 3

Amount Outstanding: $12.50

24/7 Telecirc: 800-471-0991
www.sccl.org
Thank you for visiting our library.

day, say in South Carolina, along those simmering rice-fields?"
He grew into the habit of pausing for a moment by the side
of this grave every morning and evening. "Blank Rodman. It
might easily have been John. And then, where should *I* be?"

But Blank Rodman remained silent, and the keeper, after
pulling up a weed or two and trimming the grass over his relative, went off to his duties again. "I am convinced that Blank
is a relative," he said to himself; "distant, perhaps, but still a
kinsman."

One April day the heat was almost insupportable; but
the sun's rays were not those brazen beams that sometimes
in Northern cities burn the air and scorch the pavements to
a white heat; rather were they soft and still; the moist earth
exhaled her richness, not a leaf stirred, and the whole level
country seemed sitting in a hot vapor-bath. In the early dawn
the keeper had performed his outdoor tasks, but all day he
remained almost without stirring in his chair between two
windows, striving to exist. At high noon out came a little black
bringing his supplies from the town, whistling and shuffling
along, gay as a lark. The keeper watched him coming slowly
down the white road, loitering by the way in the hot blaze,
stopping to turn a somersault or two, to dangle over a bridge
rail, to execute various impromptu capers all by himself. He
reached the gate at last, entered, and, having come all the way
up the path in a hornpipe step, he set down his basket at the
door to indulge in one long and final double-shuffle before
knocking. "Stop that!" said the keeper through the closed
blinds. The little darkey darted back; but as nothing further
came out of the window—a boot, for instance, or some other

stray missile—he took courage, showed his ivories, and drew near again. "Do you suppose I am going to have you stirring up the heat in that way?" demanded the keeper.

The little black grinned, but made no reply, unless smoothing the hot white sand with his black toes could be construed as such; he now removed his rimless hat and made a bow.

"Is it, or is it not warm?" asked the keeper, as a naturalist might inquire of a salamander, not referring to his own so much as to the salamander's ideas on the subject.

"Dunno, mars'," replied the little black.

"How do *you* feel?"

"'Spects I feel all right, mars'."

The keeper gave up the investigation, and presented to the salamander a nickel cent. "I suppose there is no such thing as a cool spring in all this melting country," he said.

But the salamander indicated with his thumb a clump of trees on the green plain north of the cemetery. "Ole Mars' Ward's place—cole spring dah." He then departed, breaking into a run after he had passed the gate, his ample mouth watering at the thought of a certain chunk of taffy at the mercantile establishment kept by Aunt Dinah in a corner of her one-roomed cabin. At sunset the keeper went thirstily out with a tin pail on his arm, in search of the cold spring. "If it could only be like the spring down under the rocks where I used to drink when I was a boy!" he thought. He had never walked in that direction before. Indeed, now that he had abandoned the town, he seldom went beyond the walls of the cemetery. An old road led across to the clump of trees, through fields run to waste, and following it he came to the place, a deserted house with tumble-down fences and overgrown garden, the out-buildings indicating that once upon a time there were many servants and a prosperous master. The house was of wood, large on the ground, with encircling piazzas; across the front door rough bars had been nailed, and the closed blinds were protected in the same manner; from long want of paint the clapboards were gray and mossy, and the floor of the piazza had fallen in here and there from decay. The keeper decided that his cemetery was a much more cheerful place than this, and then he looked around for the spring. Behind the house the ground sloped down; it must be there. He went around and came suddenly upon a man lying on an old rug outside of a back door. "Excuse me. I thought nobody lived here," he said.

"Nobody does," replied the man; "I am not much of a body, am I?"

His left arm was gone, and his face was thin and worn with long illness; he closed his eyes after speaking, as though the few words had exhausted him.

"I came for water from a cold spring you have here, somewhere," pursued the keeper, contemplating the wreck before him with the interest of one who has himself been severely wounded and knows the long, weary pain. The man waved his hand toward the slope without unclosing his eyes, and Rodman went off with his pail and found a little shady hollow, once curbed and paved with white pebbles, but now neglected, like all the place. The water was cold, however, deliciously cold. He filled his pail and thought that perhaps after all he would exert himself to make coffee, now that the sun was down; it would taste better made of this cold water. When he came up the slope the man's eyes were open.

"Have some water?" asked Rodman.

"Yes; there's a gourd inside."

The keeper entered, and found himself in a large, bare room; in one corner was some straw covered with an old counterpane, in another a table and chair; a kettle hung in the deep fireplace, and a few dishes stood on a shelf; by the door on a nail hung a gourd; he filled it and gave it to the host of this desolate abode. The man drank with eagerness.

"Pomp has gone to town," he said, "and I could not get down to the spring to-day, I have had so much pain."

"And when will Pomp return?"

"He should be here now; he is very late to-night."

"Can I get you anything?"

"No, thank you; he will soon be here."

The keeper looked out over the waste; there was no one in sight. He was not a man of any especial kindliness—he had himself been too hardly treated in life for that—but he could not find it in his heart to leave this helpless creature all alone with night so near. So he sat down on the door-step. "I will rest awhile," he said, not asking but announcing it. The man had turned away and closed his eyes again, and they both remained silent, busy with their own thoughts; for each had recognized the ex-soldier, Northern and Southern, in portions of the old uniforms, and in the accent. The war and its memories were still very near to the maimed, poverty-stricken Confederate; and the other knew that they were, and did not obtrude himself.

Twilight fell, and no one came.

"Let me get you something," said Rodman; for the face

looked ghastly as the fever abated. The other refused. Darkness came; still, no one.

"Look here," said Rodman, rising, "I have been wounded myself, was in hospital for months; I know how you feel. You must have food—a cup of tea, now, and a slice of toast, brown and thin."

"I have not tasted tea or wheaten bread for weeks," answered the man; his voice died off into a wail, as though feebleness and pain had drawn the cry from him in spite of himself. Rodman lighted a match; there was no candle, only a piece of pitch-pine stuck in an iron socket on the wall; he set fire to this primitive torch and looked around.

"There is nothing there," said the man outside, making an effort to speak carelessly; "my servant went to town for supplies. Do not trouble yourself to wait; he will come presently, and—and I want nothing."

But Rodman saw through proud poverty's lie; he knew that irregular quavering of the voice, and that trembling of the hand; the poor fellow had but one to tremble. He continued his search; but the bare room gave back nothing, not a crumb.

"Well, if you are not hungry," he said, briskly, "I am, hungry as a bear: and I'll tell you what I am going to do. I live not far from here, and I live all alone too; I haven't a servant as you have. Let me take supper here with you, just for a change; and, if your servant comes, so much the better, he can wait upon us. I'll run over and bring back the things."

He was gone without waiting for reply; the shattered ankle made good time over the waste, and soon returned, limping a little, but bravely hasting, while on a tray came the keeper's best supplies, Irish potatoes, corned beef, wheaten bread, butter, and coffee; for he would not eat the hot biscuits, the corn-cake, the bacon and hominy of the country, and constantly made little New England meals for himself in his prejudiced little kitchen. The pine-torch flared in the doorway; a breeze had come down from the far mountains and cooled the air. Rodman kindled a fire on the cavernous hearth, filled the kettle, found a saucepan, and commenced operations, while the other lay outside and watched every movement in the lighted room.

"All ready; let me help you in. Here we are now; fried potatoes, cold beef, mustard, toast, butter, and tea. Eat, man; and the next time I am laid up you shall come over and cook for me."

Hunger conquered, and the other ate, ate as he had not eaten for months. As he was finishing a second cup of tea, a slow step came around the house; it was the missing Pomp, an old negro, bent and shriveled, who carried a bag of meal and some bacon in his basket. "That is what they live on," thought the keeper.

He took leave without more words. "I suppose now I can be allowed to go home in peace," he grumbled to conscience. The negro followed him across what was once the lawn. "Fin' Mars' Ward mighty low," he said apologetically, as he swung open the gate which still hung between its posts, although the fence was down, "but I hurred and hurred as fas' as I could; it's mighty fur to de town. Proud to see you, sah; hope you'll come again. Fine fambly, de Wards, sah, befo' de war."

"How long has he been in this state?" asked the keeper.

"Ever since one ob de las' battles, sah; but he's worse sence we come yer, 'bout a mont' back."

"Who owns the house? Is there no one to see to him? has he no friends?"

"House b'long to Mars' Ward's uncle; fine place once, befo' de war; he's dead now, and dah's nobuddy but Miss Bettina, an' she's gone off somewhuz. Propah place, sah, fur Mars' Ward—own uncle's house," said the old slave, loyally striving to maintain the family dignity even then.

"Are there no better rooms—no furniture?"

"Sartin; but—but Miss Bettina, she took de keys; she didn't know we was comin'—"

"You had better send for Miss Bettina, I think," said the keeper, starting homeward with his tray, washing his hands, as it were, of any future responsibility in the affair.

The next day he worked in his garden, for clouds veiled the sun and exercise was possible; but, nevertheless, he could not forget the white face on the old rug. "Pshaw!" he said to himself, "haven't I seen tumble-down old houses and battered human beings before this?"

At evening came a violent thunderstorm, and the splendor of the heavens was terrible. "We have chained you, mighty spirit," thought the keeper as he watched the lightning, "and some time we shall learn the laws of the winds and foretell the storms; then, prayers will no more be offered in churches to alter the weather than they would be offered now to alter an eclipse. Yet back of the lightning and the wind lies the power of the great Creator, just the same."

But still into his musings crept, with shadowy persistence, the white face on the rug.

"Nonsense!" he exclaimed; "if white faces are going around as ghosts, how about the fourteen thousand white faces that went under the sod down yonder? If they could arise and walk, the whole State would be filled and no more carpet-baggers needed." So, having balanced the one with the fourteen thousand, he went to bed.

Daylight brought rain—still, soft, gray rain; the next morning showed the same, and the third likewise, the nights keeping up their part with low-down clouds and steady pattering on the roof. "If there was a river here, we should have a flood," thought the keeper, drumming idly on his window-pane. Memory brought back the steep New England hillsides shedding their rain into the brooks, which grew in a night to torrents and filled the rivers so that they overflowed their banks; then, suddenly, an old house in a sunken corner of a waste rose before his eyes, and he seemed to see the rain dropping from a moldy ceiling on the straw where a white face lay.

"Really, I have nothing else to do to-day, you know," he remarked in an apologetic way to himself, as he and his umbrella went along the old road; and he repeated the remark as he entered the room where the man lay, just as he had fancied, on the damp straw.

"The weather *is* unpleasant," said the man. "Pomp, bring a chair."

Pomp brought one, the only one, and the visitor sat down. A fire smoldered on the hearth and puffed out acrid smoke now and then, as if the rain had clogged the soot in the long-neglected chimney; from the streaked ceiling oozing drops fell with a dull splash into little pools on the decayed floor; the door would not close; the broken panes were stopped with rags, as if the old servant had tried to keep out the damp; in the ashes a corn-cake was baking.

"I am afraid you have not been so well during these long rainy days," said the keeper, scanning the face on the straw.

"My old enemy, rheumatism," answered the man; "the first sunshine will drive it away."

They talked awhile, or rather the keeper talked, for the other seemed hardly able to speak, as the waves of pain swept over him; then the visitor went outside and called Pomp out. "*Is* there any one to help him, or not?" he asked impatiently.

"Fine fambly, befo' de war," began Pomp.

"Never mind all that; is there any one to help him now—yes or no?"

"No," said the old black with a burst of despairing truthfulness. "Miss Bettina, she's as poor as Mars' Ward, an' dere's no one else. He's had noth'n but hard corn-cake for three days, an' he can't swaller it no more."

The next morning saw Ward De Rosset lying on the white pallet in the keeper's cottage, and old Pomp, marveling at the cleanliness all around him, installed as nurse. A strange asylum for a Confederate soldier, was it not? But he knew nothing of the change, which he would have fought with his last breath if consciousness had remained; returning fever, however, had absorbed his senses, and then it was that the keeper and the slave had borne him slowly across the waste, resting many times, but accomplishing the journey at last.

That evening John Rodman, strolling to and fro in the dusky twilight, paused alongside of the other Rodman. "I do not want him here, and that is the plain truth," he said, pursuing the current of his thoughts. "He fills the house; he and Pomp together disturb all my ways. He'll be ready to fling a brick at me too, when his senses come back; small thanks shall I have for lying on the floor, giving up all my comforts, and, what is more, riding over the spirit of the place with a vengeance!" He threw himself down on the grass beside the mound and lay looking up toward the stars, which were coming out, one by one, in the deep blue of the Southern night. "With a vengeance, did I say? That is it exactly—the vengeance of kindness. The poor fellow has suffered horribly in body and in estate, and now ironical Fortune throws him in my way, as if saying, 'Let us see how far your selfishness will yield.' This is not a question of magnanimity; there is no magnanimity about it, for the war is over, and you Northerners have gained every point for which you fought. This is merely a question between man and man; it would be the same if the sufferer was a poor Federal, one of the carpet-baggers, whom you despise so, for instance, or a pagan Chinaman. And Fortune is right; don't you think so, Blank Rodman? I put it to you, now, to one who has suffered the extreme rigor of the other side—those prison-pens yonder."

Whereupon Blank Rodman answered that he had fought for a great cause, and that he knew it, although a plain man and not given to speech-making; he was not one of those who had sat safely at home all through the war, and now belittled it and made light of its issues. (Here a murmur came up from the long line of the trenches, as though all the dead had cried out.) But now the points for which he had fought being gained, and strife ended, it was the plain duty of every man to encourage peace. For his part he bore no malice; he was glad the poor Confederate was up in the cottage, and he did not think any the less of the keeper for bringing him there. He would like to add that he thought more of him; but he was sorry to say that he was well aware what an effort it was, and how almost grudgingly the charity began.

If Blank Rodman did not say this, at least the keeper imagined that he did. "That is what he would have said," he thought. "I am glad you do not object," he added, pretending to himself that he had not noticed the rest of the remark.

"We do not object to the brave soldier who honestly fought for his cause, even though he fought on the other side," answered Blank Rodman for the whole fourteen thousand. "But never let a coward, a double-face, or a flippant-tongued idler walk over our heads. It would make us rise in our graves!"

And the keeper seemed to see a shadowy pageant sweep by—gaunt soldiers with white faces, arming anew against the subtle product of peace: men who said, "It was nothing! Behold, we saw it with our eyes!"—stay-at-home eyes.

The third day the fever abated, and Ward De Rosset noticed his surroundings. Old Pomp acknowledged that he had been moved, but veiled the locality: "To a frien's house, Mars' Ward."

"But I have no friends now, Pomp," said the weak voice.

Pomp was very much amused at the absurdity of this. "No frien's! Mars' Ward, no frien's!" He was obliged to go out of the room to hide his laughter. The sick man lay feebly thinking that the bed was cool and fresh, and the closed green blinds pleasant; his thin fingers stroked the linen sheet, and his eyes wandered from object to object. The only thing that broke the rule of bare utility in the simple room was a square of white drawing-paper on the wall, upon which was inscribed in ornamental text the following verse:

"Toujours femme varie,
Bien fou qui s'y fie;
Une femme souvent
N'est qu'une plume au vent."

With the persistency of illness the eyes and mind of Ward
De Rosset went over and over this distich; he knew something of French, but was unequal to the effort of translating;
the rhymes alone caught his vagrant fancy. "Toujours femme
varie," he said to himself over and over again; and when the
keeper entered, he said it to him.

"Certainly," answered the keeper; "bien fou qui s'y fie. How
do you find yourself this morning?"

"I have not found myself at all, so far. Is this your house?"

"Yes."

"Pomp told me I was in a friend's house," observed the sick
man, vaguely.

"Well, it isn't an enemy's. Had any breakfast? No? Better
not talk, then."

He went to the detached shed which served for a kitchen,
upset all Pomp's clumsy arrangements, and ordered him outside; then he set to work and prepared a delicate breakfast
with his best skill. The sick man eagerly eyed the tray as
he entered. "Better have your hands and face sponged off, I
think," said Rodman; and then he propped him up skillfully,
and left him to his repast. The grass needed mowing on the
parade-ground; he shouldered his scythe and started down the
path, viciously kicking the gravel aside as he walked. "Wasn't
solitude your principal idea, John Rodman, when you applied
for this place?" he demanded of himself. "How much of it are

you likely to have with sick men, and sick men's servants, and so forth?"

The "and so forth," thrown in as a rhetorical climax, turned into reality and arrived bodily upon the scene—a climax indeed. One afternoon, returning late to the cottage, he found a girl sitting by the pallet—a girl young and dimpled and dewy; one of the creamy roses of the South that, even in the bud, are richer in color and luxuriance than any Northern flower. He saw her through the door, and paused; distressed old Pomp met him and beckoned him cautiously outside. "Miss Bettina," he whispered gutturally; "she's come back from somewhuz, an' she's awful mad 'cause Mars' Ward's here. I tole her all 'bout 'em—de leaks an' de rheumatiz an' de hard corn-cake, but she done gone scole me; and Mars' Ward, he know now whar he is, an' he mad too."

"Is the girl a fool?" said Rodman. He was just beginning to rally a little. He stalked into the room and confronted her. "I have the honor of addressing—"

"Miss Ward."

"And I am John Rodman, keeper of the national cemetery."

This she ignored entirely; it was as though he had said, "I am John Jones, the coachman." Coachmen were useful in their way; but their names were unimportant.

The keeper sat down and looked at his new visitor. The little creature fairly radiated scorn; her pretty head was thrown back, her eyes, dark brown fringed with long dark lashes, hardly deigned a glance; she spoke to him as though he was something to be paid and dismissed like any other mechanic.

"We are indebted to you for some days' board, I believe, keeper—medicines, I presume, and general attendance. My cousin will be removed to-day to our own residence; I wish to pay now what he owes."

The keeper saw that her dress was old and faded; the small black shawl had evidently been washed and many times mended; the old-fashioned knitted purse she held in her hand was lank with long famine.

"Very well," he said; "if you choose to treat a kindness in that way, I consider five dollars a day none too much for the annoyance, expense, and trouble I have suffered. Let me see: five days—or is it six? Yes. Thirty dollars, Miss Ward."

He looked at her steadily; she flushed. "The money will be sent to you," she began haughtily; then, hesitatingly, "I must ask a little time—"

"O Betty, Betty, you know you can not pay it. Why try to disguise—But that does not excuse *you* for bringing me here," said the sick man, turning toward his host with an attempt to speak fiercely, which ended in a faltering quaver.

All this time the old slave stood anxiously outside of the door; in the pauses they could hear his feet shuffling as he waited for the decision of his superiors. The keeper rose and threw open the blinds of the window that looked out on the distant parade-ground. "Bringing you here," he repeated—"*here;* that is my offense, is it? There they lie, fourteen thousand brave men and true. Could they come back to earth they would be the first to pity and aid you, now that you are down. So would it be with you if the case were reversed; for a soldier is generous to a soldier. It was not your own heart that spoke then; it was the small venom of a woman, that here, as everywhere through the South, is playing its rancorous part."

The sick man gazed out through the window, seeing for

the first time the far-spreading ranks of the dead. He was very weak, and the keeper's words had touched him; his eyes were suffused with tears. But Miss Ward rose with a flashing glance. She turned her back full upon the keeper and ignored his very existence. "I will take you home immediately, Ward—this very evening," she said.

"A nice, comfortable place for a sick man," commented the keeper, scornfully. "I am going out now, De Rosset, to prepare your supper; you had better have one good meal before you go."

He disappeared, but as he went he heard the sick man say, deprecatingly: "It isn't very comfortable over at the old house now, indeed it isn't, Betty; I suffered"—and the girl's passionate outburst in reply. Then he closed his door and set to work.

When he returned, half an hour later, Ward was lying back exhausted on the pillows, and his cousin sat leaning her head upon her hand; she had been weeping, and she looked very desolate, he noticed, sitting there in what was to her an enemy's country. Hunger is a strong master, however, especially when allied to weakness; and the sick man ate with eagerness.

"I must go back," said the girl, rising. "A wagon will be sent out for you, Ward; Pomp will help you."

But Ward had gained a little strength as well as obstinacy with the nourishing food. "Not to-night," he said.

"Yes, to-night."

"But I can not go to-night; you are unreasonable, Bettina. To-morrow will do as well, if go I must."

"If go you must! You do not want to go, then—to go to our own home—and with me"—Her voice broke; she turned toward the door.

The keeper stepped forward. "This is all nonsense, Miss Ward," he said, "and you know it. Your cousin is in no state to be moved. Wait a week or two, and he can go in safety. But do not dare to offer me your money again; my kindness was to the soldier, not to the man, and as such he can accept it. Come out and see him as often as you please. I shall not intrude upon you. Pomp, take the lady home."

And the lady went.

Then began a remarkable existence for the four: a Confederate soldier lying ill in the keeper's cottage of a national cemetery; a rampant little rebel coming out daily to a place which was to her anathema-maranatha; a cynical, misanthropic keeper sleeping on the floor and enduring every variety of discomfort for a man he never saw before—a man belonging to an idle, arrogant class he detested; and an old black freedman allowing himself to be taught the alphabet in order to gain permission to wait on his master—master no longer in law—with all the devotion of his loving old heart. For the keeper had announced to Pomp that he must learn his alphabet or go; after all these years of theory, he, as a New-Englander, could not stand by and see precious knowledge shut from the black man. So he opened it, and mighty dull work he found it.

Ward De Rosset did not rally as rapidly as they expected. The white-haired doctor from the town rode out on horseback, pacing slowly up the graveled roadway with a scowl on his brow, casting, as he dismounted, a furtive glance down toward the parade-ground. His horse and his coat were alike old and worn, and his broad shoulders were bent with long service in the miserably provided Confederate hospitals, where he had striven to do his duty through every day and every night of those shadowed years. Cursing the incompetency in high places, cursing the mismanagement of the entire medical department of the Confederate army, cursing the reckless-ness and indifference which left the men suffering for want of proper hospitals and hospital stores, he yet went on res-olutely doing his best with the poor means in his control until the last. Then he came home, he and his old horse, and went the rounds again, he prescribing for whooping-cough or measles, and Dobbin waiting outside; the only difference was that fees were small and good meals scarce for both, not only for the man but for the beast. The doctor sat down and chatted awhile kindly with De Rosset, whose father and uncle had been dear friends of his in the bright, prosperous days; then he left a few harmless medicines and rose to go, his gaze resting a moment on Miss Ward, then on Pomp, as if he were hesitating. But he said nothing until on the walk outside he met the keeper, and recognized a person to whom he could tell the truth. "There is nothing to be done; he may recover, he may not; it is a question of strength merely. He needs no medicines, only nourishing food, rest, and careful tendance."

"He shall have them," answered the keeper briefly. And then the old gentleman mounted his horse and rode away, his first and last visit to a national cemetery.

"National!" he said to himself—"national!"

All talk of moving De Rosset ceased, but Miss Ward moved into the old house. There was not much to move: herself, her one trunk, and Marí, a black attendant, whose name probably began life as Maria, since the accent still dwelt on the curtailed last syllable. The keeper went there once, and once only, and then it was an errand for the sick man, whose fancies came sometimes at inconvenient hours—when Pomp had gone to town, for instance. On this occasion the keeper entered the mockery of a gate and knocked at the front door, from which the bars had been removed; the piazza still showed its decaying planks, but quick-growing summer vines had been planted, and were now encircling the old pillars and veiling all defects with their greenery. It was a woman's pathetic effort to cover up what can not be covered—poverty. The blinds on one side were open, and white curtains waved to and fro in the breeze; into this room he was ushered by Marí. Matting lay on the floor, streaked here and there ominously by the dampness from the near ground. The furniture was of dark mahogany, handsome in its day: chairs, a heavy pier-table with low-down glass, into which no one by any possibility could look unless he had eyes in his ankles, a sofa with a stiff round pillow of hair-cloth under each curved end, and a mirror with a compartment framed off at the top, containing a picture of shepherds and shepherdesses, and lambs with blue ribbons around their necks, all enjoying themselves in the most natural and life-like manner. Flowers stood on the high mantel-piece, but their fragrance could not overcome the faint odor of the damp straw-matting. On a table were books—a life of General Lee, and three or four shabby little volumes printed at the South during the war, waifs of prose and poetry of that highly wrought, richly colored style which seems indigenous to Southern soil.

"Some way, the whole thing reminds me of a funeral," thought the keeper.

Miss Ward entered, and the room bloomed at once; at least that is what a lover would have said. Rodman, however, merely noticed that she bloomed, and not the room, and he said to himself that she would not bloom long if she continued to live in such a moldy place. Their conversation in these days was excessively polite, shortened to the extreme minimum possible, and conducted without the aid of the eyes, at least on one side. Rodman had discovered that Miss Ward never looked at him, and so he did not look at her—that is, not often; he was human, however, and she was delightfully pretty. On this occasion they exchanged exactly five sentences, and then he departed, but not before his quick eyes had discovered that the rest of the house was in even worse condition than this parlor, which, by the way, Miss Ward considered quite a grand apartment; she had been down near the coast, trying to teach school, and there the desolation was far greater than here, both armies having passed back and forward over the ground, foragers out, and the torch at work more than once.

"Will there ever come a change for the better?" thought the keeper, as he walked homeward. "What an enormous stone has got to be rolled up hill! But at least, John Rodman, *you* need not go to work at it; *you* are not called upon to lend your shoulder."

None the less, however, did he call out Pomp that very afternoon and sternly teach him "E" and "F," using the smooth white sand for a blackboard, and a stick for chalk. Pomp's primer was a Government placard hanging on the wall of the office. It read as follows:

IN THIS CEMETERY REPOSE THE REMAINS

OF

FOURTEEN THOUSAND THREE HUNDRED AND TWENTY-ONE

UNITED STATES SOLDIERS.

"Tell me not in mournful numbers
　　Life is but an empty dream;
For the soul is dead that slumbers,
　　And things are not what they seem.

"Life is real! Life is earnest!
　　And the grave is not its goal;
Dust thou art, to dust returnest,
　　Was not written of the soul!"

"The only known instance of the Government's conde-scending to poetry," the keeper had thought, when he first read this placard. It was placed there for the instruction and edification of visitors; but, no visitors coming, he took the lib-erty of using it as a primer for Pomp. The large letters served the purpose admirably, and Pomp learned the entire quota-tion; what he thought of it has not transpired. Miss Ward came over daily to see her cousin. At first she brought him soups and various concoctions from her own kitchen—the leaky cavern, once the dining-room, where the soldier had taken refuge after his last dismissal from hospital; but the keeper's soups were richer, and free from the taint of smoke; his martial laws of neatness even disorderly old Pomp dared not disobey, and the sick man soon learned the difference. He thanked the girl, who came bringing the dishes over carefully in her own dimpled hands, and then, when she was gone, he sent them untasted away. By chance Miss Ward learned this, and wept bitter tears over it; she continued to come, but her poor little soups and jellies she brought no more.

One morning in May the keeper was working near the flag-staff, when his eyes fell upon a procession coming down the road which led from the town and turning toward the cemetery. No one ever came that way: what could it mean? It drew near, entered the gate, and showed itself to be negroes walking two and two—old uncles and aunties, young men and girls, and even little children, all dressed in their best; a very poor best, sometimes gravely ludicrous imitations of "ole mars'" or "ole miss'," sometimes mere rags bravely patched together and adorned with a strip of black calico or rosette of black ribbon; not one was without a badge of mourning. All carried flowers, common blossoms from the little gardens behind the cabins that stretched around the town on the out-skirts—the new forlorn cabins with their chimneys of piled stones and ragged patches of corn; each little darkey had his bouquet and marched solemnly along, rolling his eyes around, but without even the beginning of a smile, while the elders moved forward with gravity, the bubbling, irrepressible gayety of the negro subdued by the new-born dignity of the freedman.

"Memorial Day," thought the keeper; "I had forgotten it."

"Will you do us de hono', sah, to take de head ob de pro-cessio', sah?" said the leader, with a ceremonious bow. Now, the keeper had not much sympathy with the strewing of flow-ers, North or South; he had seen the beautiful ceremony more than once turned into a political demonstration. Here, how-

ever, in this small, isolated, interior town, there was nothing
of that kind; the whole population of white faces laid their
roses and wept true tears on the graves of their lost ones in the
village churchyard when the Southern Memorial Day came
round, and just as naturally the whole population of black
faces went out to the national cemetery with their flowers on
the day when, throughout the North, spring blossoms were
laid on the graves of the soldiers, from the little Maine village to the stretching ranks of Arlington, from Greenwood
to the far Western burial-places of San Francisco. The keeper
joined the procession and led the way to the parade-ground.
As they approached the trenches, the leader began singing
and all joined. "Swing low, sweet chariot," sang the freedmen,
and their hymn rose and fell with strange, sweet harmony—
one of those wild, unwritten melodies which the North heard
with surprise and marveling when, after the war, bands of
singers came to their cities and sang the songs of slavery, in
order to gain for their children the coveted education. "Swing
low, sweet chariot," sang the freedmen, and two by two they
passed along, strewing the graves with flowers till all the
green was dotted with color. It was a pathetic sight to see some
of the old men and women, ignorant field-hands, bent, dull-
eyed, and past the possibility of education even in its simplest
forms, carefully placing their poor flowers to the best advantage. They knew dimly that the men who lay beneath those
mounds had done something wonderful for them and for their
children; and so they came bringing their blossoms, with little
intelligence but with much love.

The ceremony over, they retired. As he turned, the keeper
caught a glimpse of Miss Ward's face at the window.

"Hope we's not makin' too free, sah," said the leader, as the procession, with many a bow and scrape, took leave, "but we's kep' de day now two years, sah, befo' you came, sah, an we's teachin' de chil'en to keep it, sah."

The keeper returned to the cottage. "Not a white face," he said.

"Certainly not," replied Miss Ward, crisply.

"I know some graves at the North, Miss Ward, graves of Southern soldiers, and I know some Northern women who do not scorn to lay a few flowers on the lonely mounds as they pass by with their blossoms on our Memorial Day."

"You are fortunate. They must be angels. We have no angels here."

"I am inclined to believe you are right," said the keeper.

That night old Pomp, who had remained invisible in the kitchen during the ceremony, stole away in the twilight and came back with a few flowers. Rodman saw him going down toward the parade-ground, and watched. The old man had but a few blossoms; he arranged them hastily on the mounds with many a furtive glance toward the house, and then stole back, satisfied; he had performed his part.

Ward De Rosset lay on his pallet, apparently unchanged; he seemed neither stronger nor weaker. He had grown childishly dependent upon his host, and wearied for him, as the Scotch say; but Rodman withstood his fancies, and gave him only the evenings, when Miss Bettina was not there. One afternoon, however, it rained so violently that he was forced to seek shelter; he set himself to work on the ledgers; he was on the ninth thousand now. But the sick man heard his step in the outer room, and called in his weak voice, "Rodman, Rodman." After a time he went in, and it ended in his staying; for the patient was nervous and irritable, and he pitied the nurse, who seemed able to please him in nothing. De Rosset turned with a sigh of relief toward the strong hands that lifted him readily, toward the composed manner, toward the man's voice that seemed to bring a breeze from outside into the close room; animated, cheered, he talked volubly. The keeper listened, answered once in a while, and quietly took the rest of the afternoon into his own hands. Miss Ward yielded to the silent change, leaned back, and closed her eyes. She looked exhausted and for the first time pallid; the loosened dark hair curled in little rings about her temples, and her lips were parted as though she was too tired to close them; for hers were not the thin, straight lips that shut tight naturally, like the straight line of a closed box. The sick man talked on. "Come, Rodman," he said, after a while, "I have read that lying verse of yours over at least ten thousand and fifty-nine times; please tell me its history; I want to have something definite to think of when I read it for the ten thousand and sixtieth."

"Toujours femme varie,
Bien fou qui s'y fie;
Une femme souvent
N'est qu'une plume au vent,"

read the keeper slowly, with his execrable English accent. "Well, I don't know that I have any objection to telling the story. I am not sure but that it will do me good to hear it all over myself in plain language again."

"Then it concerns yourself," said De Rosset; "so much the better. I hope it will be, as the children say, the truth, and long."

"It will be the truth, but not long. When the war broke out I was twenty-eight years old, living with my mother on our farm in New England. My father and two brothers had died and left me the homestead; otherwise I should have broken away and sought fortune farther westward, where the lands are better and life is more free. But mother loved the house, the fields, and every crooked tree. She was alone, and so I staid with her. In the center of the village green stood the square, white meeting-house, and near by the small cottage where the pastor lived; the minister's daughter, Mary, was my promised wife. Mary was a slender little creature with a profusion of pale flaxen hair, large, serious blue eyes, and small, delicate features; she was timid almost to a fault; her voice was low and gentle. She was not eighteen, and we were to wait a year. The war came, and I volunteered, of course, and marched away; we wrote to each other often; my letters were full of the camp and skirmishes; hers told of the village, how the widow Brown had fallen ill, and how it was feared that Squire Stafford's boys were lapsing into evil ways. Then came the day when my regiment marched to the field of its slaughter, and soon after our shattered remnant went home. Mary cried over me, and came out every day to the farmhouse with her bunches of violets; she read aloud to me from her good little books, and I used to lie and watch her profile bending over the page, with the light falling on her flaxen hair low down against the small, white throat. Then my wound healed, and I went again, this time for three years; and Mary's father blessed me, and said that when peace came he would call me son, but not before, for these were no times for marrying or giving in marriage. He was a good man, a red-hot abolitionist, and a roaring lion as regards temperance; but nature had made him so small in body that no one was much frightened when he roared. I said that I went for three years; but eight years have passed and I have never been back to the village. First, mother died. Then Mary turned false. I sold the farm by letter and lost the money three months afterward in an unfortunate investment; my health failed. Like many another Northern soldier, I remembered the healing climate of the South; its soft airs came back to me when the snow lay deep on the fields and the sharp wind whistled around the poor tavern where the moneyless, half-crippled volunteer sat coughing by the fire. I applied for this place and obtained it. That is all."

"But it is not all," said the sick man, raising himself on his elbow; "you have not told half yet, nor anything at all about the French verse."

"Oh—that? There was a little Frenchman staying at the hotel; he had formerly been a dancing-master, and was full of dry, withered conceits, although he looked like a thin and bilious old ape dressed as a man. He taught me, or tried to teach me, various wise sayings, among them this one, which pleased my fancy so much that I gave him twenty-five cents to write it out in large text for me."

"Toujours femme varie," repeated De Rosset; "but you don't really think so, do you, Rodman?"

"I do. But they can not help it; it is their nature.—I beg your pardon, Miss Ward. I was speaking as though you were not here."

Miss Ward's eyelids barely acknowledged his existence;

that was all. But some time after she remarked to her cousin that it was only in New England that one found that pale flaxen hair.

June was waning, when suddenly the summons came. Ward De Rosset died. He was unconscious toward the last, and death, in the guise of sleep, bore away his soul. They carried him home to the old house, and from there the funeral started, a few family carriages, dingy and battered, following the hearse, for death revived the old neighborhood feeling; that honor at least they could pay—the sonless mothers and the widows who lived shut up in the old houses with everything falling into ruin around them, brooding over the past. The keeper watched the small procession as it passed his gate on its way to the churchyard in the village. "There he goes, poor fellow, his sufferings over at last," he said; and then he set the cottage in order and began the old solitary life again.

He saw Miss Ward but once.

It was a breathless evening in August, when the moonlight flooded the level country. He had started out to stroll across the waste; but the mood changed, and climbing over the eastern wall he had walked back to the flag-staff, and now lay at its foot gazing up into the infinite sky. A step sounded on the gravel-walk; he turned his face that way, and recognized Miss Ward. With confident step she passed the dark cottage, and brushed his arm with her robe as he lay unseen in the shadow. She went down toward the parade-ground, and his eyes followed her. Softly outlined in the moonlight, she moved to and fro among the mounds, pausing often, and once he thought she knelt. Then slowly she returned, and he raised himself and waited; she saw him, started, then paused.

"I thought you were away," she said; "Pomp told me so."

"You set him to watch me?"

"Yes. I wished to come here once, and I did not wish to meet you."

"Why did you wish to come?"

"Because Ward was here—and because—because—never mind. It is enough that I wished to walk once among those mounds."

"And pray there?"

"Well—and if I did!" said the girl defiantly.

Rodman stood facing her, with his arms folded; his eyes rested on her face; he said nothing.

"I am going away to-morrow," began Miss Ward again, assuming with an effort her old, pulseless manner. "I have sold the place, and I shall never return, I think; I am going far away."

"Where?"

"To Tennessee."

"That is not so very far," said the keeper, smiling.

"There I shall begin a new existence," pursued the voice, ignoring the comment.

"You have scarcely begun the old; you are hardly more than a child, now. What are you going to do in Tennessee?"

"Teach."

"Have you relatives there?"

"No."

"A miserable life—a hard, lonely, loveless life," said Rodman. "God help the woman who must be that dreary thing, a teacher from necessity!"

Miss Ward turned swiftly, but the keeper kept by her side. He saw the tears glittering on her eyelashes, and his voice softened. "Do not leave me in anger," he said; "I should not have spoken so, although indeed it was the truth. Walk back with me to the cottage, and take your last look at the room where poor Ward died, and then I will go with you to your home."

"No; Pomp is waiting at the gate," said the girl, almost inarticulately.

"Very well; to the gate, then."

They went toward the cottage in silence; the keeper threw open the door. "Go in," he said. "I will wait outside."

The girl entered and went into the inner room, throwing herself down upon her knees at the bedside. "O Ward, Ward!" she sobbed; "I am all alone in the world now, Ward—all alone!" She buried her face in her hands and gave way to a passion of tears; and the keeper could not help but hear as he waited outside. Then the desolate little creature rose and came forth, putting on, as she did so, her poor armor of pride. The keeper had not moved from the door-step. Now he turned his face. "Before you go—go away for ever from this place—will you write your name in my register," he said—"the visitors' register? The Government had it prepared for the throngs who would visit these graves; but with the exception of the blacks, who can not write, no one has come, and the register is empty. Will you write your name? Yet do not write it unless you can think gently of the men who lie there under the grass. I believe you do think gently of them, else why have you come of your own accord to stand by the side of their graves?" As he said this, he looked fixedly at her.

Miss Ward did not answer; but neither did she write.

"Very well," said the keeper; "come away. You will not, I see."

"I can not! Shall I, Bettina Ward, set my name down in black and white as a visitor to this cemetery, where lie fourteen thousand of the soldiers who killed my father, my three brothers, my cousins; who brought desolation upon all our house, and ruin upon all our neighborhood, all our State, and all our country?—for the South *is* our country, and not your North. Shall I forget these things? Never! Sooner let my right hand wither by my side! I was but a child; yet I remember the tears of my mother, and the grief of all around us. There was not a house where there was not one dead."

"It is true," answered the keeper; "at the South, all went."

They walked down to the gate together in silence.

"Good-by," said John, holding out his hand; "you will give me yours or not as you choose, but I will not have it as a favor."

She gave it.

"I hope that life will grow brighter to you as the years pass. May God bless you!"

He dropped her hand; she turned, and passed through the gateway; then he sprang after her.

"Nothing can change you," he said; "I know it, I have known it all along; you are part of your country, part of the time, part of the bitter hour through which she is passing. Nothing can change you; if it could, you would not be what you are, and I should not—But you can not change. Good-by, Bettina, poor little child—good-by. Follow your path out into the world. Yet do not think, dear, that I have not seen—have not understood."

He bent and kissed her hand; then he was gone, and she went on alone.

A week later the keeper strolled over toward the old house. It was twilight, but the new owner was still at work. He was one of those sandy-haired, energetic Maine men, who, probably on the principle of extremes, were often found through the South, making new homes for themselves in the pleasant land.

"Pulling down the old house, are you?" said the keeper, leaning idly on the gate, which was already flanked by a new fence.

"Yes," replied the Maine man, pausing; "it was only an old shell, just ready to tumble on our heads. You're the keeper over yonder, an't you?" (He already knew everybody within a circle of five miles.)

"Yes, I think I should like those vines if you have no use for them," said Rodman, pointing to the uprooted greenery that once screened the old piazza.

"Wuth about twenty-five cents, I guess," said the Maine man, handing them over.

SISTER ST. LUKE

"SISTER ST. LUKE" WAS INSPIRED BY THE WINters Woolson spent in and around St. Augustine, Florida, from 1873 to 1879, for the benefit of her mother's health. Woolson loved the quaint town with its colonial Spanish character, but she loved the wild landscape then surrounding it even more. When she wasn't writing, she was sailing and boating, exploring the swamps as well as the bay with its myriad inlets and islands that fronted the Atlantic Ocean, sometimes alone but often in the company of other Northern tourists, such as the two men featured in this story. "Sister St. Luke" takes place on the barrier island that lies across the Matanzas River from St. Augustine. It is a good example of Woolson's many stories that portray women who tend to go unnoticed but possess unsuspected powers. It was first published in *The Galaxy* in April 1877 and was reprinted in *Rodman the Keeper: Southern Sketches* in 1880.

SISTER ST. LUKE

. . . .

She lived shut in by flowers and trees,
And shade of gentle bigotries;
On this side lay the trackless sea,
On that the great world's mystery;
But, all unseen and all unguessed,
They could not break upon her rest.
The world's far glories flamed and flashed,
Afar the wild seas roared and dashed;
But in her small dull paradise,
Safe housed from rapture or surprise,
    Nor day nor night had power to fright
The peace of God within her eyes.

—JOHN HAY

THEY FOUND HER THERE. "THIS IS MORE THAN I expected," said Carrington as they landed—"seven pairs of Spanish eyes at once."

"Three pairs," answered Keith, fastening the statement to fact and the boat to a rock in his calm way; "and one if not two of the pairs are Minorcan."

The two friends crossed the broad white beach toward the little stone house of the light-keeper, who sat in the doorway,

having spent the morning watching their sail cross over from
Pelican reef, tacking lazily east and west—an event of more
than enough importance in his isolated life to have kept him
there, gazing and contented, all day. Behind the broad shoulders of swarthy Pedro stood a little figure clothed in black;
and as the man lifted himself at last and came down to meet
them, and his wife stepped briskly forward, they saw that the
third person was a nun—a large-eyed, fragile little creature,
promptly introduced by Melvyna, the keeper's wife, as "Sister
St. Luke." For the keeper's wife, in spite of her black eyes,
was not a Minorcan; not even a Southerner. Melvyna Sawyer
was born in Vermont, and, by one of the strange chances of
this vast, many-raced, motley country of ours, she had traveled south as nurse—and a very good, energetic nurse too,
albeit somewhat sharp-voiced—to a delicate young wife, who
had died in the sunny land, as so many of them die; the sun,
with all his good will and with all his shining, not being able
to undo in three months the work of long years of the snows
and bleak east winds of New England.

The lady dead, and her poor thin frame sent northward
again to lie in the hillside churchyard by the side of bleak Puritan ancestors, Melvyna looked about her. She hated the lazy
tropical land, and had packed her calf-skin trunk to go, when
Pedro Gonsalvez surprised her by proposing matrimony. At
least that is what she wrote to her aunt Clemanthy, away in
Vermont; and, although Pedro may not have used the words,
he at least meant the fact, for they were married two weeks
later by a justice of the peace, whom Melvyna's sharp eyes had
unearthed, she of course deeming the padre of the little parish
and one or two attendant priests as so much dust to be tram-

pled energetically under her shoes, Protestant and number six
and a half double-soled mediums. The justice of the peace, a
good-natured old gentleman who had forgotten that he held
the office at all, since there was no demand for justice and the
peace was never broken, married them as well as he could in a
surprised sort of way; and, instead of receiving a fee, gave one,
which Melvyna, however, promptly rescued from the bridegroom's willing hand, and returned with the remark that there
was no "call for alms" (pronounced as if rhymed with hams),
and that two shilling, or mebbe three, she guessed, would be
about right for the job. This sum she deposited on the table,
and then took leave, walking off with a quick, enterprising
step, followed by her acquiescent and admiring bridegroom.
He had remained acquiescent and admiring ever since, and
now, as lighthouse-keeper on Pelican Island, he admired and
acquiesced more than ever; while Melvyna kept the house
in order, cooked his dinners, and tended his light, which,
although only third-class, shone and glittered under her daily
care in the old square tower which was founded by the Spaniards, heightened by the English, and now finished and owned
by the United States, whose Lighthouse Board said to each
other every now and then that really they must put a first-
class Fresnel on Pelican Island and a good substantial tower
instead of that old-fashioned beacon. They did so a year or two
later; and a hideous barber's pole it remains to the present day.
But when Carrington and Keith landed there the square tower
still stood in its gray old age at the very edge of the ocean, so
that high tides swept the step of the keeper's house. It was
originally a lookout where the Spanish soldier stood and fired
his culverin when a vessel came in sight outside the reef; then

the British occupied the land, added a story, and placed an iron grating on the top, where their coastguardsman lighted a fire of pitch-pine knots that flared up against the sky, with the tidings, "A sail! a sail!" Finally the United States came into possession, ran up a third story, and put in a revolving light, one flash for the land and two for the sea—a proportion unnecessarily generous now to the land, since nothing came in any more, and everything went by, the little harbor being of no importance since the indigo culture had failed. But ships still sailed by on their way to the Queen of the Antilles, and to the far Windward and Leeward Islands, and the old light went on revolving, presumably for their benefit. The tower, gray and crumbling, and the keeper's house, were surrounded by a high stone wall with angles and loopholes—a small but regularly planned defensive fortification built by the Spaniards; and odd enough it looked there on that peaceful island, where there was nothing to defend. But it bore itself stoutly nevertheless, this ancient little fortress, and kept a sharp lookout still over the ocean for the damnable Huguenot sail of two centuries before.

The sea had encroached greatly on Pelican Island, and sooner or later it must sweep the keeper's house away; but now it was a not unpleasant sensation to hear the water wash against the step—to sit at the narrow little windows and watch the sea roll up, roll up, nearer and nearer, coming all the way landless in long surges from the distant African coast, only to never quite get at the foundations of that stubborn little dwelling, which held its own against them, and then triumphantly watched them roll back, roll back, departing inch by inch down the beach, until, behold! there was a magnificent parade-ground,

broad enough for a thousand feet to tread—a floor more fresh
and beautiful than the marble pavements of palaces. There
were not a thousand feet to tread there, however; only six. For
Melvyna had more than enough to do within the house, and
Pedro never walked save across the island to the inlet once in
two weeks or so, when he managed to row over to the village,
and return with supplies, by taking two entire days for it, even
Melvyna having given up the point, tacitly submitting to loitering she could not prevent, but recompensing herself by a
general cleaning on those days of the entire premises, from
the top of the lantern in the tower to the last step in front of
the house.

You could not argue with Pedro. He only smiled back upon
you as sweetly and as softly as molasses. Melvyna, endeavoring to urge him to energy, found herself in the position of an
active ant wading through the downy recesses of a feather bed,
which well represented his mind.

Pedro was six feet two inches in height, and amiable as a
dove. His wife sensibly accepted him as he was, and he had his
two days in town—a very mild dissipation, however, since the
Minorcans are too indolent to do anything more than smoke,
lie in the sun, and eat salads heavily dressed in oil. They said,
"The serene and august wife of our friend is well, we trust?"
and, "The island—does it not remain lonely?" and then the
salad was pressed upon him again. For they all considered
Pedro a man of strange and varied experiences. Had he not
married a woman of wonder—of an energy unfathomable?
And he lived with her alone in a lighthouse, on an island;
alone, mind you, without a friend or relation near!

The six feet that walked over the beautiful beach of the

southern ocean were those of Keith, Carrington, and Sister St. Luke.

"Now go, Miss Luke," Melvyna had said, waving her energetically away with the skimmer as she stood irresolute at the kitchen door. "'Twill do you a power of good, and they're nice, quiet gentlemen who will see to you, and make things pleasant. Bless you, *I* know what they are. They ain't none of the miserable, good-for-nothing race about here! Your convent is fifty miles off, ain't it? And besides, you were brought over here half dead for me to cure up—now, warn't you?"

The Sister acknowledged that she was, and Melvyna went on:

"You see, things is different up North, and I understand 'em, but you don't. Now you jest go right along and hev a pleasant walk, and I'll hev a nice bowl of venison broth ready for you when you come back. Go right along now." The skimmer waved again, and the Sister went.

"Yes, she's taken the veil, and is a nun for good and all," explained Melvyna to her new guests the evening of their arrival, when the shy little Sister had retreated to her own room above. "They thought she was dying, and she was so long about it, and useless on their hands, that they sent her up here to the village for sea air, and to be red of her, I guess. 'Tany rate, there she was in one of them crowded, dirty old houses, and so—I jest brought her over here. To tell the truth, gentlemen—the real bottom of it—my baby died last year—and—and Miss Luke she was so good I'll never forget it. I ain't a Catholic—fur from it; I hate 'em. But she seen us coming up from the boat with our little coffin, and she came out and brought flowers to lay on it, and followed to the grave, feeble as she was; and she even put in her little black shawl, because the sand was wet—this miserable half-afloat land, you know—and I couldn't bear to see the coffin set down into it. And I said to myself then that I'd never hate a Catholic again, gentlemen. I don't love 'em yet, and don't know as I ever shell; but Miss Luke, she's different. Consumption? Well, I hardly know. She's a sight better than she was when she come. I'd like to make her well again, and, someway, I can't help a-trying to, for I was a nurse by trade once. But then what's the use? She'll only hev to go back to that old convent!" And Melvyna clashed her pans together in her vexation. "Is she a good Catholic, do you say? Heavens and earth, yes! She's *that* religious— my! I couldn't begin to tell! She believes every word of all that rubbish those old nuns have told her. She thinks it's beautiful to be the bride of heaven; and, as far as that goes, I don't know but she's right: 'tain't much the other kind is wuth," pursued Melvyna, with fine contempt for mankind in general. "As to freedom, they've as good as shoved her off their hands, haven't they? And I guess I can do as I like any way on my own island. There wasn't any man about their old convent, as I can learn, and so Miss Luke, she hain't been taught to run away from 'em like most nuns. Of course, if they knew, they would be sending over here after her; but they don't know, and them priests in the village are too fat and lazy to earn their salt, let alone caring what has become of her. I guess, if they think of her at all, they think that she died, and that they buried her in their crowded, sunken old graveyard. They're so slow and sleepy that they forget half the time who they're burying! But Miss Luke, she ought to go out in the air, and she is so afraid of everything that it don't do her no good to go alone. I haven't got the time to go; and so, if you will let her walk along the beach with you once in a while, it will do her a sight of good, and give her an appetite—although what I want her to hev an appetite for I am sure I don't know; for, ef she gets well, of course she'll go back to the convent. Want to go? *That* she does. She loves the place, and feels lost and strange anywhere else. She was taken there when she was a baby, and it is all the home she has. *She* doesn't know they wanted to be red of her, and she wouldn't believe it ef I was to tell her forty times. She loves them all dearly, and prays every day to go back there. Spanish? Yes, I suppose so; she don't know herself what she is exactly. She speaks English well though, don't she? Yes, Sister St. Luke is her name; and a heathenish name it is for a woman, in my opinion. *I* call her Miss Luke. Convert her? Couldn't any more convert her than you could convert a white gull, and make a land-bird of him. It's his nature to ride on the water and be wet all the time. Towels couldn't dry him—not if you fetched a thousand!"

"Our good hostess is a woman of discrimination, and sorely perplexed, therefore, over her *protégée*," said Keith, as the two young men sought their room, a loft under the peaked roof, which was to be their abode for some weeks, when they were not afloat. "As a nurse she feels a professional pride in curing, while as a Calvinist she would almost rather kill than cure, if her patient is to go back to the popish convent. But the little Sister looks very fragile. She will probably save trouble all around by fading away."

"She is about as faded now as a woman can be," answered Carrington.

The two friends, or rather companions, plunged into all the

phases of the southern ocean with a broad, inhaling, expanding delight which only a physique naturally fine, or carefully
trained, can feel. George Carrington was a vigorous young
Saxon, tall and broad, feeling his life and strength in every
vein and muscle. Each night he slept his eight hours dream-
lessly, like a child, and each day he lived four hours in one,
counting by the pallid hours of other men. Andrew Keith, on
the other hand, represented the physique cultured and trained
up to a high point by years of attention and care. He was a
slight man, rather undersized, but his wiry strength was more
than a match for Carrington's bulk, and his finely cut face, if
you would but study it, stood out like a cameo by the side of
a ruddy miniature in oils. The trouble is that but few people
study cameos. He was older than his companion, and "one of
those quiet fellows, you know," said the world. The two had
never done or been anything remarkable in their lives. Keith
had a little money, and lived as he pleased, while Carrington,
off now on a vacation, was junior member of a firm in which
family influence had placed him. Both were city men.

"You absolutely do not know how to walk, señora," said
Keith. "I will be doctor now, and you must obey me. Never
mind the crabs, and never mind the jelly-fish, but throw back
your head and walk off briskly. Let the wind blow in your face,
and try to stand more erect."

"You are doctor? They told me, could I but see one, well
would I be," said the Sister. "At the convent we have only Sister Inez, with her small and old medicines."

"Yes, I think I may call myself doctor," answered Keith
gravely. "What do you say, Carrington?"

"Knows no end, Miss, Miss—Miss Luke—I should say,

Miss St. Luke. I am sure I do not know why I should stumble over it when St. John is a common enough name," answered Carrington, who generally did his thinking aloud.

"No end?" repeated the little Sister inquiringly. "But there is an end in this evil world to all things."

"Never mind what he says, señora," interrupted Keith, "but step out strongly and firmly, and throw back your head. There now, there are no crabs in sight, and the beach is hard as a floor. Try it with me: one, two; one, two."

So they treated her, partly as a child, partly as a gentle being of an inferior race. It was a new amusement, although a rather mild one Carrington said, to instruct this unformed, timid mind, to open the blinded eyes, and train the ignorant ears to listen to the melodies of nature.

"Do you not hear? It is like the roll of a grand organ," said Keith as they sat on the door-step one evening at sunset. The sky was dark; the wind had blown all day from the north to the south, and frightened the little Sister as she toiled at her lace-work, made on a cushion in the Spanish fashion, her lips mechanically repeating prayers meanwhile; for never had they such winds at the inland convent, embowered in its orange-trees. Now, as the deep, low roll of the waves sounded on the shore, Keith, who was listening to it with silent enjoyment, happened to look up and catch the pale, repressed nervousness of her face.

"Oh, not like an organ," she murmured. "This is a fearful sound; but an organ is sweet—soft and sweet. When Sister Teresa plays the evening hymn it is like the sighing of angels."

"But your organ is probably small, señora."

"We have not thought it small. It remains in our chapel, by

the window of arches, and below we walk, at the hour of meditation, from the lime-tree to the white rose-bush, and back
again, while the music sounds above. We have not thought it
small, but large—yes, very large."

"Four feet long, probably," said Carrington, who was
smoking an evening pipe, now listening to the talk awhile,
now watching the movements of two white heron who were
promenading down the beach. "I saw the one over in the village church. It was about as long as this step."

"Yes," said the Sister, surveying the step, "it is about as long
as that. It is a very large organ.

"Walk with me down to the point," said Keith—"just once
and back again."

The docile little Sister obeyed; she always did immediately
whatever they told her to do.

"I want you to listen now; stand still and listen—listen to
the sea," said Keith, when they had turned the point and stood
alone on the shore. "Try to think only of the pure, deep, blue
water, and count how regularly the sound rolls up in long, low
chords, dying away and then growing louder, dying away and
then growing louder, as regular as your own breath. Do you
not hear it?"

"Yes," said the little Sister timorously.

"Keep time, then, with your hand, and let me see whether
you catch the measure."

So the small brown hand, nerveless and slender, tried to
mark and measure the roar of the great ocean surges, and at
last succeeded, urged on by the alternate praises and rebukes
of Keith, who watched with some interest a faint color rise in
the pale oval face, and an intent listening look come into the

soft, unconscious eyes, as, for the first time, the mind caught the mighty rhythm of the sea. She listened, and listened, standing mute, with head slightly bent and parted lips.

"I want you to listen to it in that way every day," said Keith, as he led the way back. "It has different voices: sometimes a fresh, joyous song, sometimes a faint, loving whisper; but always something. You will learn in time to love it, and then it will sing to you all day long."

"Not at the dear convent; there is no ocean there."

"You want to go back to the convent?"

"Oh, could I go! could I go!" said the Sister, not impatiently, but with an intense yearning in her low voice. "Here, so lost, so strange am I, so wild is everything. But I must not murmur"; and she crossed her hands upon her breast and bowed her head.

THE TWO YOUNG MEN led a riotous life; they rioted with the ocean, with the winds, with the level island, with the sunshine and the racing clouds. They sailed over to the reef daily and plunged into the surf; they walked for miles along the beach, and ran races over its white floor; they hunted down the center of the island, and brought back the little brown deer who lived in the low thicket on each side of the island's backbone. The island was twenty miles long and a mile or two broad, with a central ridge of shell-formed rock about twenty feet in height, that seemed like an Appalachian chain on the level waste; below, in the little hollows on each side, spread a low tangled thicket, a few yards wide; and all the rest was barren sand, with movable hills here and there—hills a few feet in height,

blown up by the wind, and changed in a night. The only vegetation besides the thicket was a rope-like vine that crept over
the sand, with few leaves far apart, and now and then a dull
purple blossom—a solitary tenacious vine of the desert, satisfied with little, its growth slow, its life monotonous; yet try
to tear it from the surface of the sand, where its barren length
seems to lie loosely like an old brown rope thrown down at
random, and behold, it resists you stubbornly. You find a mile
or two of it on your hands, clinging and pulling as the strong
ivy clings to a stone wall; a giant could not conquer it, this
seemingly dull and half-dead thing; and so you leave it there
to creep on in its own way, over the damp, shell-strewn waste.
One day Carrington came home in great glory; he had found
a salt marsh. "Something besides this sand, you know—a
stretch of saw-grass away to the south, the very place for fat
ducks. And somebody has been there before us, too, for I saw
the mast of a sail-boat some distance down, tipped up against
the sky."

"That old boat is ourn, I guess," said Melvyna. "She drifted
down there one high tide, and Pedro he never would go for
her. She was a mighty nice little boat, too, ef she *was* cranky."

Pedro smiled amiably back upon his spouse, and helped
himself to another hemisphere of pie. He liked the pies,
although she was obliged to make them, she said, of such out-
landish things as figs, dried oranges, and pomegranates. "If
you could only see a pumpkin, Pedro," she often remarked,
shaking her head. Pedro shook his back in sympathy; but, in
the mean time, found the pies very good as they were.

"Let us go down after the boat," said Carrington. "You
have only that old tub over at the inlet, Pedro, and you really

need another boat." (Carrington always liked to imagine that he was a constant and profound help to the world at large.) "Suppose anything should happen to the one you have?" Pedro had not thought of that; he slowly put down his knife and fork to consider the subject.

"We will go this afternoon," said Keith, issuing his orders, "and you shall go with us, señora."

"And Pedro, too, to help you," said Melvyna. "I've always wanted that boat back, she was such a pretty little thing: one sail, you know, and decked over in front; you sat on the bottom. I'd like right well to go along myself; but I suppose I'd better stay at home and cook a nice supper for you."

Pedro thought so, decidedly.

When the February sun had stopped blazing down directly overhead, and a few white afternoon clouds had floated over from the east to shade his shining, so that man could bear it, the four started inland toward the backbone ridge, on whose summit there ran an old trail southward, made by the fierce Creeks three centuries before. Right up into the dazzling light soared the great eagles—straight up, up to the sun, their unshrinking eyes fearlessly fixed full on his fiery ball.

"It would be grander if we did not know they had just stolen their dinners from the poor hungry fish-hawks over there on the inlet," said Carrington.

Sister St. Luke had learned to walk quite rapidly now. Her little black gown trailed lightly along the sand behind her, and she did her best to "step out boldly," as Keith directed; but it was not firmly, for she only succeeded in making a series of quick, uncertain little paces over the sand like bird-tracks. Once Keith had taken her back and made her look at her own uneven footsteps. "Look—no two the same distance apart," he said. The little Sister looked and was very much mortified. "Indeed, I *will* try with might to do better," she said. And she did try with might; they saw her counting noiselessly to herself as she walked, "One, two; one, two." But she had improved so much that Keith now devoted his energies to teaching her to throw back her head and look about her. "Do you not see those soft banks of clouds piled up in the west?" he said, constantly directing her attention to objects above her. But this was a harder task, for the timid eyes had been trained from childhood to look down, and the head was habitually bent, like a pendant flower on its stem. Melvyna had deliberately laid hands upon the heavy veil and white band that formerly encircled the small face. "You can not breathe in them," she said. But the Sister still wore a light veil over the short dark hair, which would curl in little rings upon her temples in spite of her efforts to prevent it; the cord and heavy beads and cross encircled her slight waist, while the wide sleeves of her nun's garb fell over her hands to the finger-tips.

"How do you suppose she would look dressed like other women?" said Carrington one day. The two men were drifting in their small yacht, lying at ease on the cushions, and smoking.

"Well," answered Keith slowly, "if she was well dressed—very well, I mean, say in the French style—and if she had any spirit of her own, any vivacity, you might, with that dark face of hers and those eyes—you *might* call her piquant."

"Spirit? She has not the spirit of a fly," said Carrington, knocking the ashes out of his pipe and fumbling in an embroidered velvet pouch, one of many offerings at his shrine, for a fresh supply of the strong aromatic tobacco he affected, Keith meanwhile smoking nothing but the most delicate cigarettes. "The other day I heard a wild scream; and rushing down stairs I found her half fainting on the steps, all in a little heap. And what do you think it was? She had been sitting there, lost in a dream—mystic, I suppose, like St. Agnes—

> Deep on the convent roof the snows
> Are sparkling to the moon:
> My breath to heaven like vapor goes.
> May my soul follow soon—

and that sort of thing."

"No," said Keith, "there is nothing mystical about the Luke maiden; she has never even dreamed of the ideal ecstasies of deeper minds. She says her little prayers simply, almost mechanically, so many every day, and dwells as it were content in the lowly valleys of religion."

"Well, whatever she was doing," continued Carrington, "a great sea crab had crawled up and taken hold of the toe of her little shoe. Grand tableau—crab and Luke maiden! And the crab had decidedly the better of it."

"She *is* absurdly timid," admitted Keith.

And absurdly timid she was now, when, having crossed the stretch of sand and wound in and out among the low hillocks, they came to the hollow where grew the dark green thicket, through which they must pass to reach the Appalachian range, the backbone of the island, where the trail gave them an easier way than over the sands. Carrington went first and hacked out a path with his knife; Keith followed, and held back the branches; the whole distance was not more than twelve feet; but its recesses looked dark and shadowy to the little Sister, and she hesitated.

"Come," said Carrington; "we shall never reach the salt marsh at this rate."

"There is nothing dangerous here, señora," said Keith. "Look, you can see for yourself. And there are three of us to help you."

"Yes," said Pedro—"three of us." And he swung his broad bulk into the gap.

Still she hesitated.

"Of what are you afraid?" called out Carrington impatiently.

"I know not, indeed," she answered, almost in tears over her own behavior, yet unable to stir. Keith came back, and saw that she was trembling—not violently, but in a subdued, help-less sort of way which was pathetic in its very causelessness.

"Take her up, Pedro," he ordered; and, before she could object, the good-natured giant had borne her in three strides through the dreaded region, and set her down safely upon the ridge. She followed them humbly now, along the safe path, trying to step firmly, and walk with her head up, as Keith had directed. Carrington had already forgotten her again, and even Keith was eagerly looking ahead for the first glimpse of green.

"There is something singularly fascinating in the stretch of a salt marsh," he said. "Its level has such a far sweep as you stand and gaze across it, and you have a dreamy feeling that there is no end to it. The stiff, drenched grasses hold the salt which the tide brings in twice a day, and you inhale that fresh, strong, briny odor, the rank, salt, invigorating smell of the sea;

the breeze that blows across has a tang to it like the snap of a whip-lash across your face, bringing the blood to the surface, and rousing you to a quicker pace."

"Ha!" said Carrington; "there it is. Don't you see the green? A little farther on, you will see the mast of the boat."

"That is all that is wanted," said Keith. "A salt marsh is not complete without a boat tilted up aground somewhere, with its slender dark mast outlined against the sky. A boat sailing along in a commonplace way would blight the whole thing; what we want is an abandoned craft, aged and deserted, aground down the marsh with only its mast rising above the waste."

"*Bien!* there it is," said Carrington; "and now the question is, how to get to it."

"You two giants will have to go," said Keith, finding a comfortable seat. "I see a mile or two of tall wading before us, and up to your shoulders is over my head. I went duck-shooting with that man last year, señora. 'Come on,' he cried—'splendid sport ahead, old fellow; come on.'

"'Is it deep?' I asked from behind. I was already up to my knees, and could not see bottom, the water was so dark.

"'Oh, no, not at all; just right,' he answered, striding ahead. 'Come on.'

"I came; and went in up to my eyes."

But the señora did not smile.

"You know Carrington is taller than I am," explained Keith, amused by the novelty of seeing his own stories fall flat.

"Is he?" said the Sister vaguely.

It was evident that she had not observed whether he was or not.

Carrington stopped short, and for an instant stared blankly at her. What every one noticed and admired all over the country wherever he went, this little silent creature had not even seen!

"He will never forgive you," said Keith laughing, as the two tall forms strode off into the marsh. Then, seeing that she did not comprehend in the least, he made a seat for her by spreading his light coat on the Appalachian chain, and, leaning back on his elbow, began talking to her about the marsh. "Breathe in the strong salt," he said, "and let your eyes rest on the green, reedy expanse. Supposing you were painting a picture, now—does any one paint pictures at your convent?"

"Ah, yes," said the little nun, rousing to animation at once. "Sister St. James paints pictures the most beautiful on earth. She painted for us Santa Inez with her lamb, and Santa Rufina of Sevilla, with her palms and earthen vases."

"And has she not taught you to paint also?"

"Me! Oh, no. I am only a Sister young and of no gifts. Sister St. James is a great saint, and of age she has seventy years."

"Not requisites for painting, either of them, that I am aware," said Keith. "However, if you were painting this marsh, do you not see how the mast of that boat makes the feature of the landscape the one human element; and yet, even that abandoned, merged as it were in the desolate wildness of the scene?"

The Sister looked over the green earnestly, as if trying to see all that he suggested. Keith talked on. He knew that he talked well, and he did not confuse her with more than one subject, but dwelt upon the marsh; stories of men who had been lost in them, of women who had floated down in boats and never returned; descriptions clear as etchings; studies of the monotone of hues before them—one subject picture over and over again, as, wishing to instruct a child, he would have drawn with a chalk one letter of the alphabet a hundred times, until the wandering eyes had learned at last to recognize and know it.

"Do you see nothing at all, feel nothing at all?" he said. "Tell me exactly."

Thus urged, the Sister replied that she thought she did feel the salt breeze a little.

"Then take off that shroud and enjoy it," said Keith, extending his arm suddenly, and sweeping off the long veil by the corner that was nearest to him.

"Oh!" said the little Sister—"oh!" and distressfully she covered her head with her hands, as if trying to shield herself from the terrible light of day. But the veil had gone down into the thicket, whither she dared not follow. She stood irresolute.

"I will get it for you before the others come back," said Keith. "It is gone now, however, and, what is more, you could not help it; so sit down, like a sensible creature, and enjoy the breeze."

The little nun sat down, and confusedly tried to be a sensible creature. Her head, with its short rings of dark hair, rose childlike from the black gown she wore, and the breeze swept freshly over her; but her eyes were full of tears, and her face so pleading in its pale, silent distress, that at length Keith went down and brought back the veil.

"See the cranes flying home," he said, as the long line dotted the red of the west. "They always seem to be flying right into the sunset, sensible birds!"

The little Sister had heard that word twice now; evidently the cranes were more sensible than she. She sighed as she fastened on the veil; there were a great many hard things out in the world, then, she thought. At the dear convent it was not expected that one should be as a crane.

The other two came back at length, wet and triumphant, with their prize. They had stopped to bail it out, plug its cracks, mend the old sail after a fashion, and nothing would do but that the three should sail home in it, Pedro, for whom there was no room, returning by the way they had come. Carrington, having worked hard, was determined to carry out his plan; and said so.

"A fine plan to give us all a wetting," remarked Keith.

"You go down there and work an hour or two yourself, and see how *you* like it," answered the other, with the irrelevance produced by aching muscles and perspiration dripping from every pore.

This conversation had taken place at the edge of the marsh where they had brought the boat up through one of the numerous channels.

"Very well," said Keith. "But mind you, not a word about danger before the Sister. I shall have hard enough work to persuade her to come with us as it is."

He went back to the ridge, and carelessly suggested returning home by water.

"You will not have to go through the thicket then," he said.

Somewhat to his surprise, Sister St. Luke consented immediately, and followed without a word as he led the way. She was mortally afraid of the water, but, during his absence, she had been telling her beads, and thinking with contrition of two obstinacies in one day—that of the thicket and that of the veil—she could not, she would not have three. So, commending herself to all the saints, she embarked.

"Look here, Carrington, if ever you inveigle me into such danger again for a mere fool's fancy, I will show you what I think of it. You knew the condition of that boat, and I did not," said Keith, sternly, as the two men stood at last on the beach in front of the lighthouse. The Sister had gone within, glad to feel land underfoot once more. She had sat quietly in her place all the way, afraid of the water, of the wind, of everything, but entirely unconscious of the real danger that menaced them. For the little craft would not mind her helm; her mast slipped about erratically; the planking at the bow seemed about to give way altogether; and they were on a lee shore, with the tide coming in, and the surf beating roughly on the beach. They were both good sailors, but it had taken all they knew to bring the boat safely to the lighthouse.

"To tell the truth, I did not think she was so crippled," said Carrington. "She really is a good boat for her size."

"Very," said Keith sarcastically.

But the younger man clung to his opinion; and, in order to verify it, he set himself to work repairing the little craft. You would have supposed his daily bread depended upon her being made seaworthy, by the way he labored. She was made over from stem to stern: a new mast, a new sail; and, finally, scarlet and green paint were brought over from the village, and out she came as brilliant as a young paroquet. Then Carrington took to sailing in her. Proud of his handy work, he sailed up and down, over to the reef, and up the inlet, and even persuaded Melvyna to go with him once, accompanied by the meek little Sister.

"Why shouldn't you both learn how to manage her?" he said in his enthusiasm. "She's as easy to manage as a child—"

"And as easy to tip over," replied Melvyna, screwing up her lips tightly and shaking her head. "You don't catch me out in her again, sure's my name's Sawyer."

For Melvyna always remained a Sawyer in her own mind, in spite of her spouse's name; she could not, indeed, be anything else—*noblesse oblige.* But the Sister, obedient as usual, bent her eyes in turn upon the ropes, the mast, the sail, and the helm, while Carrington, waxing eloquent over his favorite science, delivered a lecture upon their uses, and made her experiment a little to see if she comprehended. He used the simplest words for her benefit, words of one syllable, and unconsciously elevated his voice somewhat, as though that would make her understand better; her wits seemed to him always of the slowest. The Sister followed his directions, and imitated his motions with painstaking minuteness. She did very well until a large porpoise rolled up his dark, glistening back close alongside, when, dropping the sail-rope with a scream, she crouched down at Melvyna's feet and hid her face in her veil. Carrington from that day could get no more passengers for his paroquet boat. But he sailed up and down alone in his little craft, and, when that amusement palled, he took the remainder of the scarlet and green paint and adorned the shells of various sea-crabs and other crawling things, so that the little Sister was met one afternoon by a whole procession of unearthly creatures, strangely variegated, proceeding gravely in single file down the beach from the pen where they had been confined. Keith pointed out to her, however, the probability of their being much admired in their own circles as long as the hues lasted, and she was comforted.

They strolled down the beach now every afternoon, sometimes two, sometimes three, sometimes four when Melvyna had no cooking to watch, no bread to bake; for she rejected with scorn the omnipresent hot biscuit of the South, and kept her household supplied with light loaves in spite of the difficulties of yeast. Sister St. Luke had learned to endure the crabs, but she still fled from the fiddlers when they strayed over from their towns in the marsh; she still went carefully around the great jelly-fish sprawling on the beach, and regarded from a safe distance the beautiful blue Portuguese men-of-war, stranded unexpectedly on the dangerous shore, all their fair voyagings over. Keith collected for her the brilliant sea-weeds, little flecks of color on the white sand, and showed her their beauties; he made her notice all the varieties of shells, enormous conches for the tritons to blow, and beds of wee pink ovals and cornucopias, plates and cups for the little web-footed fairies. Once he came upon a sea-bean.

"It has drifted over from one of the West Indian islands," he said, polishing it with his handkerchief—"one of the islands— let us say Miraprovos—a palmy tropical name, bringing up visions of a volcanic mountain, vast cliffs, a tangled gorgeous forest, and the soft lapping wash of tropical seas. Is it not so, señora?"

But the señora had never heard of the West Indian islands. Being told, she replied: "As you say it, it is so. There is, then, much land in the world?"

"If you keep the sea-bean for ever, good will come," said Keith, gravely presenting it; "but, if after having once accepted it you then lose it, evil will fall upon you."

The Sister received the amulet with believing reverence. "I will lay it up before the shrine of Our Lady," she said, carefully placing it in the little pocket over her heart, hidden among the folds of her gown, where she kept her most precious treasures—a bead of a rosary that had belonged to some saint who lived somewhere some time, a little faded prayer copied in the handwriting of a young nun who had died some years before and whom she had dearly loved, and a list of her own most vicious faults, to be read over and lamented daily; crying evils such as a perverse and insubordinate bearing, a heart froward and evil, gluttonous desires of the flesh, and a spirit of murderous rage. These were her own ideas of herself, written down at the convent. Had she not behaved herself perversely to the Sister Paula, with whom one should be always mild on account of the affliction which had sharpened her tongue? Had she not wrongfully coveted the cell of the novice Felipa, because it looked out upon the orange walk? Had she not gluttonously longed for more of the delectable marmalade made by the aged Sanchita? And, worse than all, had she not, in a spirit of murderous rage, beat the yellow cat with a palm-branch for carrying off the young doves, her especial charge? "Ah, my sins are great indeed," she sighed daily upon her knees, and smote her breast with tears.

Keith watched the sea-bean go into the little heart-pocket almost with compunction. Many of these amulets of the sea, gathered during his winter rambles, had he bestowed with formal warning of their magic powers, and many a fair hand had taken them, many a soft voice had promised to keep them "for ever." But he well knew they would be mislaid and forgotten in a day. The fair ones well knew it too, and each knew that the other knew, so no harm was done. But this sea-bean, he thought, would have a different fate—laid up in some little nook before the shrine, a witness to the daily prayers of the simple-hearted little Sister. "I hope they may do it good," he thought vaguely. Then, reflecting that even the most depraved bean would not probably be much affected by the prayers, he laughed off the fancy, yet did not quite like to think, after all, that the prayers were of no use. Keith's religion, however, was in the primary rocks.

Far down the beach they came upon a wreck, an old and long hidden relic of the past. The low sand-bluff had caved away suddenly and left a clean new side, where, imbedded in the lower part, they saw a ponderous mast. "An old Spanish galleon," said Keith, stooping to examine the remains. "I know it by the curious bolts. They ran ashore here, broadside on, in one of those sudden tornadoes they have along this coast once in a while, I presume. Singular! This was my very place for lying in the sun and letting the blaze scorch me with its clear scintillant splendor. I never imagined I was lying on the bones of this old Spaniard."

"God rest the souls of the sailors!" said the Sister, making the sign of the cross.

"They have been in—wherever they are, let us say, for about three centuries now," observed Keith, "and must be used to it, good or bad."

"Nay; but purgatory, señor."

"True. I had forgotten that," said Keith.

One morning there came up a dense, soft, southern-sea fog, "The kind you can cut with a knife," Carrington said. It lasted for days, sweeping out to sea at night on the land breeze, and lying in a gray bank low down on the horizon, and then rolling in again in the morning enveloping the water and the island in a thick white cloud which was not mist and did not seem damp even, so freshly, softly salt was the feeling it gave to the faces that went abroad in it. Carrington and Keith, of course, must needs be out in it every moment of the time. They walked down the beach for miles, hearing the muffled sound of the near waves, but not seeing them. They sailed in it not knowing whither they went, and they drifted out at sunset and watched the land breeze lift it, roll it up, and carry it out to sea, where distant ships on the horizon line, bound southward, and nearer ones, sailing northward with the Gulf Stream, found themselves enveloped and bothered by their old and baffling foe. They went over to the reef every morning, these two, and bathed in the fog, coming back by sense of feeling, as it were, and landing not infrequently a mile below or above the lighthouse; then what appetites they had for breakfast! And, if it was not ready, they roamed about, roaring like young lions. At least that is what Melvyna said one morning when Carrington had put his curly head into her kitchen door six times in the course of one half hour.

The Sister shrank from the sea fog; she had never seen one before, and she said it was like a great soft white creature that came in on wings, and brooded over the earth. "Yes, beautiful, perhaps," she said in reply to Keith, "but it is so strange—and—and—I know not how to say it—but it seems like a place for spirits to walk, and not of the mortal kind."

They were wandering down the beach, where Keith had lured her to listen to the sound of the hidden waves. At that moment Carrington loomed into view coming toward them. He seemed of giant size as he appeared, passed them, and disappeared again into the cloud behind, his voice sounding muffled as he greeted them. The Sister shrank nearer to her companion as the figure had suddenly made itself visible. "Do you know it is a wonder to me how you have ever managed to live so far," said Keith smiling.

"But it was not far," said the little nun. "Nothing was ever far at the dear convent, but everything was near, and not of strangeness to make one afraid; the garden wall was the end. There we go not outside, but our walk is always from the lime-tree to the white rose-bush and back again. Everything we know there—not roar of waves, not strong wind, not the thick, white air comes to give us fear, but all is still and at peace. At night I dream of the organ, and of the orange-trees, and of the doves. I wake, and hear only the sound of the great water below."

"You will go back," said Keith.

He had begun to pity her lately, for her longing was deeper than he had supposed. It had its roots in her very being. He had studied her and found it so.

"She will die of pure homesickness if she stays here much longer," he said to Carrington. "What do you think of our writing down to that old convent and offering—of course unknown to her—to pay the little she costs them, if they will take her back?"

"All right," said Carrington. "Go ahead."

He was making a larger sail for his paroquet boat. "If none

of you will go out in her, I might as well have all the sport I can," he said.

"Sport to consist in being swamped?" Keith asked.

"By no means, croaker. Sport to consist in shooting over the water like a rocket; I sitting on the tilted edge, watching the waves, the winds, and the clouds, and hearing the water sing as we rush along."

Keith took counsel with no one else, not even with Melvyna, but presently he wrote his letter and carried it himself over to the village to mail. He did good deeds like that once in a while, "to help humanity," he said. They were tangible always; like the primary rocks.

At length one evening the fog rolled out to sea for good and all, at least as far as that shore was concerned. In the morning there stood the lighthouse, and the island, and the reef, just the same as ever. They had almost expected to see them altered, melted a little.

"Let us go over to the reef, all of us, and spend the day," said Keith. "It will do us good to breathe the clear air, and feel the brilliant, dry, hot sunshine again."

"Hear the man!" said Melvyna laughing. "After trying to persuade us all those days that he liked that sticky fog too!"

"Mme. Gonsalvez, we like a lily; but is that any reason why we may not also like a rose?"

"Neither of 'em grows on this beach as I'm aware of," answered Melvyna dryly.

Then Carrington put in his voice, and carried the day. Women never resisted Carrington long, but yielded almost unconsciously to the influence of his height and his strength, and his strong, hearty will. A subtiler influence over them,

however, would have waked resistance, and Carrington himself would have been conquered far sooner (and was conquered
later) by one who remained unswayed by those influences, to
which others paid involuntary obeisance.

Pedro had gone to the village for his supplies and his two
days of mild Minorcan dissipation, and Melvyna, beguiled
and cajoled by the chaffing of the two young men, at last consented, and not only packed the lunch-basket with careful
hand, but even donned for the occasion her "best bonnet," a
structure trimmed in Vermont seven years before by the experienced hand of Miss Althy Spears, the village milliner, who
had adorned it with a durable green ribbon and a vigorous
wreath of artificial flowers. Thus helmeted, Mme. Gonsalvez
presided at the stern of the boat with great dignity. For they
were in the safe, well-appointed little yacht belonging to
the two gentlemen, the daring paroquet having been left at
home tied to the last of a low heap of rocks that jutted out into
the water in front of the lighthouse, the only remains of the
old stone dock built by the Spaniards long before. Sister St.
Luke was with them of course, gentle and frightened as usual.
Her breath came quickly as they neared the reef, and Carrington with a sure hand guided the little craft outside into
the surf, and, rounding a point, landed them safely in a miniature harbor he had noted there. Keith had counted the days,
and felt sure that the answer from the convent would come
soon. His offer—for he had made it his alone without Carrington's aid—had been liberal; there could be but one reply.
The little Sister would soon go back to the lime-tree, the white
rose-bush, the doves, the old organ that was "so large"—all
the quiet routine of the life she loved so well; and they would

see her small oval face and timid dark eyes no more. So he took her for a last walk down the reef, while Melvyna made coffee, and Carrington, having noticed a dark line floating on the water, immediately went out in his boat, of course, to see what it was.

The reef had its high backbone, like the island. Some day it would be the island, with another reef outside, and the lighthouse beach would belong to the mainland. Down the stretch of sand toward the sea the pelicans stood in rows, toeing a mark, solemn and heavy, by the hundreds—a countless number—for the reef was their gathering-place.

"They are holding a conclave," said Keith. "That old fellow has the floor. See him wag his head."

In and out among the pelicans, and paying no attention to them and their conclave, sped the sickle-bill curlews, actively probing everywhere with their long, grotesque, sickle-shaped bills; and woe be to the burrowing things that came in their way! The red-beaked oyster-bird flew by, and close down to the sea skimmed the razor-bill shear-water, with his head bent forward and his feet tilted up, just grazing the water with his open bill as he flew, and leaving a shining mark behind, as though he held a pencil in his mouth and was running a line. The lazy gulls, who had no work to do, and would not have done it if they had, rode at ease on the little wavelets close in shore. The Sister, being asked, confessed that she liked the lazy gulls best. Being pressed to say why, she thought it was because they were more like the white doves that sat on the old stone well-curb in the convent garden.

Keith had always maintained that he liked to talk to women. He said that the talk of any woman was more piquant than the conversation of the most brilliant men. There was only one obstacle: the absolute inability of the sex to be sincere, or to tell the truth, for ten consecutive minutes. Today, however, as he wandered to and fro whither he would on the reef, he also wandered to and fro whither he would in the mind, and the absolutely truthful mind too, of a woman. Yet he found it dull! He sighed to himself, but was obliged to acknowledge that it *was* dull. The lime-tree, the organ, the Sisters, the Sisters, the lime-tree, the organ; it grew monotonous after a while. Yet he held his post, for the sake of the old theory, until the high voice of Melvyna called them back to the little fire on the beach and the white cloth spread with her best dainties. They saw Carrington sailing in with an excited air, and presently he brought the boat into the cove and dragged ashore his prize, towed behind—nothing less than a large shark, wounded, dead, after a struggle with some other marine monster, a sword-fish probably. "A man-eater," announced the captor. "Look at him, will you? Look at him, Miss Luke!"

But Miss Luke went far away, and would not look. In truth he was an ugly creature; even Melvyna kept at a safe distance. But the two men noted all his points; they measured him carefully; they turned him over, and discussed him generally in that closely confined and exhaustive way which marks the masculine mind. Set two women to discussing a shark, or even the most lovely little brook-trout, if you please, and see how far off they will be in five minutes!

But the lunch was tempting, and finally its discussion called them away even from that of the shark. And then they all sailed homeward over the green and blue water, while the white sand-hills shone silvery before them, and then turned red in the sunset. That night the moon was at its full. Keith went out and strolled up and down on the beach. Carrington was playing fox-and-goose with Mme. Gonsalvez on a board he had good-naturedly constructed for her entertainment when she confessed one day to a youthful fondness for that exciting game. Up stairs gleamed the little Sister's light. "Saying her prayers with her lips, but thinking all the time of that old convent," said the stroller to himself, half scornfully. And he said the truth.

The sea was still and radiant; hardly more than a ripple broke at his feet; the tide was out, and the broad beach silvery and fresh. "At home they are buried in snow," he thought, "and the wind is whistling around their double windows." And then he stretched himself on the sand, and lay looking upward into the deep blue of the night, bathed in the moonlight, and listening dreamily to the soft sound of the water as it returned slowly, slowly back from the African coast. He thought many thoughts, and deep ones too, and at last he was so far away on ideal heights, that, coming home after midnight, it was no wonder if, half unconsciously, he felt himself above the others; especially when he passed the little Sister's closed door, and thought, smiling not unkindly, how simple she was.

The next morning the two men went off in their boat again for the day, this time alone. There were still a few more questions to settle about that shark, and, to tell the truth, they both liked a good day of unencumbered sailing better than anything else.

About four o'clock in the afternoon Melvyna, happening

to look out of the door, saw a cloud no bigger than a man's hand low down on the horizon line of the sea. Something made her stand and watch it for a few moments. Then, "Miss Luke! Miss Luke! Miss Luke! Miss Luke!" she called quickly. Down came the little Sister, startled at the cry, her lace-work still in her hand.

"Look!" said Melvyna.

The Sister looked, and this is what she saw: a line white as milk coming toward them on the water, and behind it a blackness.

"What is it?" she asked.

"A tornader," said Melvyna with white lips. "I've only seen one, and then I was over in the town; but it's awful! We must run back to the thicket." Seizing her companion's arm, the strong Northern woman hurried her across the sand, through the belt of sand-hills, and into the thicket, where they crouched on its far side close down under the projecting backbone. "The bushes will break the sand, and the ridge will keep us from being buried in it," she said. "I dursn't stay on the shore, for the water'll rise."

The words were hardly spoken before the tornado was upon them, and the air was filled with the flying sand, so that they could hardly breathe. Half choked, they beat with their hands before them to catch a breath. Then came a roar, and for an instant, distant as they were, they caught a glimpse of the crest of the great wave that followed the whirlwind. It seemed to them mountain-high, and ready to ingulf the entire land. With a rushing sound it plunged over the keeper's house, broke against the lower story of the tower, hissed across the sand, swallowed the sand-hills, and swept to their very feet, then sullenly receded with slow, angry muttering. A gale of wind came next, singularly enough from another direction, as if to restore the equipoise of the atmosphere. But the tornado had gone on inland, where there were trees to uproot, and houses to destroy, and much finer entertainment generally.

As soon as they could speak, "Where are the two out in the sail-boat?" asked the Sister.

"God knows!" answered Melvyna. "The last time I noticed their sail they were about a mile outside of the reef."

"I will go and see."

"Go and see! Are you crazy? You can never get through that water."

"The saints would help me, I think," said the little Sister.

She had risen, and now stood regarding the watery waste with the usual timid look in her gentle eyes. Then she stepped forward with her uncertain tread, and before the woman by her side comprehended her purpose she was gone, ankle-deep in the tide, knee-deep, and finally wading across the sand up to her waist in water toward the lighthouse. The great wave was no deeper, however, even there. She waded to the door of the tower, opened it with difficulty, climbed the stairway, and gained the light-room, where the glass of the windows was all shattered, and the little chamber half full of the dead bodies of birds, swept along by the whirlwind and dashed against the tower, none of them falling to the ground or losing an inch of their level in the air as they sped onward, until they struck against some high object, which broke their mad and awful journey. Holding on by the shattered casement, Sister St. Luke gazed out to sea. The wind was blowing fiercely, and the waves were lashed to fury. The sky was inky black. The reef was under water, save one high knob of its backbone, and to that two dark objects were clinging. Farther down she saw the wreck of the boat driving before the gale. Pedro was over in the village; the tide was coming in over the high sea, and night was approaching. She walked quickly down the rough stone stairs, stepped into the water again, and waded across where the paroquet boat had been driven against the wall of the house, bailed it out with one of Melvyna's pans, and then, climbing in from the window of the sitting-room, she hoisted the sail, and in a moment was out on the dark sea.

Melvyna had ascended to the top of the ridge, and when the sail came into view beyond the house she fell down on her knees and began to pray aloud: "O Lord, save her; save the lamb! She don't know what's she is doing, Lord. She's as simple as a baby. Oh, save her, out on that roaring sea! Good Lord, good Lord, deliver her!" Fragments of prayers she had heard in her prayer-meeting days came confusedly back into her mind, and she repeated them all again and again, wringing her hands as she saw the little craft tilt far over under its all too large sail, so that several times, in the hollows of the waves, she thought it was gone. The wind was blowing hard but steadily, and in a direction that carried the boat straight toward the reef; no tacks were necessary, no change of course; the black-robed little figure simply held the sail-rope, and the paroquet drove on. The two clinging to the rock, bruised, exhausted, with the waves rising and falling around them, did not see the boat until it was close upon them.

"By the great heavens!" said Keith.

His face was pallid and rigid, and there was a ghastly cut across his forehead, the work of the sharp-edged rock. The next moment he was on board, brought the boat round just in time, and helped in Carrington, whose right arm was injured.

"You have saved our lives, señora," he said abruptly.

"By Jove, yes," said Carrington. "We could not have stood it long, and night was coming." Then they gave all their attention to the hazardous start.

Sister St. Luke remained unconscious of the fact that she had done anything remarkable. Her black gown was spoiled, which was a pity, and she knew of a balm which was easily compounded and which would heal their bruises. Did they think Melvyna had come back to the house yet? And did they know that all her dishes were broken—yes, even the cups with the red flowers on the border? Then she grew timorous again, and hid her face from the sight of the waves.

Keith said not a word, but sailed the boat, and it was a wild and dangerous voyage they made, tacking up and down in the gayly painted little craft, that seemed like a toy on that angry water. Once Carrington took the little Sister's hand in his, and pressed his lips fervently upon it. She had never had her hand kissed before, and looked at him, then at the place, with a vague surprise, which soon faded, however, into the old fear of the wind. It was night when at last they reached the lighthouse; but during the last two tacks they had a light from the window to guide them; and when nearly in they saw the lantern shining out from the shattered windows of the tower in a fitful, surprised sort of way, for Melvyna had returned, and, with the true spirit of a Yankee, had immediately gone to work at the ruins.

The only sign of emotion she gave was to Keith. "I saw it all," she said. "That child went right out after you, in that terrible wind, as natural and as quiet as if she was only going across the room. And she so timid a fly could frighten her! Mark my words, Mr. Keith, the good Lord helped her to do it! And I'll go to that new mission chapel over in the town every Sunday after this, as sure's my name is Sawyer!" She ceased abruptly, and, going into her kitchen, slammed the door behind her. Emotion with Melvyna took the form of roughness.

Sister St. Luke went joyfully back to her convent the next day, for Pedro, when he returned, brought the letter, written, as Keith had directed, in the style of an affectionate invitation. The little nun wept for happiness when she read it. "You see how they love me—love me as I love them," she repeated with innocent triumph again and again.

"It is all we can do," said Keith. "She could not be happy anywhere else, and with the money behind her she will not be neglected. Besides, I really believe they do love her. The sending her up here was probably the result of some outside dictation."

Carrington, however, was dissatisfied. "A pretty return we make for our saved lives!" he said. "I hate ingratitude." For Carrington was half disposed now to fall in love with his preserver.

But Keith stood firm.

"Addios," said the little Sister, as Pedro's boat received her. Her face had lighted so with joy and glad anticipation that they hardly knew her. "I wish you could to the convent go with me," she said earnestly to the two young men. "I am sure you would like it." Then, as the boat turned the point, "I am sure you would like it," she called back, crossing her hands on her breast. "It is very heavenly there—very heavenly."

That was the last they saw of her.

Carrington sent down the next winter from New York a large silver crucifix, superbly embossed and ornamented. It was placed on the high altar of the convent, and much admired and reverenced by all the nuns. Sister St. Luke admired it too. She spoke of the island occasionally, but she did not tell the story of the rescue. She never thought of it. Therefore, in the matter of the crucifix, the belief was that a special grace had touched the young man's heart. And prayers were ordered for him. Sister St. Luke tended her doves, and at the hour of meditation paced to and fro between the lime-tree and the bush of white roses. When she was thirty years old her cup was full, for then she was permitted to take lessons and play a little upon the old organ.

Melvyna went every Sunday to the bare, struggling little Presbyterian mission over in the town, and she remains to this day a Sawyer.

But Keith remembered. He bares his head silently in reverence to all womanhood, and curbs his cynicism as best he can, for the sake of the little Sister—the sweet little Sister St. Luke.

"MISS GRIEF"

W OOLSON'S FIRST EUROPEAN STORY, "'MISS
Grief'" was written sometime after her departure from
the United States in December 1879, when she was
still grieving the death of her mother earlier that year.
It marks the transition from her identity as a dutiful
daughter, writing to support herself and her mother,
to that of an independent artist living in Europe.
Although the story is set in Rome, Woolson had not
yet visited that city. Nor had she met Henry James, who
shares many superficial similarities with the story's narrator. Woolson had a letter of introduction from James's
cousin and had gone to his home in London almost
as soon as she arrived, but he was out of the country.
"'Miss Grief'" suggests the complex feelings she had
as she anticipated making his acquaintance. Above all,
Woolson hoped for a mutual recognition of their dis-
parate strengths as writers. (Her writing was known for

its originality and force, his for its exquisite polish.) She pointed up their differences in her portrait of a poor, starving woman writer who has been unable to publish (unlike Woolson herself, whose writings were well regarded) approaching a successful male writer who has everything he could desire, simply because, he realizes, his style of writing is preferred by the public and the gatekeepers of the literary world. "'Miss Grief'" was first published in *Lippincott's* in May 1880 and chosen by Scribner's for volume four of its *Stories by American Authors*, published in 1884.

"MISS GRIEF"

. . . .

"A CONCEITED FOOL" IS A NOT UNCOMMON EXPRES-
sion. Now, I know that I am not a fool, but I also know that
I am conceited. But, candidly, can it be helped if one hap-
pens to be young, well and strong, passably good-looking,
with some money that one has inherited and more that one
has earned—in all, enough to make life comfortable—and if
upon this foundation rests also the pleasant superstructure of
a literary success? The success is deserved, I think: certainly it
was not lightly gained. Yet even with this I fully appreciate its
rarity. Thus, I find myself very well entertained in life: I have
all I wish in the way of society, and a deep, though of course
carefully concealed, satisfaction in my own little fame; which
fame I foster by a gentle system of non-interference. I know
that I am spoken of as "that quiet young fellow who writes
those delightful little studies of society, you know"; and I live
up to that definition.

A year ago I was in Rome, and enjoying life particularly.
I had a large number of my acquaintances there, both Amer-
ican and English, and no day passed without its invitation.
Of course I understood it: it is seldom that you find a literary

man who is good-tempered, well-dressed, sufficiently provided with money, and amiably obedient to all the rules and
requirements of "society." "When found, make a note of it";
and the note was generally an invitation.

One evening, upon returning to my lodgings, my man
Simpson informed me that a person had called in the afternoon, and upon learning that I was absent had left not a card,
but her name—"Miss Grief." The title lingered—Miss Grief!
"Grief has not so far visited me here," I said to myself, dismiss-
ing Simpson and seeking my little balcony for a final smoke,
"and she shall not now. I shall take care to be 'not at home' to
her if she continues to call." And then I fell to thinking of Isabel Abercrombie, in whose society I had spent that and many
evenings: they were golden thoughts.

The next day there was an excursion; it was late when I
reached my rooms, and again Simpson informed me that Miss
Grief had called.

"Is she coming continuously?" I said, half to myself.

"Yes, sir: she mentioned that she should call again."

"How does she look?"

"Well, sir, a lady, but not so prosperous as she was, I should
say," answered Simpson, discreetly.

"Young?"

"No, sir."

"Alone?"

"A maid with her, sir."

But once outside in my little high-up balcony with my
cigar, I again forgot Miss Grief and whatever she might rep-
resent. Who would not forget in that moonlight, with Isabel
Abercrombie's face to remember?

The stranger came a third time, and I was absent; then she let two days pass, and began again. It grew to be a regular dialogue between Simpson and myself when I came in at night: "Grief to-day?"

"Yes, sir."

"What time?"

"Four, sir."

"Happy the man," I thought, "who can keep her confined to a particular hour!"

But I should not have treated my visitor so cavalierly if I had not felt sure that she was eccentric and unconventional—qualities extremely tiresome in a woman no longer young or attractive. If she were not eccentric she would not have persisted in coming to my door day after day in this silent way, without stating her errand, leaving a note, or presenting her credentials in any shape. I made up my mind that she had something to sell—a bit of carving or some intaglio supposed to be antique. It was known that I had a fancy for oddities. I said to myself, "She has read or heard of my 'Old Gold' story, or else 'The Buried God,' and she thinks me an idealizing ignoramus upon whom she can impose. Her sepulchral name is at least not Italian; probably she is a sharp country-woman of mine, turning, by means of the present æsthetic craze, an honest penny when she can."

She had called seven times during a period of two weeks without seeing me, when one day I happened to be at home in the afternoon, owing to a pouring rain and a fit of doubt concerning Miss Abercrombie. For I had constructed a careful theory of that young lady's characteristics in my own mind, and she had lived up to it delightfully until the previous evening, when with one word she had blown it to atoms and taken flight, leaving me standing, as it were, on a desolate shore, with nothing but a handful of mistaken inductions wherewith to console myself. I do not know a more exasperating frame of mind, at least for a constructor of theories. I could not write, and so I took up a French novel (I model myself a little on Balzac). I had been turning over its pages but a few moments when Simpson knocked, and, entering softly, said, with just a shadow of a smile on his well-trained face, "Miss Grief." I briefly consigned Miss Grief to all the Furies, and then, as he still lingered—perhaps not knowing where they resided—I asked where the visitor was.

"Outside, sir—in the hall. I told her I would see if you were at home."

"She must be unpleasantly wet if she had no carriage."

"No carriage, sir: they always come on foot. I think she *is* a little damp, sir."

"Well, let her in; but I don't want the maid. I may as well see her now, I suppose, and end the affair."

"Yes, sir."

I did not put down my book. My visitor should have a hearing, but not much more: she had sacrificed her womanly claims by her persistent attacks upon my door. Presently Simpson ushered her in. "Miss Grief," he said, and then went out, closing the curtain behind him.

A woman—yes, a lady—but shabby, unattractive, and more than middle-aged.

I rose, bowed slightly, and then dropped into my chair again, still keeping the book in my hand. "Miss Grief?" I said interrogatively as I indicated a seat with my eyebrows.

"Not Grief," she answered—"Crief: my name is Crief."

She sat down, and I saw that she held a small flat box.

"Not carving, then," I thought—"probably old lace, something that belonged to Tullia or Lucrezia Borgia." But as she did not speak I found myself obliged to begin: "You have been here, I think, once or twice before?"

"Seven times; this is the eighth."

A silence.

"I am often out; indeed, I may say that I am never in," I remarked carelessly.

"Yes; you have many friends."

"—Who will perhaps buy old lace," I mentally added. But this time I too remained silent; why should I trouble myself to draw her out? She had sought me; let her advance her idea, whatever it was, now that entrance was gained.

But Miss Grief (I preferred to call her so) did not look as though she could advance anything; her black gown, damp with rain, seemed to retreat fearfully to her thin self, while her thin self retreated as far as possible from me, from the chair, from everything. Her eyes were cast down; an old-fashioned lace veil with a heavy border shaded her face. She looked at the floor, and I looked at her.

I grew a little impatient, but I made up my mind that I would continue silent and see how long a time she would consider necessary to give due effect to her little pantomime. Comedy? Or was it tragedy? I suppose full five minutes passed thus in our double silence; and that is a long time when two persons are sitting opposite each other alone in a small still room.

At last my visitor, without raising her eyes, said slowly,

"You are very happy, are you not, with youth, health, friends, riches, fame?"

It was a singular beginning. Her voice was clear, low, and very sweet as she thus enumerated my advantages one by one in a list. I was attracted by it, but repelled by her words, which seemed to me flattery both dull and bold.

"Thanks," I said, "for your kindness, but I fear it is undeserved. I seldom discuss myself even when with my friends."

"I am your friend," replied Miss Grief. Then, after a moment, she added slowly, "I have read every word you have written."

I curled the edges of my book indifferently; I am not a fop, I hope, but—others have said the same.

"What is more, I know much of it by heart," continued my visitor. "Wait: I will show you"; and then, without pause, she began to repeat something of mine word for word, just as I had written it. On she went, and I—listened. I intended interrupting her after a moment, but I did not, because she was reciting so well, and also because I felt a desire gaining upon me to see what she would make of a certain conversation which I knew was coming—a conversation between two of my characters which was, to say the least, sphinx-like, and somewhat incandescent as well. What won me a little, too, was the fact that the scene she was reciting (it was hardly more than that, though called a story) was secretly my favorite among all the sketches from my pen which a gracious public has received with favor. I never said so, but it was; and I had always felt a wondering annoyance that the aforesaid public, while kindly praising beyond their worth other attempts of mine, had never noticed the higher purpose of this little shaft, aimed not at the balconies and lighted windows of society, but straight up toward the distant stars. So she went on, and presently reached the conversation: my two people began to talk. She had raised her eyes now, and was looking at me soberly as she gave the words of the woman, quiet, gentle, cold, and the replies of the man, bitter, hot, and scathing. Her very voice changed, and took, though always sweetly, the different tones required, while no point of meaning, however small, no breath of delicate emphasis which I had meant, but which the dull types could not give, escaped an appreciative and full, almost overfull, recognition which startled me. For she had understood me—understood me almost better than I had understood myself. It seemed to me that while I had labored to interpret, partially, a psychological riddle, she, coming after, had comprehended its bearings better than I had, though confining herself strictly to my own words and emphasis. The scene ended (and it ended rather suddenly), she dropped her eyes, and moved her hand nervously to and fro over the box she held; her gloves were old and shabby, her hands small.

I was secretly much surprised by what I had heard, but my ill-humor was deep-seated that day, and I still felt sure, besides, that the box contained something which I was expected to buy.

"You recite remarkably well," I said carelessly, "and I am much flattered also by your appreciation of my attempt. But it is not, I presume, to that alone that I owe the pleasure of this visit?"

"Yes," she answered, still looking down, "it is, for if you had not written that scene I should not have sought you. Your other sketches are interiors—exquisitely painted and delicately finished, but of small scope. *This* is a sketch in a few bold, masterly lines—work of entirely different spirit and purpose."

I was nettled by her insight. "You have bestowed so much of your kind attention upon me that I feel your debtor," I said, conventionally. "It may be that there is something I can do for you—connected, possibly, with that little box?"

It was impertinent, but it was true; for she answered, "Yes."

I smiled, but her eyes were cast down and she did not see the smile.

"What I have to show you is a manuscript," she said after a pause which I did not break; "it is a drama. I thought that perhaps you would read it."

"An authoress! This is worse than old lace," I said to myself in dismay.—Then, aloud, "My opinion would be worth nothing, Miss Crief."

"Not in a business way, I know. But it might be—an assistance personally." Her voice had sunk to a whisper; outside, the rain was pouring steadily down. She was a very depressing object to me as she sat there with her box.

"I hardly think I have the time at present—" I began.

She had raised her eyes and was looking at me; then, when I paused, she rose and came suddenly toward my chair. "Yes, you will read it," she said with her hand on my arm—"you will read it. Look at this room; look at yourself; look at all you have. Then look at me, and have pity."

I had risen, for she held my arm, and her damp skirt was brushing my knees.

Her large dark eyes looked intently into mine as she went on; "I have no shame in asking. Why should I have? It is my last endeavor; but a calm and well-considered one. If you refuse I shall go away, knowing that Fate has willed it so. And I shall be content."

"She is mad," I thought. But she did not look so, and she had spoken quietly, even gently.—"Sit down," I said, moving away from her. I felt as if I had been magnetized; but it was only the nearness of her eyes to mine, and their intensity. I drew forward a chair, but she remained standing.

"I cannot," she said in the same sweet, gentle tone, "unless you promise."

"Very well, I promise; only sit down."

As I took her arm to lead her to the chair I perceived that she was trembling, but her face continued unmoved.

"You do not, of course, wish me to look at your manuscript now?" I said, temporizing; "it would be much better to leave it. Give me your address, and I will return it to you with my written opinion; though, I repeat, the latter will be of no use to you. It is the opinion of an editor or publisher that you want."

"It shall be as you please. And I will go in a moment," said Miss Grief, pressing her palms together, as if trying to control the tremor that had seized her slight frame.

She looked so pallid that I thought of offering her a glass of wine; then I remembered that if I did it might be a bait to bring her there again, and this I was desirous to prevent. She rose while the thought was passing through my mind. Her pasteboard box lay on the chair she had first occupied; she took it, wrote an address on the cover, laid it down, and then, bowing with a little air of formality, drew her black shawl round her shoulders and turned toward the door.

I followed, after touching the bell. "You will hear from me by letter," I said.

Simpson opened the door, and I caught a glimpse of the maid, who was waiting in the anteroom. She was an old woman, shorter than her mistress, equally thin, and dressed like her in rusty black. As the door opened she turned toward it a pair of small, dim blue eyes with a look of furtive suspense. Simpson dropped the curtain, shutting me into the inner room; he had no intention of allowing me to accompany my visitor further. But I had the curiosity to go to a bay-window in an angle from whence I could command the street-door, and presently I saw them issue forth in the rain and walk away side by side, the mistress, being the taller, holding the umbrella: probably there was not much difference in rank between persons so poor and forlorn as these.

It grew dark. I was invited out for the evening, and I knew that if I should go I should meet Miss Abercrombie. I said to myself that I would not go. I got out my paper for writing, I made my preparations for a quiet evening at home with myself; but it was of no use. It all ended slavishly in my going. At the last allowable moment I presented myself, and—as a punishment for my vacillation, I suppose—I never passed a more disagreeable evening. I drove homeward in a murky temper; it was foggy without, and very foggy within. What Isabel really was, now that she had broken through my elaborately-built theories, I was not able to decide. There was, to tell the truth, a certain young Englishman—But that is apart from this story.

I reached home, went up to my rooms, and had a supper. It was to console myself; I am obliged to console myself scientifically once in a while. I was walking up and down afterward, smoking and feeling somewhat better, when my eye fell upon the pasteboard box. I took it up; on the cover was written an address which showed that my visitor must have walked a long distance in order to see me: "A. Crief."—"A Grief," I thought; "and so she is. I positively believe she has brought all this trouble upon me: she has the evil eye." I took out the manuscript and looked at it. It was in the form of a little volume, and clearly written; on the cover was the word "Armor" in German text, and, underneath, a pen-and-ink sketch of a helmet, breastplate, and shield.

"Grief certainly needs armor," I said to myself, sitting down by the table and turning over the pages. "I may as well look over the thing now; I could not be in a worse mood." And then I began to read.

Early the next morning Simpson took a note from me to the given address, returning with the following reply: "No; I prefer to come to you; at four; A. CRIEF." These words, with their three semicolons, were written in pencil upon a piece of coarse printing-paper, but the handwriting was as clear and delicate as that of the manuscript in ink.

"What sort of a place was it, Simpson?"

"Very poor, sir, but I did not go all the way up. The elder person came down, sir, took the note, and requested me to wait where I was."

"You had no chance, then, to make inquiries?" I said, knowing full well that he had emptied the entire neighborhood of any information it might possess concerning these two lodgers.

"Well, sir, you know how these foreigners will talk, whether one wants to hear or not. But it seems that these two persons have been there but a few weeks; they live alone, and are uncommonly silent and reserved. The people round there call them something that signifies 'the Madames American, thin and dumb.'"

At four the "Madames American" arrived; it was raining again, and they came on foot under their old umbrella. The maid waited in the anteroom, and Miss Grief was ushered into my bachelor's parlor. I had thought that I should meet her with great deference; but she looked so forlorn that my deference changed to pity. It was the woman that impressed me then, more than the writer—the fragile, nerveless body more than the inspired mind. For it was inspired: I had sat up half the night over her drama, and had felt thrilled through and through more than once by its earnestness, passion, and power.

No one could have been more surprised than I was to find myself thus enthusiastic. I thought I had outgrown that sort of thing. And one would have supposed, too (I myself should have supposed so the day before), that the faults of the drama, which were many and prominent, would have chilled any liking I might have felt, I being a writer myself, and therefore critical; for writers are as apt to make much of the "how," rather than the "what," as painters, who, it is well known, prefer an exquisitely rendered representation of a commonplace theme to an imperfectly executed picture of even the most striking subject. But in this case, on the contrary, the scattered rays of splendor in Miss Grief's drama had made me forget the dark spots, which were numerous and disfiguring; or, rather, the splendor had made me anxious to have the spots removed. And this also was a philanthropic state very unusual with me. Regarding unsuccessful writers, my motto had been "Væ victis!"

My visitor took a seat and folded her hands; I could see, in spite of her quiet manner, that she was in breathless suspense. It seemed so pitiful that she should be trembling there before me—a woman so much older than I was, a woman who possessed the divine spark of genius, which I was by no means sure (in spite of my success) had been granted to me—that I felt as if I ought to go down on my knees before her, and entreat her to take her proper place of supremacy at once. But there! one does not go down on one's knees, combustively, as it were, before a woman over fifty, plain in feature, thin, dejected, and ill-dressed. I contented myself with taking her hands (in their miserable old gloves) in mine, while I said cordially, "Miss Crief, your drama seems to me full of original power. It has roused my enthusiasm: I sat up half the night reading it."

The hands I held shook, but something (perhaps a shame for having evaded the knees business) made me tighten my hold and bestow upon her also a reassuring smile. She looked at me for a moment, and then, suddenly and noiselessly, tears rose and rolled down her cheeks. I dropped her hands and retreated. I had not thought her tearful: on the contrary, her voice and face had seemed rigidly controlled. But now here she was bending herself over the side of the chair with her head resting on her arms, not sobbing aloud, but her whole frame shaken by the strength of her emotion. I rushed for a glass of wine; I pressed her to take it. I did not quite know what to do, but, putting myself in her place, I decided to praise the drama; and praise it I did. I do not know when I have used so many adjectives. She raised her head and began to wipe her eyes.

"Do take the wine," I said, interrupting myself in my cataract of language.

"I dare not," she answered; then added humbly, "that is, unless you have a biscuit here or a bit of bread."

I found some biscuit; she ate two, and then slowly drank the wine, while I resumed my verbal Niagara. Under its influence—and that of the wine too, perhaps—she began to show new life. It was not that she looked radiant—she could not—but simply that she looked warm. I now perceived what had been the principal discomfort of her appearance heretofore: it was that she had looked all the time as if suffering from cold.

At last I could think of nothing more to say, and stopped. I really admired the drama, but I thought I had exerted myself sufficiently as an anti-hysteric, and that adjectives enough, for the present at least, had been administered. She had put down her empty wine-glass, and was resting her hands on the broad cushioned arms of her chair with, for a thin person, a sort of expanded content.

"You must pardon my tears," she said, smiling; "it was the revulsion of feeling. My life was at a low ebb: if your sentence had been against me it would have been my end."

"Your end?"

"Yes, the end of my life; I should have destroyed myself."

"Then you would have been a weak as well as wicked woman," I said in a tone of disgust. I do hate sensationalism.

"Oh no, you know nothing about it. I should have

destroyed only this poor worn tenement of clay. But I can well understand how *you* would look upon it. Regarding the desirableness of life the prince and the beggar may have different opinions.—We will say no more of it, but talk of the drama instead." As she spoke the word "drama" a triumphant brightness came into her eyes.

I took the manuscript from a drawer and sat down beside her. "I suppose you know that there are faults," I said, expecting ready acquiescence.

"I was not aware that there were any," was her gentle reply.

Here was a beginning! After all my interest in her—and, I may say under the circumstances, my kindness—she received me in this way! However, my belief in her genius was too sincere to be altered by her whimsies; so I persevered. "Let us go over it together," I said. "Shall I read it to you, or will you read it to me?"

"I will not read it, but recite it."

"That will never do; you will recite it so well that we shall see only the good points, and what we have to concern ourselves with now is the bad ones."

"I will recite it," she repeated.

"Now, Miss Crief," I said bluntly, "for what purpose did you come to me? Certainly not merely to recite: I am no stage-manager. In plain English, was it not your idea that I might help you in obtaining a publisher?"

"Yes, yes," she answered, looking at me apprehensively, all her old manner returning.

I followed up my advantage, opened the little paper volume and began. I first took the drama line by line, and spoke of the faults of expression and structure; then I turned back and touched upon two or three glaring impossibilities in the plot. "Your absorbed interest in the motive of the whole no doubt made you forget these blemishes," I said apologetically.

But, to my surprise, I found that she did not see the blemishes—that she appreciated nothing I had said, comprehended nothing. Such unaccountable obtuseness puzzled me. I began again, going over the whole with even greater minuteness and care. I worked hard: the perspiration stood in beads upon my forehead as I struggled with her—what shall I call it—obstinacy? But it was not exactly obstinacy. She simply could not see the faults of her own work, any more than a blind man can see the smoke that dims a patch of blue sky. When I had finished my task the second time she still remained as gently impassive as before. I leaned back in my chair exhausted, and looked at her.

Even then she did not seem to comprehend (whether she agreed with it or not) what I must be thinking. "It is such a heaven to me that you like it!" she murmured dreamily, breaking the silence. Then, with more animation, "And *now* you will let me recite it?"

I was too weary to oppose her; she threw aside her shawl and bonnet, and, standing in the centre of the room, began.

And she carried me along with her: all the strong passages were doubly strong when spoken, and the faults, which seemed nothing to her, were made by her earnestness to seem nothing to me, at least for that moment. When it was ended she stood looking at me with a triumphant smile.

"Yes," I said, "I like it, and you see that I do. But I like it because my taste is peculiar. To me originality and force are everything—perhaps because I have them not to any marked degree myself—but the world at large will not overlook as I do your absolutely barbarous shortcomings on account of them. Will you trust me to go over the drama and correct it at my pleasure?" This was a vast deal for me to offer; I was surprised at myself.

"No," she answered softly, still smiling. "There shall not be so much as a comma altered." Then she sat down and fell into a reverie as though she were alone.

"Have you written anything else?" I said after a while, when I had become tired of the silence.

"Yes."

"Can I see it? Or is it *them?*"

"It is *them*. Yes, you can see all."

"I will call upon you for the purpose."

"No, you must not," she said, coming back to the present nervously. "I prefer to come to you."

At this moment Simpson entered to light the room, and busied himself rather longer than was necessary over the task. When he finally went out I saw that my visitor's manner had sunk into its former depression: the presence of the servant seemed to have chilled her.

"When did you say I might come?" I repeated, ignoring her refusal.

"I did not say it. It would be impossible."

"Well, then, when will you come here?" There was, I fear, a trace of fatigue in my tone.

"At your good pleasure, sir," she answered humbly.

My chivalry was touched by this: after all, she was a

woman. "Come to-morrow," I said. "By the way, come and dine with me then; why not?" I was curious to see what she would reply.

"Why not, indeed? Yes, I will come. I am forty-three: I might have been your mother."

This was not quite true, as I am over thirty: but I look young, while she—Well, I had thought her over fifty. "I can hardly call you 'mother,' but we might compromise upon 'aunt,'" I said, laughing. "Aunt what?"

"My name is Aaronna," she gravely answered. "My father was much disappointed that I was not a boy, and gave me as nearly as possible the name he had prepared—Aaron."

"Then come and dine with me to-morrow, and bring with you the other manuscripts, Aaronna," I said, amused at the quaint sound of the name. On the whole, I did not like "aunt."

"I will come," she answered.

It was twilight and still raining, but she refused all offers of escort or carriage, departing with her maid, as she had come, under the brown umbrella. The next day we had the dinner. Simpson was astonished—and more than astonished, grieved—when I told him that he was to dine with the maid; but he could not complain in words, since my own guest, the mistress, was hardly more attractive. When our preparations were complete I could not help laughing: the two prim little tables, one in the parlor and one in the anteroom, and Simpson disapprovingly going back and forth between them, were irresistible.

I greeted my guest hilariously when she arrived, and, fortunately, her manner was not quite so depressed as usual: I could never have accorded myself with a tearful mood. I had thought that perhaps she would make, for the occasion, some change in her attire; I have never known a woman who had not some scrap of finery, however small, in reserve for that unexpected occasion of which she is ever dreaming. But no: Miss Grief wore the same black gown, unadorned and unaltered. I was glad that there was no rain that day, so that the skirt did not at least look so damp and rheumatic.

She ate quietly, almost furtively, yet with a good appetite, and she did not refuse the wine. Then, when the meal was over and Simpson had removed the dishes, I asked for the new manuscripts. She gave me an old green copybook filled with short poems, and a prose sketch by itself; I lit a cigar and sat down at my desk to look them over.

"Perhaps you will try a cigarette?" I suggested, more for amusement than anything else, for there was not a shade of Bohemianism about her; her whole appearance was puritanical.

"I have not yet succeeded in learning to smoke."

"You have tried?" I said, turning round.

"Yes: Serena and I tried, but we did not succeed."

"Serena is your maid?"

"She lives with me."

I was seized with inward laughter, and began hastily to look over her manuscripts with my back toward her, so that she might not see it. A vision had risen before me of those two forlorn women, alone in their room with locked doors, patiently trying to acquire the smoker's art.

But my attention was soon absorbed by the papers before me. Such a fantastic collection of words, lines, and epithets I had never before seen, or even in dreams imagined. In truth, they were like the work of dreams: they were *Kubla Khan*, only

more so. Here and there was radiance like the flash of a diamond, but each poem, almost each verse and line, was marred
by some fault or lack which seemed wilful perversity, like the
work of an evil sprite. It was like a case of jeweller's wares
set before you, with each ring unfinished, each bracelet too
large or too small for its purpose, each breastpin without its
fastening, each necklace purposely broken. I turned the pages,
marvelling. When about half an hour had passed, and I was
leaning back for a moment to light another cigar, I glanced
toward my visitor. She was behind me, in an easy-chair before
my small fire, and she was—fast asleep! In the relaxation of
her unconsciousness I was struck anew by the poverty her
appearance expressed; her feet were visible, and I saw the miserable worn old shoes which hitherto she had kept concealed.

After looking at her for a moment I returned to my task and
took up the prose story; in prose she must be more reasonable.
She was less fantastic perhaps, but hardly more reasonable.
The story was that of a profligate and commonplace man
forced by two of his friends, in order not to break the heart of
a dying girl who loves him, to live up to a high imaginary ideal
of himself which her pure but mistaken mind has formed. He
has a handsome face and sweet voice, and repeats what they
tell him. Her long, slow decline and happy death, and his own
inward ennui and profound weariness of the rôle he has to
play, made the vivid points of the story. So far, well enough,
but here was the trouble: through the whole narrative moved
another character, a physician of tender heart and exquisite
mercy, who practised murder as a fine art, and was regarded
(by the author) as a second Messiah! This was monstrous.
I read it through twice, and threw it down; then, fatigued,

I turned round and leaned back, waiting for her to wake. I could see her profile against the dark hue of the easy-chair.

Presently she seemed to feel my gaze, for she stirred, then opened her eyes. "I have been asleep," she said, rising hurriedly.

"No harm in that, Aaronna."

But she was deeply embarrassed and troubled, much more so than the occasion required; so much so, indeed, that I turned the conversation back upon the manuscripts as a diversion. "I cannot stand that doctor of yours," I said, indicating the prose story; "no one would. You must cut him out."

Her self-possession returned as if by magic. "Certainly not," she answered haughtily.

"Oh, if you do not care—I had labored under the impression that you were anxious these things should find a purchaser."

"I am, I am," she said, her manner changing to deep humility with wonderful rapidity. With such alternations of feeling as this sweeping over her like great waves, no wonder she was old before her time.

"Then you must take out that doctor."

"I am willing, but do not know how," she answered, pressing her hands together helplessly. "In my mind he belongs to the story so closely that he cannot be separated from it."

Here Simpson entered, bringing a note for me: it was a line from Mrs. Abercrombie inviting me for that evening—an unexpected gathering, and therefore likely to be all the more agreeable. My heart bounded in spite of me; I forgot Miss Grief and her manuscripts for the moment as completely as though they had never existed. But, bodily, being still in the same room with her, her speech brought me back to the present.

"You have had good news?" she said.

"Oh no, nothing especial—merely an invitation."

"But good news also," she repeated. "And now, as for me, I must go."

Not supposing that she would stay much later in any case, I had that morning ordered a carriage to come for her at about that hour. I told her this. She made no reply beyond putting on her bonnet and shawl.

"You will hear from me soon," I said; "I shall do all I can for you."

She had reached the door, but before opening it she stopped, turned and extended her hand. "You are good," she said: "I give you thanks. Do not think me ungrateful or envious. It is only that you are young, and I am so—so old." Then she opened the door and passed through the anteroom without pause, her maid accompanying her and Simpson with gladness lighting the way. They were gone. I dressed hastily and went out—to continue my studies in psychology.

Time passed; I was busy, amused and perhaps a little excited (sometimes psychology is exciting). But, though much occupied with my own affairs, I did not altogether neglect my self-imposed task regarding Miss Grief. I began by sending her prose story to a friend, the editor of a monthly magazine, with a letter making a strong plea for its admittance. It should have a chance first on its own merits. Then I forwarded the drama to a publisher, also an acquaintance, a man with a taste for phantasms and a soul above mere common popularity, as his own coffers knew to their cost. This done, I waited with conscience clear.

Four weeks passed. During this waiting period I heard

nothing from Miss Grief. At last one morning came a letter from my editor. "The story has force, but I cannot stand that doctor," he wrote. "Let her cut him out, and I might print it." Just what I myself had said. The package lay there on my table, travel-worn and grimed; a returned manuscript is, I think, the most melancholy object on earth. I decided to wait, before writing to Aaronna, until the second letter was received. A week later it came. "Armor" was declined. The publisher had been "impressed" by the power displayed in certain passages, but the "impossibilities of the plot" rendered it "unavailable for publication"—in fact, would "bury it in ridicule" if brought before the public, a public "lamentably" fond of amusement, "seeking it, undaunted, even in the cannon's mouth." I doubt if he knew himself what he meant. But one thing, at any rate, was clear: "Armor" was declined.

Now, I am, as I have remarked before, a little obstinate. I was determined that Miss Grief's work should be received. I would alter and improve it myself, without letting her know: the end justified the means. Surely the sieve of my own good taste, whose mesh had been pronounced so fine and delicate, would serve for two. I began; and utterly failed.

I set to work first upon "Armor." I amended, altered, left out, put in, pieced, condensed, lengthened; I did my best, and all to no avail. I could not succeed in completing anything that satisfied me, or that approached, in truth, Miss Grief's own work just as it stood. I suppose I went over that manuscript twenty times: I covered sheets of paper with my copies. But the obstinate drama refused to be corrected; as it was it must stand or fall.

Wearied and annoyed, I threw it aside and took up the prose story: that would be easier. But, to my surprise, I found that that apparently gentle "doctor" would not out: he was so closely interwoven with every part of the tale that to take him out was like taking out one especial figure in a carpet: that is, impossible, unless you unravel the whole. At last I did unravel the whole, and then the story was no longer good, or Aaronna's: it was weak, and mine. All this took time, for of course I had much to do in connection with my own life and tasks. But, though slowly and at my leisure, I really did try my best as regarded Miss Grief, and without success. I was forced at last to make up my mind that either my own powers were not equal to the task, or else that her perversities were as essential a part of her work as her inspirations, and not to be separated from it. Once during this period I showed two of the short poems to Isabel, withholding of course the writer's name. "They were written by a woman," I explained.

"Her mind must have been disordered, poor thing!" Isabel said in her gentle way when she returned them—"at least, judging by these. They are hopelessly mixed and vague."

Now, they were not vague so much as vast. But I knew that I could not make Isabel comprehend it, and (so complex a creature is man) I do not know that I wanted her to comprehend it. These were the only ones in the whole collection that I would have shown her, and I was rather glad that she did not like even these. Not that poor Aaronna's poems were evil: they were simply unrestrained, large, vast, like the skies or the wind. Isabel was bounded on all sides, like a violet in a garden-bed. And I liked her so.

One afternoon, about the time when I was beginning to see that I could not "improve" Miss Grief, I came upon the maid. I was driving, and she had stopped on the crossing to let the carriage pass. I recognized her at a glance (by her general forlornness), and called to the driver to stop: "How is Miss Grief?" I said. "I have been intending to write to her for some time."

"And your note, when it comes," answered the old woman on the crosswalk fiercely, "she shall not see."

"What?"

"I say she shall not see it. Your patronizing face shows that you have no good news, and you shall not rack and stab her any more on *this* earth, please God, while I have authority."

"Who has racked or stabbed her, Serena?"

"Serena, indeed! Rubbish! I'm no Serena: I'm her aunt. And as to who has racked and stabbed her, I say you, *you*—YOU literary men!" She had put her old head inside my carriage, and flung out these words at me in a shrill, menacing tone. "But she shall die in peace in spite of you," she continued. "Vampires! you take her ideas and fatten on them, and leave her to starve. You know you do—*you* who have had her poor manuscripts these months and months!"

"Is she ill?" I asked in real concern, gathering that much at least from the incoherent tirade.

"She is dying," answered the desolate old creature, her voice softening and her dim eyes filling with tears.

"Oh, I trust not. Perhaps something can be done. Can I help you in any way?"

"In all ways if you would," she said, breaking down and

beginning to sob weakly, with her head resting on the sill of the carriage-window. "Oh, what have we not been through together, we two! Piece by piece I have sold all."

I am good-hearted enough, but I do not like to have old women weeping across my carriage-door. I suggested, therefore, that she should come inside and let me take her home. Her shabby old skirt was soon beside me, and, following her directions, the driver turned toward one of the most wretched quarters of the city, the abode of poverty, crowded and unclean. Here, in a large bare chamber up many flights of stairs, I found Miss Grief.

As I entered I was startled: I thought she was dead. There seemed no life present until she opened her eyes, and even then they rested upon us vaguely, as though she did not know who we were. But as I approached a light came into them: she recognized me, and this sudden revivification, this return of the soul to the almost deserted body, was the most wonderful thing I ever saw. "You have good news of the drama?" she whispered as I bent over her: "tell me. I *know* you have good news."

What was I to answer? Pray, what would you have answered, puritan?

"Yes, I have good news, Aaronna," I said. "The drama will appear." (And who knows? Perhaps it will in some other world.)

She smiled, and her now brilliant eyes did not leave my face.

"He knows I'm your aunt: I told him," said the old woman, coming to the bedside.

"Did you?" whispered Miss Grief, still gazing at me with a smile. "Then please, dear Aunt Martha, give me something to eat."

Aunt Martha hurried across the room, and I followed her. "It's the first time she's asked for food in weeks," she said in a husky tone.

She opened a cupboard-door vaguely, but I could see nothing within. "What have you for her?" I asked with some impatience, though in a low voice.

"Please God, nothing!" answered the poor old woman, hiding her reply and her tears behind the broad cupboard-door. "I was going out to get a little something when I met you."

"Good Heavens! is it money you need? Here, take this and send; or go yourself in the carriage waiting below."

She hurried out breathless, and I went back to the bedside, much disturbed by what I had seen and heard. But Miss Grief's eyes were full of life, and as I sat down beside her she whispered earnestly, "Tell me."

And I did tell her—a romance invented for the occasion. I venture to say that none of my published sketches could compare with it. As for the lie involved, it will stand among my few good deeds, I know, at the judgment-bar.

And she was satisfied. "I have never known what it was," she whispered, "to be fully happy until now." She closed her eyes, and when the lids fell I again thought that she had passed away. But no, there was still pulsation in her small, thin wrist. As she perceived my touch she smiled. "Yes, I am happy," she said again, though without audible sound.

The old aunt returned; food was prepared, and she took

some. I myself went out after wine that should be rich and pure. She rallied a little, but I did not leave her: her eyes dwelt upon me and compelled me to stay, or rather my conscience compelled me. It was a damp night, and I had a little fire made. The wine, fruit, flowers, and candles I had ordered made the bare place for the time being bright and fragrant. Aunt Martha dozed in her chair from sheer fatigue—she had watched many nights—but Miss Grief was awake, and I sat beside her.

"I make you my executor," she murmured, "as to the drama. But my other manuscripts place, when I am gone, under my head, and let them be buried with me. They are not many—those you have and these. See!"

I followed her gesture, and saw under her pillows the edges of two more copybooks like the one I had. "Do not look at them—my poor dead children!" she said tenderly. "Let them depart with me—unread, as I have been."

Later she whispered, "Did you wonder why I came to you? It was the contrast. You were young—strong—rich—praised—loved—successful: all that I was not. I wanted to look at you—and imagine how it would feel. You had success—but I had the greater power. Tell me, did I not have it?"

"Yes, Aaronna."

"It is all in the past now. But I am satisfied."

After another pause she said with a faint smile, "Do you remember when I fell asleep in your parlor? It was the good and rich food. It was so long since I had had food like that!"

I took her hand and held it, conscience-stricken, but now she hardly seemed to perceive my touch. "And the smoking?" she whispered. "Do you remember how you laughed? I saw it. But I had heard that smoking soothed—that one was no longer tired and hungry—with a cigar."

In little whispers of this sort, separated by long rests and pauses, the night passed. Once she asked if her aunt was asleep, and when I answered in the affirmative she said, "Help her to return home—to America: the drama will pay for it. I ought never to have brought her away."

I promised, and she resumed her bright-eyed silence.

I think she did not speak again. Toward morning the change came, and soon after sunrise, with her old aunt kneeling by her side, she passed away.

All was arranged as she had wished. Her manuscripts, covered with violets, formed her pillow. No one followed her to the grave save her aunt and myself; I thought she would prefer it so. Her name was not "Crief," after all, but "Moncrief;" I saw it written out by Aunt Martha for the coffin-plate, as follows: "Aaronna Moncrief, aged forty-three years, two months, and eight days."

I never knew more of her history than is written here. If there was more that I might have learned, it remained unlearned, for I did not ask.

And the drama? I keep it here in this locked case. I could have had it published at my own expense; but I think that now she knows its faults herself, perhaps, and would not like it.

I keep it; and, once in a while, I read it over—not as a *memento mori* exactly, but rather as a memento of my own good fortune, for which I should continually give thanks. The want of one grain made all her work void, and that one grain was given to me. She, with the greater power, failed—I, with the less, succeeded. But no praise is due to me for that. When

I die "Armor" is to be destroyed unread: not even Isabel is to see it. For women will misunderstand each other; and, dear and precious to me as my sweet wife is, I could not bear that she or any one should cast so much as a thought of scorn upon the memory of the writer, upon my poor dead, "unavailable," unaccepted "Miss Grief."

A FLORENTINE
EXPERIMENT

WRITTEN SHORTLY AFTER WOOLSON FIRST MET
Henry James in Florence in April 1880, "A Florentine
Experiment" revisits many of the places they toured
together and provides echoes of their discussions
about art and nature, capturing something of the tensions and pleasures of their initial encounter as the
two writers observed each other closely. It also reflects
Woolson's interest in James's writing, for in it she con-
sciously set out to write the type of story at which he
was considered to excel—the society tale in which the
talk is more important than the plot and in which,
she felt, manner was placed above matter. Woolson
sent the story to William Dean Howells, editor of
the *Atlantic Monthly*, who had previously objected to
strains of idealism in some of her work. He thought
it her best story yet and published it in October 1880.

Although she was chagrined by his response, she also showed that she could invest the drawing-room drama with some of the feeling she felt it often lacked. The story was republished in *Dorothy and Other Italian Stories* in 1896.

A FLORENTINE
EXPERIMENT

. . . .

ONE AFTERNOON, THREE YEARS AGO, TWO LADIES were talking together on the heights of Fiesole overlooking Florence. They occupied the stone bench which bears the inscription of its donor, an appreciative Englishman, who in a philanthropical spirit has had it placed there for the benefit of the pilgrims from all nations who come to these heights to see the enchanting view. The two ladies were not speaking of the view, however, but of something more personal. It seemed to be interesting.

"He is certainly much in love with you," said one, who was taller and darker than her companion. As she spoke, she gave back a letter which she had been reading.

"Yes, I think he is," said the other, reflectively, replacing it in its envelope.

"I suppose you are so accustomed to it, Beatrice, that it does not make much impression upon you," continued the first speaker, her glance as she spoke resting not upon her companion, but upon the lovely levels beneath, with the violet-hued mountains rising softly up round about them, so softly that one forgot they were mountains until the eye caught the gleam of snow on the summits towards the east. There was a pause after this question, and it lasted so long that the questioner at length removed her eyes from the landscape and turned them upon her friend; to her surprise she saw that the friend was blushing.

"Why, Beatrice!" she exclaimed, "is it possible—"

"No," said Beatrice, "it is not possible. I know that I am blushing; but you must not think too much of that. I am not as strong as I was, and blush at everything; I am taking iron for it. In the present case, it only means that—" She paused.

"That you like him," suggested the other, smiling.

"I like a number of persons," said Mrs. Lovell, tranquilly, gazing in her turn down the broad, slightly winding valley, dotted with its little white villages, and ending in a soft blue haze, through which the tawny Arno, its course marked by a line of tall, slender, lightly foliaged, seemingly branchless trees, like tall rods in leaf, went onward towards the west.

"I know you do," said the first speaker. "And I really wish," she added, with a slight touch of vehemence, "that your time would come—that I should see you at last liking some one person really and deeply and jealously, and to the exclusion of all the rest."

"I don't know why you should wish me unhappiness, Margaret. You have beautiful theories, I know; but in my *experience*" (Mrs. Lovell slightly underlined this word as if in opposition to the "theories" of her friend) "the people who have those deeper sort of feelings you describe are almost always very unhappy."

Margaret turned her head, and looked towards the waving line of the Carrara mountains; in her eyes there was the reflection of a sudden inward pain. But she knew that she could indulge in this momentary expression of feeling; the mountains would not betray her, and the friend by her side did not realize that anything especial could have happened to "Margaret." In excuse for Mrs. Lovell it may be said that so much that was very especial had always happened, and still continued to happen, to her, that she had not much time for the more faintly colored episodes of other people.

Beatrice Lovell was an unusually lovely woman. The adjective is here used to signify that she inspired love. Not by an effort, word, action, or hardly interest of her own; but simply because she was what she was. Her beauty was not what is called striking; it touched the eye gently at first, but always grew. People who liked to analyze said that the secret lay in the fact that she had the sweetness, the tints, the surface texture as it were, and even sometimes the expression, of childhood still; and then, when you came to look deeper, you found underneath all the richer bloom of the woman. Her golden hair, not thick or long, but growing in little soft wavelets upon her small head; her delicate rose-leaf skin, showing the blue veins; her little teeth and the shape of her sweet mouth— all these were like childhood. In addition, she was dimpled and round, with delicately cut features, and long-lashed violet eyes, in whose soft depths lay always an expression of gentle trust. This beautiful creature was robed to-day in widow's mourning-garb made in the severest fashion, without one attempt to decorate or lighten it. But the straight-skirted, untrimmed garments, the little close bonnet, and the heavy veil pinned over it with straight crape-pins, only brought out more vividly the tints of her beauty.

"No," she continued, as her companion did not speak, "I by no means wish for the feelings you invoke for me. I am better off as I am; I keep my self-possession. For instance, I told this Sicily person that it was in very bad taste to speak to me in that way at such a time—so soon after Mr. Lovell's death; and that I was much annoyed by it."

"It has not prevented his writing," said Margaret, coming back slowly from the Carrara mountains, and letting her eyes rest upon the tower of the Palazzo Vecchio below, springing above the city roofs like the stem of a flower.

"They always write, I think," said Mrs. Lovell, simply.

"I know they do—to *you*," said Margaret. She turned as she spoke, and looked at her friend with the same old affection and admiration which she had felt for her from childhood, but now with a sort of speculative curiosity added. How must it feel to live such a life—to be constantly surrounded and accompanied by an atmosphere of devotion and enthralment such as that letter had expressed? Beatrice seemed to divine something of her friend's thought, and answered it after her fashion.

"It is such a comfort to be with you, Margaret," she said, affectionately; "it has always been a comfort, ever since we were children. I can talk freely to you, and as I can talk to no one else. You understand; you do not misunderstand. But all the other women I meet invariably do; or, at least, pretend to enough to excuse their being horribly disagreeable."

Margaret took her hand. They had taken off their gloves, as the afternoon was warm, and they had the heights to themselves; it was early in March, and the crowd of tourists who come in the spring to Italy, and those more loitering travellers who had spent the winter in Naples or Rome, had not yet reached Florence, although it may be said that they were at the door. Mrs. Lovell's hands, now destitute of ornament save the plain band of the wedding-ring, were small, dimpled, very white; her friend Miss Stowe had hands equally small, but darker and more slender.

"You have been happy all your life, have you not, Beatrice?" said Margaret, not questioningly so much as assertively.

"Yes," answered Mrs. Lovell, "I think I have. Of course I was much shocked by Mr. Lovell's death; he was very kind to me."

"Mr. Lovell," as his wife always called him, had died four months previously. He was fifty-six years of age, and Beatrice had been his wife for a little more than a year. He had been very happy with her, and had left her his fortune and his blessing; with these, and his memory, she had come abroad, and had been for six weeks in Sicily, with some elderly friends. She had stopped in Florence to see Miss Stowe, who was spending the winter there with an aunt; but she was not to remain. In her present state of seclusion she was to visit Venice and the Lakes in advance of the season, and spend the summer in "the most quiet village" which could be discovered for her especial benefit on the Brittany coast. The friends had not met for two years, and there had been much to tell—that is, for Beatrice to tell. Her always personal narratives were saved from tedious-

ness, however, because they were not the usual decorated feminine fancies, but plain masculine facts (oh, very plain!); and
because, also, the narrator was herself quite without the vanity which might naturally have accompanied them. This last
merit seemed to her admirers a very remarkable one; in reality
it was only that, having no imagination, she took a simple,
practical view of everything, themselves included. This last,
however, they never discovered, because her unfailing tact and
gentleness lay broadly and softly over all.

"And what shall you do about your Sicily person?" said
Margaret, not in the least, however, associating the remark,
and knowing also that Beatrice would not associate it, with
"Mr. Lovell" and his "memory" (it was quite well understood
between them about "Mr. Lovell").

"Of course I shall not answer."

"And if he follows you?"

"He will hardly do that—now. Besides, he is going to
America; he sails to-morrow. Our having been together in
Sicily was quite by chance, of course; he knows that, and he
knows also that I intend to pay, in every way, the strictest
respect to Mr. Lovell's memory. That will be fully two years."

"And then?"

"Oh, I never plan. If things do not assert themselves, they
are not worth a plan."

"You certainly are the most delightful little piece of
common-sense I ever met," said Margaret, laughing, and kiss-
ing her. "I wish you would give me a share of it! But come—it
is late; we must go."

As they went down the slope together towards the village where their carriage was waiting, they looked not unlike the two seventeen-year-old school-girls of eight years before; Beatrice was smiling, and Margaret's darker face was lighted by the old animation which had always charmed her lovely but unanimated friend. It may here be remarked that the greatest intellectual excitements which Beatrice Lee had known had been when Margaret Stowe had let loose her imagination, and carried her friend up with her, as on strong wings, to those regions of fancy which she never attained alone; Beatrice had enjoyed it, wondered over it, and then had remained passive until the next time.

"Ah well—poor Sicily person!" said Margaret, as they took their places in the carriage. "I know just what you will do with him. You will write down his name in a memorandum-book, so as not to forget it; you will safely burn his poor letter, as you have safely burned so many others; and you will go gently on to Brittany without even taking the ashes!"

"Keep it for me!" said Mrs. Lovell, suddenly, drawing the letter from her pocket and placing it in Margaret's hand. "Yes," she repeated, enjoying her idea and dwelling upon it, delighted to find that she possessed a little fancy of her own, after all, "keep it for me, and read it over once in a while. It is quite well written, and will do you good, because it is not one of your theories, but a fact. There is nothing disloyal in my giving it to you, because I always tell you everything, and this Sicily person has no claim for exemption in that regard. He has gone back to America, and you will not meet him. No—positively, I will not take it. You must keep it for me."

"Very well," said Margaret, amused by this little unexpected flight. "But as I may go back to America also, I want to be quite sure where I stand. Did you happen to mention to this Sicily person my name, or anything about me?"

"No," replied Mrs. Lovell, promptly. "We did not talk on such subjects, you know."

"And he had no idea that you were to stop in Florence?"

"No; he supposed I was to take the steamer at Naples for Marseilles. You need not be so scrupulous; everything is quite safe."

"And when shall I return the epistle?"

"When I ask for it," said Mrs. Lovell, laughing.

The next morning she went northward to Venice.

TWO WEEKS LATER MISS STOWE formed one of the company at a reception, or, rather, a musical party. She looked quite unlike the "Margaret" of Fiesole as she sat on a small, faded purple satin sofa, listening, rather frowningly, to the rippling movement that follows the march in Beethoven's sonata, opus twenty-six; she had never liked that rippling movement, she did not pretend to like it now. Her frown, however, was slight—merely a little line between her dark eyebrows; it gave her the appearance of attention rather than of disapprobation. The "Margaret" of Fiesole had looked like an animated, almost merry, young girl; the "Miss Stowe" of the reception appeared older than she really was, and her face wore an expression of proud reserve, which, although veiled by all the conventional graciousness required by society, was not on that account any the less apparent. She was richly dressed; but the general effect of her attire was that of simplicity. She fanned herself slowly with a large fan, whose sticks were of carved amber, and the upper part of soft gray ostrich plumes, curled; closed or open, as she used it or as it lay beside her, this fan was an object of beauty. As the music ceased a lady came fluttering across the room, and, with a whispered "Permit me," introduced a gentleman, whose name, in the hum of released conversation, Miss Stowe did not hear.

"He understands *everything* about old pictures, and you *know* how ignorant *I* am!" said this lady, half closing her eyes, and shaking her ringleted head with an air of abnegation. "*I* have but *one* inspiration; there is room in me but for *one*. I bring him, therefore, to *you*, who have so many! We *all* know your love for the early masters—may I not say, the *earliest?*"

Madame Ferri was an American who had married a Florentine; she was now a little widow of fifty, with gray ringlets and emotions regarding music almost too ineffable to be expressed. I say "almost," because she did, after all, express them, as her friends knew. She was a useful person in Florence because she indefatigably knew everybody—the English and Americans as well as the Florentines; and she spent her time industriously at work mingling these elements, whether they would or no. No one thanked her for this especially, or remembered it after it was done; if republics are ungrateful, even more so is a society whose component parts are transient, coming and departing day by day. But Madame Ferri herself appreciated the importance of her social combinations if no one else did; and, like many another chemist, lived on content in the consciousness of it.

"I know very little about old pictures," said the stranger, with a slight smile, finding himself left alone beside Miss Stowe.

"And I—do not like them," she replied.

"If, more than that, you dislike them, we shall have something to talk about. Dislike can generally express itself very well."

"On the contrary, I think it is one of those feelings we do not express—but conceal."

"You are thinking of persons, perhaps. I was speaking of things. Pictures are things."

Miss Stowe felt herself slightly displeased; and the feeling was not lessened when, with a "Will you allow me?" the stranger took a seat at the end of her sofa, in the space left free by the gray silken sweep of her dress. There was in reality an abundance of room for him; other men were seated, and there was no chair near. Still, the sofa was a small one; the three Italians and two Frenchmen who had succeeded each other in the honor of standing beside her for eight or ten minutes' conversation had not thought of asking for the place so calmly taken by this new-comer. She looked at him as he began talking; he was quite unlike the three Italians and two Frenchmen. He was not ruddy enough for an Englishman of that complexion; he had a lethargic manner which was un-American. She decided, however, that he was, like herself, an American; but an American who had lived much abroad.

He was talking easily upon the various unimportant subjects in vogue at a "small party"; she replied in the same strain.

Margaret Stowe was not beautiful; "pretty" was the last word that could have been applied to her. Her features were irregular; she had a well-shaped, well-poised head, and a quantity of dark hair which she wore closely braided in a low knot behind. She was tall, slender, and rather graceful; she had dark eyes. As has been said before, she was not beautiful; but within the past two years she had acquired, her friends thought, an air of what is called distinction. In reality this was but a deep indifference, combined with the wish at the same time to maintain her place unchanged in the society in which she moved. Indifference and good manners taken together, in a tall and graceful person, will generally give that air. Beatrice Lovell had not perceived this change in her friend, but on that day at Fiesole Miss Stowe had been simply the "Margaret" of old.

In accordance with what we have called her good manners, Miss Stowe now gave to the stranger beside her easy replies, several smiles, and a fair amount of intelligent attention. It was all he could have expected; but, being a man of observation, he perceived her indifference lying broadly underneath, like the white sand under a shallow river.

During the same week she met him at a dinner-party, and they had some conversation. Later he was one of the guests at a reception which she attended, and again they talked together awhile. She now mentioned him to her aunt, Miss Harrison, to whom she generally gave, every few days, a brief account of the little events in the circle to which they belonged. She had learned his name by this time; it was Morgan.

"I wonder if he is a grandson of old Adam Morgan," said Miss Harrison, who was genealogical and reminiscent. "If he is, I should like to see him. Has he a Roman nose?"

"I think not," said her niece, smiling.

"Well, describe him, then."

"He is of medium height, neither slender nor stout; he is light, with rather peculiar eyes because they are so blue—a deep, dull blue, like old china; but they are not large, and he does not fully open them. He has a long, light mustache, no beard, and very closely cut hair."

"He must be good-looking."

"No; he is not, especially. He may be anywhere between thirty and forty; his hair in a cross-light shows a slight tinge of gray. He looks fatigued; he looks cynical. I should not be surprised if he were selfish. I do not like him."

"But if he should be the grandson of old Adam, I should have to invite him to dinner," said Miss Harrison, reflectively. "I could not do less, I think."

"I won't poison the soup. But Morgan is a common name, Aunt Ruth; this is the fourth Morgan I have met here this spring. There isn't one chance in a thousand that he belongs to the family you know." She was smiling as she spoke, but did not explain her smile; she was thinking that "Morgan" was also the name signed to that letter locked in her writing-desk—a letter whose expressions she now knew quite well, having obeyed Mrs. Lovell's injunction to "read it over" more than once. They were ardent expressions; it might be said, indeed, that they were very ardent.

But now and then that one chance in a thousand, so often summarily dismissed, asserts its existence and appears upon the scene. It turned out in the present case that the stranger was the grandson of the old Adam Morgan whom Miss Harrison remembered. Miss Stowe, in the meantime, had continued to meet him; but now she was to meet him in a new way—when he would be more upon her hands, as it were; for Miss Harrison invited him to dinner.

Miss Ruth Harrison was an invalid of nearly sixty years of age; she had been for ten years in Europe, but had only had her orphaned niece with her during the past eighteen months. She had a large fortune, and she gave Margaret every luxury; especially she liked to see her richly dressed. But it was quite well understood between them that the bulk of her wealth was to go to another relative in America who bore her family name. It was understood between them, but it was not understood outside. On the contrary, it was generally believed in Florence that Miss Stowe would inherit the whole. It is just possible that this belief may have had a remote influence in shaping the opinion which prevailed there—namely, that this young lady was "handsome" and "gracious," when, in truth, she was neither. But Mr. Morgan, the new-comer, exhibited so far, at least, no disposition to fall in with this fiction. In his estimation Miss Stowe was a conventionally agreeable, inwardly indifferent young lady of twenty-six, who carried herself well, but was too ironical as well as too dark. He came to dinner. And did not change his opinion.

A few days after the dinner Miss Harrison invited her new acquaintance to drive; she was able to go out for an hour or two in the afternoon, and she had a luxurious carriage and fine horses. Miss Stowe did not accompany them; she went off by herself to walk in the Boboli Garden.

Miss Harrison returned in good-humor. "I like him," she announced, as the maid removed her bonnet. "Yes, I think I may hope that the grandson of old Adam is not going to be a disappointment."

"The grandson of Adam—I suppose his name is Adam also—is a fortunate person, Aunt Ruth, to have gained your liking so soon; you do not often take likings to strangers."

"His name is not Adam," pursued Miss Harrison, "and that is a pity; there is character as well as association in Adam. He has a family name—Trafford. His mother was a Miss Trafford, of Virginia, it seems."

Miss Stowe was selecting flowers from a fragrant heap before her to fill the wide-mouthed vases which stood on the floor by her side; but now she stopped. "Trafford Morgan" was the name signed at the end of that letter! It must be he; it was not probable that there were two names of that special combination; it seemed a really remarkable chance. And evidently he had not gone to America, in spite of Mrs. Lovell's belief. She began to smile and almost to laugh, bending her head over a great soft purple heap of Florence lilies in order that her aunt might not observe it. But the large room was dusky, and Miss Harrison near-sighted; she observed nothing. The two ladies occupied an apartment in a house which, if it had not been so new, would have been called a "palace." Although modern, the measurements had been after the old Florentine pattern, and the result was that the occupants moved about in rooms which could have contained entire, each one, a small American house. But they liked the vastness. After a moment Miss Stowe went on arranging her blossoms, but inwardly she was enjoying much entertainment; she was going over in her own mind the expressions of that letter, which now took on quite a new character, coming no longer from some formless stranger, but from a gentleman with whom she had spoken, a person she had met and would meet again. "I never should have dreamed that he was capable of it," she said to herself. "He has seemed indifferent, *blasé*. But it places *me* in a nice position! Especially now that Aunt Ruth has taken a fancy to him. I must write to Beatrice immediately, and ask her to take back the stupid letter." She wrote during the same evening.

The next day she was attacked by a severe illness—severe, although short. No one could tell what was the matter with her; even the physician was at fault. She did not eat or sleep, she seemed hardly to know what they said when they spoke to her. Her aunt was alarmed. But at the end of the week, as suddenly as she had fallen ill, she came back to life again, rose, ordered the maid to braid her hair, and appeared at Miss Harrison's lonely little dinner-table quite herself, save that she was tremulous and pale. But by the next day even these signs were no longer very apparent. It was decided that she had had an attack of "nervous prostration"; "although why in the world you should have been seized by it just now, and here, I am at a loss, Margaret, to imagine," said her aunt.

On the day of her reappearance at the dinner-table there came a letter from Beatrice which bore the postmark of a village on one of the Channel islands. Mrs. Lovell had changed her plans, and gone yachting for a month or two with a party of friends, a yacht probably being considered to possess attributes of seclusion more total than even the most soundless village on the Brittany shore. Of course she had not received Margaret's letter, nor could she receive one—their route being uncertain, but nevertheless to the southward—until her return. Communication between them for the present was therefore at an end.

On the afternoon after Margaret's reappearance Madame

Ferri was making a visit of congratulation upon the recovery of "our dear girl." It was a cool day, a heavy rain had fallen, and fresh snow gleamed on the summits of the Apennines; our dear girl, very unresponsive and silent, was dressed in black velvet, whose rich, plain folds brought out her slenderness, and made more apparent than usual the graceful shape of her head and hair. But the unrelieved black made her look extremely pale, and it was her recent illness, probably, which made her look also tired and languid. Madame Ferri, who kept constantly in practice her talent for being charming (she was always spoken of as "charming"), looked at her for a time while conversing; then she rose, took all the crimson roses from a vase, and, going to her, placed one in her hair, meditatively; another in a button-hole of the closely fitting high corsage; and, after a moment's reflection, all the others in a bunch in a velvet loop which was on the side of the skirt not quite half-way down, rapidly denuding herself of pins for the purpose as she proceeded. "There!" she said, stepping back a few paces to survey her handiwork, with her head critically on one side, "*now* you are a picture. Look, dear Miss Harrison, pray look."

Miss Harrison put up her glass and approved. And then, while this climax still lasted, Madame Ferri took her departure; she liked to depart in a climax.

She had hardly gone when another card was brought in: "Mr. Trafford Morgan." He, too, had come to pay his respects to Miss Harrison upon the change for the better in her niece; he had not expected to see the latter person, he had merely heard that there was "an improvement." After he had been there twenty minutes he said to himself that there was, and in more ways than one. She not only looked much better than usual (this may have been owing to the roses), but there was a new gentleness about her; and she listened with a perceptible increase of attention to what he said. Not that he cared much for this; he had not admired Miss Stowe; but any man (this he remarked to himself) likes to be listened to when he is talking better than the contrary; and as the minutes passed he became conscious that Miss Stowe was not only listening, but bestowing upon him also what seemed an almost serious attention. She did not say much—Miss Harrison said more; but she listened to and looked at him. She had not looked at him previously; people can turn their eyes upon one without really looking, and Miss Stowe had excelled in this accomplishment.

During the next week he met her at a dinner-party; she went to these entertainments with a friend of her aunt's, a lady who was delighted to act as chaperon for the heiress. The spring season was now at its height in Florence, and the members of the same circle perforce constantly met each other; on each separate occasion during the two weeks that followed Trafford Morgan was conscious that Miss Stowe was honoring him, although in a studiously guarded and quiet way, with much of a very observant attention. This, in the end, excited in him some curiosity. He had as good an opinion of himself as most men have; but he did not think it probable that the heiress had suddenly fallen in love with him without rhyme or reason, as it were, the "rhyme" being that he was neither an Apollo, an Endymion, nor a military man; the "reason," that he had never in the least attempted to make himself agreeable to her. Of course, if he *had* attempted—But he had not. She was not in need of entertainment; she had enough of that, of all sorts, including apparently the sort given by suitors. She showed no sign of having troublesomely impulsive feelings; on the contrary, she seemed cold. "She is playing some game," he thought; "she has some end in view. But if she wishes to make use of me she must show her hand more. I may assist her, and I may not; but, at any rate, I must understand what it is—I will not be led." He made up his mind that her aim was to excite remark in their circle; there was probably some one in that circle who was to be stimulated by a little wholesome jealousy. It was an ancient and commonplace method, and he had not thought her commonplace. But human nature at heart is but a commonplace affair, after all, and the methods and motives of the world have not altered much, in spite of the gray lapse of ages.

Morgan was an idle man; at present he was remaining in Italy for a purpose, and had nothing to do there. The next time he met Miss Stowe he followed out his theory and took the lead; he began to pay her attention which might, if pursued, have aroused observation. To his surprise she drew back, and so completely that he was left stranded. He tried this three times on three different occasions, and each time met the same rebuff. It became evident, therefore, that Miss Stowe did not wish for the kind of attention which he had supposed was her point; but as, whenever she could do it unobserved, she continued to turn upon him the same quiet scrutiny, he began to ask himself whether she wished for any other. An opportunity occurred which made him think that she did.

It was in the Boboli Garden, where he had gone to walk off a fit of weariness; here he came upon Miss Stowe. There seemed to be no one in the garden save themselves—at least, no one whom they knew; only a few stray tourists wander-

ing about, with Baedeker, Horner, and Hare. The world of
fashion was at the Cascine that day, where races were going
on. Morgan did not feel like talking; he exchanged the usual
phrases with Miss Stowe, and then prepared to pass on. But
she said, gently, "Are you going now? If not, why not stroll
awhile with me?"

After this, as he mentally observed, of course he was forced
to stroll awhile. But, on the whole, he found himself entertained, because his companion gave him an attention which
was almost devout. Its seriousness, indeed, compelled him to
be serious likewise, and made him feel as though he were in
an atmosphere combining the characteristics of a church and
a school; he was partly priest, partly pedagogue, and the sensation was amusing. She asked him what he liked best in Florence; and she called it, gravely, "enchanting Florence."

"Giotto and Botticelli," he answered.

"I wish you would be in earnest; I am in earnest."

"With all the earnestness in the world, Miss Stowe, I could
only repeat the same reply."

"What is it you find to like in them? Will you tell me?"

"It would take an age—a full half-hour; you would be
quite tired out. Women are so much quicker in their mental
processes than we are that you would apprehend what I was
going to say before I could get it out; you would ascend all
the heights, scour all the plains, and arrive at the goal before
I came even in sight, where you would sit waiting, patiently
or impatiently, as I, slowly and with mortified perception,
approached."

"Yes, we are quick; but we are superficial. I wish you would
tell me."

He glanced at her; she was looking at him with an expression in her eyes which was extremely earnest. "I cannot deliver a discourse while walking," he said. "I require a seat."

"Let us go to the amphitheatre; I often sit there for a while on the stone benches under the old statues. I like to see them standing around the circle; they are so serenely indifferent to the modern pencil-scrawlings on their robes, so calmly certain that their time will come again."

"What you say is entirely charming. Still, I hardly think I can talk to the statues. I must have something more— more secluded." He was aware that he was verging upon a slight impertinence; but he wished to see whether she would accede—what she would do. He made no effort to find the seclusion of which he spoke; he left that to her.

She hesitated a moment; then, "We might go to a seat there is under a tree at the top of the slope," she said. "It is a pleasant place."

He assented; and they went up the path by the side of the tall, stately hedges, and past the fountain and the great statue of Abbondanza. The stone bench was not one of those sought for; it was not in front, but on the western side. It commanded a view of the city below, with the Duomo and Giotto's lovely bell-tower; of the fruit-trees, all in flower on the outskirts; of the treetops of the Cascine, now like a cloud of golden smoke with their tender brown leaflets, tasselled blossoms, and winged seeds; of the young grain, springing greenly down the valley; and the soft, velvety mountains rising all around. "How beautiful it is!" she said, leaning back, closing her parasol and folding her hands.

"Beautiful—yes; but barren of human interest save to those

who are going to sell the fruit, or who depend upon the growth of the grain. The beauty of art is deeper; it is all human."

"I must be quite ignorant about art," she answered, "because it does not impress me in that way; I wish it did. I wish you would instruct me a little, Mr. Morgan."

"Good!" he thought. "What next?" But although he thought, he of course was obliged to talk also, and so he began about the two art masters he had mentioned. He delivered quite an epic upon Giotto's two little frescos in the second cloister of Santa Maria Novella, and he openly preferred the third there—the little Virgin going up the impossible steps—to Titian's splendid picture of the same subject, in Venice. He grew didactic and mystic over the round Botticelli of the Uffizi and the one in the Prometheus room at the Pitti; he invented as he went along, and amused himself not a little with his own unusual flow of language. His companion listened, and now and then asked a question. But her questions were directed more towards what he thought of the pictures (after a while he noticed this), and what impressions they made upon him, than to the pictures themselves or their claims to celebrity. As he went on he made some slight attempts to diverge a little from the subject in hand, and skirt, if ever so slightly, the borders of flirtation; he was curious to see if she would follow him there. But she remained unresponsive; and, while giving no sign of even perceiving his digressions, she brought him back to his art atmosphere, each time he left it, with a question or remark very well adapted for the purpose; so well, indeed, that it could not have been by chance.

She declined his escort homeward, pretexting a visit she wished to pay; but she said, of her own accord, that she would sing for him the next time he came. He knew this was a favor she did not often grant; Madame Ferri had so informed him.

He went, without much delay; and she sang several songs in the dusky corner where her piano stood while he sat near. The light from the wax candles at the other end of the large room, where Miss Harrison was knitting, did not penetrate here; but she said she liked to sing in a semi-darkness, as she had only a twilight voice. It was in truth not at all powerful; but it was sweet and low, and she sang with much expression. Trafford Morgan liked music; it was not necessary to make up a conviction or theory about that; he simply had a natural love for it, and he came more than once to hear Miss Stowe sing.

In the meantime Miss Harrison continued to like "the grandson of old Adam," and again invited him to drive. A month went by, and, by the end of it, he had seen in one way and another a good deal of these two ladies. The "later manner" (as he mentally called it) of Miss Stowe continued; when they were in company, she was as she had been originally, but when they were unobserved, or by themselves, she gave him the peculiar sober attention which he did not quite comprehend. He had several theories about it, and varied between them. He was a man who did not talk of persons, who never told much. If questioned, while answering readily and apparently without reserve, it was noticed afterwards that he had told nothing. He had never spoken of Sicily, for instance, but had talked a good deal of Sweden. This reticence, so exasperating to many women, seemed agreeable to Miss Stowe, who herself did not tell much, or talk of persons—that is, generally. One person she talked about, and with persistence. Morgan was hardly ever with her that she did not, sooner or later, begin to talk to him about himself. Sometimes he was responsive, sometimes not; but responsive or unresponsive, in society or out of it, he had talked, all told, a goodly number of hours with Miss Stowe when May attained its zenith and the season waned.

The tourists had gone to Venice; the red gleam of guide-books along the streets and the conscientiousness of woollen travelling-dresses in the galleries were no longer visible. Miss Stowe now stepped over the boundary-line of her caution a little; many of the people she knew had gone; she went with Trafford to the Academy and the Pitti; she took him into cool, dim churches, and questioned him concerning his creed; she strolled with him through the monastery of San Marco, and asked what his idea was of the next world. She said she liked cloisters; she would like to walk in one for an hour or two every day.

He replied that there were a number of cloisters in Florence; they might visit them in succession and pace around quietly. The effect would be heightened if she would read aloud, as they paced, short sentences from some ancient, stiff-covered little book like *De Contemptu Mundi*.

"Ah," she said, "you are not in earnest. But I am!"

And she seemed to be; he said to himself that he had hardly had a look or word from her which was not only earnest, but almost portentously so. She now began to do whatever he asked her to do, whether it was to sing Italian music or to read Dante's *Vita Nuova*, both of which she had said she did not like. It is probable that he asked her to do a number of things about this time which he did not especially care for, simply to see if she would comply; she always did.

"If she goes on in this sort of way," he thought, "never showing the least opposition, or personal moods different from mine, I really don't know where we shall end!"

But at last she did show both. It was in the evening, and she was at the piano; after one or two ballads he asked her to sing a little English song he had found among her music, not printed, but in manuscript.

"Oh, that is nothing," she said, putting out her hand to take it from him. "I will sing this of Schumann's instead; it is much prettier."

But he maintained his point. "I like this better," he said. "I like the name—of course it is impossible, but it is pleasant—'Semper Fidelis.'"

She took it, looked at it in silence for a moment, and then, without further reply, began to sing. There was nothing remarkable in the words or the music; she did not sing as well as usual, either; she hurried the time.

"SEMPER FIDELIS

"Dumb and unchanged my thoughts still round thee
    hover,
            Nor will be moved;
E'en though I strive, my heart remains thy lover,
        Though unbeloved;
    Yet there is sad content in loyalty,
    And, though the silent gift is naught to thee,
            It changes never—
            Faithful forever."

This was the verse; but at the fifth line she faltered, stopped, and then, rising abruptly, left the room.

"Margaret is very uneven at times," said Miss Harrison, apologetically, from her easy-chair.

"All interesting persons are uneven," he replied. He went over and took a seat beside his hostess, remaining half an hour longer; but as he went back to his hotel he said to himself that Miss Stowe had been for many weeks the most even woman he had ever known, showing neither variation nor shadow of turning. She had been as even as a straight line.

On this account her sudden emotion made an impression upon him. The next day he mentioned that he was going to Trieste.

"Not Venice?" said Miss Harrison. "I thought everybody went to Venice."

"Venice," he replied, "is pre-eminently the place where one needs either an actual, tangible companionship of the dearest sort, or a memory like it. I, who have neither, keep well away from Venice!"

"I rather think, Mr. Morgan, that you have had pretty much what you wanted, in Venice or elsewhere," said Miss Harrison, with a dry humor she sometimes showed. Here she was called from the room to see a poor woman whom she befriended; Miss Stowe and Morgan were left alone.

He was looking at her; he was noting what effect, if any, the tidings of his departure (he had named to-morrow) would have upon her. She had not been conventional; would she resort to conventionality now?

Her gaze was bent upon the floor; after a while she looked

up. "Where shall you be this summer?" she said, slowly. "Perhaps we shall be there too." Her eyes were fixed upon his face, her tone was hardly above a whisper.

Perhaps it was curiosity that made him do what he did; whether it was or not, mingled with it there was certainly a good deal of audacity. He rose, went to her, and took her hand. "Forgive me," he said; "I am in love with some one else."

It implied much. But had not her manner implied the same, or more?

She rose; they were both standing now.

"What do you mean?" she demanded, a light coming into her eyes—eyes usually abstracted, almost dull.

"Only what I have said."

"Why should you say it to me?"

"I thought you might be—interested."

"You are mistaken. I am not in the least interested. Why should I be?"

"Are you not a little unkind?"

"Not more unkind than you are insolent."

She was very angry. He began to be a little angry himself.

"I ask your pardon with the deepest humility, Miss Stowe. The insolence of which you accuse me was as far as possible from my mind. If I thought you might be somewhat interested in what I have told you, it was because you have honored me with some small share of your attention during the past week or two; probably it has spoiled me."

"I have; and for a month or two, not a week or two. But there was a motive—It was an experiment."

"You have used me for experimental purposes, then?"

"Yes."

"I am immensely grateful to have been considered worthy of a part in an experiment of yours, even although a passive one. May I ask if the experiment is ended?"

"It is."

"Since when? Since I made that confession about some one else?"

Miss Stowe's face was pale, her dark eyes were brilliant. "I knew all the while that you were in love—hopelessly in love—with Mrs. Lovell," she said, with a proud smile. "That was the reason that, for my experiment, I selected *you*."

A flush rose over his face as she spoke. "You thought you would have the greater triumph?" he asked.

"I thought nothing of the kind. I thought that I should be safe, because you would not respond."

"And you did not wish me to respond?"

"I did not."

"Excuse me—we are speaking frankly, are we not?—but do you not contradict yourself somewhat? You say you did not wish me to respond; yet, have you not tried to make me?"

"That was not my object. It was but a necessary accompaniment of the experiment."

"And if I *had* responded?" he said, looking at her.

"I knew you could not. I knew quite well—I mean I could imagine quite well—how much you loved Beatrice. But it has all been a piece of folly upon my part—I see it now." She turned away, and went across to the piano. "I wish you would go now," she said, in a low voice, vaguely turning over the music. "*I* cannot, because my aunt will think it strange to find me gone."

Instead of obeying her, he crossed the room and stood

beside her; and then he saw in the twilight that her eyes were full of tears and her lips quivering, in spite of her effort to prevent it.

"Margaret," he said, suddenly, and with a good deal of feeling in his voice, "I am not worth it! Indeed I am not!" And again he touched her hand.

But she drew it from him. "Are you by any chance imagining that my tears are for *you?*" she said, in a low tone, but facing him like a creature at bay. "Have you interpreted me in that way? I have a right to know; speak!"

"I am at a loss to interpret you," he said, after a moment's silence.

"I will tell you the whole, then—I must tell you; your mistake forces it from me." She paused, drew a quick breath, and then went on, rapidly: "I love some one else. I have been very unhappy. Just after you came I received a letter which told me that he was soon to be married; he *is* married now. I had an illness in consequence. You may remember my illness? I made up my mind then that I would root out the feeling if possible, no matter at what cost of pain and effort and long patience. You came in my way. I knew you were deeply attached elsewhere—"

"How did you know it?" he said. He was leaning against the piano watching her; she stood with her hands folded, and pressed so tightly together that he could see the force of the pressure.

"Never mind how; but quite simply and naturally. I said to myself that I would try to become interested in you, even if only to a small degree; I would do everything in my power to forward it. It would be an acquired interest; still, acquired interests can be deep. People can become interested in music, in pictures, in sports, in that way; why not, then, in persons also, since they are more human?"

"That is the very reason—because they are too human," he answered.

But she did not heed. "I have studied you; I have tried to find the good in you; I have tried to believe in you, to idealize you. I have given every thought that I could control to you, and to you alone, for two long months," she said, passionately, unlocking her hands, reddened with their pressure against each other, and turning away.

"It has been a failure?"

"Complete."

"And if you had succeeded?" he asked, folding his arms as he leaned against the piano.

"I should have been glad and happy. I should never have seen *you* again, of course; but at least the miserable old feeling would have been laid at rest."

"And its place filled by another as miserable!"

"Oh no; it could never have been *that*," she said, with an emphasis of scorn.

"You tried a dangerous remedy, Margaret."

"Not so dangerous as the disease."

"A remedy may be worse than a disease. In spite of your scornful tone, permit me to tell you that if you had succeeded at all, it would have been in the end by loving me as you loved—I mean love—this other man. While I, in the meantime, am in love (as you are kind enough to inform me—hopelessly) with another woman! Is Beatrice a friend of yours?"

"My dearest friend."

"Has it never occurred to you that you were playing towards her rather a traitorous part?"

"Never."

"Supposing, during this experiment of yours, that I had fallen in love with you?"

"It would have been nothing to Beatrice if you had," responded Mrs. Lovell's friend instantly and loyally, although remembering, at the same moment, that Fiesole blush. Then, in a changed voice, and with a proud humility which was touching, she added, "It would have been quite impossible. Beatrice is the loveliest woman in the world; any one who had loved *her* would never think of me."

At this moment Miss Harrison's voice was heard in the hall; she was returning.

"Good-bye," said Morgan. "I shall go to-morrow. You would rather have me go." He took her hand, held it an instant, and then raised it to his lips. "Good-bye," he said, again. "Forgive me, Margaret. And do not entirely—forget me."

When Miss Harrison returned they were looking at the music on the piano. A few moments later he took leave.

"I am sorry he has gone," said Miss Harrison. "What in the world is he going to do at Trieste? Well, so goes life! nothing but partings! One thing is a consolation, however—at least, to me; the grandson of old Adam did not turn out a disappointment, after all."

"I do not think I am a judge," replied Miss Stowe.

IN JUNE MISS HARRISON went northward to Paris, her niece accompanying her. They spent the summer in Switzerland; in the autumn returned to Paris; and in December went south-ward to Naples and Rome.

Mrs. Lovell had answered Margaret's letter in June. The six weeks of yachting had been charming; the yacht belonged to an English gentleman, who had a country-seat in Devonshire. She herself, by-the-way, might be in Devonshire during the summer; it was so quiet there. Could not Miss Harrison be induced to come to Devonshire? That would be *so* delightful. It had been extremely difficult to wear deep mourning at sea; but of course she had persisted in it. Much of it had been completely ruined; she had been obliged to buy more. Yes—it *was* amusing—her meeting Trafford Morgan. And so unexpected, of course. Did she like him? No, the letter need not be returned. If it troubled her to have it, she might destroy it; perhaps it was as well it should be destroyed. There were some such pleasant qualities in English life; there was not so much opportunity, perhaps, as in America—"That blush meant nothing, then, after all," thought the reader, lifting her eyes from the page, and looking musingly at a picture on the wall. "She said it meant only a lack of iron; and, as Beatrice always tells the truth, she did mean that, probably, and not irony, as I supposed." She sat thinking for a few moments, and then went back to the letter: There was not so much opportunity, perhaps, as in America; but there was more stability, more certainty that things would continue to go on. There were various occurrences which she would like to tell; but she never wrote that sort of thing, as Margaret knew. If she would only come to Devonshire for the summer—and so forth, and so forth.

But Beatrice did sometimes write "that sort of thing," after all. During the next February, in Rome, after a long silence,

Margaret received a letter from her which brought the tidings of her engagement. He was an Englishman. He had a country-seat in Devonshire. He owned a yacht. Beatrice seemed very happy. "We shall not be married until next winter," she wrote. "I would not consent, of course, to anything earlier. I have consistently endeavored to do what was right from the beginning, and shall not waver now. But by next January there can be no criticism, and I suppose that will be the time. How I wish you were here to advise me about a hundred things! Besides, I want you to know him; you will be sure to like him. He is"—and so forth, and so forth.

"She is following out her destiny," thought the reader in Rome.

In March Miss Harrison found the Eternal City too warm, and moved northward as far as Florence. Madame Ferri was delighted to see them again; she came five times during the first three days to say so.

"You will find *so* many whom you knew last year here again as well as yourselves," she said, enthusiastically. "We shall have some of our *charming* old reunions. Let me see—I think I can tell you." And she ran over a list of names, among them that of "Mr. Morgan."

"What, not the grandson of Adam?" said Miss Harrison.

"He is not *quite* so old as that, is he?" said Madame Ferri, laughing. "It is the one who dined with you several times last year, I believe—Mr. Trafford Morgan. I shall have great pleasure in telling him this very day that you are here."

"Do you know whether he is to remain long?" said Miss Stowe, who had not before spoken.

"I am sorry to say he is not; Mr. Morgan is always an addition, I think—don't you? But he told me only yesterday that he was going this week to—to Tarascon, I think he said."

"Trieste and Tarascon—he selects the most extraordinary places!" said Miss Harrison. "The next time it will be Tartarus."

Madame Ferri was overcome with mirth. "*Dear* Miss Harrison, you are *too* droll! *Isn't* she, dear Miss Stowe?"

"He probably chooses his names at random," said Miss Stowe, with indifference.

The next day, at the Pitti, she met him. She was alone, and returned his salutation coldly. He was with some ladies who were standing near, looking at the "Madonna of the Chair." He merely asked how Miss Harrison was, and said he should give himself the pleasure of coming to see her very soon; then he bowed and returned to his friends. Not long afterwards she saw them all leave the gallery together.

Half an hour later she was standing in front of one of Titian's portraits, when a voice close beside her said, "Ah! the young man in black. You are not admiring it?"

There had been almost a crowd in the gorgeous rooms that morning. She had stood elbow to elbow with so many persons that she no longer noticed them; Trafford Morgan had been able, therefore, to approach and stand beside her for several minutes without attracting her recognition. As he spoke she turned, and, in answer to his smile, gave an even slighter bow than before; it was hardly more than a movement of the eyelids. Two English girls, with large hats, sweet, shy eyes, and pink cheeks, who were standing close beside them, turned away towards the left for a minute to look at another picture.

"Do not treat me badly," he said. "I need kindness. I am not very happy."

"I can understand that," she answered. Here the English girls came back again.

"I think you are wrong in admiring it," he said, looking at the portrait; "it is a quite impossible picture. A youth with that small, delicate head and face could never have had those shoulders; they are the shoulders of quite another type of man. This is some boy whom Titian wished to flatter; but he was artist enough to try and hide the flattery by that over-coat. The face has no calm; you would not have admired it in life."

"On the contrary, I should have admired it greatly," replied Miss Stowe. "I should have adored it. I should have adored the eyes."

"Surely there is nothing in them but a sort of pugnacity."

"Whatever it is, it is delightful."

The English girls now turned away towards the right.

"You are quite changed," he said, looking at her.

"Yes, I think I am. I am much more agreeable. Every one will tell you so; even Madame Ferri, who is obliged to recon-cile it with my having been always more agreeable than any one in the world, you know. I have become lighter. I am no longer heavy."

"You mean you are no longer serious."

"That is it. I used to be absurdly serious. But it is an age since we last met. You were going to Trieste, were you not? I hope you found it agreeable?"

"It is not an age; it is a year."

"Oh, a great deal can happen in a year," said Miss Stowe, turning away.

She was as richly dressed as ever, and not quite so plainly. Her hair was arranged in little rippling waves low down upon her forehead, which made her look, if not what might be called more worldly, at least more fashionable, since previously she had worn it arranged with a simplicity which was neither. Owing to this new arrangement of her hair, her eyes looked larger and darker.

He continued to walk beside her for some moments, and then, as she came upon a party of friends, he took leave.

In the evening he called upon Miss Harrison, and remained an hour. Miss Stowe was not at home. The next day he sent to Miss Harrison a beautiful basket of flowers.

"He knows we always keep the rooms full of them," remarked Miss Stowe, rather disdainfully.

"All the same, I like the attention," said Miss Harrison. And she sent him an invitation to dinner. She liked to have one guest.

He came. During the evening he asked Miss Stowe to sing. "I have lost my voice," she answered.

"Yes," said Miss Harrison, "it is really remarkable; Margaret, although she seems so well, has not been able to sing for months—indeed, for a full year. It is quite sad."

"I am not sad about it, Aunt Ruth; I am relieved. I never sang well—I had not voice enough. There was really nothing in it but expression; and that was all pretence."

"You are trying to make us think you very artificial," said Morgan.

"I can make you think what I please, probably. I can fol-low several lines of conduct, one after the other, and make you believe them all." She spoke lightly; her general tone was much lighter than formerly, as she herself had said.

"Do you ever walk in the Boboli Garden now?" he asked, later.

"Occasionally; but it is a dull place. And I do not walk as much as I did; I drive with my aunt."

"Yes, Margaret has grown indolent," said Miss Harrison; "and it seems to agree with her. She has more color than for-merly; she looks well."

"Wonderfully," said Morgan. "But you are thinner than you were," he added, turning towards her.

"And darker!" she answered, laughing. "Mr. Morgan does not admire arrangements in black and white, Aunt Ruth; do not embarrass him." She wore that evening a white dress, unrelieved by any color.

"I see you are bent upon being unkind," he said. It was supposed to be a society remark.

"Not the least in the world," she answered, in the same tone.

He met her several times in company, and had short con-versations with her. Then, one afternoon, he came upon her unexpectedly in the Cascine; she was strolling down the broad path alone.

"So you do walk sometimes, after all," he said.

"Never. I am only strolling. I drove here with Aunt Ruth, but, as she came upon a party of American friends who are going to-morrow, I gave up my place, and they are driving around together for a while, and no doubt settling the entire affairs of Westchester County."

"I am glad she met them; I am glad to find you alone. I have something I wish much to say to you."

"Such a beginning always frightens me. Pray postpone it."

"On the contrary, I shall hasten it. I must make the most of this rare opportunity. Do you remember when you did me the honor, Miss Stowe, to make me the subject of an experiment?"

"You insist upon recalling that piece of folly?" she said, opening her parasol. Her tone was composed and indifferent.

"I recall it because I wish to base something upon it. I wish to ask you—to allow yourself to be passively the subject of an experiment on *my* part, an experiment of the same nature."

She glanced at him; he half smiled. "Did you imagine, then, that mine was in earnest?" she said, with a fine, light scorn, light as air.

"I never imagine anything. Imaginations are useless."

"Not so useless as experiments. Let yours go, and tell me rather what you found to like in—Trieste."

"I suppose you know that I went to England?"

"I know nothing. But yes—I do know that you are going to—Tarascon."

"I shall not go if you will permit what I have asked."

"Isn't it rather suddenly planned?" she said, ironically. "You did not know we were coming."

"Very suddenly. I have thought of it only since yesterday."

They had strolled into a narrow path which led by one of those patches of underwood of which there are several in the Cascine—little bosky places carefully preserved in a tangled wildness which is so pretty and amusing to American eyes, accustomed to the stretch of real forests.

"You don't know how I love these little patches," said Miss Stowe. "There is such a good faith about them; they are charming."

"You were always fond of nature, I remember. I used to tell you that art was better."

"Ah! did you?" she said, her eyes following the flight of a bird.

"You have forgotten very completely in one year."

"Yes, I think I have. I always forget, you know, what it is not agreeable to remember. But I must go back; Aunt Ruth will be waiting." They turned.

"I will speak more plainly," said Morgan. "I went to England during July last—that is, I followed Mrs. Lovell. She was in Devonshire. Quite recently I have learned that she has become engaged in—Devonshire, and is soon to be married there. I am naturally rather down about it. I am seeking some other interest. I should like to try your plan for a while, and build up an interest in—you."

Miss Stowe's lip curled. "The plans are not alike," she said. "Yours is badly contrived. *I* did not tell *you* beforehand what I was endeavoring to do!"

"I am obliged to tell you. You would have discovered it."

"Discovered what a pretence it was? That is true. A woman can act a part better than a man. *You* did not discover! And what am I to do in this little comedy of yours?"

"Nothing. It is, in truth, nothing to you; you have told me that, even when you made a great effort towards that especial object, it was impossible to get up the slightest interest in me. Do not take a violent dislike to me; that is all."

"And if it is already taken?"

"I shall have to conquer that. What I meant was—do not take a fresh one."

"There is nothing like precedent, and therefore I repeat your question: what if you should succeed—I mean as regards yourself?" she said, looking at him with a satirical expression.

"It is my earnest wish to succeed."

"You do not add, as I did, that in case you do succeed you will of course never see me again, but that at least the miserable old feeling will be at rest?"

"I do not add it."

"And at the conclusion, when it has failed, shall you tell me that the cause of failure was—the inevitable comparisons?"

"Beatrice is extremely lovely," he replied, turning his head and gazing at the Arno, shining through an opening in the hedge. "I do not attempt to pretend, even to myself, that she is not the loveliest woman I ever knew."

"Since you do not pretend it to yourself you will not pretend it to me."

She spoke without interrogation; but he treated the words as a question. "Why should I?" he said. And then he was silent.

"There is Aunt Ruth," said Miss Stowe; "I see the horses. She is probably wondering what has become of me."

"You have not altogether denied me," he said, just before they reached the carriage. "I assure you I will not be in the least importunate. Take a day or two to consider. After all, if there is no one upon whom it can really infringe (of course I know you have admirers; I have even heard their names), why should you not find it even a little amusing?"

Miss Stowe turned towards him, and a peculiar expression came into her eyes as they met his. "I am not sure but that I shall find it so," she answered. And then they joined Miss Harrison.

The day or two had passed. There had been no formal question asked, and no formal reply given; but as Miss Stowe had not absolutely forbidden it, the experiment may be said to have been begun. It was soon reported in Florence that Trafford Morgan was one of the suitors for the hand of the heiress; and, being a candidate, he was of course subjected to the searching light of Public Inquiry. Public Inquiry discovered that he was thirty-eight years of age; that he had but a small income; that he was indolent, indifferent, and cynical. Not being able to find any open vices, Public Inquiry considered that he was too *blasé* to have them; he had probably exhausted them all long before. All this Madame Ferri repeated to Miss Harrison, not because she was in the least opposed to Mr. Morgan, but simply as part of her general task as gatherer and disseminator.

"Trafford Morgan is not a saint, but he is well enough in his way," replied Miss Harrison. "I am not at all sure that a saint would be agreeable in the family."

Madame Ferri was much amused by this; but she carried away the impression also that Miss Harrison favored the suitor.

In the meantime nothing could be more quiet than the manner of the supposed suitor when he was with Miss Stowe. He now asked questions of her; when they went to the churches, he asked her impressions of the architecture;

when they visited the galleries, he asked her opinions of the pictures. He inquired what books she liked, and why she liked them; and sometimes he slowly repeated her replies.

This last habit annoyed her. "I wish you would not do that," she said, with some irritation. "It is like being forced to look at one's self in a mirror."

"I do it to analyze them," he answered. "I am so dense, you know, it takes me a long time to understand. When you say, for instance, that Romola is not a natural character because her love for Tito ceases, I, who think that the unnatural part is that she should ever have loved him, naturally dwell upon the remark."

"She would have continued to love him in life. Beauty is all powerful."

"I did not know that women cared much for it," he answered. Then, after a moment, "Do not be too severe upon me," he added; "I am doing my best."

She made no reply.

"I thought certainly you would have answered, 'By contrast?'" he said, smiling. "But you are not so satirical as you were. I cannot make you angry with me."

"Have you tried?"

"Of course I have tried. It would be a step gained to move you—even in that way."

"I thought your experiment was to be all on one side?" she said. They were sitting in a shady corner of the cloisters of San Marco; she was leaning back in her chair, following with the point of her parasol the lines of the Latin inscription on the slab at her feet over an old monk's last resting-place.

"I am not so consistent as I should be," he answered, rising and sauntering off, with his hands in the pockets of his short morning-coat, to look at St. Peter the Martyr.

At another time they were in the Michael Angelo chapel of San Lorenzo. It was past the hour for closing, but Morgan had bribed the custode to allow them to remain, and the old man had closed the door and gone away, leaving them alone with the wondrous marbles.

"What do they mean?" he said. "Tell me."

"They mean fate, our sad human fate: the beautiful Dawn in all the pain of waking; the stern determination of the Day; the recognition of failure in Evening; and the lassitude of dreary, hopeless sleep in Night. It is one way of looking at life."

"But not your way?"

"Oh, I have no way; I am too limited. But genius takes a broader view, and genius, I suppose, must always be sad. People with that endowment, I have noticed, are almost always very unhappy."

He was sitting beside her, and, as she spoke, he saw a little flush rise in her cheeks; she was remembering when Mrs. Lovell had used the same words, although in another connection.

"We have never spoken directly, or at any length, of Beatrice," she said, suddenly. "I wish you would tell me about her."

"Here?"

"Yes, here and now; Lorenzo shall be your judge."

"I am not afraid of Lorenzo. He is not a god; on the contrary, he has all our deepest humanity on his musing face; it is for this reason that he impresses us so powerfully. As it is the first time you have expressed any wish, Miss Stowe, I suppose I must obey it."

"Will it be difficult?"

"It is always difficult, is it not, for a man to speak of an unhappy love?" he said, leaning his elbow on the back of the seat, and shading his eyes with his hand as he looked at her.

"I will excuse you."

"I have not asked to be excused. I first met Mrs. Lovell in Sicily. I was with her almost constantly during five weeks. She is as lovable as a rose—as a peach—as a child." He paused.

"Your comparisons are rather remarkable," said Miss Stowe, her eyes resting upon the grand massiveness of Day.

"They are truthful. I fell in love with her; and I told her so because there was that fatal thing, an opportunity—that is, a garden-seat, starlight, and the perfume of flowers. Of course these were irresistible."

"Indeed?"

"Do not be contemptuous. It is possible that you may not have been exposed to the force of the combination as yet. She rebuked me with that lovely, gentle softness of hers, and then she went away; the Sicilian days were over. I wrote to her—"

He was sitting in the same position, with his hand shading his eyes, looking at her; as he spoke the last phrase he perceived that she colored, and colored deeply.

"You knew the story generally," he said, dropping his arm and leaning forward. "But it is not possible you saw that letter!"

She rose and walked across, as if to get a nearer view of Day. "I admire it so much!" she said, after a moment. "If it should stretch out that great right arm, it could crush us to atoms." And she turned towards him again.

As she did she saw that he had colored also; a deep, dark flush had risen in his face, and covered even his forehead.

"I am safe—very safe!" he said. "After reading such a letter as that, written to another woman, you are not likely to bestow much regard upon the writer, try as he may!"

Miss Stowe looked at him. "You are overacting," she said, coldly. "It is not in your part to pretend to care so soon. It was to be built up gradually."

"Lorenzo understands me," he said, recovering himself. "Shall I go on?"

"I think I must go now," she answered, declining a seat; "it is late."

"In a moment. Let me finish, now that I have begun. I had thought of returning to America; indeed, Beatrice had advised it; she thought I was becoming expatriated. But I gave it up and remained in Italy because I did not wish to appear too much her slave (women do not like men who obey them too well, you know). After this effort I was consistent enough to follow her to England. I found her in—Devonshire, lovelier than ever; and I was again fascinated; I was even ready to accept beforehand all the rules and embargo of the strictest respect to the memory of Mr. Lovell."

Miss Stowe's eyes were upon Day; but here, involuntarily, she glanced towards her companion. His face remained unchanged.

"I was much in love with her. She allowed me no encouragement. But I did not give up a sort of vague hope I had until this recent change. Then, of course, I knew that it was all over for me."

"I am sorry for you," replied Miss Stowe after a pause, still looking at Day.

"Of course I have counted upon that—upon your sympathy. I knew that you would understand."

"Spare me the quotation, 'A fellow-feeling,' and so forth," she said, moving towards the door. "I am going; I feel as though we had already desecrated too long this sacred place."

"It is no desecration. The highest heights of art, as well as of life, belong to love," he said, as they went out into the cool, low hall, paved with the gravestones of the Medici.

"Don't you always think of them lying down below?" she said. "Giovanni in his armor, and Leonore of Toledo in her golden hair?"

"Since when have you become so historical? They were a wicked race."

"And since when have you become so virtuous?" she answered. "They were at least successful."

Time passed. It has a way of passing rapidly in Florence; although each day is long and slow and full and delightful, a month flies. Again the season was waning. It was now believed that Mr. Morgan had been successful, although nothing definite was known. It was remarked how unusually well Miss Stowe looked: her eyes were so bright and she had so much color that she really looked brilliant. Madame Ferri repeated this to Miss Harrison.

"Margaret was always brilliant," said her aunt.

"Oh, extremely!" said Madame Ferri.

"Only people never found it out," added Miss Harrison.

She herself maintained a calm and uninquiring demeanor. Sometimes she was with her niece and her niece's supposed suitor, and sometimes not. She continued to receive him with the same affability which she had bestowed upon him from the first, and occasionally she invited him to dinner and to drive. She made no comment upon the frequency of his visits, or the length of his conversations upon the little balcony in the evening, where the plash of the fountain came faintly up from below. In truth she had no cause for solicitude; nothing could be more tranquil than the tone of the two talkers. Nothing more was said about Mrs. Lovell; conversation had sunk back into the old impersonal channel.

"You are very even," Morgan said one evening. "You do not seem to have any moods. I noticed it last year."

"One is even," she replied, "when one is—"

"Indifferent," he suggested.

She did not contradict him.

Two things she refused to do: she would not sing, and she would not go to the Boboli Garden.

"As I am especially fond of those tall, ceremonious old hedges and serene statues, you cut me off from a real pleasure," said Morgan.

It was on the evening of the 16th of May; they were sitting by the open window; Miss Harrison was not present.

"You can go there after we have gone," she said, smiling. "We leave to-morrow."

"You leave to-morrow!" he repeated. Then, after an instant, "It is immensely kind to tell me beforehand," he said, ironically. "I should have thought you would have left it until after your departure!"

She made no reply, but fanned herself slowly with the beautiful gray fan.

"I suppose you consider that the month is more than ended, and that you are free?"

"You have had all you asked for, Mr. Morgan."

"And therefore I have now only to thank you for your generosity, and let you go."

"I think so."

"You do not care to know the result of my experiment— whether it has been a failure or a success?" he said. "You told me the result of yours."

"I did not mean to tell you. It was forced from me by your misunderstanding."

"Misunderstandings, because so slight that one cannot attack them, are horrible things. Let there be none between us now."

"There is none."

"I do not know." He leaned back in his chair and looked up at the soft darkness of the Italian night. "I have one more favor to ask," he said, presently. "You have granted me many; grant me this. At what hour do you go to-morrow?"

"In the afternoon."

"Give me a little time with you in the Boboli Garden in the morning."

"You are an accomplished workman, Mr. Morgan; you want to finish with a polish; you do not like to leave rough ends. Be content; I will accept the intention as carried out, and suppose that all the last words have been beautifully and shiningly spoken. That will do quite as well."

"Put any construction upon it you please," he answered. "But consent."

But it was with great difficulty that he obtained that consent.

"There is really nothing you can say that I care to hear," she declared, at last.

"The king is dead! My time is ended, evidently! But, as there *is* something you can say which *I* care to hear, I again urge you to consent."

Miss Stowe rose, and passed through the long window into the lighted empty room, decked as usual with many flowers; here she stood, looking at him, as he entered also.

"I have tried my best to prevent it," she said.

"You have."

"And you still insist?"

"I do."

"Very well; I consent. But you will not forget that I tried," she said. "Good-night."

The next morning at ten, as he entered the old amphitheatre, he saw her; she was sitting on one of the upper stone seats, under a statue of Diana.

"I would rather go to our old place," he said, as he came up; "the seat under the tree, you know."

"I like this better."

"As you prefer, of course. It will be more royal, more in state; but, to be in accordance with it, you should have been clothed in something majestic, instead of that soft, yielding hue."

"That is hardly necessary," she answered.

"By which you mean, I suppose, that your face is not yielding. And indeed it is not."

She was dressed in cream color from head to foot; she held open, poised on one shoulder, a large, heavily fringed, cream-colored parasol. Above this soft drapery and under this soft shade the darkness of her hair and eyes was doubly apparent.

He took a seat beside her, removed his hat, and let the breeze play over his head and face; it was a warm summer morning, and they were in the shadow.

"I believe I was to tell you the result of my experiment," he said, after a while, breaking the silence which she did not break.

"You wished it; I did not ask it."

If she was cool, he was calm; he was not at all as he had been the night before; then he had seemed hurried and irritated, now he was quiet. "The experiment has succeeded," he said, deliberately. "I find myself often thinking of you; I like to be with you; I feel when with you a sort of satisfied content. What I want to ask is—I may as well say it at once—Will not this do as the basis of a better understanding between us?"

She was gazing at the purple slopes of Monte Morello opposite. "It might," she answered.

He turned; her profile was towards him, he could not see her eyes.

"I shall be quite frank," he continued; "under the circumstances it is my only way. You have loved some one else. I have loved some one else. We have both been unhappy. We should therefore, I think, have a peculiar sympathy for and comprehension of each other. It has seemed to me that these, combined with my real liking for you, might be a sufficient foundation for—let us call it another experiment. I ask you to make this experiment, Margaret; I ask you to marry me. If it fails—if you are not happy—I promise not to hold you in the slightest degree. You shall have your liberty untrammelled, and, at the same time, all shall be arranged so as to escape comment. I will be with you enough to save appearances; that is all. In reality you shall be entirely free. I think you can trust my word."

"I shall have but little from my aunt," was her answer, her eyes still fixed upon the mountain. "I am not her heiress, as you suppose."

"You mean that to be severe; but it falls harmless. It is true that I did suppose you were her heiress; but the fact that you are not makes no difference in my request. We shall not be rich, but we can live; it shall be my pleasure to make you comfortable."

"I do not quite see why you ask this," she said, with the same slow utterance and her eyes turned away. "You do not love me; I am not beautiful; I have no fortune. What, then, do you gain?"

"I gain," he said—"I gain—" Then he paused. "You would not like me to tell you," he added; and his voice was changed.

"I beg you to tell me." Her lips were slightly compressed, a tremor had seized her; she seemed to be exerting all her powers of self-control.

He watched her a moment, and then, leaning towards her while a new and beautiful expression of tenderness stole into his eyes, "I gain, Margaret," he said, "the greatest gift that can be given to a man on this earth, a gift I long for—a wife who really and deeply loves me."

The hot color flooded her face and throat; she rose, turning upon him her blazing eyes. "I was but waiting for this," she said, her words rushing forth, one upon the other, with the unheeding rapidity of passion. "I felt sure that it would come. With the deeply-rooted egotism of a man you believe that I love you; you have believed it from the beginning. It was because I knew this that I allowed this experiment of yours to go on. I resisted the temptation at first, but it was too strong for me; you yourself made it so. It was a chance to make you conscious of your supreme error; a chance to have my revenge. And I yielded. You said, not long ago, that I was even. I answered that one was even when one was—You said 'indifferent,' and I did not contradict you. But the real sentence was that one was even when one was pursuing a purpose. I have pursued a purpose. This was mine: to make you put into words your egregious vanity, to make you stand convicted of your dense and vast mistake. But towards the end a better impulse rose, and the game did not seem worth the candle. I said to myself that I would go away without giving you, after all, the chance to stultify yourself, the chance to exhibit clearly your insufferable and amazing conceit. But you insisted, and the impulse vanished; I allowed you to go on to the end. *I* love you! *You!*"

He had risen also; they stood side by side under the statue of Diana; some people had come into the amphitheatre below. He had turned slightly pale as she uttered these bitter words, but he remained quite silent. He still held his hat in his hand; his eyes were turned away.

"Have you nothing to say?" she asked, after some moments had passed.

"I think there is nothing," he answered, without turning.

Then again there was a silence.

"You probably wish to go," he said, breaking it; "do not let me detain you." And he began to go down the steps, pausing, however, as the descent was somewhat awkward, to give her his hand.

To the little Italian party below, looking at the Egyptian obelisk, he seemed the picture of chivalry, as, with bared head, he assisted her down; and as they passed the obelisk, these children of the country looked upon them as two of the rich Americans, the lady dressed like a picture, the gentleman distinguished, but both without a gesture or an interest, and coldly silent and pale.

He did not accompany her home. "Shall I go with you?" he said, breaking the silence as they reached the exit.

"No, thanks. Please call a carriage."

He signalled to a driver who was near, and assisted her into one of the little rattling Florence phaetons.

"Good-bye," she said, when she was seated.

He lifted his hat. "Lung' Arno Nuovo," he said to the driver.

And the carriage rolled away.

COUNTRIES ATTRACT US in different ways. We are comfortable in England, musical in Germany, amused in Paris (Paris is a country), and idyllic in Switzerland; but when it comes to the affection, Italy holds the heart—we keep going back to her. Miss Harrison, sitting in her carriage on the heights of Bellosguardo, was thinking this as she gazed down upon Flor-

ence and the valley below. It was early in the next autumn—
the last of September; and she was alone.

A phaeton passed her and turned down the hill; but she
had recognized its occupant as he passed, and called his
name—"Mr. Morgan!"

He turned, saw her, bowed, and, after a moment's hesita-
tion, ordered his driver to stop, sprang out, and came back to
speak to her.

"How in the world do you happen to be in Florence at this
time of year?" she said, cordially, giving him her hand. "There
isn't a soul in the place."

"That is the reason I came."

"And the reason we did, too," she said, laughing. "I am
delighted to have met you; one soul is very acceptable. You
must come and see me immediately. I hope you are going
to stay."

"Thanks; you are very kind. But I leave to-morrow
morning."

"Then you must come to-night; come to dinner at seven. It
is impossible you should have another engagement when there
is no one to be engaged to—unless it be the pictures; I believe
they do not go away for the summer."

"I really have an engagement, Miss Harrison; you are very
kind, but I am forced to decline."

"Dismiss your carriage, then, and drive back with me; I
will set you down at your hotel. It will be a visit of some sort."

He obeyed. Miss Harrison's fine horses started, and moved
with slow stateliness down the winding road, where the beggars had not yet begun to congregate; it was not "the season"
for beggars; they were still at the sea-shore.

Miss Harrison talked on various subjects. They had been in Switzerland, and it had rained continuously; they had seen nothing but fog. They had come over the St. Gothard, and their carriage had broken down. They had been in Venice, and had found malaria there. They had been in Padua, Verona, and Bologna, and all three had become frightfully modern and iconoclastic. Nothing was in the least satisfactory, and Margaret had not been well; she was quite anxious about her.

Mr. Morgan "hoped" that it was nothing serious.

"I don't know whether it is or not," replied Miss Harrison. "Margaret is rather a serious sort of a person, I think."

She looked at him as if for confirmation, but he did not pursue the subject. Instead, he asked after her own health.

"Oh, I am as usual. It is only your real invalids who are always well; they enjoy their poor health, you know. And what have you been doing since I last saw you? I hope nothing out of the way. Let me see—Trieste and Tarascon; you have probably been in—Transylvania?"

"That would be somewhat out of the way, wouldn't it? But I have not been there; I have been in various nearer places, engaged rather systematically in amusing myself."

"Did you succeed? If you did you are a man of genius. One must have a rare genius, I think, to amuse one's self in that way at forty. Of course I mean thirty-five, you know; but forty is a better conversational word—it classifies. And you were amused?"

"Immensely."

"So much so that you have to come to Florence in September to rest after it!"

"Yes."

Miss Harrison talked on. He listened, and made the necessary replies. The carriage entered the city, crossed the Carraja bridge, and turned towards his hotel.

"Can you not come for half an hour this evening, after your engagement is over?" she said. "I shall be all alone, for Margaret cannot be there before midnight; she went into the country this morning with Madame Ferri—some sort of a fête at a villa, a native Florentine affair. You have not asked much about her, I think, considering how constantly you were with her last spring," she added, looking at him calmly.

"I have been remiss; pardon it."

"It is only forgetfulness, of course. That is not a fault nowadays; it is a virtue, and, what is more, highly fashionable. But there is one little piece of news I must tell you about my niece: she is going to be married."

"That is not little; it is great. Please present to her my sincere good wishes and congratulations."

"I am sorry you cannot present them yourself. But at least you can come and see *me* for a little while this evening—say about ten. The grandson of your grandfather should be very civil to old Ruth Harrison for old times' sake." Here the carriage stopped at his door. "Remember, I shall expect you," she said, as he took leave.

At about the hour she had named he went to see her; he found her alone, knitting. It was one of her idiosyncrasies to knit stockings "for the poor." No doubt there were "poor" enough to wear them; but as she made a great many, and as they were always of children's size and black, her friends sometimes thought, with a kind of amused dismay, of the regiment of little funereal legs running about for which she was responsible.

He had nothing especial to say; his intention was to remain the shortest time possible; he could see the hands of the clock, and he noted their progress every now and then through the twenty minutes he had set for himself.

Miss Harrison talked on various subjects, but said nothing more concerning her niece; nor did he, on his side, ask a question. After a while she came to fashions in art. "It is the most curious thing," she said, "how people obediently follow each other along a particular road, like a flock of sheep, no matter what roads, equally good and possibly better, open to the right and the left. Now there are the wonderfully spirited frescos of Masaccio at the Carmine, frescos which were studied and copied by Raphael himself and Michael Angelo. Yet that church has no vogue; it is not fashionable to go there; Ruskin has not written a maroon-colored pamphlet about it, and Baedeker gives it but a scant quarter-page, while the other churches have three and four. Now it seems to me that—"

But what it seemed Morgan never knew, because here she paused as the door opened. "Ah, there is Margaret, after all," she said. "I did not expect her for three hours."

Miss Stowe came across the large room, throwing back her white shawl and taking off her little plumed hat as she came. She did not perceive that any one was present save her aunt; the light was not bright, and the visitor sat in the shadow.

"It was very stupid," she said. "Do not urge me to go again." And then she saw him.

He rose, and bowed. After an instant's delay she spoke his

name, and put out her hand, which he took as formally as she gave it. Miss Harrison was voluble. She was "so pleased" that Margaret had returned earlier than was expected; she was "so pleased" that the visitor happened to be still there. She seemed indeed to be pleased with everything, and talked for them both; in truth, save for replies to her questions, they were quite silent. The visitor remained but a short quarter of an hour, and then took leave, saying good-bye at the same time, since he was to go early in the morning.

"To Trent?" said Miss Harrison.

"To Tadmor, I think, this time," he answered, smiling.

The next morning opened with a dull gray rain. Morgan was late in rising, missed his train, and was obliged to wait until the afternoon. About eleven he went out, under an umbrella, and, after a while, tired of the constant signals and clattering followings of the hackmen, who could not comprehend why a rich foreigner should walk, he went into the Duomo. The vast church, never light even on a bright day, was now sombre, almost dark, the few little twinkling tapers, like stars, on an altar at the upper end, only serving to make the darkness more visible. He walked down to the closed western entrance, across whose wall outside rises slowly, day by day, the new façade under its straw-work screen. Here he stood still, looking up the dim expanse, with the dusky shadows, like great winged, formless ghosts, hovering over him.

One of the south doors, the one near the choir, was open, and through it a slender ray of gray daylight came in, and tried to cross the floor. But its courage soon failed in that breadth and gloom, and it died away before it had gone ten feet. A blind beggar sat in a chair at this entrance, his patient face faintly outlined against the ray; there seemed to be no one else in the church save the sacristan, whose form could be dimly seen moving about, renewing the lights burning before the far-off chapels.

The solitary visitor strolled back and forth in the shadow. After a while he noted a figure entering through the ray. It was that of a woman; it had not the outlines of the usual church beggar; it did not stoop or cringe; it was erect and slender, and stepped lightly; it was coming down towards the western end, where he was pacing to and fro. He stopped and stood still, watching it. It continued to approach—and at last brushed against him. Coming in from the daylight, it could see nothing in the heavy shadow.

"Excuse me, Miss Stowe," he said; "I should have spoken. My eyes are accustomed to this light, and I recognized you; but of course you could not see me."

She had started back as she touched him; now she moved away still farther.

"It is grandly solitary here on a rainy day, isn't it?" he continued. "I used often to come here during a storm. It makes one feel as if already disembodied—as if he were a shade, wandering on the gray, unknown outskirts of another world."

She had now recovered herself, and, turning, began to walk back towards the ray at the upper door. He accompanied her. But the Duomo is vast, and cannot be crossed in a minute. He went on talking about the shadows; then stopped.

"I am glad of this opportunity to give you my good wishes, Miss Stowe," he said, as they went onward. "I hope you will be quite happy."

"I hope the same, certainly," she answered. "Yet I fail to

see any especially new reason for good wishes from you just at present."

"Ah, you do not know that I know. But Miss Harrison told me yesterday—told me that you were soon to be married. If you have never forgiven me, in the light of your present happiness I think you should do so now."

She had stopped. "My aunt told you?" she said, while he was still speaking. But now, as he paused, she walked on. He could not see her face; although approaching the ray, they were still in the shadow, and her head was turned from him.

"As to forgiveness, it is I who should ask forgiveness from you," she said, after some delay, during which there was no sound but their footsteps on the mosaic pavement.

"Yes, you were very harsh. But I forgave you long ago. I was a dolt, and deserved your sharp words. But I want very much to hear *you* say that you forgive *me*."

"There is nothing to forgive."

"That is gently spoken. It is your marriage present to me, and I feel the better for it."

A minute later they had reached the ray and the door. He could see her face now. "How ill you look!" he said, involuntarily. "I noticed it last evening. It is not conventional to say so, but it is at least a real regret. He should take better care of you."

The blind beggar, hearing their footsteps, had put out his hand. "Do not go yet," said Morgan, giving him a franc. "See how it is raining outside. Walk with me once around the whole interior for the sake of the pleasant part of our Florentine days—for there *was* a pleasant part; it will be our last walk together."

She assented silently, and they turned into the shadow again.

"I am going to make a confession," he said, as they passed the choir; "it can make no difference now, and I prefer that you should know it. I did not realize it myself at the time, but I see now—that is, I have discovered since yesterday—that I was in love with you, more or less, from the beginning."

She made no answer, and they passed under Michael Angelo's grand, unfinished statue, and came around on the other side.

"Of course I was fascinated with Beatrice; in one way I was her slave. Still, when I said to you, 'Forgive me; I am in love with some one else,' I really think it was more to see what you would say or do than any feeling of loyalty to her."

Again she said nothing. They went down the north aisle.

"I wish you would tell me," he said, leaving the subject of himself and turning to her, "that you are fully and really happy in this marriage of yours. I hope you are, with all my heart; but I should like to hear it from your own lips."

She made a gesture as if of refusal; but he went on. "Of course I know I have no right; I ask it as a favor."

They were now in deep obscurity, almost darkness; but something seemed to tell him that she was suffering.

"You are not going to do that wretched thing—marry without love?" he said, stopping abruptly. "Do not, Margaret, do not! I know you better than you know yourself, and you will not be able to bear it. Some women can; but you could not. You have too deep feelings—too—"

He did not finish the sentence, for she had turned from

him suddenly, and was walking across the dusky space in the centre of the great temple whose foundations were so grandly laid six centuries ago.

But he followed her and stopped her, almost by force, taking both her hands in his. "You must not do this," he said; "you must not marry in that way. It is dangerous; it is horrible; for you, it is a crime." Then, as he stood close to her and saw two tears well over and drop from her averted eyes, "Margaret! Margaret!" he said, "rather than that, it would have been better to have married even me."

She drew her hands from his, and covered her face; she was weeping.

"Is it too late?" he whispered. "Is there a possibility—I love you very deeply," he added. And, cold and indifferent as Florence considered him, his voice was broken.

WHEN THEY CAME ROUND to the ray again, he gave the blind beggar all the small change he had about him; the old man thought it was a paper golconda.

"You owe me another circuit," he said; "you did not speak through fully half of the last one."

So they went around a second time.

"Tell me when you first began to think about me," he said, as they passed the choir. "Was it when you read that letter?"

"It was an absurd letter."

"On the contrary, it was a very good one, and you know it. You have kept it?"

"No; I burned it long ago."

"Not so very long! However, never fear; I will write you plenty more, and even better ones. I will go away on purpose."

They crossed the east end, under the great dome, and came around on the other side.

"You said some bitter things to me in that old amphitheatre, Margaret; I shall always hate the place. But after all—for a person who was quite indifferent—were you not just a little *too* angry?"

"It is easy to say that now," she answered.

They went down the north aisle.

"Why did you stop and leave the room so abruptly when you were singing that song I asked for—you know, the 'Semper Fidelis'?"

"My voice failed."

"No; it was your courage. You knew then that you were no longer 'fidelis' to that former love of yours, and you were frightened by the discovery."

They reached the dark south end.

"And now, as to that former love," he said, pausing. "I will never ask you again; but here and now, Margaret, tell me what it was."

"It was not 'a fascination'—like yours," she answered.

"Do not be impertinent, especially in a church. Mrs. Lovell was not my only fascination, I beg to assure you; remember, I am thirty-six years old. But now—what was it?"

"A mistake."

"Good; but I want more."

"It was a will-o'-the-wisp that I thought was real."

"Better; but not enough."

"You ask too much, I think."

"I shall always ask it; I am horribly selfish; I warn you before-hand that I expect everything, in the most relentless way."

"Well, then, it was a fancy, Trafford, that I mistook for—" And the Duomo alone knows how the sentence was ended.

As they passed, for the third time, on their way towards the door, the mural tablet to Giotto, Morgan paused. "I have a sort of feeling that I owe it to the old fellow," he said. "I have always been his faithful disciple, and now he has rewarded me with a benediction. On the next high-festival his tablet shall be wreathed with the reddest of roses and a thick bank of heliotrope, as an acknowledgment of my gratitude."

It was; and no one ever knew why. If it had been in "the season," the inquiring tourists would have been rendered dis-tracted by the impossibility of finding out; but to the native Florentines attending mass at the cathedral, to whom the Latin inscription, "I am he through whom the lost Art of Painting was revived," remains a blank, it was only a tribute to some "departed friend."

"And he is as much my friend as though he had not departed something over five centuries ago," said Trafford; "of that I feel convinced."

"I wonder if he knows any better, now, how to paint an angel leaning from the sky," replied Margaret.

"HAVE YOU ANY IDEA why Miss Harrison invented that enor-mous fiction about you?" he said, as they drove homeward.

"Not the least. We must ask her."

They found her in her easy-chair, beginning a new stocking. "I thought you were in Tadmor," she said, as Trafford came in.

"I started; but came back to ask a question. Why did you tell me that this young lady was going to be married?"

"Well, isn't she?" said Miss Harrison, laughing. "Sit down, you two, and confess your folly. Margaret has been ill all summer with absolute pining—yes, you have, child, and it is a woman's place to be humble. And you, Trafford, did not look especially jubilant, either, for a man who has been immensely amused during the same space of time. I did what I could for you by inventing a sort of neutral ground upon which you could meet and speak. It is very neutral for the other man, you know, when the girl is going to be married; he can speak to her then as well as not! I was afraid last night that you were not going to take advantage of my invention; but I see that it has succeeded (in some mysterious way out in all this rain) better than I knew. It was, I think," she concluded, as she commenced on a new needle, "a sort of experiment of mine—a Florentine experiment."

Trafford burst into a tremendous laugh, in which, after a moment, Margaret joined.

"I don't know what you two are laughing at," said Miss Harrison, surveying them. "I should think you ought to be more sentimental, you know."

"To confess all the truth, Aunt Ruth," said Trafford, going across and sitting down beside her, "Margaret and I have tried one or two of those experiments already!"

IN SLOANE STREET

THE ONLY STORY WOOLSON SET IN ENGLAND, "In Sloane Street" conveys her conflicted feelings about that country—its climate and people could be dreary, but it was also the home of the culture and literature she loved. More than that, however, the story reflects her complex views on family and art. In its many references to women writers and artists, spinsters and married women, and writing for money versus writing for art's sake, it explores from another perspective the questions raised by Henry James in "The Lesson of the Master" (1888). In that story, James approached the problem of the married male writer who must support his family, as viewed from the outside by an ambitious male friend, who is also a writer. Woolson, on the other hand, portrays an unmarried woman who channels her ambitions into a male friend whose wife cares nothing for literature. The triangle they create suggests how excluded intellectual, literary women could feel from both the world of literature and family life. "In Sloane Street" appeared in *Harper's Bazar* in June 1892. It has never been republished until now.

IN SLOANE STREET

. . . .

"WELL, I'VE SEEN THE NATIONAL GALLERY, AND *that's* over," said Mrs. Moore, taking off her smart little bonnet and delicately drying with her handkerchief two drops which were visible on its ribbons. "And I think I'm very enterprising. You would never have got *Isabella* to go in such a rain."

"Of course not. Isabella likes to stay at home and read *Memorials of a Quiet Life*; it makes her feel so superior," answered Gertrude Remington.

"Superior?" commented Mrs. Moore, contemptuously. "Mary would not have gone, either."

"No. But Mary—that's another affair. Mary would not touch the *Memorials* with the tip of her finger, and she wouldn't have minded the rain; but she doesn't care for galleries. With her great love for art, she prefers a book, or, rather, certain books, about pictures, to the pictures themselves. For she thinks that painters, as a rule, are stupid—have no ideas; whereas the art critics—that is, the two or three she likes— really know what a picture means."

"Better than the painters themselves?"

"Oh, far!" answered Miss Remington. "Mary thinks that the work of the painters themselves is merely mechanical; it is the art critic—always her two or three—who discovers the soul in their productions."

"The only art critics I know are Mrs. Jameson and Ruskin," remarked Mrs. Moore, in a vague tone, as she drew off her closely fitting jacket by means of a contortion.

"To Mary, those two are Tupper and *Sandford and Merton*," responded Miss Remington. "And I agree with her about Ruskin: all his later books are the weakest twaddle in the world—violent, ignorant, childish."

But Mrs. Moore's interest in the subject was already exhausted. "It's too dreadful that we're forced to be at sea on Christmas day," she said, complainingly. "Philip ought to have done something—arranged it in some other way. At home, already they are busy with the presents and everything. And by the 22d the whole house will be fragrant with the spices and the fruit and the wine for the plum-pudding. If we could only have some oysters, it would not be quite so dreadful. But I have not seen anything I could call an oyster since I came abroad." She sat poised on the edge of the sofa, as though she intended to rise the next moment. Her small boots, splashed with mud, were visible under her skirt.

"The oysters are rather dwarfish," replied Gertrude Remington. "But as England is the home of the plum-pudding, I dare say you can have that, if you like; we could anticipate Christmas by a week or two."

"There's an idea! Do ring." (To the entering servant.) "Oh, Banks, I should like to speak to Mrs. Sharpless for a moment. She is out? Then send up the cook."

"Mrs. Pollikett, mum? Yes, mum," answered Banks, disappearing.

Presently they heard a heavy step coming up the stairs. It stopped outside the door while Mrs. Pollikett regained her breath; then there was a knock.

"Come in," said Mrs. Moore. "Oh, cook, we have taken a fancy to have a plum-pudding, as we shall be at sea on Christmas day! Do you think that you can give us a good one to-morrow night for dinner? Or, if that is not possible, the day after?"

"Hany time, mum; to-day, if you like," responded Mrs. Pollikett, with the suggestion of a courtesy—it was little more than a trembling of the knees for a moment. She wore a print gown, and a cap adorned with cherry ribbons; her weight was eighteen stone, or two hundred and fifty-two pounds.

"To-day? How can you possibly have it to-day? It's afternoon already," said Mrs. Moore, surveying the big woman (as she always did) with fascinated eyes.

"I've one on hand, mum," replied cook, with serene pride. "And an hexcellent one 'tis. 'Twere made a little over a year ago, and the materials being hof the best, 'tis better now than 'tever was; they himprove with keeping, mum. It's large, but what's left you can take with you in a tin box. With care 'twill be as good as hever another year, if you don't require to heat it all now, mum."

Mrs. Moore gave a gasping glance at Miss Remington. Then she laughed, putting the veil which she held in her hand to her lips, to hide in part her merriment.

"I'll let you know later, cook," she said. "I'll send word by nurse."

And Mrs. Pollikett, unconscious of ridicule, calmly withdrew. Amy Moore put her head down upon the pile of sofa cushions beside her, and ground it into them as if in desperation.

"Plum-pudding a year old, and warranted to keep another year! Hard as a stone, of course, and black as lead. Think of ours at home! Think how light it will be, almost like a *soufflé!* And its delicate color and fragrance!" She took up her jacket, lifted her bonnet, and pinned the little lace veil to it with the long bonnet-pin; then, still laughing, she rose. On her way to the door her eyes caught sight of a figure which was passing the window outside. "There is Philip going out again. How he does slouch!"

"Slouch?" said Miss Remington, inquiringly. She also had seen the figure from her chair by the fire.

"I don't mean slouch exactly; I mean that he is so bent. Curiously enough, it isn't his back either. But up at the top of his shoulders behind, between there and the head, there's a stoop, or rather a lunge forward. But there's no hollow; it's a roll of flesh. The truth is that Philip is growing too stout."

"That bend you speak of is the scholar's stoop," observed Miss Remington.

"I suppose you mean writer's. He could stand when he writes, couldn't he? But probably it's too late now. How do *you* manage to be always so tremendously straight, Gertrude?"

"Don't you know that spinsters—those at least who have conquered the dejection of their lot—are always straight-backed?" said Miss Remington. "Their one little pride is a stiff spine and light step. Because, you know, the step of their married contemporaries is sometimes rather heavy."

"You think you can say that because I happen to weigh only ninety-eight pounds," answered Amy Moore. "But let me tell you one thing—*you* overdo your straightness; your shoulders in those tailor-made dresses you are so fond of look as though they were moulded of iron plate. You'd be a great deal more attractive and comfortable to look at, Gertrude, if you had a few cozy little habits, nice homelike little ways. You never lounge; you never lean back against anything—that is, with any thorough enjoyment. Who ever saw *you* stretched out lazily in a rocking chair by the fire, with a box of chocolate creams and a novel?"

Miss Remington laughed. "But if I don't care for chocolates?"

"That's just what I am saying: if you cared for them, you'd be much more cozy. A tall thin woman in a tailor-made gown, with her hair dragged tightly back from her face, and all sorts of deep books—why, naturally, all men are afraid of her."

"Are you kind enough to be still thinking of matrimonial hopes for me?" inquired Miss Remington.

"Oh no! For what would become of Philip then?" said Philip's wife. "You are his chief incense-burner; you're awfully valuable to me just for that." She was opening the door as she said this; she went out, closing it after her.

Left alone in the large room, Miss Remington took a newspaper from the table by her side, and vaguely glanced at its page. Her eyes rested by chance upon a series of short lines, each line beginning with a capital letter, like a poem. It was headed "Commercial Matters," and the first four lines were as follows:

"Wool is weaker.

Leather is slow.

Hides are easy.

Rice is low."

Presently the door opened, and Philip Moore entered.

"Oh, you've come back," she said, letting the paper drop to her lap.

"Only went to the corner to put a letter in the box."

"Very wet still, isn't it?"

"Very."

Moore sat down before the fire, extended his legs, and watched the combat between the heat and the dampness of his trousers.

After a while Miss Remington remarked, "We've been to the National Gallery since lunch."

He made no answer.

"We had intended to go to Highgate also," she went on; "but it was too wet for so long a drive."

"To Highgate?"

"Yes. To George Eliot's grave."

Moore's gloom was lightened for the moment by a short laugh.

"You think that's absurd," said his companion.

"Well—yes. Thoughts suitable for the occasion were to have been the attraction, I suppose. But if you can conjure them up in one place, why can't you in another, and save your cab fare? It was your idea, I know—the going to Highgate. Amy is not devoted to such excursions."

"I suppose it was my idea," answered Gertrude. "I thought you liked George Eliot," she went on, after a moment.

"Do you mean her ghost? How can I like a person I have never seen?"

"I mean her books."

"The first two, perhaps," answered Moore, frowning impatiently. "I suppose I may have said so once—ages before the flood, and you never forget anything, you are merciless about that. But women's books—what are they? Women can't write. And they ought not to try."

"What *can* you mean?"

"What I say," answered Philip Moore. "Children's stories—yes; they can write for children, and for young girls, extremely well. And they can write little sketches and episodes if they will confine themselves rigidly to the things they thoroughly know, such as love-stories, and so forth. But the great questions of life, the important matters, they cannot render in the least. How should they? And when in their ignorance they begin, in addition, to preach—good heavens, what a spectacle!" Happening to look up and see the expression of his companion's face, he added, laughing: "*You* need not be troubled, you have never tried. And I'm thankful you haven't. It would be insupportable to me to have any of my personal friends among that band."

"No, I have never tried," Gertrude answered. She hesitated a moment, then added, "My ambition is all for other people."

"You mean my things, of course. I should like you much better if you had never read a word of them," responded Moore, his impatience returning. "After they're once done I care nothing about them, they are no longer a part of me; they are detached—gone. By the time they're printed—and that is when *you* get hold of them—I'm taken up with something else, and miles away. Yet you always try to drag me back."

Miss Remington bit her lip, a slight flush rose in her cheeks. But it faded as quickly as it had come, and her companion did not see it; he was staring at the fire.

He was a man of forty-five, with heavy features and thick dark hair. His eyes and head were fine. His forehead wore almost habitually a slight frown. He was somewhat under medium height, and his wife's description of his figure and bearing was true enough.

But Gertrude Remington saw him as he once was—the years when he had been full of life and hope and vigor. She also saw another vision of him as he might be now, perhaps, as he would be (so she told herself) under different influences. It was this possible vision which constantly haunted her, troubled her, tossed her about, and beckoned her hither and thither. She was three years younger than Philip, and she had known him from childhood, as her father's house was next to the house of the elder Philip Moore, in the embowered street of the Massachusetts town which was the home of both. When Philip married, he brought his little wife, the golden-haired, blue-eyed Amy, home to this old house, now his own, owing to the death of his father, and the intimacy of the two families had continued. It was almost a matter of course, therefore, that Miss Remington should be one of the party when the Moores came abroad for six months, their second visit to the Old World. Amy was twelve years younger than her husband, and nine years younger than Gertrude Remington.

To Moore's accusation, "You always try to drag me back," Gertrude had replied in a light tone: "That is because one doesn't stop to think. 'Never talk to an author about his books.' I saw that given somewhere as a wise maxim only the other day."

"I saw it too, and in the very review in which you saw it," replied Moore, in a sarcastic tone. "But you have not given the whole quotation; there was more of it. 'Never talk to an author about his books unless you really believe (or can make him feel you believe) that they are the greatest of the great; he will accept *that!*' In your case there is no hypocrisy, I exonerate you on that score; you really do think my things the greatest of the great. And that's the very trouble with you, Gertrude; you have no sense of proportion, no discrimination. If I had believed you, I should have been a fool; I should have been sure that my books were the finest of the century, instead of their being what they are—and I know it, too—half failures, all of them." He got up, went to the window, and looked out. Then he left the room.

Miss Remington lifted the newspaper from her lap, and again perused unconsciously the same column. This time her eyes rested on the second four lines:

> "Beans are steady.
> Sugars are down.
> Truck is in good demand.
> Sweet-potatoes are firm."

This last item brought Florida to her mind, and she thought for a moment of the gray-white soil which produces the sweet potatoes; of the breezy sweep of the pine-barrens, with their carpet of wild flowers; of the blue Florida sky. Then she put down the sheet (it was an American paper), rose, and going to the window in her turn, looked out. It was the 13th of December. The autumn had been warm, and even now it was not cold, though the air was damp and chilling; fine gray rain had been falling steadily ever since the sluggish daylight—slow and unwilling—had dawned over vast London. The large house was in the London quarter called S.W.; it stood at a corner of Sloane Street, and these American travellers were occupying, temporarily, its ground-floor; it was literally a ground-floor, for there was only one step at the outer door. Miss Remington surveyed Sloane Street. Its smooth wooden pavement was dark and slippery; the houses opposite had a brown-black hue—brown in the centre of each brick and black at its edges; a vine was attached to one of these dwellings, and its leaves, though dripping, had a dried appearance, which told of the long-lasting dusts of the summer. Omnibuses, with their outside seats empty, and their drivers enveloped in oil-skins, constantly succeeded each other; the glass of their windows was obscured by damp, and their sides bore advice (important in the blackest of towns) about soap; each carried on its top something that looked like a broomstick, from which floated mournfully a wet rag. Among the pedestrians, the women all had feet that appeared to be entirely unelastic, like blocks of wood; they came clumping and pounding along, clutching at their skirts behind with one hand, and holding an open umbrella with the other; the clutch was always ineffectual, the skirts were always draggled. These women all wore small black bonnets; and the bonnets attached to the heads of the poorer class had a singularly battered appearance, as though they had been kicked across the floor—or even the street— more than once. Hansom cabs passed and repassed. The horse belonging to those which were empty walked slowly, his head hanging downward; the horse of those that carried a fare moved onward with a gait which had the air of being rapid, because he continually turned his high-held nose to the right or the left, according to the guidance of his driver, making a pretence at the same time of turning his body also; this last, however, he never really did unless compelled, for it would have been one step more. Huge covered carts, black and drip- ping, devoted (so said the white lettering on their sides) to the moving of furniture, rolled slowly by, taking with cyni- cal despotism all the space they required, like Juggernauts. A red-faced milk-woman appeared, wearing a dirty white apron over her drabbled short skirt, with indescribable boots, and the inevitable small battered black bonnet. The gazer, finding the milk-woman more depressing even than the hansom cab- horses, turned and went to a fourth window, which overlooked the narrow street at the side of the house. Here the battered stone pavement held shallow pools of yellow water in each of its numerous depressions. On the opposite corner a bak- er's shop displayed in its windows portly loaves, made in the shape of the Queen's crown—loaves of a clay-colored hue, and an appearance which suggested endurance. There were also glass jars containing lady's-fingers of immemorial age, and, above these, a placard announcing "Mineral Waters." Next came a green-grocer's stall, with piles of small, hard, dark green apples. Miss Remington imagined a meal composed of one of the clay-colored loaves, the mineral waters, the lady's-fingers, and the hard apples. A hideous child now appeared, with a white face streaked with dirt, and white eyelashes; it wore a red feather in its torn wet gypsy hat, and it carried a skipping-rope, with which, drearily, it began to skip, after a while, in the rain. A younger child followed, equally hideous and dirty; it was sucking an orange as it trailed after its sister. Neither of the two looked hungry; but, oh! so unhealthy, so depraved. Miss Remington gave it up; she returned to her place by the fire.

Ten minutes later the door opened, and Mrs. Moore came in, freshly dressed. She drew an easy-chair forward and seated herself, putting out two dainty little shoes towards the blaze.

"Those English people upstairs are too ghastly," she announced. "They do nothing but drink tea."

"They have the best of it, then," answered Miss Remington. "For probably they like it, and perhaps it is good. Whereas what we want—the coffee—is atrocious."

"Just wait till I get home," responded Amy, drumming noiselessly on the arm of her chair with her finger-tips, the motion drawing sparkles from her diamond rings. "I have only found one place in Europe where the coffee is as good as ours, and that is Vienna. But as regards tea, they do keep at it, that family upstairs. First, they all drink it for breakfast. Then again with luncheon. Then it goes in a third time at five or six, with piles of bread-and-butter. Then they have it in the evening after dinner. And if they go to the theatre or anything of that sort, they have a cup after they come home. In addition, if any one has a cold, or is tired, or has been out in the rain, there are extra supplies ordered. I should think it would make them nervous enough to fly."

"It doesn't appear to," answered Gertrude. "We look far more nervous than they do. They are remarkably handsome, and pictures of health each one."

"I am sure *I* don't want to look like them," responded Amy.

Miss Remington made no reply. Amy's firm belief that she had still the beauty of twelve or fifteen years before always rankled a little in the older woman's mind. Amy had been a very pretty girl, the pet of a large family circle, who thought that she had conferred a wonderful favor when she gave her hand to Philip Moore. Through the years which had passed, they had never concealed this opinion. And sometimes it was apparent also that Amy (in her own mind at least) agreed with them. At present her beauty was gone; in appearance she was insignificant. Her small figure was wasted, her little face was pallid, her blue eyes had lost their bright color, and the golden hair had grown ominously thin.

Presently she began again. "When one is abroad, if it rains, one is ended; one can't get up home occupations in deadly rooms like these; at least I can't. To-night there is *Cavalleria*, but between that and this nothing. Have you any books?"

"I have *Vapour* upstairs. Shall I get it?"

"That analytical thing? I hate analytical novels, and can't imagine why any one writes them. Why don't you talk? You're as dumb as an owl."

"What shall I say?"

"Anything you like. Why people write analytical novels will do as a starter."

Miss Remington, who was embroidering, lifted her eyes. "I

suppose you could tell me a great deal about Philip's disposition, couldn't you? All sorts of queer unexpected little ins and outs; oddities; surprises; and trip-you-up-in-the-dark places?"

"I rather think I could," answered Amy, laughing.

"And well as I and all our family believe that we know him, I dare say you could astonish us with details and instances which would show him in lights which we have never suspected?"

"Of course I could."

"Well, if all that you know should be carefully written down, it would be a study of Philip's character which would be very interesting to those who think they know him. My idea is that the persons who write analytical novels, and those also who like to read them, are interested in the study of character generally, as you and I are interested in Philip's in particular."

Amy yawned. "But they put such *little* things in those novels—such trifles!"

"When Philip refused to buy that exquisite little drawing of Du Maurier's that was for sale in Bond Street the other day—refused, though he was longing for it, simply because he had said that he would not buy another article of any kind or description, not even a pin, as long as he was abroad—was it not as vivid an example of his obstinacy (especially as that unexpected check from home had made it perfectly easy for him to indulge his longing) as if he had refused a Senatorship because he had said some time that he would never live in Washington?"

"Oh, I hope he has not said *that!*" answered Mrs. Moore. "Because if he has, he will stick to it, and I shall have endless trouble to persuade him out of it. For there is nothing I should

like better than to live in Washington—I've been thinking of
it for a long time. He need not have anything to do with the
government, you know."

"And when he flung that footstool of yours through the
window into the garden last spring, breaking all the glass,
wasn't that as much an instance of uncontrollable temper as if
he had knocked a man down?"

"The footstool was the embroidered velvet one," answered
Amy, "and it was completely spoiled—out all night in the
rain. I have to have footstools, because I'm so short; *I* can't
stretch my legs all over the room, as you can. I was sitting in
the study for an hour or two that day while they were sweeping the drawing-room, and I told Rosa to bring me one; and
then when I went out, I forgot it, and there it staid. But it was
a very little thing, I am sure, to be so furious about."

"If it had happened only once, yes," answered Gertrude,
smiling. "But I seem to have heard before of footstools forgotten in the middle of the floor in the study, and its master
coming in after dark in a hurry, and not expecting to find
them there."

"Ten times. Ten times at least," responded Amy, gleefully.
"It's the funniest thing in the world. There's a perfect fatality
about it."

The door opened, and a little boy and girl came in. They
were very beautiful children, although slender and rather pale.
They went to their mother and kissed her, climbing to her lap
and the arm of her chair.

"A story!" demanded the boy. "About the dog who had a
house up in a tree."

"No," said the girl. "About Wolla Kersina, the fairy."

"But it isn't story-time," answered Mrs. Moore. "If you have them now, there'll be none when you go to bed."

Fritz and Polly considered this statement thoughtfully; they decided to wait until bed-time.

"Come on, Poll; let's play water-cure," said the boy.

"Well," answered the girl, assentingly. She went to a closet and drew out a box, from which she took forty small china dolls, arrayed in silks and laces. "Here's the passhints," she said, arranging them on the floor.

"I'm the head doctor," said the boy. "Is the passhints ready?" he inquired, in a gruff tone. Kneeling down, he extended his forefinger menacingly towards the first doll. "Good-morning. How are yer? You have a turrible fever, an' you must take twenty baths, and a sitz and a pack before eating a *mossel*."

"Fritzy Moore, she'll die with all that," said the girl, indignantly, rescuing the doll. "That's Grace Adelaide, and she's delicate."

Fritz went on to the next one. "Fer you, a shower-bath, and needles, and the deuce, every five minutes."

"I've no appetite, doctor," said Polly, speaking in a very weak voice for a doll whom she drew from the line. "I've been rather anxious because my ten children" (here she hustled forward rapidly ten of the smaller dolls) "have all had typhoid fever most *dangerously* for more than *three* years."

"Vegetubble baths and the *mind*-cure," ordered Fritz.

"I'm going to play I'm a lady who has come with her child to call on a passhint," said the girl. She took a large doll from the closet, drew her own lips tightly together, and, speaking in a melancholy voice, said: "I'm *very* sorry, Maud Violet, that we accepturred Mrs. Razzers's invitation to stay to dinner at this water-cure, for Mrs. Razzers isn't very rich; I don't think she has got more than twenty-five cents; and so we must be very careful. Eat just as little as you *possibly* can, Maud Violet, an' say 'no-thank-yer' to everything, just 'cep' meat and pota-toes." Dragging the doll by its hand, she walked with digni-fied steps towards the side window, where she seated herself on the floor with her back against the wall, the doll by her side. "No-thank-yer," she said, as if speaking to a servant; "no soup. (Maud Violet, say 'no-thank-yer'!)"

Mrs. Moore, meanwhile, had glanced towards the table. "French again? Why are you forever reading French books?"

"Aren't they the cleverest?"

"They have so many s'écriais—he or she s'écriaid—as I always translate that 'shriek,' they go shrieking all down the page," answered Amy. She made a long stretch and took two paper-covered volumes from the table. "Lemaitre? Who is he? Oh, it isn't a novel. And this other one is that Bashkirtseff thing! The most perfectly unnatural book I have ever read."

"I thought it so natural."

"Mercy!"

"I don't mean that it was natural to write it for publication, or even, perhaps, to write it at all; I referred to the ideas, merely. If some invisible power should reproduce with exact truthful-ness each one of our secret thoughts, do you think we should come out of it so infinitely better than Marie Bashkirtseff?"

"What extraordinary notions you invent! If I thought that Polly would ever have such ideas as that girl's—But she won't.

You spinsters are too queer. You are either so prudish that one can't look at you, or else you're so emancipated that Heaven alone knows what you'll say next! It all comes from your ignorance, I suppose."

"Yes; that answer is always flung at us," responded Gertrude, holding her embroidery at arm's-length for a moment, in order to inspect it critically.

Polly, having overheard her name, had come to her mother's knee. "Want me, mamma?"

"No. Go back to your play."

"We're not playing. Fritzy won't."

"'Cause you're so selfish with your old dolls," said Fritz. "You said they was passhints. Then you came an' yanked 'em all away."

Polly made a face at him. Fritz responded with another, and one of preternatural hideousness, rolling his eyes up to the whites, and stretching out his tongue. This seemed to soothe him, for he demanded, after the effort was over:

"Where's the Noah's ark? You get it, and we'll play crocodile."

"I had happened to read the *Life of Louisa Alcott* just before I began the Bashkirtseff journal," Gertrude went on. "What a contrast! It is true that the Russian girl was but twenty-four when she died, but one feels that she would have been the same at fifty. Miss Alcott worked all her life as hard as she possibly could, turning her hand to anything that offered, no matter what; and her sole motive was to assist her parents and her family, those who were dear to her; of herself she never thought at all. Marie Bashkirtseff's behavior to her mother and aunt showed indifference, and often scorn; her one thought was herself—her own attractions, her own happiness, her own celebrity, and the persons who could perhaps add to the latter two. Her egotism—"

"Children, what *are* you about?" interrupted Mrs. Moore, turning her head; for Fritz and Polly were lying on the floor flat upon their stomachs, and in this position wriggling in zigzags across the room, with low roars, directing their course towards the animals of Noah's ark, who were drawn up in a line before the sofa.

"We're crocodiles," called Fritz. "We're 'vancing to *scrunch* 'em!"

"Polly, get up instantly; look at your nice white frock! Fritz—Oh, here's Christine at last. Christine, do see to the children," said Mrs. Moore.

The German nurse, who had entered, lifted Polly to her feet and smoothed down her skirts. Fritz sprang up and rushed to the window, for he heard music outside: a street band composed of four men of depressed aspect had begun to play before the house the strains associated with the words:

> "Ever be hap-*pee*,
> Wherever thou art,
> Pride of the pirate's heart—"

"How ridiculous to be tooting away in all this rain!" said Mrs. Moore, irritably.

"It isn't raining now, mamma," called Polly, her nose also as well as Fritz's pressed against the pane.

"As it ees no rain, meeses, I might take de childrens to see dat leedle boy at Norteeng Hill?" suggested the nurse, respectfully.

"Has it really stopped?" answered Mrs. Moore, turning to look. "Well, perhaps it would be better for them to go out. Put on their cork-soled shoes and their water-proofs, and you must be back by five o'clock, or half past—not later."

"I veel at mine vatch look, and take de train shoost in time to be back at half past five," answered Christine, in her earnest, careful fashion. "It ees not much meeneets to Norteeng Hill."

She put the animals back in the ark, and placed it, with the box of dolls, in the closet.

"Take this shilling and give it to that dreadful band. Tell them to go away immediately," said Mrs. Moore.

"Yes, meeses." And taking the children with her, Christine left the room, softly closing the door behind her.

"I do wish Philip *would* go to Washington," said Mrs. Moore, after some minutes of silence.

The band had ceased its wailed good wishes for the pride of the pirate's heart; the room without the chatter of the children seemed suddenly very still; a coal dropping from the grate made a loud sound.

Miss Remington did not answer.

"It's the very place for me," pursued Amy. "There are all sorts of people there—foreigners and Southerners as well as Northerners. Not the seven deadly families, always the same, month after month, that we everlastingly have in New Edinburgh. I love variety and I love gayety, and I especially love dinner parties. I should like to dine out five nights in the week, and have friends to dine with us the other two. I don't see,

after all, why we shouldn't go this very winter," she went on,
with animation. "I have all these lovely new things from Paris,
you know. Think of their being wasted in New Edinburgh!"

"They won't be wasted," said Gertrude. "Everybody will
profoundly admire them."

"Profoundly criticize, you mean. Because they are all plain-
looking themselves, they think it frivolous to care for looks;
and because they are all dull and serious by nature, they think
nobody ought to be gay; it's a good strong position, and I
dare say they believe it's a moral one! Philip fancies that New
Edinburgh is perfect, simply because he has his library there.
But books can be moved, can't they? And it is his duty to
remember *me* now and then. I suppose he can't appreciate that
I have any such needs, because his mother and his five sisters are so different. Dear me! if girls could only know! They
never think, when they marry, about the mother and sisters.
But no matter what a husband may be as a man out in the
world among men, when he thinks of his wife's requirements
he seldom gets much beyond what his mother and sisters did
and had. Of course Philip's sisters don't long for Washington.
Imagine them there! But that's no reason for *me*."

"Philip himself would be a lion in Washington," said Gertrude, her face looking obstinate as she threaded her needle.

"You mean among the literary set? I should not care to
have anything to do with *them*, and Philip wouldn't either. I
know, because whenever I do succeed in forcing him out, he
always likes my kind of people ever so much better. I suppose
it wouldn't be hard to get a furnished house as a beginning;
one with a good dining-room? But, dear me! what is the use
of planning? I might as well be old and stupid and ugly! Philip

will stick to New Edinburgh, and stick to New Edinburgh. *You* will like that; you adore the place, with its horrid clubs, and papers read aloud, and poky old whist!"

"I don't think Philip cares for New Edinburgh in itself," answered Miss Remington. "But he has the house, and it is a large place, with all the ground about it. And you know he has spent a great deal in alterations and improvements of many sorts, including all the new furniture."

"And I suppose you charge me with that? But I maintain that I'm not extravagant in the least," said Amy. "I must have things about me dainty and pretty, because I have all those tastes; I was born with them, and they are a part of me; people who haven't them, of course don't understand the necessity. But there's one thing to be said; there is no merit in going without the things one doesn't care for. Philip's sisters are perfectly willing to live forever with nailed-down carpets, hideous green lambrequins and furniture, because they don't know they are hideous. But just attack them on what they *do* care for—their Spanish and German lessons, their contributions to the 'Harvard Annex,' and the medical colleges for women, and there would be an outcry! As to money, Philip could easily make ever so much more a year, if he chose; those syndicate people do nothing but write to him."

"But you would not wish to see him descend to a lower grade of work, would you?" Gertrude's voice was indignant as she said this; but she kept her eyes on her work, and drew her stitches steadily.

"I don't know what you call a lower grade. *I* call it a lower grade to keep us in New Edinburgh, and a higher grade to give us a nice home in Washington—as it's Washington I happen to fancy. Philip *could* make this larger income; even you acknowledge that. Well, then, I say he ought. Other men do—I mean other authors. Look at Gray Tucker!"

"*Philip* to write in the style of Gray Tucker!"

"Now you're furious," said Amy, laughing. "But I'm afraid Philip couldn't do it even if he should try; he hasn't that sort of knack. Of course you are scornful; but, all the same, I can tell you plainly that *I* like Gray Tucker's books ever so much; they're easy to read, and they make one laugh, and I think that's what a novel is for. Everybody reads Gray Tucker's books, and they sell in thousands and thousands."

Miss Remington remained silent for several moments. Then, in a guarded voice, she said, "But if Philip has not that sort of knack, as you call it, surely you would not advise him to tie himself down at so much a year to produce just so many pages?"

"Why not?—if the sum offered is a good one."

"Just so many pages, whether good or bad?"

"They needn't be bad, I suppose. I don't see why he shouldn't keep on writing in the same style as now, but produce more. It simply depends upon his own determination."

"It isn't purely mechanical work, you know," answered Miss Remington.

"Your face is red!" said Amy, watching her with amused eyes. "There is nothing so funny as to see you get in a rage about Philip. It's a pity he doesn't appreciate it more. Now, Gertrude, listen to me for a moment. I am not in the least frivolous, though you always have a manner that seems to show that you think I am. I have more common-sense than Philip has; I am the practical one, not he. What *is* the use of his persistingly writing books that nobody reads, or, at least, only a very few? To me it seems that a man can have no higher aim than to do splendidly for his own family—for the people that belong to him and depend upon him. I am his wife, am I not? And Fritz and Polly are his children. To give his wife the home she wishes, to educate his children in the very best way, and lay up a good generous sum for them—I confess this seems to me more important than the sort of fame his books may have in the future when we're all dead. For as to fame in the *present* there is no question, that hangs over the volumes that sell; the fame of to-day belongs always to the books that are popular. I know you don't think I'm clever at all; whether I am or not, that's my opinion."

"You're only too clever," said Gertrude, rolling up her work. "If there is any word I loathe, it's that lying term 'popular.'"

"Your eyes are brimming over, you absurd creature!" said Amy, not unkindly. "Yet somehow," she added, as Gertrude rose, "it only makes you look stiffer."

"Oh, do forget my stiffness!" said Miss Remington, angrily. She crossed the room, and began to rearrange the sofa cushions and chairs which the children had pulled about.

The door opened and Philip Moore came in.

"I thought you were writing?" said his wife.

"I can't write on a toilet table or the mantel-piece. Where are the children?"

"They have gone to Notting Hill to see Walter Carberry."

"Did they go by the underground?"

"Yes; Christine, you know, has the whole line at her fingers' ends. She once lived for two years at Hackney."

"Hackney?"

"Well, perhaps it was Putney. Such names! Imagine living at Tooting, or Barking, or Wormwood Scrubs! And then they talk to us about *our* names! But I have something to show them; I saw it in the *Times* yesterday, cut it out, and put it in my purse; here it is. Listen: 'November 28th, at St. Peter's Church, Redmile, Leicestershire, by the Rev. James Terry, rector of *Clarby-cum-Normanby-le-Wold*, Lincolnshire, Algernon Boothby, Esquire, to Editha, daughter of the Rev. J. Trevor Aylmar, rector of *Carlton-Scroop-cum-Normanton-on-Cliffe*, Lincolnshire.' There now! What do you say to that?"

"I don't like their going by the underground," said Moore.

"With Christine they are safe," answered his wife. "Where are our seats to-night?"

"Oh, I forgot to tell you, I've taken a box, after all. I met Huntley and Forrester, and asked them to join us."

"That is just like you, Philip. If I had not happened to ask, you would never have told me at all! Of course for a box I shall dress more," Amy added. "I'll do it for a *box*. And I'd better go and get it done now, by-the-bye, as there is no light upstairs but dull glimmering candles." She rose. "I suppose you are superior to dress, Gertrude?"

"Superior or inferior, whichever you like," answered Miss Remington.

Mrs. Moore went out.

"Do you care about this opera?" inquired Gertrude, returning to the fire.

"Can't say I do," answered Moore. "But they tell me it's pretty, and I thought it might amuse Amy." He had taken an evening paper from his pocket—the *St. James Gazette*; he began to look over the first page.

Gertrude sat down, took up a book, and opened it. "Amy wishes to live in Washington," she said.

"Yes, I know," replied Moore.

"Perhaps the fancy won't last," his companion went on. She closed the book (it was *Marie Bashkirtseff's Journal*), and with a pencil began to make a row of little rosettes on the yellow cover. "Washington life would not suit you, Philip," she said. "You do not enjoy society; it does not amuse you, but only tires you. That has been proved again and again. And you would not be able to avoid it, either. The circumstances of the case would force you into it. Why isn't New Edinburgh the best place, with your large house, and your library all arranged, and that beautiful garden, and the grove and brook for the children?"

"It's dull for Amy," Moore replied, still reading. "She has been very unselfish about it. I should like to give her a change, if I could. But the first step would have to be to sell the place, and a purchaser for a place of that kind is not easily found."

"You will never get back half that you have spent upon it. New Edinburgh doesn't seem to me so dull," Gertrude continued.

"Amy is so much younger than we are that her ideas are different," answered Moore. He cut open the pages of the *St. James* jaggedly with the back of his hand, turned the leaf, and went on with his reading.

Miss Remington made five more little rosettes in a straight line on the cover. "Why not at least stay until your new book is finished," she said—"the one we all care so much about?" She hurried on, after this suggestion, to another subject. "Washington would only be safe for the children for part of the year.

It would be necessary to take them away in April, and they could not return before November. That would be six months of travelling for you every summer—hotels, and all that. You have just said that you could not write on a mantel-piece," she added, forcing a laugh.

"It's very good of you to interest yourself so much in our affairs," said Moore, coldly. "The children would do very well in Washington in the winter; for the summer, I could look up some old farm-house in the mountains not very far away, where they could run wild. That would be even better for them than New Edinburgh. I should like it, too, myself."

"Then you have decided?" said Gertrude, quickly.

"Decided? I don't know whether I have or not," answered Moore.

Banks now appeared with a lamp and a large tea-tray. He placed the tray on a low table which stood in a corner, and drew the table towards Miss Remington; then he set out the cups and saucers in careful symmetry, and after waiting a moment to see if anything more was required, with noiseless step left the room. When the door was closed, Moore turned his head, glancing at the corpulent teapot, the piled sugar-bowl, the large plate covered with slices of bread-and-butter as thin as a knife blade, and arranged with mathematical precision.

"Do any of us ever touch it?" he inquired.

"Never," Gertrude answered. "Yet they send it in every afternoon in exactly the same way. It's a fixed rule, I suppose; like the house-maids always scrubbing the door-steps on their knees, instead of using a long-handled scrubbing-brush; and like the cold toast in the morning."

No more was said. She laid aside her pencil and the book,

and took up a newspaper. It proved to be the same one she had had earlier in the day, and mechanically she read another four lines of the commercial poem:

> "Grass seed is middling.
> Pork has movement.
> Lemons have reacted.
> Molasses is strong."

After a while, Amy came in. "When do you intend to dress?" she said to her husband as she sat down by the fire.

"I'm waiting for the children. They ought not to be out after dark."

"It isn't late; they will be here in a few minutes; Christine is like a clock." She lifted her silk skirt and shook it. "It is creased a little, in spite of all the care they took in packing it. But it's a perfectly lovely dress! You need not look up, Gertrude, with that duty expression, as though you were trying to think of something admiring to say; I don't dress for you; or for Philip either, for that matter; he hasn't a particle of taste. I dress for myself—to satisfy my own ideal. And *this* is my ideal of a costume for the opera (that is, if one has a box)—delicate, Parisian, pretty. Philip, do you know what idea came to me upstairs? I want to go home by the White Star Line, instead of the Cunard."

No answer came from behind the *St. James's Gazette*; Moore had found at last a paragraph that interested him.

"Philip, Philip, I say! Why don't you listen?"

"Yes," said Moore.

"You are reading still; you are not listening one bit. Wake up!"

"Well, what is it?"

"I want to go home by the White Star Line instead of the Cunard."

Moore's eyes had glanced at his wife over the top of the newspaper, but there was not full comprehension in his glance.

"When you're absent-minded like that, you look about sixty years old," said Amy. "You've taken to stooping lately, and to scowling. If you add absent-mindedness, too—dear me!"

Moore let his newspaper drop, keeping a corner of it in his left hand, while with his right he rubbed his forehead, as if to rouse himself to quicker modes of thought.

"*Must* I say it again?" inquired Amy, in resigned despair. "You and Gertrude will end by making me lose my voice. No matter what my subject is, yours is always another. I said that I wished to go home by the White Star Line instead of the Cunard."

"But we can't. Our cabins on the *Etruria* have been engaged for weeks," replied her husband.

"They can be changed. At this season there's no crowd."

"But why?"

"I want to see the other line for myself, with my own eyes, so that the next time we cross we can make an intelligent choice."

"The next time? We needn't hurry about that. And it's too late to change now," said Moore, returning to his paper.

"It isn't in the least too late, if you cared to please me. And it's a very little thing, I'm sure. Don't you see that if we are to live in Washington, we must go away early every summer?

We ought not to stay there a day after April, on account of the children. So, as I like going abroad better than any of the summer resorts, we shall be over here often. I don't see why we should not cross every year. So far, the three times we have crossed already, you have kept me tied to the Cunards. But I think that's narrow—to know only one line. It's like the New Edinburgh narrowness. They always quote Boston, and go to Boston, as though New York didn't exist. If you see about it immediately—to-morrow morning—I dare say you can arrange it. Promise me you will?"

"No; it's too late; they wouldn't do it. It's unreasonable to ask it."

A flush of anger rose in Amy's thin little face. "I suppose you mean that I'm unreasonable? But if there's anything I'm not, it's that. I always have a motive for everything I do. You have not a single reason for holding to the Cunard, except the trouble it will be to change, while I have an excellent one for wishing to try the White Star. Unreasonable!"

Here there was a knock at the door, and Banks appeared with a scared look in his eyes. "Please, sir, will you step out for a moment?" he murmured, but preserving his correct attitude in spite of his alarm.

Moore threw down his paper, and hurried into the hall, closing the door behind him. Amy, however, had instantly followed him.

A policeman standing at the street door delivered his message: "There is a child injured at the underground station. Don't know how bad it is. The nurse said it lived here at this number."

"Good God!" said Moore. And pushing by the man, he ran down the street towards the station.

Amy, who had overheard where she stood at the end of the hall, gave a gasp, and leaned for an instant against the wall. Then she too, bareheaded, darted out, and rushed down the lighted street. Miss Remington now appeared at the sitting-room door; seeing the policeman, and catching from Banks the words "child" and "station," she ran back, seized a shawl of her own which was lying on a chair, and then followed the others, Banks accompanying her, but hardly able to keep up with her swiftness.

The Sloane Square Station was near. The stairway leading to the tracks at this station is one of the longest possessed by the underground railway; it does not turn, but goes straight down, down, as if descending to the bowels of the earth. The wicket at the bottom was open, and Gertrude ran through it and out on the lighted platform. There was a group at a distance; something told her that it surrounded the injured child. But before she could reach it, her eyes caught sight of Philip Moore leading, or trying to lead, Amy in the opposite direction, away from this group. Gertrude joined them, speechless.

"It's some other child," said Philip, as she came up. "From our house, apparently. Belongs to that family above us, I suppose. Amy, do come this way; come into the shadow. Think of those poor people who will be here in a moment, and don't let them see you crying."

But Amy seemed incapable of listening. He put his arm round her, and half carried her down the platform towards the deep shadow at the end.

"There is nothing the matter with any of *us*, Amy. Polly and Fritz are safe, and will be here soon. Don't cry so."

But the shock had been too great. Amy could not stop. She clung to her husband in a helpless tremor, sobbing: "Don't leave me, Philip. Stay with me! Stay with me!"

"Leave you?" He kissed her forehead in the darkness. "I'm not dreaming of leaving you. Aren't you more to me than all the world?" He soothed her tenderly, stroking her hair as her head lay on his breast—the thin golden hair, artificially waved to hide its thinness.

Gertrude stood beside them in silence. After a minute she held out the shawl.

"Yes," said Philip, "I am afraid she has already taken cold, with her head bare, she is so delicate." There was deep love in his eyes as he drew the soft folds closely round his little wife, and lifted a corner to cover her bowed head. Then, still keeping his arm about her, he turned her so that she stood with her back toward the distant group, and also toward the stairway by which the other parents must descend.

They came a moment afterwards, poor things! But the noise of an arriving train on the other side covered the sounds that followed—if there were any. Philip, glancing over his shoulder, saw the child borne into one of the waiting-rooms, whose door was immediately shut upon the gazing crowd.

Now came a train on their side—the one from Notting Hill. It stopped, and Christine, composed and cool, emerged, holding Fritz's arm firmly with one hand, and Polly's with the other.

"Don't stop to kiss them now," said Moore; "let us get away from here. Christine, take the children home as fast as possible." He followed the surprised nurse (surprised, but instantly obedient), supporting Amy up the long stairway directly behind Polly's little legs and the knickerbockers of Fritz.

Gertrude ascended behind them. She too was bareheaded; but no one had noticed that. At the door of the station stood Banks. Composedly he presented Philip Moore's hat.

The injured child recovered, though not for many long months. The Moores, however, left the house the next day, for the accident had made the place unpleasant to Amy. They went to the Bristol, Burlington Gardens.

On the passenger list of the White Star steamer Teutonic, January 6, 1892, were the following names: "Philip Moore and wife; two children and nurse. Miss Remington."

Gertrude Remington does not keep a diary. But in a small almanac she jots down occasional brief notes. This is one of them: "New Edinburgh, February 20, 1892. Philip and A. gone to Washington. House here closed."

NOTES

FOREWORD

1. Constance Fenimore Woolson [hereinafter CFW] to Harriet Benedict Sherman, [1887], *The Complete Letters of Constance Fenimore Woolson*, ed. Sharon L. Dean (Gainesville: University Press of Florida, 2012), 349–50.

2. CFW to Samuel Livingston Mather, April 10, 1880, *Complete Letters*, 138.

3. CFW to Samuel Mather, April 11, [1891], *Complete Letters*, 449.

4. CFW to unidentified recipient, [1880], *Complete Letters*, 136.

5. CFW to Katharine Livingston Mather, July 2, 1893, *Complete Letters*, 517.

6. CFW to Katharine Livingston Mather, August 20, 1893, *Complete Letters*, 520.

7. Lyndall Gordon, *A Private Life of Henry James* (London: Chatto & Windus, 1998), 217.

8. CFW to Samuel Mather, March 20, [1880], *Complete Letters*, 130.

9. CFW to Arabella Washburn, no date, *Complete Letters*, 25.

10. Gordon., 172–73.

11. Ibid., 250.

INTRODUCTION

1. I discuss the critical response to her works in *Constance Fenimore Woolson: Portrait of a Lady Novelist* (New York: W. W. Norton, 2016), from which the material for this introduction as a whole is derived. "Novelist laureate" from *The Boston Globe* quoted in a Harper & Brothers advertisement that ran nationally after the publication of *For the Major* (1883) and in the back of most of her subsequent books, all published by Harper & Brothers. See also the reference to her as America's "foremost novelist" in "Recent Fiction," *The Independent* 38 (December 1886): 11; and the remark that she "easily takes the first place among American female novelists" in "Miss Woolson's Stories," *Harper's Bazar* 19 (November 20, 1886): 758. That article continues, "Among English women George Eliot alone takes a higher rank." Henry James, "Miss Woolson," *The American Essays of Henry James*, ed. Leon Edel (Princeton, N.J.: Princeton University Press, 1989), 164. Helen Gray Cone, "Woman in American Literature," *Century Illustrated Magazine* 40 (October 1890): 927.

2. Henry Mills Alden, "Constance Fenimore Woolson," *Harper's Weekly* 38 (February 3, 1894): 113; "Constance Fenimore Woolson," *New York Tribune*, January 28, 1894, 14; and Charles Dudley Warner, "Editor's Study," *Harper's New Monthly Magazine* 88 (May 1894): 967.

3. M. H., Letter to the *New York Times* Saturday Review of Books, *The New York Times*, June 2, 1906, BR358; Shan F. Bullock, "Miss Woolson Had a Conscience," unidentified newspaper clipping, August 1, 1920 (the clipping is taped into a copy of Woolson's *East Angels* in the Clare Benedict Collection, Western Reserve Historical Society, Cleveland).

4. I discuss this phenomenon at length in Anne E. Boyd,

Writing for Immortality: Women and the Emergence of High Literary Culture in America (Baltimore: Johns Hopkins University Press, 2004).

5. See, for instance, Fred Lewis Pattee, *A History of American Literature Since 1870* (New York: Century, 1915); Fred Lewis Pattee, "Constance Fenimore Woolson and the South." *The South Atlantic Quarterly* 38 (April 1939): 130–41; John Hervey, "Sympathetic Art." *Saturday Review of Literature* 12 (October 1929): 268; John Dwight Kern, *Constance Fenimore Woolson: Literary Pioneer* (Philadelphia: University of Pennsylvania Press, 1934); Arthur Hobson Quinn, *American Fiction: An Historical and Critical Survey* (New York: Appleton-Century, 1936); Lyon N. Richardson, "Constance Fenimore Woolson, 'Novelist Laureate' of America," *The South Atlantic Quarterly* 39 (January 1940): 20–36; Jay B. Hubbell, "Some New Letters of Constance Fenimore Woolson," *New England Quarterly* 14 (December 1941): 715–35; Van Wyck Brooks, *The Dream of Arcadia: American Writers and Artists in Italy, 1760–1915* (New York: E. P. Dutton, 1958); Rayburn S. Moore, *Constance F. Woolson* (New York: Twayne, 1963); and Leon Edel, *Henry James: The Middle Years, 1882–1895* (Philadelphia: J. B. Lippincott, 1962).

6. See, for instance, Sharon Dean, "Constance Fenimore Woolson and Henry James: The Literary Relationship," *Massachusetts Studies in English* 7 (1980): 1–9; Sharon Dean, "Constance Fenimore Woolson's Southern Sketches," *Southern Studies* 25 (Fall 1986): 274–83; Sharon Dean, *Constance Fenimore Woolson: Homeward Bound* (Knoxville: University of Tennessee Press, 1995); Joan Myers Weimer, ed., *Women Artists, Women Exiles: "Miss Grief" and Other Stories* (New Brunswick, N.J.: Rutgers University Press, 1988); Cheryl Torsney, *Constance Fenimore Woolson: The Grief of Artistry* (Athens: University of Georgia Press, 1989); Cheryl Torsney, ed., *Critical Essays on Constance*

Fenimore Woolson (New York: G. K. Hall, 1992); Victoria Brehm, "Island Fortresses: The Landscape of the Imagination in the Great Lakes Fiction of Constance Fenimore Woolson," *American Literary Realism* 22 (1990): 51–66; and Victoria Brehm, ed., *Constance Fenimore Woolson's Nineteenth Century: Essays* (Detroit: Wayne State University Press, 2001).

7. Charles Dudley Warner, "Editor's Study," *Harper's New Monthly Magazine* 88 (May 1894): 967.

8. Constance Fenimore Woolson [hereinafter CFW] to Samuel Mather, December 10, [1893], in *The Complete Letters of Constance Fenimore Woolson*, ed. Sharon Dean (Gainesville: University Press of Florida, 2012), 535.

9. CFW to Arabella Carter Washburn, undated fragment, in ibid., 561.

10. Inscription in Stopford A. Brooke, ed., *Poems from Shelley* (London: Macmillan, 1880), Non-Catholic Cemetery in Rome.

11. CFW to Henry Mills Alden, January 17, 1890, in *Complete Letters*, 397.

12. CFW to Edmund Clarence Stedman, August 10, [1889], in ibid., 376.

13. CFW to Edmund Clarence Stedman, April 30, [1883], in ibid., 239.

14. James, "Miss Woolson," 168.

15. CFW to Miss Farnian, April 17, 1875, in *Complete Letters*, 33; CFW to Arabella Carter Washburn, [1874?], in ibid., 26; and CFW to Samuel Mather, April 25, [1875], in ibid., 34.

16. CFW to Henry James, February 12, [1882], in ibid., 190.

17. CFW to James, February 12, [1882]; CFW, *East Angels* (New York: Harper & Brothers, 1886), 356.

ST. CLAIR FLATS

3 **Captain Kidd**: Captain William Kidd (1645–1701), a Scottish seaman who was captured in Boston and sent to England, where he was executed for murder and piracy.

4 **flags**: Wild irises, which possess sword-like leaves.

7 **Flying Dutchmen**: The Flying Dutchman was a legendary ghost ship that was forced to sail forever and never make port.

10 **"In the kingdom . . ."**: Slightly altered lines from the poem "Annabel Lee" (1849) by Edgar Allan Poe.

16 **Apollyon**: The destroyer or angel of the bottomless pit, from Revelation 9:11.

20 **shake-downs**: Beds of straw.

21 **crash towels**: Coarse linen towels.

21 **if you sing . . .** : Proverb meaning if you are happy in the morning, your mood will change by the evening.

22 **"The heavens declare . . ."**: The chant is adapted from the Psalms: "The heavens declare . . . ," 19:1; "Joy cometh . . . ," 30:5; "As a bridegroom . . . As a strong man . . . ," 19:5; "The outgoings . . . ," 65:8; "Like a pelican . . . Like a sparrow . . . ," 102:6–7.

23 **Napoleon on St. Helena**: Emperor Napoleon Bonaparte (1769–1821) was exiled to the remote island of St. Helena in the South Atlantic after his defeat by the British at the Battle of Waterloo in 1815. He died there six years later.

24 **"The moping bittern . . ."**: Slightly misquoted lines from "The Haunted House" (1844) by the British poet Thomas Hood (1799–1845). Rather than a "bittern," Hood writes of a "moping heron." Woolson seems to have taken her lines from an article on bitterns in *The American Naturalist* in 1870 (vol. 3, p. 177).

26 **a ramified answer**: This wording was maintained in book and magazine versions, but Woolson may have meant "rarified."

28 *Faust*: In a German legend, the scholar Faust makes a bargain with the devil: in exchange for all knowledge and earthly pleasure for a period of twenty-four years, Faust will accept eternal damnation. The most famous adaptation of the legend was the play *Faust* by Johann Wolfgang von Goethe; the first part was published in 1808, the second in 1832. The opera *Faust* by Charles Gounod premiered in 1859.

28 **the Punic wars**: Wars fought between Rome and Carthage from 264 B.C. to 146 B.C.

28 **Belshazzar**: Prince of Babylon in the sixth century B.C., mentioned in Daniel in the Old Testament.

29 *Te Deum*: A Christian hymn of praise sung to God.

30 **Mount Tabor**: Located west of the Sea of Galilee, Mount Tabor was believed to be the site of Christ's Transfiguration.

31 **Jacob Bœhmen . . . spiritualism**: Jacob Boehme (1575–1624) was an untutored German mystic who believed in the divinity of humanity; his first book was *Aurora* (1612) or "dawn." Chiliastic is a Greek word for the belief (also known as millennialism) that Jesus will reign for one thousand years before the day of judgment. Modern spiritualism refers to the popular nineteenth-century belief that communication with the dead was possible, usually through a spiritual medium.

31 **"Much learning . . ."**: A twist on "Much learning hath made thee mad" (Acts 26:24); the original refers to Paul.

32 **Prime**: William Cowper Prime (1825–1905), American journalist and travel writer, wrote *I Go A-Fishing* (1873), a narrative of various fishing expeditions.

33 **Bret Harte's "Melons"**: In "Melons" (1870), by the American writer Bret Harte (1836–1902), a boy whistles the tune

to "John Brown's Body," a popular song about the American militant abolitionist who raided Harper's Ferry in 1859. The tune would become the music for Julia Ward Howe's "The Battle Hymn of the Republic" (1862).

35 **delaine**: A high-quality wool fabric made from delaine sheep.

35 **chirk**: Cheerful.

37 **our evening was over**: When Woolson republished "St. Clair Flats" in *Castle Nowhere*, she deleted here a conversation between the narrator and Raymond in which they disagree about the wisdom of Roxanna and Samuel's marriage. Raymond argues that the union of such an "ignorant, commonplace woman" and "a poetical, imaginative man" inevitably leads to misery, while the narrator believes that Samuel would be in a lunatic asylum without Roxanna's "tender care." He argues, "Her love for him is something sublime: her poor, plain face, her dull eyes, and her rough hands, are transformed into something higher than beauty."

38 **"He came flying . . ."**: Adapted from Psalms 18:10.

38 **Hebrew poet**: King David, who composed many of the sacred poems in the Psalms.

40 **"folded their tents . . ."**: From "The Day Is Done" (1845) by Henry Wadsworth Longfellow (1807–1882).

SOLOMON

43 **glow-worm lamps**: Lamps made of jars containing fireflies, or glowworms.

44 **"Western Reserve"**: An area of 3.3 million acres in northeastern Ohio that was reserved by the state of Connecticut when it ceded its claim to the Northwest Territory in 1786. The land was largely settled by Connecticut immi-

grants, and was ceded to Ohio in 1800. The names in the next two sentences are various tracts in Ohio. "Moravian Lands" refers to three 4000-acre tracts of land granted to Moravian missionaries by the Continental Congress in 1787.

45 **Käse-lab:** Woolson probably means Käse-laib, which is German for "wheel of cheese."

46 **huts of the Black Forest:** Small huts built by peasants of rough logs were common throughout the mountainous Black Forest in southwestern Germany.

47 **Mound-Builders:** Ancient indigenous peoples of North America who lived around the Great Lakes and the Mississippi Valley and built ceremonial mounds throughout the region.

47 **C——:** Cleveland, from which Woolson also hailed; it lies about seventy-five miles north of Zoar.

48 **linsey-woolsey:** A coarse fabric made of linen or cotton and wool.

48 **list slippers:** Slippers made from fabric edging, or selvage, which made them very quiet.

50 **Sandy:** Sandusky, a town on Lake Erie.

50 **Queen of Sheby:** An Arabian ruler mentioned in the Bible, the Queen of Sheba visited King Solomon in Jerusalem, bearing great gifts and asking him to solve a number of riddles.

51 **Solomon:** In the Bible, Solomon was the king of Israel and the son of David. He was known for great power and wisdom, but also for idolatry. In Kings, he is described as being influenced by his wives to turn away from God. A later Old Testament book, the "Song of Solomon" or "Song of Songs," comprises a song sung between two lovers about the joys of sexual love.

51 **Judy, Ruth, Esthy**: Three women who appear in the Old Testament. The Biblical story of Judith seducing and beheading Holfernes in order to save her people was portrayed many times in Renaissance art. Ruth was the great-grandmother of David. Esther, who was Jewish and known for her great beauty, married a Persian king and persuaded him to rescind an order to execute all Jews.

52 **chany**: China, or decorated porcelain dishes.

52 **open-work stockings**: Fancy stockings made of fabric with decorative openings.

52 **cambric**: A fine linen or cotton cloth that is tightly woven.

53 ***Où la vanité va-t-elle se nicher?***: In French, Where is the vanity going to hide?

53 **the Lorelei**: The German legend of a maiden who lures sailors on the Rhine River to their deaths with her beautiful music. It was set to music many times. The opening lines cited just above—translated as, "I don't know what it means / That I am so sad"—come from "Die Lorelei" (1824) by the poet Heinrich Heine (1797–1856).

54 **"She is quite sure . . . had her day"**: From "Maud" (1855) by Alfred, Lord Tennyson (1809–1892). The lines read in the original: "Before I am quite sure / That there is one to love me; / Then let come what may / To a life that has been so sad, / I shall have had my day."

54 **"A man's a man"**: "A Man's a Man for A' That" (1795) by Robert Burns (1759–1796).

59 **kobold**: A household sprite from German folklore that can appear in the form of an animal.

61 **my rose of Sharon**: Song of Solomon 2:1: "I am the rose of Sharon, and the lily of the valleys."

62 **Tuscarora**: A Native American tribe and member of the Iroquois League. The Tuscarora originally came from the

Great Lakes region, and the tribe now has members in New York, North Carolina, and Canada. The name was used for place-names throughout the upper Midwest.

64 **Dux nascitur**: Latin for born leader.

RODMAN THE KEEPER

73 **"The long years . . ."**: Excerpted from "Spring in New England" by Thomas Bailey Aldrich (1836–1907), published in the *Atlantic Monthly* in June 1875.

76 **estate with philosophic eyes**: In the magazine version of the story, the following sentence appeared here: "He no longer felt warming within him his early temptations to put in the missing nail or pick up the rusting axe; 'for if they did these things in a green tree, what will they do in a dry?' he thought." The quotation is from Luke 23:31.

90 **Federal**: A Union soldier.

90 **carpet-baggers**: Northerners who came to the South after the Civil War for political or economic gain, often carrying bags made of carpet; the term was pejorative.

90 **pagan Chinamen**: Chinese immigrants along the West Coast of the United States, many of whom worked in railroad construction. They were often portrayed negatively in the nineteenth-century press.

92 **"Toujours femme varie . . . plume au vent"**: French: "Women always vary, / He who trusts them is quite mad; / Often a woman / is only a feather in the wind."

96 **anathema-maranatha**: Cursed or condemned, incurring God's wrath; from 1 Corinthians 16:22: "If any man not love the Lord Jesus Christ, let him be Anathema-Maranatha."

98 **The furniture was of dark mahogany**: A pier-table is made to stand against a wall between two windows. Low-down

glass is a mirror that stands against the back side of the table, between the top and a shelf that is close to the ground. Hair-cloth is a stiff fabric woven of horsehair.

100 **"Tell me not . . .":** The opening to the poem "A Psalm of Life" (1838) by Henry Wadsworth Longfellow (1807–1882).

110 **at the South, all went:** The following passage appears here in the magazine version, but was cut from the book version:

> "Grief covers our land."
>
> "Yes; for a mighty wrong brings ever in its train a mighty sorrow."
>
> Miss Ward turned upon him fiercely. "Do you, who have lived among us, dare to pretend that the state of our servants is not worse this moment than it ever was before?"
>
> "Transition."
>
> "A horrible transition!"
>
> "Horrible, but inevitable; education will be the savior. Had I fifty millions to spend on the South to-morrow, every cent should go for schools, and for schools alone."
>
> "For the negroes, I suppose," said the girl with a bitter scorn.
>
> "For the negroes, and for the whites also," answered John Rodman gravely. "The lack of general education is painfully apparent everywhere th[r]oughout the South; it is from that cause more than any other that your beautiful country now lies desolate."
>
> "Desolate,—desolate indeed," said Miss Ward.

SISTER ST. LUKE

115 **"She lived shut in . . .":** "Sister Saint Luke" by the states-
man and poet John Milton Hay (1838–1905), written specif-
ically for this story when it was republished in *Rodman the
Keeper: Southern Sketches.*

115 **Minorcan:** The Minorcans are inhabitants of Minorca, one
of the Spanish Balearic Islands. A large group of Minorcan indentured servants was brought to Florida in 1767 by a
Scottish entrepreneur to work his indigo plantation. After
much cruel treatment, they petitioned the British colonial
governor in St. Augustine for their freedom, which they
won, along with a tract of land on which their descendants
lived for generations.

116 **as Sister St. Luke:** The nun is named after St. Luke, or
Luke the Evangelist, the author of the Gospel according
to Luke in the New Testament of the Bible. A disciple of
Paul, Luke is referred to in the Bible as a physician and was
regarded by Catholics as the patron saint of artists, doctors,
and students.

117 **first-class Fresnel:** A Fresnel lens, invented by Augustin-
Jean Fresnel in 1822, contained many concentric rings that
reflected light for greater distances than any previous lens.

117 **Pelican Island:** A name invented by Woolson.

117 **a hideous barber's pole:** The history Woolson describes is
that of the St. Augustine lighthouse, which was completed
in October 1874. It is decorated with black and white stripes
to this day. It sits on Anastasia Island, which is fourteen
miles long and one mile wide—about the size of Pelican
Island in the story. The island was developed in the twentieth century, except for the 1500-acre Anastasia State Park.

118 **Queen of the Antilles:** A nickname for Cuba. The Wind-